"He comes!"

The shout made Senset spin around, jerking her hand from Aram's.

"The bridegroom comes!"

Someone else walked toward them, but from a side street running parallel to the temple itself. He strode confidently, surrounded by a group of children, boys and girls running around him laughing and tossing flowers and green leaves into the air. The crowd cheered and some were also throwing petals. He laughed and held out his hands.

The sun gleamed off his golden mask.

Michael. Senset felt her knees weaken. *At last.*

As he neared where Senset and Aram stood, the children flung the last of their flowers. Their laughter stopped as they ran into the crowd to waiting parents holding out their arms to hug them tightly.

"My brother…" Aram stepped forward, offering Senset's hand. "I bring your bride to you."

Michael held out his hand and Aram placed Senset's in it.

"Come, my bride."

Praise

"I enjoyed it so much I found it daunting to write a review. I know, I sound silly saying that, but it's true. How do you adequately convey your opinions on a story that's so rich with feeling in such a brief write up?…Ms. Sweeney is the mistress of her craft…5 stars."

~*2Lips*

~*~

"…I enjoyed this book and would highly recommend it to anyone who enjoys going back into a time of chariots and the land where history began. 4.5 Stars."

~*Penelope Adams, PRG*

~*~

"…Judaism plays a big role in this story. Their names, the history, the dress, the one God. The reason for the curse. Since I am of Jewish faith, some of the story made me cry, but it might not do this so much to others, who would not realize all this story had to offer. 5 Stars."

~*Gloria Lakritz, PRG Senior Reviewer*

Mask of the Beast

by

Toni V. Sweeney

Mask of the Beast

Cover Art by *Lisa Dawn MacDonald*

The Wild Rose Press, Inc.
PO Box 708
Adams Basin, NY 14410-0708
Visit us at www.thewildrosepress.com

Publishing History
First Edition, 2023
Trade Paperback ISBN 978-1-5092-5328-9
Digital ISBN 978-1-5092-5329-6

Published in the United States of America

Dedication

In Memory of Esther Cohen,
a dear lady and a good friend

Above all, love each other deeply,
because love covers over a multitude of sins.
1 Peter 4:8

Part 1: Beast Man's Bride

Chapter 1

"He comes. The General has returned. Reshep be praised!"

The slave Hinep gave a perfunctory knock to the brassbound door. Without waiting for permission, she burst into the royal princess' apartments, flinging herself to the floor before her mistress.

"His Highness Horem is back, my lady. Triumphant."

"What? When?" Asanath paused in the act of tossing the pair of finely-polished bone dice.

"He rides even now through the city gate." Hinep dared raise her head, pointing in a vague westerly direction.

Dropping the dice onto the playing board, Asanath pushed Bubash off her lap and struggled to her feet.

The cat landed with ease, baring fangs in a yowl at having its nap disturbed, as it stretched, seeming to lengthen by a foot.

"Help me." Asanath held out her hand to her sister-in-law. "*Great Taweret,*" she puffed at Senset. "Truly, this child has the weight of a river rock."

Wondering cynically how much of her haste was to see her returning husband and how much to simply disrupt the game of Monkeys and Cranes they'd been

1

playing, Senset seized Asanath's arm and hauled her pregnant bulk upright. She'd been winning, the princess losing, and she had a feeling her brother's wife had been looking for some excuse to quit playing.

Asanath didn't like to lose.

Silently, Senset made certain her sister-in-law was steady on her feet, then straightened the disarranged draperies of her gown and followed her through the open archway onto the balcony. After a moment's hesitation, Hinep got to her feet and scurried after them, the cat trailing.

Hinep should've assisted her mistress. Lazy wench. She ought be the one making certain her robes are arranged modestly, not I. The thought flitted rebelliously through Senset's mind, rankling a little. Lesser children often performed tasks below their status simply because they were *lesser*...and they were expected to do it without comment.

By this time, Asanath was outside on the balcony, dropping heavily onto the stone bench set before the balustrade.

Babush leaped onto the seat beside her.

Her hand went to Bubash's neck, unconsciously stroking around its collar of elaborately interlaced jade, turquoise, and carnelian lozenges as she looked down at the gathering crowd. The cat shook her head, sending the golden ring in her left ear swinging.

The royal palace was built on the slope of a foothill. Unlike those buildings below, it was constructed of granite and marble, made to last forever as it towered above the city of Usaset. From their vantage point, they could see over the tops of the flat-roofed, sunbaked brick buildings into the marketplace itself.

There was more movement than usual for this hour of the morning, a hubbub of excitement and activity. People were gathering on the sides of the main street, pressing into the stalls and shop doors to make room for the returning army. Vendors scooped up their wares, pushing them out of the way for the spectators taking their places.

A low rumble trembled in the distance, many feet trampling the ground. As it grew closer, a cheer arose, swelling and rushing from the city gate through the crowd and up the hillside.

"I can't see him." Seizing the stone baluster, Asanath pulled herself to her feet, standing on tiptoe, craning her neck.

Deprived of her stroking hand, Bubash began washing a paw, showing unconcern that her mistress couldn't find her husband. Like most felines, she appeared scornful in her view of humans, royal or otherwise. All simply existed for her well-being, be it a caressing hand or offering a bowl of goat's milk.

"Hinep, are you certain of this?" the princess asked.

"Oh yes, my lady. The general sent a messenger to his noble father, telling him he'd be arriving at any moment."

"And you know this...how?" Senset raised a skeptical brow.

"I...happened to be walking past the audience hall when the messenger arrived, my lady." The slave flicked Senset a smile as she spoke.

"More likely you were lurking in the gallery, eavesdropping." Senset retorted, returning the smile.

The old woman had learned long ago sharp ears earned favors. Listening at locks and hearing whispers while crouched in corners was something at which she'd become expert. It could also be reason for punishment if she were caught hearing the wrong thing, but so far she'd been lucky. As yet, Hinep brought only harmless information to her mistress.

"His Majesty ordered me to inform my lady of my noble lord's arrival."

"As you walked past." Senset made the words as ironic as possible.

"As you say, my lady." Hinep inclined her head slightly. "As I walked past."

Assuming the slave was somewhere nearby, eavesdropping, Aseti-Ra had merely called out, "Inform the Princess Asanath, Hinep," in a loud voice as he dismissed the messenger to the barracks before ordering his advisors to begin preparations for a welcoming banquet for his son, and calling for his own slaves to help him prepare for their coming meeting. Mentally, he also made a note that when the next encounter of any true import occurred, he should order the guards to check the gallery and other hiding places and make certain no snooping slaves were about.

"Hush, you two…" Asanath's hiss cut short their exchange. "Senset, can you see?"

Impatient to be assured of her husband's safe return, she looked to the girl. It had been six months since she'd seen Horem, on the day he rode through that same gate to meet the beast men on the Plain of Arriah.

By this time, Senset had hiked up her own skirts and climbed from the stone bench to the rim of an urn thick with sprouting bamboo canes. As she released them, the folds of linen fluttered around her knees, the breeze swirling inside the cloth. It tickled and she laughed quietly. Immodest, she admitted, but there was no one to see but Asanath and the slave, so what did it matter?

Clasping her arms around the pillar next to the urn, she stared toward the open city gates.

"I don't…no, wait…yes, yes, I do. He's here, Asanath."' Her voice rose with excitement. "Truly."

"I wish he'd hurry…so I could see." Asanath pounded one fist against the baluster in irritation. "If only I wasn't so short."

"Listen."

Now they could hear the slow, steady beat of drums. *…boom…boom…*

The morning had been cool, but the sun now beat down. Below, the heat rose in visible waves from the rooftops.

Asanath shifted impatiently, raising one hand to brush at the trickle of sweat appearing under the edge of her wig. She'd foolishly selected a heavy wig to wear. With its weight and that of her royal coronet, she now regretted her choice.

"Yes." She cocked her head slightly. "I hear the heralds."

The drummers came into view, five men with shoulder harnesses holding heavy round drums in place. Swinging their arms in a steady rhythm, they struck padded antelope-hide mallets against the stretched skin covers on the wooden half-tubs.

… boom… boom… boom…

Like the dull echo of thunder, the thuds reverberated up the slope, as another sound added itself, a rapid *rat-a-tat-tat*.

Behind the drummers marched a second set beating snare drums hanging from chest straps and balanced at their hips. The short, sharp tattoo of the wooden sticks against the drum faces made a rousing counterpoint to the loud bass beats.

...rat-a-tat-tat... boom... rat-a-tat-tat... boom... boom...

There was a blast of trumpets as the royal buglers appeared, blaring the notes of a triumphant processional.

...ta-rahhh...

The crowd cheered, some raising their hands and shaking them in welcome.

"Here he comes." Senset pointed.

A crimson-painted chariot trimmed in gold leaf rumbled into view, pulled by two white horses. Standing beside his armored charioteer, Horem, general of the Ægysian army and crown prince of Usaset, raised a hand in acknowledgement of the crowd's adulation.

"Can you see him now?"

"No. I…" Asanath stretched, craned. "Yes."

She waved, arms flailing. The figure didn't respond.

"Oh, he can't see *me*."

"Give him a moment, Asa," Senset cautioned. "He's just inside the gates. Let him get closer."

With the reins in one hand, the charioteer guided the horses through the avenue of bodies. He raised his free hand, waving to the crowd, then indicating Horem, and the shouts grew louder.

Horem smiled; from his movements, the watching women could see he was laughing out loud. The sun reflected off his leather armor and its tiny metal brads, gleaming up the hillside to dazzle their eyes. It shone off his helmet, glittering on the sinuous figure of Wadjet encircling his head, and Nekhbet's falcon wings draped protectively on either side of his lean face.

His right arm, banded with a metal vambrace, lifted, hand clenched into a fist. He shook it dramatically. Thrown from an upstairs window, a cascade of acacia flowers floated down, spilling over him. He looked up, catching a handful of petals, touching them to his lips before tossing them back into the air.

"Horem!" Someone shouted his name and the crowd picked it up, "Ho-rem! Ho-rem!" until it became a river of sound, the returning hero's name flowing through the city.

"Horem!" From higher up, several female voices rose above the shouts of the crowd.

Asanath looked up. On the next terrace, the general's two lesser wives and three concubines waved frantically.

"You there. Shut up." She shook her fist, her own voice rising above theirs. "I'm prime wife and it's my privilege to welcome my husband, not you five. Get yourselves back inside."

"Hah!" floated down to her from a plump little Assran named Xena. "We've as much right as you. Maybe it'll be one of us he'll celebrate with tonight, Big-belly!" She jumped up and down, making her bound breasts jiggle. "I've certainly more to offer him."

"Why, you—"

Asanath clambered to her feet, overbalanced and fell back onto the bench, nearly sitting on Bubash and sending the cat leaping from the bench and stalking back inside with a *rowr* of displeasure. Briefly, true vexation reddened the princess' face, shining through the rice powder used to whiten her complexion.

"Impudent wench."

Laughter floated down. Xena stuck out her tongue,

7

blowing against it and making a rude *blluuuuhhh.*

"Come, Asa." Senset climbed down from the urn. She caught her arm, patting soothingly.

Asanath was too close to giving birth to become upset. She released her sister-in-law to wipe at the sweat beading her own chin and slowly dripping onto the cloth banding her breasts. Glancing at her hand, she saw it held a dark smear. The kohl outlining her eyes was streaking in the heat.

It's getting too hot. I must get Asa back inside. Soon.

"Forget them. Look. Horem's below us now."

The charioteer was guiding the white horses under the arch with its double figures of Horus, the god facing himself on the upright pillars leading into the palace courtyard. Asanath leaned over the baluster, looking down, her gaze worshipful.

"Horem…" That whispered word held adoration.

At that moment, he looked up, saw her, and his smiling expression changed into a delighted grin. The clenched fist opened. Horem waved to his prime wife. His lips moved. They couldn't hear what he said but it looked as if he spoke her name.

Asanath waved back.

As the chariot went under the arch and out of their sight, she looked up, smirking.

"Guess we know who he was waving to, don't we?" To Senset, she went on, "Now the troops will come. I don't care to see—"

There was another shout from the crowd, a burst of surprise swelling into a roar of fear.

"Wait." Sensdet looked back. "What's that?"

"Where?" Asanath looked past her pointing finger. The next moment, she clutched Senset's arm, fingers

8

digging into her flesh. "Benevolent Ra. It's a prisoner. Senset, they've captured one of the beast men."

Between the approaching lines of foot soldiers, two white mules were led down the street, one soldier on either side of the animals, holding a bridle's cheekpiece. Tied to the harnesses on the animals' bodies were several ropes stretching from one mule to the other, and between them…

…a wild creature, a mass of tangled hair and fur on two legs. Ropes wrapped around its neck and chest held it between the animals. Its fur-covered paws bound together, it fought its bindings, digging in its heels and refusing to move, roaring its rage.

For a shocked moment, the crowd fell silent. Then, the mules continued their steady movement forward. The creature was jerked off its feet and dragged several yards before it regained its footing again.

That broke the spell and the people yelled their triumph as the beast screamed again, the sound so full of fury it crashed up the hill like an angry wave.

Her heart pounding, Senset leaned forward, squinting to get a better look.

The shouts of the people increased, became louder, filled with anger.

Someone darted out of the crowd, bent and picked up a clod of dirt from the street, flinging it at the creature. It struck the side of the shaggy head and the beast flinched, jerking backward before shrieking again. Others began throwing things…rocks, dirt…

Neither the mules' handlers nor the officer riding at the front of the following line of men did anything to stop them.

A townsman flicked a coin to a fruit vendor,

selecting an over-ripe peach and lobbing it at the beast. It struck the hairy chest and burst, spraying sticky fruit and fragments of pulp everywhere. Bits spattered the creature's face, clinging to its skin.

Shaking its head, it screamed again, and, with a heave, pulled its paws loose from its bonds, lunging at someone getting too close. His claws caught in the neck of the man's robe, lifting him off his feet, and dragging him toward an open mouth and bared teeth.

Immediately, the captain barked out a command. Two foot soldiers broke from formation, flipping their spears backward, using the butts to jab at the creature. The ends caught the beast in the ribs, making him drop the man. As his intended victim scrambled to his feet and staggered back into the crowd, the procession marched on, dragging the beast toward the courtyard gate while the soldiers continued to beat at it with their spears.

He screamed once more, fury and pain in the sound. One paw swiped at a spear. Immediately, he cringed, arms wrapped around his head protectively as one of the soldiers drew his sword, striking him on the shoulders with the flat of the blade. He fell again, was dragged through the dirt, his body making a dark smear in the hard-packed soil before regaining his feet.

A disturbing sense of pity welled inside Senset.

Why should I feel sorry for that creature? He and his kind have waged war on us for years, and killed many of our people. He deserves whatever he gets.

"Oh." Asanath's sudden cry made her glance at her sister-in-law. She was leaning against the balustrade, face white. "Senset…"

"What is it? Are you ill?"

"That horrid creature. It frightens me. I shouldn't be

seeing it. It might mark my child. Help me inside. Quickly."

"Of course, Asa. Come." Senset put her arm around her sister-in-law's waist, lifting her off the bench.

She knew she had to get her inside as soon as possible. Nothing must endanger her brother's expected son, and a fright such as the one Asanath could receive from seeing the beast man might do that. This child was Horem's seventh but it was no less important to him.

"Hinep, help me."

With the slave's assistance, she guided Asanath inside, to the couch where she'd been lounging when Hinep arrived with her announcement.

Once she was seated and Hinep had supplied her with a draft of lemon water poured from an alabaster pitcher sitting near the gaming board, Senset asked, anxiously, "Do you feel better now? Shall I summon the physician?"

Asanath took a long slow drink before answering. Her color was returning. "No, I don't wish that bothersome old man around. Not just now."

"But, Asa, if you've been upset by that creature," Senset protested, "Horem would wish it."

"Horem doesn't have to know about this, and I'm fine now." Asanath waved her concern away, taking another deep swallow. She thrust the cup at Senset, releasing it before the girl had it within her grasp so she had to catch it to prevent its striking the floor and spilling. "I've too much to do."

"Like what?" Senset set the cup on the table.

"I must prepare myself to receive my lord. Hinep, summon my bath slaves. Have water drawn and heated. I'll want attar of lilies and that wonderful new perfumed unguent my lord gave me for my natal anniversary. I'll wear the embroidered linen with the cloth-of-gold applications. And my best jeweled collar." Fully recovered from her fright, Asanath rattled off orders at breakneck speed, Hinep nodding frantically in reply. "Horem will be coming to me after he reports to his lord father, and I must look my best." She heaved a heavy sigh. "Ah, I've missed him so. We'll have such a reunion tonight."

"Asa…" As Hinep bowed and scurried away, Senset spoke quietly, pointing out the obvious. "You're nearly nine months with child. How much of a reunion can you have?"

"Oh, my dear little sister…" Asanath's darkly drawn brows rose as her carmined mouth twisted into a smirk. "There are ways, believe me…" She patted her belly. "Even when nine months with child. Hinep!"

"Mistress?" At the door, the slave paused, looking back.

"After you've gotten the bath slaves, you'll wait by my lord's door and give him this message when he arrives at his chambers: *My lord, my loving master, your handmaiden and adoring wife awaits your pleasure. Come to me, my stallion, your little mare shivers in anticipation. She longs for the nip of your teeth and the feel of your strong thighs.*"

Cheeks flushing, Hinep stared at her, not moving.

Senset hid a smile behind her hand. *Not so little, anymore,* came her uncomplimentary thought.

"Do you understand? Repeat it back to me."

Obediently, Hinep recited Asanath's words. Her withered cheeks reddened at the intimacy of their meaning, as well as seeing Senset's smirk from where

12

she stood behind her sister-in-law.

"Good." Asanath nodded, satisfied, and waved a hand in dismissal. "Now go."

Hinep disappeared through the door.

"You may leave me, also, Senset. I wish to be alone, to settle myself into contemplation before my bath." Asanath looked perturbed. "I forgot to tell Hinep to order refreshments for my lord and myself. He'll be famished. Would you do that for me? Tell the cook to prepare his favorites."

"Of course." Bowing, Senset also made her escape.

Chapter 2

Outside in the corridor, Senset shook her head as she thought again of Asanath's message.

What a bunch of rubbish... Loving rubbish, to be sure, but so silly. And yet...she was certain Horem would be delighted, and quite possibly aroused by that ridiculous speech, especially the part comparing him to a stallion.

Men are so odd in those things pleasing them.

Senset loved her brother. Though he was the eldest son and thus prince and heir to the throne, and she was the child of a lesser wife and a mere daughter, he'd always been pleasant to her. He'd been seven when she was born, and even then was enchanted with this particular half-sibling. Perhaps it was because, of his three sisters, she was the only one younger than he. When she'd been a child, he'd played with her, taking her with him in his chariot and driving around the stable yards while her mother and nurse fretted loudly about her safety. The time she'd been ill with that ever-present river fever, he'd risked his own precious health by bringing her fresh fruit because the physician suggested it might make her heal faster. When he married Asanath, he'd asked that she be included in the wedding party as one of the flower bearers walking with his bride into the temple.

There were other brothers—both whole and half-siblings—but Horem and Senset had a unique bond between them existing with none of the others.

Ægys was a small kingdom in the heart of a large, mostly forested continent, though the girl and the majority of her people had no idea of its vast size or knowledge of the many other inhabitants spread across its coasts. Only the court historians and some of the very, very old were aware of their descent from a great empire on the desert banks of a large river running northward, a kingdom from which their ancestors had been exiled millennia before.

They had been gone so long from that other place that the common people could no longer recall what had caused their exodus from the land of their ancestors and sent them into the wilds of the heart of the continent...nor did they care. The old kingdom was called *Ta-Sheme'aw,* "Land of the Rushes." They called their new one Ægys, because the god Ra-Harakhty had placed his *ægis* or shield over them to protect them.

With their separation from that larger kingdom, the Ægysian rulers had chosen to bring with them its gods, laws, and customs, and to follow most of the ways of their former homeland...with certain exceptions. In the *Home Empire*—as they chose to call it whenever anyone spoke of their origins—inheritance came through the female line, automatically demanding the heir marry his eldest sister in order to become ruler. With the ascension to the throne of Horem's eight-times-great-grandfather and the beginning of the Asetiran Dynasty, that custom came to an end. Aseti-Ra the First had believed his children should be used to form political alliances outside Ægys, to strengthen its power by making allies of its neighbors through marriage. Thus, he married a foreign princess, and bonded his sisters, brothers, and offspring to foreigners as needed. Only if it could be proven the match would be a propitious one was an Ægysian marriage allowed within the royal family. Of course, that didn't account for lesser wives and concubines, so any native-born female finding herself in favor with a royal son might be added to his intimate retinue in another status. That was the way many nobles actually found true love.

Such hadn't been the case with Horem and Asanath. It was an arranged marriage, to be sure, but it had been lust—quickly followed by love—at first sight for the young prince and his bride. Though her noble father-in-law, Aseti-Ra the Fourth, allowed foreign wives to keep some of their own customs, Asanath gladly gave up any mention of her people to follow her husband's beliefs.

Horem might have lesser wives and concubines as duty ordered, but he spent every night possible on his prime wife's couch. When he wasn't away fighting the beast men, that is.

The Ægysians came from a heritage of warriors and were always prepared to fight. That was the way they had claimed and settled the land south of the Plain of Arriah. Conquered tribes became allies through treaties followed by marriage, and the entire area in which the Plain was situated was a fairly peaceful place now, except for the beast men.

No one knew where they came from or if they'd been there all along and had suddenly discovered their own military might. In fact, it was sometimes questioned if they had any true battle sense at all or were simply so fierce they didn't know when to surrender. Whatever the reason, at studied intervals, the Ægysians and their allies had fought the beast men for several hundred years, generally losing most of the battles.

It was always the same. They would swoop down from the mountains, entering the plain to fight with ferocious and deadly violence, then retreat. Sometimes, the Ægysians were victorious, and fighting would cease for a score of years or so; more often, the beast men won, and when that happened, whatever land they'd taken over would house another huddle of buildings as a village sprang up and another bit of the Plain of Arriah fell to the creatures. If attempts were made to reclaim the lost land, the beast men defended it successfully. They appeared to be intent on acquiring the entire valley for themselves, no matter how long it took. Ægys was the only power preventing this, but there was always the chance that could change.

Senset thought the beasts' battle tactics showed more intelligence than anyone gave credit, but of course, no one asked her opinion. In fact, she wasn't even supposed to know that fact, but Horem had spoken of it to Asanath and she, in turn, while bragging of her beloved's confiding in *her*, as opposed to any of his other wives or concubines, told the girl. Asanath had no doubt Horem would eventually slay all the beast men, and peace—*true* peace—would be accomplished in her husband's lifetime.

Perhaps she was right. Once again, Horem had beaten back the horde and this time had captured one of the creatures. Surely that was a *Sign*…a signal from the all-powerful gods that the terror those animal-men wrought was about to come to an end.

Chapter 3

Stomach grumbling, Senset decided since she was on the way to the kitchens, she should nourish herself while there. It had been a long time since she had broken her fast, dining early that morning with the other women on the floor above Asanath's suite.

An orange and a square of flatbread don't last long.

As prime wife, Asa had private apartments where her husband might visit her. All the others, with their female children, lived in a community dwelling with small cell-like rooms where they slept in private, though they spent most of their time in the grand chamber, gossiping, bathing, tending their babies, and playing games, when not called into their husbands' presences. No males, except infant sons, were allowed on that floor; the guards were all female, mercenary amazons hired from the city of Pontus on the shores of the Euxine Sea. Boy-children stayed with their mothers until the age of five, at which time they were given their own suites and servants elsewhere in the palace as their educations began.

Senset was certain she could wheedle some sweetmeats or pastries from the kitchen help, but if not...

Perhaps I'll go into the garden and pick a couple of peaches.

That made her think of the fruit thrown at the beast, how it had burst apart on impact, of the bits of pulp clinging to its fur.

She had to pass through the upper gallery of the audience chamber, where her lord father was even then sitting upon his throne awaiting his returning son.

I wish I could hear Horem tell Father of the battle.

She could almost see him, so handsome in his armor, kneeling before his father, waiting for permission to rise and speak.

Aseti-Ra, no less tall than his royal son, though not quite so slim now but still a fine figure of a monarch, would be adorned in his linen robes, head held high and neck stiff to support the heavy woven-cane crown holding the same symbols as his son's helmet. He would be seated on a throne situated between larger-than-life statues of Muut, goddess of truth and order, Mafdet, bringer of justice, Bastet the cat-headed and Nekhbet, both protectors of the king, and Hathor-Menkaure-Bat, the triad of gods giving him the right to rule. He would leave his throne, coming down the steps with arms held wide to embrace his son as he got to his feet…

At least, that's the way Senset envisioned Aseti-Ra's meeting with Horem.

Why is it women are never allowed to be present when important guests arrive? Females were rarely allowed in the audience hall, not even Aseti-Ra's own prime wife. *Why are we always the ones to organize banquets, whether we attend them or not?*

Though Senset herself would never be invited to a feast because of her low rank in the royal birth pecking-order, she had once dared ask her father that very question and was surprised by his answer.

Women have no need to hear such serious talk as men must say when they come to see me, Daughter. We speak of war or trade or other subjects of a business nature. What advice or input could a female offer? When honoring our guests or making celebration giving homage to the gods, then a woman's in her element, for who else can know better what to say and do to make the atmosphere congenial and the manner of things proper for the occasion?

Senset had accepted his answer and bowed. With a pat to her bewigged head, Aseti-Ra sent her on her way, thinking his reply a wise one and that it had been accepted. He was completely unaware of his third daughter's rebellious thoughts.

I don't want to arrange dinners and banquets. Let the dining-hall stewards do that. I want to hear Horem tell of how he fought the beast men and killed them and came back to us unharmed. I'd like to be his charioteer and drive his horses while he nocks his arrows and sends them into beast men's hearts.

Those thoughts came back to her as she paused on the gallery.

Hinep hides here and spies, and Father allows it. What if I—

A scuff of thick-soled sandals on the stairs told her guards approached.

I mustn't be found here. Where can I hide? A quick look around told her the only place was in one of the niches behind the statues guarding either side of the gallery. Before she could move, the two guards were through the doorway.

"Hold there," one called out, raising his spear. "Who are you and what are you doing here?"

"Calm down," the other told him.

Senset recognized him. A young guard called

Amasis. He smiled at her, bowing.

"Hello, my lady."

She nodded, returning the smile, as the first guard demanded, "You know this girl?"

"This isn't just a *girl*, stupid. This is Lady Sensete-Ra, His Majesty's third daughter and tenth child. Her mother is Princess Yashmina."

"I beg your pardon, my lady." The guard was immediately on one knee, head bowed. "Forgive me."

"Please, get up." Since she was rarely in the public eye or even a private one, Senset was never comfortable with such homage.

The guard scrambled to his feet. He dipped his head in another bow as he said, "May I ask why you're here?"

"I was on my way to the kitchens," Senset replied. She looked from one to the other, raising eyebrows haughtily. "Why are *you* here?"

"Why…uh…" The guard stuttered under her stare, uncertain if he'd made another error.

Amasis, accustomed to her teasing, came to his rescue. "We've been sent by His Majesty to make certain no curious slaves lurk about to eavesdrop on his audience with General Horem. And we'd better get to it."

He nudged his companion in the ribs and bowed before turning away.

"Hinep's on errands for the princess," Senset called after him as he and the other guard began to check behind the curtains and in the niches. She started down the corridor.

"You'd better learn to recognize His Majesty's offspring," she heard Amasis say. "Otherwise you may get into trouble for challenging the wrong person."

"How was I to know the girl was his daughter? Hell,

he's got so many children, he probably doesn't even know their names," came the retort.

Whatever else he said was lost as Senset rounded a corner in the hallway and the stairs to the kitchens loomed ahead.

That's certainly not true, she thought.

For a man with so many wives and concubines, Aseti-Ra kept himself well supplied with information on his many children, not only their birthdates but on the progress in their educations, how his sons were doing in their military training, and how their wives were faring as well. He was often seen in the palace's many gardens playing with his grandchildren or speaking with his daughters-in-law.

She went through the open hallway connecting the kitchen to the palace.

It was a bright, sunny place, a series of roofed archways draped with heavy wisteria vines whose fragrance now wafted over her. To the left, in a small courtyard were several high, round-roofed ovens where breads and cakes were baked to keep the kitchen itself from being so hot. Two of the cook's apron-clad helpers stood in front of them, baking shovels ready to lift out the loaves as soon as they were done. Just ahead loomed the kitchen door where the scents of roasting meats mingled with the smell of baking bread and the wisteria's delicate scent.

Mmm, smells like fruit-bread. Senset took a deep breath as she walked through the doorway. *I hope Cook will let me have some.*

****

Cook had been very generous. Since fruit-bread was one of Horem's favorites and she, with proper

22

anticipation, was in the midst of preparing the meal to be sent to Asanath's suite for her "reunion" with her beloved, she'd stopped long enough to cut the girl a large slice from one of the loaves, then sent her on her way.

Senset sat on one of the stone benches near the ovens to eat her treat.

Though the ovens were only a few feet away, she was shielded from their heat by the shade from the wisteria above her head.

Senset fell to eating with gusto. Cook had cut her a large slice, almost a *hunk,* of the honey-sweetened bread. It was filled with glaced fruit—figs, de-seeded grapes, and plums—and dusted with honey, crystallized then beaten into powder. It had long been her favorite pastry, as well as her brother's, and she was certain he was going to enjoy it tonight.

If he gets a chance to eat it, she thought.

Knowing Asanath, he'd probably have little opportunity to partake of any kind of food until after he and his wife had risen from their marital couch. Senset was aware of the intimacies of marriage; they had been explained to her when she reached bleeding age, but the knowledge wasn't very detailed. Briefly, she wondered exactly what they could do with Asanath in such clumsy shape, then shrugged.

I suppose once I'm a wife, I'll learn for myself...if I ever become a wife.

The thought nagged a moment before she pushed it away. She was seventeen now. Aseti-Ra's other two daughters had been wives and mothers long before that age while she remained unmarried, and even unbetrothed. There were no more kingdoms needing to be allied with Ægys. All south of the Plain of Arriah had been conquered and aligned.

Once, when she'd lamented that fact, Asanath had snapped, "For heaven's sake, Senset. Do you want your noble father to have a war just so you can get a husband?"

No, Senset didn't want that, but she did want to fulfill her destiny as a royal daughter by making a marriage pleasing her father.

There weren't any eligible young Ægysian men presently available, either. Still, Senset was confident someone would appear for her, some prince, perhaps even from a foreign land not wanting to engage in war with her father but merely having heard of its strength and wishing to offer allegiance.

That thought made her smile as she nibbled the last scrap of bread.

Oh yes, I'm more than confident…

On the evening of her last natal anniversary, she waited until everyone was asleep, then took a candle and knelt before the polished metal mirror on its stand in her room.

She'd closed her eyes and prayed to Neith the great Mother Goddess to send her someone, and then she'd waited for a count of ten before opening them again. Holding the flame of the candle close to the mirror, Senset peered into its depths, expecting to see the face of her intended. For a moment, she saw nothing, then over her reflected shoulder, something moved…an image appeared…a pointed ear sporting a golden ring…sharp teeth…furry face…

Gasping, Senset whirled.

Bubash clung to one of the ledges cut into the wall, having leaped to it from the doorway.

"Oh, you silly cat. You startled me."

Bubash merely licked her paw, not bothered at all that she'd interrupted Senset's seeking of her true love and frightened his image from the mirror.

No matter. *He'll come. When the Mother Goddess is ready to send him to me.*

It would be soon. She was certain. This victory of Horem's was connected to her betrothed somehow. She could feel it in her heart.

Senset swallowed the last bit of bread and stood to brush the crumbs from the folds of her linen gown.

****

Wishing she'd been given the charge of taking Asanath's message to Horem, Senset had no true reason to find herself at the door to her brother's suite. Except that she wanted to see him, and—just as Asanath would also do—assure herself he was truly all right. Though he'd appeared unharmed as he stood beside his charioteer, she wanted to be certain he hadn't been wounded in any way, and no bandages were hidden under his armor.

Asanath would be angered she'd seen Horem first, but Senset didn't care.

Asanath got her way too much. Being prime wife to the Prince Royal, adored by her husband, and with child most of the time enabled her to have that.

If Horem's audience with his father went as it usually did, the prince was by now in his own apartments, resting and being prepared to go to his wife. Senset took a deep breath as she approached the tall, metal-encased double doors.

On the transom, Nekhbet again spread her protective wings over the entrance to the prince's chambers. From

25

his perch on the left side of the doorframe, Bes, the dwarfed demigod, stared at his own image on the right. Lotus blossoms and figures of slaves bearing baskets of flowers and fruits walked the wall of the fresco around the door.

Raising her fist, she struck the door panel in the customary three knocks announcing someone requesting entrance, then waited.

"Who's there, disturbing my noble master's rest?" Khonsu, Horem's personal manservant, spoke from the other side of the door.

"Sensete-Ra," Senset answered. "Wishing to enter and bid my noble brother welcome."

There was a pause while Khonsu relayed that message to Horem. Then, the door swung open to reveal the N'juban servant standing there, massive in his white linen robes, bowing so the bead-wrapped curls of his wig fell forward to strike his ebony cheeks as he stepped back to allow her entrance.

"Welcome, Sensete-Ra. Your noble brother is at his bath. He bids you come to him."

He gestured to an open door on the right, and Senset walked through it, for the moment ignoring the gilded-wood furniture and sculptures in the suite's common room.

The bathing room was no less well appointed. Foot-square tiles of aqua and white decorated the floor as well as three feet up the walls in a ceramic wainscoting. The ceiling was supported by statues of Nut, Ra-Horakhty, Toth, and Shu, gods of the night, the dawn, the sun and the moon, and the air. On the high border traversing the walls near the ceiling crawled hundreds of figures of Khepra, the sacred scarab, his hard-shelled back iridescent with the mingled colors of the rising dawn.

In this room, the frescoes were of lake scenes, water lilies, fish, cranes, and water birds, the pattern repeated again in the large-tiled tub in its center. On a low couch next to the tub, Horem lay on his belly, chin resting on his crossed arms. He was naked, a female slave massaging the muscles of his thighs while another poured oil into her hands and kneaded his slim buttocks.

Senset's step didn't hesitate, though she carefully averted her eyes from her brother's body to his face. Though the common clothing of Ægysian men was light linens and generally only a knee-length hip-kilt with a wide, bejeweled girdle, she'd never had occasion to see a man's body completely bare. Asanath had regaled her many times with words of adoration for her husband's physique, as well as his lovemaking ability, though the girl always managed to distract her before she got too graphic.

Long ago, Senset had decided she wanted to learn some things first-hand, not from her sister-in-law. She didn't want her own brother to be the first man whose *Most Treasured Possession* she saw, either.

"Little sister!" Horem raised his head from his arms and held out a hand to her. "It's good to see you."

She ran to the couch, caught his hand and pressed it to her forehead, dipping a short bob of a curtsey. "It's good to see you, also, brother. I'm most joyed at your safe return."

Then she simply stood there, looking at him, glad he was home and safe. He returned his arm to the couch, resting his chin against it and closing his eyes. He looked tired, she thought, but that was only natural. She doubted one got much sleep while fighting a war. Or many chances to bathe or shave, either, and she was certain that distressed him since the Ægysians were, by nature, a fastidious people.

Horem had already bathed, as was evidenced by the wet sponges collected in the basket lying on the tiles near the tub, and the damp towels on the floor yet to be gathered by slaves at Khonsu's direction. He hadn't been shaved, however, and the dark shadowing on his head and the stubbling on his cheeks and chin revealed he hadn't been near a barber in some time.

He looks so odd.

Vaguely, Senset wondered how Horem would appear if he allowed his hair to grow. There was no room for a wig under his war helmet, but in the palace, he wore elaborate ones, with beaded and braided locks hanging to his waist, as well as ear disks and jeweled collars so heavy she wondered how he managed to walk while wearing them.

"Has Asanath sent you with more messages?" He opened his eyes, glancing at her. They held laughter, crinkling at the corners, telling her he was well aware how embarrassing she considered his wife's verbal worship. "Perhaps more words of adoration? Lauding my amatory efforts? Or my physical attributes?"

"No, thank the heavens. Honestly, Horem, how do you stand it?"

"I stand it because I love her. *Rub harder, damn it*…I've been standing in a chariot for nearly six months nonstop. My muscles are rock-bound."

It was a moment before Senset realized he was directing those last words to the slave working the oil into his calves.

"Besides, it strokes my ego to know she thinks of

28

me that way. So…if you aren't my beloved wife's message-bearer, why are you here?"

"Do I need a reason to be in my brother's company…other than the fact you've been absent for six months?"

"I guess not," he conceded. "Especially since I'm your favorite brother—at least I hope I still am—as you, little princess, are my favorite sister."

"I'm your *only* sister, now that Nephrys and Tetera are wives."

Aseti-Ra had made certain his two eldest daughters were Prime Wives to their husbands. That way they had more prestige in their adopted countries and he, in turn, had more influence with his sons-in-law. He also required they return to visit him twice a year so he could ensure himself of their well-being and get reports from the slaves he had sent with them as spies.

"True," Horem agreed. "But I don't miss them as I'll miss you when you marry and move away."

"That doesn't appear to be happening anytime soon." Senset's answer was a grumble.

"It'll come soon enough." He patted the couch near his shoulder. "Come, sit with me and let's talk. I know you want to hear all about the battles. What is it about warfare that interests you so? Females shouldn't be concerned with such violence, unless they're like Father's amazons." He raised his head to give her a slightly startled look. "You don't wish to become one of those, do you?"

"Of course not, silly."

She dropped onto the couch beside him, still careful not to let her gaze stray past his shoulders. They were broad and heavily muscled, tapering to a slim waist, and

Asanath had described their breadth in great length on several occasions. Senset caught his hand, squeezing it before letting him return it to propping up his chin.

"What I'd really like to know about is the beast man."

"What beast man?" He spoke as if he had no idea what she meant.

"Don't be that way!" She slapped his shoulder lightly with her open palm.

Horem grinned.

"The prisoner. Did you capture him yourself? What are you going to do with him? Put him in the zoo? Question him? What?"

"Oh, *that* beast man." Horem hesitated as if debating how much to say before replying with false modesty, "Yes, I captured him."

"Tell me about it."

"Really, Senset, I don't think…"

"Please." She seized his hand again, shaking it. "I know you won't be telling Asanath. Not in her delicate condition, and I know you want to brag, so tell *me*. You've a willing audience. I want to hear."

"Well…" That was all he'd been waiting for.

He'd already given his father his report. Within two days, there would be a banquet celebrating the victory, by which time a scribe would've written down the entire story. A minstrel would sing it to their guests, with loud laudatory exclamations, but Senset was the only one Horem was able to actually talk to about the things he'd seen and done on his campaigns, though he generally didn't give her the complete, gory details.

"It was just a little after dawn four days ago…"

It seemed the beast men liked to strike at that

particular time of day, expecting their foes to be immersed in sleep and sluggish to respond. By now, of course, the Ægysians were accustomed to it, so they were startled when nothing happened, uneasy as the day wore on, and on edge when night came and the enemy still hadn't appeared. They had just settled into sleep, crouching around their campfires with weapons still drawn, when an ear-rending scream split the air, and the creatures were upon them.

"Luckily, the horses were still harnessed, so Ramasis and I leaped into the chariot, and I drew my bow."

All around them, men were fighting as the other war-chariots rolled into action. Horem could see arrows flying, beasts falling with shafts sunk deep into their chests. His own chariot was too hemmed in for him to aim his bow, however, so he abandoned it and drew his sword. With it in his right hand and spear in his left, he fought while Ramasis guided the chariot through the press of bodies.

"And then—out of nowhere—this beast was riding straight toward me! He looked as if he wasn't even guiding his horse. I don't know how they do it."

Instead of using chariots, the beasts actually rode their horses, giving them an advantage. Horem's grandfather had tried to get his own men to learn to ride, but the ability to control an animal and use a weapon at the same time took too much divided concentration, especially when aiming an arrow. Standing in a chariot with someone else driving, so the warrior could center his attention on his weapon and only that, was considered best by the Ægysians, so the idea was abandoned.

"He swung his sword at me, knocking my own out

of my hand. I spun my spear, catching him in the ribs."
Horem raised himself off the couch to gesture. "It
knocked him off his horse, but the creature whirled so he
fell directly into the chariot with us."

Horem took a deep breath. Abruptly, he twisted to
glare over his shoulder at the two slaves. "Did I tell you
to stop and listen? Get to work on those muscles in my
shoulders. And you…"

He looked at the one bent over his legs.
"Concentrate on my ankles."

Hurriedly, the two went back to work.

"Where was I?" Horem lay down again.

"The beast fell into the chariot," Senset prompted.
"It didn't turn over, did it? Oh, Horem, you might have
been trampled—"

"I wasn't, thank the gods."

*The chariot rocked, Ramasis thrown against its side,
nearly dropping the reins as the beast tumbled to the
floor. Horem clung to the handhold on his side of the
chariot wall, his spear flailing, the beast lying stunned
beneath their feet. The horses were galloping wildly, the
chariot careening and teetering on only two wheels. For
a sickening moment, Horem was certain it was going to
topple and they would be dragged and crushed. Then, it
righted itself, and Ramasis regained control of the
animals.*

"Before the beast could recover, I drove my spear
into his shoulder with all my strength." He raised himself
on his elbows, making a stabbing motion with one hand
fisted on top of the other.

Senset winced. Horem looked at her, mouth
quirking.

"It pinned him to the chariot floor. And then…it was

over."

"Wh-what do you mean?" Senset stared at him. She'd almost been able to see it…the madly out-of-control chariot, the horses wild-eyed and stampeding, Ramasis and Horem struggling to stay inside while the beast rolled about on the floor between them.

"The moment my spear went into the creature's shoulder, a great cry went up." There was a look of wonder on her brother's face as if he still couldn't believe it. "Though they continued fighting, some of their fierceness disappeared, and we began to drive them back."

"Why?"

"The gods alone know, little sister."

"The prisoner…was he their leader?"

That would be a good reason. If their leader was killed or captured, they'd have no one to tell them to fight. She'd been told that was the way lions hunted gazelles, by killing the leader and throwing the herd into panic.

Horem shook his head. "I don't think so. There was another, just as wild and fierce. He wore a golden mask. I think he was their leader. "

Senset shuddered. "What manner of creature is so hideous he hides his face from his own people?"

Her brother shrugged. "If I had an answer to that, I might be able to unravel the riddle of these animals, little sister."

"So now you have a prisoner. What are you going to do with him?" Senset repeated her earlier question. "Will you question him?"

"For what purpose?"

"Why…to find out more about his people."

"Senset, the creature's dumb. He can only scream and grunt and make loud noises. Besides, there's nothing I wish to know about those animals, except how to kill them."

"Will you put him in the zoo?"

"Hardly." Horem laughed at that suggestion. "He's too wild. He'd probably disrupt all the other animals, and they're mostly a docile group. Besides, he's a little too smart to be put permanently in a cage. I imagine he'd find a way to get out."

"How do you mean?"

"Remember how those wild baboons learned to pick the lock on the orchard gate so they could get in and steal figs? Until the gardener set two of my hunting lions upon them?"

She nodded, remembering hearing the screams in the night and the lions' roars as they ran after and caught the thieving simians.

"Beast men have a certain cunning, Senset."

"Are you certain they're animals, then?" Senset questioned. "I mean…they make war, they use weapons, they ride horses. You say this one might learn how to get out of a cage…doesn't that show they're intelligent?"

"Not much. You've seen how the street entertainers teach their dogs to do tricks? For a little bit, you'd believe those animals were intelligent, but it's just something they've learned. Hell, even Bubash figured out how to open a door by watching Asanath do it. As for riding a horse… I've seen wild monkeys leap onto gazelles' backs and ride them from one tree to another instead of swinging through the branches. These creatures are smart, to be sure, Senset, but they're still animals. They're just dirty, hairy, stinking animals."

"So what's going to happen to him, if you aren't going to put him in the zoo?" Even as she asked the question, Senset felt a sinking in the pit of her stomach. She was certain she already knew the answer.

"Three days from now is the Celebration of Ra-Horakhty. Father's holding my victory feast that night. I plan to sacrifice the beast to the god and ask him to give us peace in exchange for the creature's life essence."

"Everyone attends the part of the Celebration taking place at the temple." Senset reminded him. "Do you want Asanath to see something like that?"

"Of course not." Horem said, with certainty. "Neither my noble father nor the priests would wish my child endangered by forcing its mother to attend. And you won't be there, either. I'll tell Father you need to stay with Asanath."

"No." Senset shook her head. In the moments before Horem ended its life, it would be her only chance to see the beast up close. "I'll be there. To honor you, my brother, as well as the god."

"Thank you, little sister." Horem rolled over onto his back, closing his eyes. He put his arms behind his head, cradling it in his hands.

Senset saw that his chest, as well as his armpits, was also bristly with hair, and there was a shadowy trail running toward his thighs. Like her own hair, if allowed to grow, it would be a very dark brown with reddish sunlights. She looked away, not daring to let her eyes explore further.

"Khonsu."

"Master?" The slave moved from the spot near the pool where he'd been standing during Horem's narrative.

"Where's that barber? He was notified over an hour

35

ago."

"I left him sharpening his razors, my lord. He should be along directly."

"Good." Horem raised a hand, running it across the dark bristle on his head, scratching lightly. His nails made a rasping sound as they scraped over his scalp. "I want to be rid of this itchy stuff as soon as possible. From my head as well as the rest of my body. When I go to my wife tonight, I want my balls as smooth and clean as a baby's! Go now, little sister. I thank you for coming to me."

He closed his eyes. One of the female slaves lifted his left arm, resting his wrist against her breast as she caught it between her arm and side and began to knead his bicep.

Effectively dismissed, Senset turned and hurried to the door.

As she opened it and stepped out, she met the barber, carrying his case of razors.

Chapter 4

I must see the creature before he dies.

That thought had been going around and around in her head since Horem told her his plan. Now, as she lay on her couch trying to sleep, Senset knew she wouldn't rest until she'd seen the beast man up close.

As soon as she was certain everyone was asleep, she slid from her bed. Wrapping a sleeping robe around herself, she made certain it was fastened securely, then tiptoed from her cell, through the common room, and to the door.

"Where do you think you're going, mistress?" One of the amazons, a tall redhead who towered over Senset by nearly a foot, asked. She was fairly comely but big and muscular, and the heavy armor she was wearing did nothing to make her look any smaller.

"I-I can't sleep," Senset stuttered.

The warrior women always intimidated her. In spite of her own wish to be her brother's charioteer, she'd never understood why a female would want to actually *fight.*

"I thought I'd walk in the garden a while."

"One of us will go with you." The redhead looked at her fellow guard, a buxom blonde with a long braid hanging over one shoulder. "Amaris?"

"N-no, that's all right," Senset assured her quickly. "I really wish to be alone right now." The redhead looked skeptical, appearing about to protest, so she went on quickly, "I-I'm…just…you know…having cramps… It's almost my Time…" She let her voice trail away as if in embarrassment.

"Ah…" The guard looked sympathetic. "I understand. " She nodded. "Yes, a walk in the cool night air would be good for that. Very well, mistress. Go on your way then. But if you're not back within two hours, I'll come to check on you."

"Of course. I appreciate that." Senset backed away as she spoke. "You're very conscientious. Thank you."

She turned and walked quickly down the corridor toward the stairs.

Behind her, she heard the redhead say, "Gods, I'm glad we're deprived of that little benefit once we become warriors."

"Life does have its blessings, doesn't it?" her companion muttered.

****

Once out of the guards' sight, Senset turned left instead of right, following the corridor to the doors leading down a flight of stairs to the dungeon. Initially, they were of normal size, but at the second landing, they narrowed, until by the time the fourth landing and the actual door leading into the caverns under the palace were reached, the flight of stairs was no wider than one man could traverse.

There was no lighting, no torches or lamps set into the walls, and she had to move slowly, fearful a misstep might send her tumbling into the darkness.

What am I doing? Do I really want to see this creature? What does it matter if I only get a glimpse of it before it dies? What if the dungeon master's there?

Surely he won't let me pass. And he'll probably tell Father and then I'll have to make up a good reason for being here.

Nevertheless, she didn't turn back but continued until her feet struck a flat surface that didn't slope downward and she walked through a darkened archway into the dungeon itself.

For a moment, Senset stood still, staring into the room. There was no one around. The dungeon master must be off somewhere having his supper. She hoped.

It was very dark, the only light trickling dimly through an open square high in the wall, just a few inches above the outside ground level. She could see motes of dust swirling thickly as the outside air stirred them. Her gaze followed the pale beam of moonlight to where it widened slightly, illuminating a bulky object in the center of the room.

A cage…a large cage fashioned of iron slats woven together. On one side, she could see a smaller rectangle, a door with chains wrapped through the slats, a U-shaped padlock holding them together. The dust swirled faster, and she felt the wind as it swooped into the cage and out again, bringing with it a thick smell of urine-soaked straw, blood, and sweat.

The center of the cage was dark, but in one corner…

She thought she could see a huddled shape, thick, wiry fur standing upright, like the way Bubash's hair spiked when she was angry or displeased. It wasn't moving, however.

Is the beast sleeping?

One of the soldiers had struck it with the flat of his sword. It had already been wounded. Could it have died from the soldiers' abuse?

Carefully, she tiptoed into the room. Hugging the wall, she stopped in the shadows cloaking the walls and simply stood there, staring.

She felt a brief disappointment. She'd expected the creature to be clawing at the walls of the cage, screaming its rage at being imprisoned. As it was, she could barely see anyth—

"Are you going to stay there in the shadows staring at me, or are you coming out where I can see you?"

Senset jumped. For a fraction of a second, she didn't move; then, before she realized it, she had taken a step toward the cage.

"You can speak?"

"I'm talking to you, aren't I?" The beast turned his head.

She thought she saw the glow of eyes reflecting the shifting light.

"So apparently, I can speak, and more than just AEgyn, too."

"But you're a *beast*," she protested. "Horem said you couldn't talk, except to make sounds and grunts."

"Then he's mistaken, isn't he?" There was a rustle of straw as he rolled over so he was facing her.

With a groan, he rose to his knees. The movement sent the mix of smells toward her again.

She became aware he was much larger than she'd originally thought. He must have been curled up in the straw. His voice was rough and harsh, like a hound who'd bayed itself hoarse.

"He was right about one thing." Senset raised a hand, flapping it in front of her to wave the odors away. "You *are* dirty, smelly, and hairy!"

He gave something that might have been a bark…or

a grating laugh…and shook his head, a shaggy head with its beard hiding most of his face.

"I've been fighting a war, little mistress. I've been wounded, beaten, and dragged through your none-too-clean streets. Should I smell as if I've just been bathed by my handmaidens and anointed with fragrant oils?"

"You have handmaidens?" Her memory of him lashing out at the villager imposed itself over an image of him splashing in a pool-bath while slave women shrieked and fled in terror.

Would he like water any more than Bubash did? Would his fur stand on end like the cat's, before being slicked to a sodden mass?

He crawled closer, looking up at her, one hand against the woven bars. It was a *real* hand, she saw, with four grimy, bloody fingers and a thumb. There was dirt under the broken nails. From his knuckles upward was covered by torn leather wrapped in fur…a lion's paw, the claws still embedded in it.

"More than I need." A smirk touched the bearded face. "Or want."

"Horem says that same thing." Senset wrinkled her nose. Not so much at the smell. She was getting accustomed to that. It wasn't any worse than being in the stables, really. The gesture was to emphasize her next words. "Men. You're all alike."

"Get past the smell and the hair, and I imagine I'm as much a man as your beloved general." His hand tightened on the slats as he hauled himself to his feet with a swallowed grunt. "Maybe more so."

"Don't disparage Horem." She was quick to defend her brother. "He's our hero."

"And has one stalwart worshipper, it seems." He

41

was upright now, towering over her. He was even taller than Horem. A giant.

Senset forced herself not to scurry backward into the shadows.

"He's my brother."

"I beg pardon, your little majesty." He bowed slightly and nearly fell, clutching at the bars again.

It was difficult to read his expression through the gloom, the dirt, and that beard. Senset had never seen a man with hair on his face before, except for that little stubble Horem and her father sported before the royal barber shaved it off.

It was oddly fascinating.

"Half-brother, really," she was surprised to hear herself explain. "I'm just the daughter of a seventh wife. But he knows my name. He speaks to me."

"You're double-blessed then, aren't you? Aram."

It took her a moment to realize he'd given her his name.

"Sensete-Ra." She executed a clumsy dip of a bow.

"*She who carries Ra before her*. A name which can be interpreted in many ways."

It shouldn't have surprised her that he knew the meaning of her name. Still, it did. This beast wasn't fitting anything she'd heard about his kind at all.

He shambled closer. One hand cradled his side, and he winced as he moved. He stepped into the little cone of moonlight and she saw that the fur on his arms and body, like that on his hands, wasn't really his. He was wearing an animal skin, several of them, sewn together. They were laced over what appeared to be a leather tunic of some kind. Soft leather boots held in place by wrapped rawhide strips covered from toes to knees, with heavily muscled thighs showing beneath the tail of the tunic. The garments and his legs were covered with dried mud and grass.

He staggered slightly, falling against the wall of the cage, and inhaled quickly and sharply as he regained his balance by clinging to the slats again.

"You're hurt." The fur covering his upper body was torn and bloody, as was the shoulder beneath it. Why was she shocked? She knew that already.

"Told...you." The words came out breathlessly. "Didn't I...say...I'd been wounded? You should listen to what people say, little mistress." He took his hand from the slat long enough to gesture. "The general did that with his spear. The soldiers beat me when I fell. Broke a couple of ribs, I think."

"You need a physician." Senset's gentle nature awoke. No one, not even an enemy, should suffer so.

That earned her a grimace that might have been a smile. "I'd rather be fed. Didn't bring any meat scraps to feed the animals, did you?"

"I'm sorry. I didn't."

"Hm." He cocked his head slightly, reminding her how the hunting pups acted when she spoke to them. Not that he looked like one of the pups. They were slim and sleek. "Does anyone know you're here, Sensete-Ra?"

"No."

Why would he want to know that?

"You shouldn't admit it," he cautioned. "I could kill you and no one would know."

He was right. Though he was in a cage, he could easily reach through the bars and catch her before she could move.

Why was I stupid enough to get so close?

She imagined that dirty, blood-encrusted hand seizing her…choking the life from her…shaking her as Bubash did one of the rats she caught in the stables' granary.

"What good would that do you? Then you'd be down here with a corpse. Unless…" She paused, then dared asked, "You don't eat…people…do you?"

"No. Though I'll admit you appear a tasty morsel." His tongue came out, traveling slowly across his cracked and bruised lower lip.

Again, she managed not to take a step backward, stifling the shudder trying to shiver through her.

"You're not afraid of me, are you?" He regarded her with startling admiration.

It was so dark she couldn't see the color of his eyes, just that they were shaded with pain and the beginnings of fever.

"Not really," she bluffed.

"Why are you here, Sensete-Ra?" he asked. "Did you come to jeer? Throw rotten fruit at me as your fellow townspeople did earlier?"

"No."

"Why then?" He sounded as if he truly wanted to know.

She decided to tell him the truth. "I…I was curious."

"So you decided to brave the dungeon and see the beast up close," he finished for her.

She nodded.

"Well, you've seen me." The look he gave her now was speculative. "What happens if someone finds out you've been here?"

"I'll be punished, I suppose." She shrugged, trying to appear nonchalant. She'd be punished all right…beaten, probably, then locked in her room, away from everyone, to consider her disobedience.

His head went up, turning toward the doorway. "You'd better go before they get here."

"Who?"

"My captors. They should be coming soon. Listen." His head turned so one ear was toward the door.

Senset copied his gesture. She heard nothing.

"They're on the way. Go."

She stepped away from the cage, into the shadows again. Aram backed away from the slats. No sooner was she hidden by the gloom than three men appeared in the archway. One carried a torch and a truncheon, the other two held spears. The spear-carriers wore uniforms.

"There he is," said the one who was the dungeon master, gesturing with his torch. "Do what you want. Just don't kill him. That honor belongs to General Horem."

One flipped his spear around, thrusting it through the bars, butt-first. Aram tried to dodge and failed. The spear struck him and he flinched, giving a grunt of pain. The other soldier and the dungeon master moved to opposite sides of the cage. She could see the truncheon and the second spear moving in the dim light.

Back against the dark wall, Senset edged away. As she reached the stairs and darted up them, she heard Aram cry out, the sound an odd counterpoint to the sound of wood meeting flesh and the soldiers' laughter.

Chapter 5

Senset slept little that night, and when she did finally drift into slumber, she dreamed of Aram in his dark, stinking cage…

…a different Aram from the beast, however. He was dressed in white linen robes, standing in the midst of the filthy straw. A shaft of sunlight surrounded him, making his body glow. On his head was a gilded headdress, similar to those her father wore, though it bore no sacred symbols. His face was clean shaven, but blurred so she was unable to see his features. Straps ran from the temple-plates of the helmet, securing a woven false beard into place on his chin, the symbol of a king…

"Senset. My little majesty." Aram held out his hand. It was clean, the nails smoothed and hennaed a dark red.

She reached out to place her own in it…

"Senset, look out!" Horem appeared behind her, hurling his spear. It struck Aram in the chest, but it was no longer Aram. A raging beast stood in his place, tearing at the headdress, blood spurting from its wound…

With a gasp, Senset jerked herself from sleep. She stared into the darkness, trembling.

What a nightmare.

Why had she dreamed it? Why would her sleeping mind make Aram into the figure of a king? Had the gods sent her this dream as some kind of message?

If so, what does it mean and what must I do?

She had no answers to her own questions. She only knew one thing. She had to see Aram again before he died.

****

Senset fretted through the next day. As usual, Asanath requested her presence, though much later in the day, since she managed to keep Horem with her until the morning drifted into early afternoon. Then, he reluctantly left her side to go into counsel with his father and Aseti-Ra's advisors, and Senset was called to keep his wife entertained.

She wasn't very successful. Thoughts of her nightmare and of Aram lying at her feet skewered by Horem's spear kept intruding, until Asanath exclaimed petulantly, "What's the matter with you, Senset? I've asked you twice to pour me a cup of lemon water and you sit there, staring into space. Are you ill?"

She glared at Hinep, who hastily poured the water and presented it to her mistress.

Accepting it, Asanath went on without waiting for Senset to answer. "If so, go to your rooms and get away from me. I can't afford to be stricken by any sickness this close to my lying-in."

That pulled Senset from her thoughts. "I'm sorry, Asa. I didn't sleep well last night. I had horrid nightmares."

"Brought on by seeing that beast, no doubt." Her sister-in-law sniffed, finishing the drink. "He *was* horrid, even from so far away. I probably would've been terrified, if I hadn't thought of being encircled by my beloved's strong arms. Oh, Senset, he's so…"

"You're right. I should go and let you rest." Senset

cut into Asanath's speech, not giving her a chance to begin extolling Horem's virtues. With a bow, she ran for the door, leaving Asanath sitting there, mouth open.

Back in her own room, she lay upon her couch but didn't sleep, just kept thinking of her dream and what she was going to do once night fell.

Chapter 6

Once again Senset left the apartments, this time using her nightmare as her excuse. Perhaps watching the fish swim in the garden pool and smelling the subtle fragrance of lotus blossoms might soothe her mind and help her sleep, she said. The redheaded guard agreed. With the same warning as before, she allowed Senset to leave.

This time, the girl made a detour to the little orchard on the side of the palace, picking three of the sweetest peaches she could find.

Clutching the soft-fuzzed globes against her chest, she hurried to the dungeon. Her robe, tied carelessly in her haste, came untied, baring her bosom, and Senset paused, placing the peaches on the steps as she rearranged and closed its folds. When she slept, she abandoned the linen binding flattening her breasts. Freed, as they were now, they bounced as she walked and she was acutely aware of their heaviness.

The Ægysian concept of feminine beauty was of a slim, small-hipped female with flat breasts. Most of the women from other tribes fulfilled those requirements, but Asanath, coming from far to the south of the Plain of Ariah, and Senset—whose mother had been from an equally southern kingdom—were both round-hipped and buxom and dutifully bound their breasts in order to conform...though Asanath, usually bigger-breasted with pregnancy, swore Horem extolled her *lush and milk-rounded globes* loudly when they made love.

It came to Senset she was being very foolish in appearing before Aram in her sleeping-wear with her bosom unbound.

He's in a cage, what danger can he be?

After all, he'd made no offer of violence the night before.

Still, he's male and I should probably have dressed... But he's wounded and no doubt in worse shape tonight than yesterday...

Convincing herself her manner of dress didn't matter, she knotted the belt tightly and continued down the steps.

Once more, luck went her way. The dungeon master was again absent, and this time, she stepped boldly into the room, calling out, "Aram? Do you sleep?"

The shadows in the cage moved, rose, and staggered toward her.

"Little majesty. You grace me with your presence. Again." He seemed to weave slightly before grasping the bar with his good hand.

She wanted to ask him how he felt, and if he was in pain, but decided that was foolish. He'd been beaten twice in one day, as well as being wounded, and she doubted if anyone had called a physician.

Instead, she said, "Where's your jailer?"

"That one?" He glanced in the direction of the door, then shook his head. A strong air current of old blood and filth swept around her. Senset held her breath, fighting the desire to gag.

How can he stand to smell himself? Perhaps he can't?

"Around sundown, he eats his supper and drinks his beer, then heads to the barracks for a couple of games of cards with his soldier friends. It seems he was lucky last night. That's why he brought his friends back with him. To celebrate by beating the captive."

He turned his head and she saw the bruises on his cheeks and the split skin across his nose, the broken edges dark and ugly where they disappeared into the tangle of his beard. She wanted to put her hand through the bars and touch his face, pat it reassuringly.

"I'm sorry."

"Thanks for that, anyway." His voice was a little less hoarse now. It sounded young. She thought he might be around Horem's age, twenty-four natals. She wanted to ask but realized it didn't matter. Within one more day, he'd be no age at all.

Aram was still talking, rubbing his cheek. "Might not have been so bad if the bastard had shared some of his meal with me first."

Senset tightened her hold on the peaches and that brought his gaze to her breasts.

"What have you there, little majesty?"

A hand reached toward her. She backed away, then realized he was reaching for a peach.

"Is that for me?"

She was startled to see him begin to drool, moisture dripping out of the corners of his mouth to soak into the hair on his chin.

He must be starving.

She nodded.

He pulled it from her grasp.

She'd never seen anyone eat anything so fast. He bit into the peach with the ferocity he'd used on the attacking peasant, chewed, swallowed, and consumed the entire fruit in five bites before sucking the remaining flesh from the pit and tossing it into the straw.

"Good." It was mumbled through chewed pulp. His hand shot out. "Another?"

She gave him the other two and he alternated taking bites from each, finishing them as quickly. When he leaned against the bars with a sigh, wiping his sticky mouth with equally juice-stained fingers, he looked down at her and smiled.

It was shocking, that smile. So beautiful on that dirty, hairy face.

"Thank you. Been better if it was meat but good, anyway. It doesn't appear they're going to feed me any time soon."

Senset looked away.

"Do you know what they plan for me?" Aram continued talking, not noticing how she avoided his gaze. "What's my fate, little majesty?" When she didn't answer, he went on, "I mean…will your brother ransom me? Or am I to become an object of curiosity? His Majesty's pet beast? Is your beloved brother going to put a chain around my neck and parade me before his guests at parties, teach me tricks to keep them entertained?"

She looked back at him, eyes brimming with tears. She hadn't intended to cry. She'd simply planned to tell him what Horem intended, at least prepare him for what was to happen.

Unbidden, a tear rolled down her cheek.

"Here, what's this?" The dirty hand chucked her under the chin, lifting her head, and she didn't flinch, just leaned her cheek against it briefly, startled by how warm it felt, how the fur on his gauntlet rubbed rough against her skin.

Another tear joined the first, striking his fingers. Somehow, he understood.

"Horem isn't planning on keeping me alive, is he?"

"He plans to sacrifice you to Ra-Horakhty." She spoke through teeth gritted to prevent sobs. "Two days from now. He believes the god will end the war with your people if he does this."

"That's something I wish also, but not with me as the offering."

She was startled at the way he accepted this news.

"I suppose there's no changing his mind? My people will pay to get me back, you know."

The way he said it told her he knew whatever had been decided couldn't be changed.

"Aram, I'm so sorry." Senset began to cry in earnest, leaning her forehead against the bars, holding on to them.

"Thank you for your tears, little majesty." His hand brushed hers in what might have been a caress. Then, he turned away. "If you don't mind, I need to be alone now."

"What are you going to do?"

"Not much I can do. Except pray for the strength not to shame myself and my people as I die. I'll ask God to give me that strength."

"You have gods?" Somehow, she'd never thought of that, his having gods or religion or anything else resembling what her people possessed. What else did the beasts have making them human?

He shouldn't die. We should try to learn more about them from him.

"*God*," he corrected. "One god, the True One, and he's more powerful than all your false ones put

53

together."

She should've been angry at that, should've defended her religion at those insulting words. Instead, all she felt was confusion, and despair.

"If your God's so powerful, have him free you. Ask him not to let you die."

"Perhaps this is His plan for me," came his quiet answer. "Though I don't particularly want it." There was a sigh. "Thank you for the food, Senset. It'll give my body strength for what comes. Now, I must pray for my mind to find sustenance, also."

With that, he sank to his knees in the dirty straw, head turned away. Senset stood a moment longer, then hurried from the dungeon. At the doorway, she looked back.

Silhouetted against the wall, Aram leaned against the bars, hands clasped together, his forehead resting upon them. His shoulders drooped in defeat, shaking slightly.

As she ran up the stairs, she thought she heard hastily whispered words, followed by a harsh sob.

Chapter 7

Another sleepless night. Another tedious and anxious day filled with reprimands from Asanath, sharp words dared to be spoken by Hinep, and sneers from the cat. As the evening approached, Senset became frantic. With each movement of the sun across the sky, Aram had one less hour to live…and she could do nothing.

She'd tried.

She'd gone to Horem's apartments, requesting to see him. Khonsu explained her brother was closeted with his father and the council. He was too busy to see her, making plans for the sacrifice of the prisoner, as well as a new battle strategy. So certain was Horem that the god would grant his request and assure them conquest of their long-time enemy, he had called in his commanding officers and was planning an assault into the foothills of the mountain itself, bearding the beasts in their own territory.

"After the ceremony tomorrow, he'll have plenty of time for you, mistress," the slave said. "He plans to rest for several weeks before returning to annihilate these creatures once and for all."

"After the ceremony will be too late." Senset was ready to plead if she had to. "Please, Khonsu, tell him I *have* to see him. *Tonight*."

"I'm sorry, mistress." Khonsu shook his head. He looked as if he truly regretted refusing her, though he didn't understand the reason for her agitation. "He plans to spend this evening with the princess and has given orders nothing must disturb them. He—"

Nodding, Senset turned away, not letting the slave finish his explanation. Shoulders slumping, she made her way to the balcony outside Horem's suite. Sitting on one of the stone benches, she stared up at the sky, letting the sun burn her eyes until she could see nothing but large, dark splotches.

Ra-Harakhty, do something. This man mustn't die. I don't know why, but I feel it's important he live.

Briefly, a cloud obscured the sun and tears blurred her vision. For a long time, she stared at nothing, while the day lengthened and shadows fell over the terrace. At last, with a sigh, she stood and returned to her room.

The evening meal was an ordeal. The chatter of the other women, so lighthearted and inconsequential, was torture.

Senset wanted to shout at them. *How can you be so uncaring? A man will die tomorrow, a man we're treating as an animal, sacrificing him as we would a goat or a bull.*

When one of them dared start discussing what she was going to wear to the ceremony, she could stand it no longer. Jumping to her feet, she ran to her room.

"What's wrong with Senset?" Someone's question trailed after her.

"Who knows?" another replied. "She's been acting odd for days. It's probably just her Time approaching."

"Poor thing. I know how that is." The first speaker went back to her description of the robes she would wear to witness Aram's death.

Senset stayed in her room until the tables were

cleared and the others distracted by their children or preparing to sleep. She'd been thinking long and frantically, and one thought kept coming into her mind.

I must get Aram out of here. He mustn't die.

A wild and foolhardy idea came into her head, and she allowed it to carry her, not stopping to think it through and see its ill-planning. She went to Satis, head slave in charge of caring for the wives and concubines. The old woman was seated on cushions between two of the windows, three of her underlings with her, sewing garments for two of Aseti-Ra's wives.

"Good evening, little mistress," Satis greeted her cordially. "How may I serve you?"

"I've been having trouble sleeping," Senset answered.

"Ah." The old woman nodded. "Is that the reason you've been so out of sorts…taking those long walks in the garden and coming back so late each night?"

Senset nodded. After that first night, she'd thought it wise to let Satis know where she was going, though she lied to her as she had to the guards. "I thought perhaps you could give me a sleeping potion."

"Of course, mistress." Satis laid down her sewing, reaching for a nearby covered basket. Opening it, she surveyed its contents…small corked bottles filled with various herbs and powders. "Are you having bad dreams or are you simply restless at night?"

"Both." Senset decided to get the strongest sleeping concoction she could. "I think my restlessness is causing the bad dreams."

Satis nodded. "You'll need a special mixture."

Taking a mortar and pestle out of the basket, she extracted two of the little bottles, opening both. From one, she took small pieces of dried root, dropping it into the mortar's bowl; from the other, she shook tiny black grains onto her palm and placed them in the bowl also. Then, she took the pestle and crushed the two together.

"Valerian root and poppy seeds," she explained. She took a third bottle from the basket. This one had a lid with holes punched in it and she shook it once over the bowl's contents. "And a dash of dried, crushed lotus bulb. That should do the trick."

Lifting the mortar, she shook the mixture into a tiny vial, scraping out the last bit with her finger. Then, she poured in water from a nearby pitcher, corked the vial, and shook it vigorously. She presented the little container to Senset.

"There you are, mistress. Mix that with some fruit water and drink before you retire. You should have a good night's sleep and no bad dreams."

"Thank you, Satis." Senset took the vial, studying it.
Do I dare? Have I enough courage to do this?
"How long does it take to work?"

"Not long," Satis assured her. "Best be lying down when you drink it, else you may not make it to your couch."

"That fast?" Senset was shocked. "Then I think I'll take a walk in the garden beforehand. To help settle my mind."

"A wise idea," the slave agreed. "A soothed mind accepts the herbs' sleeping caress more easily."

Nodding, Senset went to the door, the vial clutched in her fist.
I will do this. I must.

By now, the guards were accustomed to seeing her leave, thought generally not this early. She paused a moment to speak to them, explaining about Satis's potion and her reason for walking in the garden before evening came. They sent her on her way with the usual admonitions.

Once out of sight, she headed to the dungeons. This early in the evening, the dungeon master would be there, keeping an eye on the prisoner. She'd never seen the man, never having been to the dungeons before her curiosity about Aram got the best of her, but she now knew what she *had* to do.

Aram had said the jailer ate his supper at sundown before abandoning his post to gamble with the soldiers. She had to get there before he left, somehow slip the sleeping potion into his beer, and wait for it to take effect. Then, she would let Aram out of that cage. She had no idea what she was going to say to the jailer nor how she would explain why she was in the dungeons. Royal children, especially female ones, weren't usually visitors to such a place. How she was going to get him to drink drugged beer was another problem.

Senset knew her plan wasn't well thought out. She was acting on mere hope.

Ra-Harakhty, please help me. Yes, help me cheat you of a sacrifice, of the one thing making you grant my brother's wish while it makes me a traitor to my people.

Aram mustn't die. Of that one fact, she was determined.

She was extra quiet going down the stairs, taking off her sandals and creeping down the stone steps on bare feet so there would be no telltale scuff of sole upon stone. The doorway was open as usual, though it appeared brighter this time.

Tiptoeing over to it, she peeped in, being careful not

to lean in too far and be seen. She immediately saw the source of the light. There was a lamp sitting on the floor, a large round urn filled with oil, a wick soaking in it, flame glowing from its tip. It lit the room brightly…all the corners and walls, highlighting Aram huddled in the straw on the far side of the cage, and the jailer sitting on his stool by the door. There was a small table beside him. Both it and the stool had previously gone unnoticed in the usual gloom of the place.

Sitting on the table was a tankard filled with dark amber liquid, and a folded-back square of cloth on which lay a half loaf of bread, some figs, and what appeared to be a slab of sausage. Next to the tankard was his ring of keys.

While she watched, the jailer picked up the sausage, bit off a hunk, and followed it with a mouthful of bread. Chewing, he lifted the tankard, taking a long swallow to wash down the two.

"Ahhh."

At the sound, Aram raised his head. His gaze swung to the food.

Poor thing. He's probably hungry.

On hands and knees, he crawled to the side of the cage near his jailer. One hand went through the bars, fingers spread. "Give me some."

"Shut up and get back." A sandaled foot kicked at his hand.

Aram's fingers recoiled, clenching into a fist. The jailer ate a fig, chewing loudly and making slurping noises, as if to torture his prisoner.

Senset knew she didn't make a sound, but suddenly, Aram's eyes swung toward the door, widening as he saw her crouched there. She put her finger to her lips.

She could see the question in his eyes—*Little majesty, what are you doing here?*—and the worry also, distracting him momentarily from his own danger. *What if the jailer discovers you?*

Nodding at the jailer, she made frantic motions with her hands.

Aram's brow furrowed. He scowled; it made him look more beast-like than ever. He looked from her to the jailer and back again, raising his shaggy brows.

Doesn't he understand I want him to distract the man? Oh...

She nodded again, pointing, then held up the vial, making a pouring motion with it, then pulled out the cork. Looking puzzled, he backed away to the other side of the cage, getting to his feet. Slowly, he nodded, then seized the bars, and gave a bellow so loud and sudden she jumped.

So did the jailer, dropping his sausage onto the table. Aram whirled, throwing himself at the bars in front of the man, shaking them violently.

"Here now, what's the matter with you?" The jailer got to his feet, picking up the truncheon lying beside his stool. "Be quiet or I'll give you something to yell about."

He raised the big stick.

That seemed to make Aram even more violent. He backed away from the bars only to throw himself at them again, yelling loudly. He beat on the bars with his fists.

"All right. Don't say I didn't warn you." Holding up the truncheon, the jailer advanced on the cage. He struck the bars. Aram struck back, snarling.

While the jailer's back was turned, Senset darted into the room, heading for the table. Luckily it was close enough to the door so she didn't have to run far. She reached out, tilting the vial, splashing its contents into the tankard. Over the jailer's shoulder, Aram watched anxiously as he dodged the big stick. She hurried back through the doorway to crouch in the shadows again.

As soon as she was out of sight, Aram backed out of reach, crawling into the safety of his corner. The truncheon stopped in midair, falling to the jailer's side as he spun and lumbered back to the stool.

"Crazy animal. Ought to just knock out his brains. Not wait for His Lordship to do it…"

Muttering to himself, he dropped onto the stool, seized the tankard, and downed half of it in one swallow. He wiped his mouth, then finished the rest of the sausage and the beer. When he set down the tankard, he just sat there.

Why isn't he falling asleep? Satis said it worked quickly.

From the cage, Aram glanced from the jailer to her, being careful not to let the man see where his gaze was directed. Senset met his eyes desperately.

Is it because he's so much bigger than I? Or because he ate food along with it? It isn't going to work.

Just as she was ready to burst into tears and run back up the steps, there was a crash.

Aram was on his feet instantly as the jailer toppled, taking the stool, the table, and the tankard with him to the floor.

Senset dashed through the door. She didn't hesitate but ran directly to the unconscious man and scooped up the keys lying on the floor. With the ring in her hand, she hurried to the other side of the cage. It took only minutes to find which key opened the padlock, and while Aram waited in disbelief, she swung the door open.

"Come on." When he didn't move, she dared seize his arm, tugging on it. "We have to go."

"What are you doing?" He didn't move.

"Getting you out of here," she snapped. "Unless you want to die tomorrow."

That seemed to break whatever was keeping him still. He leaped through the doorway. Dropping the keys, she started to the dungeon entrance, Aram following. He didn't question again why she was helping him, just came with her without speaking.

For the first time in her life, Senset was glad she was a lesser child who was not so carefully watched but had been allowed to run through the palace as she wished. She had discovered many little-used passageways and secrets openings, ways to get in and out without notice, escape routes if the unthinkable happened and the palace was ever stormed. She was going to use one now to get Aram to the stables.

Their progress was slow. Bent over and favoring his ribs, Aram had to stop often to rest. By some miracle, no one saw them. Only when they were standing inside the first stable, looking at the rows and rows of horses in their stalls, did he speak.

"Why are you doing this?"

"Isn't it obvious? I don't want you to die." Her answer was sharp. "Ask another stupid question like that and I'll begin to doubt your intellect."

"I mean, *why* are you doing this?" His emphasis on that one word changed its meaning. "Why help your brother's prize escape? It won't go well with you when they find out."

"I know that, and I must be mad, but I had a dream, Aram, and though I don't understand it, I think it means you must live."

"So…" He surprised her by accepting that and looking around. "What do we do now? How long do you suppose that jailer will sleep, anyway?"

"I've no idea. The draft was for me, so it may not be as long as I'd hope. As for what happens now…I give you a mount and you ride out of here."

He shook his head. "That won't work."

"Why not?" She wanted to seize and shake him, though he towered over her by nearly a foot.

"Your horses have never had men on their backs. None will let me ride them. They'll fight as if I were an attacking lion."

"Oh no…" She hadn't thought of that, and the look on her face told him so. "Do you think you can get back to your people on foot?"

"In this condition?" He spread his arms, grimacing as the movement pulled on his ribs.

His wound had dried, but through the tear in the animal hide and his breastplate, she could see a raw, red furrow, pus welling in it.

"I won't get very far. Your brother's men will probably catch me in a few hours." He shook his head and staggered, putting out a hand to brace against the wall. "I'm sick, little majesty. I've a fever, and infection is setting in. Even if I could hide in the jungle, I'll probably die if I don't get treatment."

"You're not going to die. Hear me?" She did catch him by the shoulders then, shaking him so violently he went white, gave a sharp gasp, and hugged his ribs. She jumped back, letting him go. "Aram, I'm sorry. I—" A sudden bray cut off what she was about to say. Senset whirled. "That's it!"

She started in the direction of the sound, Aram shambling behind her.

"What?"

"A mule." She approached the stall where one of the mules was stabled, one of those to which Aram had been tied. "He's accustomed to carrying burdens. A man should be no more than an extra-heavy pack to him."

Pulling open the stall door, she lead the mule out as she spoke. It came docilely, rubbing its nose against her hand. Raising dark eyes to Aram, it snorted, and stood there.

He reached for one of the bridles hanging on the wall, placing a hand on the mule's crest. The bit went easily into its mouth, and it waited patiently as he slid the brow band over its ears and across its forehead.

Walking on each side of the mule, they left the stable, and Senset led Aram to the garden across the courtyard from the stable. Pushing aside the shielding group of three lantana shrubs, she indicated a low door fitted into the wall. It hadn't been opened in some time and the hinges groaned as he helped her pull it inward. Outside, the flat, open wilderness that was the beginning of the Plain of Ariah beckoned.

Senset led the mule through the doorway. She placed the reins in Aram's hand.

"Can you mount by yourself?"

"This would be easier if I had a saddle."

"What's that?"

"Never mind. I'll get on, don't worry. Senset, I—" He leaned toward her, then appeared to realize he had to hurry. "Thank you."

Seizing the mule by its short bristle of mane, he heaved himself onto its back. The movement made him cry out. The creature staggered slightly under his weight, then righted itself and stood there, unperturbed.

Aram slapped its shoulders with the end of the reins, and it leaped forward, broke into a gallop and sprinted into the night.

Senset turned and ran back inside. She wanted to stay and watch him ride away, wanted to see him disappear into the darkness, but she knew that soon enough the jailer would awaken and there would be a hue and cry and the hunt would be on. If Aram were caught this time, he wouldn't live to become Ra-Harakhty's sacrifice.

As she closed the gate and let the shrubs fall back into place, her only thought was, *Great Ra, what have I done?* Nevertheless, her heart felt lighter.

Chapter 8

Senset awoke to a swarming of angry bees, the hum changing to human voices as she came to full consciousness.

"What is it? What's all the fuss?" Wrapping her robe about her, she stumbled from her room into the common area. She shook her head, dispelling the confusion of dreams still clinging to her.

"Oh, little mistress." After bowing to the women huddled among a grouping of floor pillows, Satis hurried over. "Such a shock."

"What is?" Senset looked around, rubbing her eyes.

The women were in their usual places, lying among cushions, reclining on couches, a few splashing in the pool, but they were all talking, the drone of their voices rising and falling.

"The prisoner escaped last night." The slave made it an announcement of the highest import.

For anyone to escape from the king's dungeon was a rarity, and though she already knew, Senset still managed to look startled. "B-but how...?"

"That fool of a jailer got drunk and the creature filched his keys and got out of his cell." Satis shook her head, but whether at the dungeon master's stupidity or the beast's intelligence, Senset couldn't tell. "Well, he'll get his reward for that soon enough."

"What do you mean?" That remark brought Senset

fully awake.

"His Majesty's passing sentence even now." Satis gave her a look as if the answer should be obvious.

"What? Oh no." Once again, she hadn't thought ahead, that someone would be punished—*had* to be punished—if Aram escaped.

The jailer was the logical one. He'd been in charge of the prisoner, responsible for him.

Whirling, she ran back into her room, leaving the slave standing there, mouth open. It took only a few moments to fling off the wrap and gather the linen folds of a gown about her. Then she hurried past Satis and across the common room to the doors.

"Little mistress, where are you going?"

"I must speak to my noble father."

"But…you're wearing no jewels…your face needs cosmetics…"

"Never mind that."

Stupid cow. Does she think painting my face is more important than a man's life?

Senset felt a violent twisting in her gut as she pulled the doors open and dashed into the corridor.

"Good morning, little mistress, what's the rush?"

Ignoring the call from the guard, she ran down the hall to the Audience Chamber, the violence in her stomach increasing.

Mighty Ra-Harakhty, forgive me. Don't let that man die for my crime.

Would the god hear her plea? Would he grant the prayer of one who'd cheated him of his sacrifice?

****

"Miserable creature, you'll pay for this insult to Ra-Harakhty."

Before she reached the doorway, she could hear her father's voice, loud and calm, though the rage in it was evident.

"Mercy, master! I swear I wasn't drunk." That cringing, desperate voice had to belong to the jailer.

"In that case, did you deliberately let the beast out of its cage?" Horem's fury wasn't as well-contained as his royal father's. "You cheated our supreme god of his tribute on purpose?"

"No…I…" For a moment, the jailer groped for an answer. "I had no more than my one mug of beer, Royal General. I swear. It's never made me drunk before. It shouldn't have this time." Desperate certainty crept in. "It must've been tainted. Y-you should look to the royal brewmaster. He gave me bad beer and it made me swoon…"

"Bah! Don't try to lay the blame on others." Horem swept his excuses aside.

Senset aimed herself for the doors. The guards saw her coming and lowered their lances, crossing them before the open doorway.

On any other day, she would've allowed herself to be turned away. Today, she lowered her head, caught the staffs of the weapons, and flung them upward, dashing through the opening into the audience chamber. Startled, the guards caught their sailing lances and ran after her.

"Horem, stop. Don't harm him." Inside the door, she skidded to a halt.

Behind her, the first of the guards nearly crashed against her. He recovered and seized her arm.

Dressed in linen *shendyt* and gilded leather girdle, her brother stood in front of the jailer, his curved sword raised. The hapless dungeon master cowered before him on the tiled floor. His arms were held by two more guards, their hands on his neck, forcing his head down. He twisted, looking up fearfully at the blade hovering above him.

Both the general and the accused stared at Senset.

"I beg your mercy, Majesty. The girl got by us." That was so obvious, the guard's explanation died away. His hand tightened on Senset's arm, making her wince.

Aseti-Ra ignored him, making a dismissive gesture with the hand holding the flail, symbol of his right to dispense justice to his people. At the moment, he was only interested in what his daughter had said. His advisor, standing at his right hand, remained silent.

"Why shouldn't my son punish this fool for what he's done?"

"B-because…" Senset pulled away from the guard. Hand falling from her arm, he let her go but stood, still tense, beside the other one. She took a deep breath. "Because I set the prisoner free."

"You *what?*" Horem's exclamation drowned out the gasps made by the others. He stalked around the jailer's cringing body, heading for Senset, sword still raised. "Why? How?"

"I told Satis I couldn't sleep. She made a potion, and I took it and put it in the jailer's beer."

"Why didn't you tell me this?" Horem spun around, glaring at the man on the floor.

"I-I…" He looked from the general to Senset. For a moment, she thought she saw a lie hovering on his frightened lips. Then he shook his head. "I never saw her, Noble General. Would I deliberately drink drugged beer?"

"You're lying." Horem didn't hesitate to accuse her.

"The beast saw me. He screamed and the jailer was distracted. I ran in, poured the potion into his mug, and ran out again."

"Idiot girl, do you know what you've done?" Horem shook his head, waving the sword. "Why would you do such a thing, Senset?"

"He didn't deserve to die, Horem." She managed to keep the quaver out of her voice. She wanted to cower away but forced herself not to move. "So I let him go."

"Who are you to decide who lives and who dies?" Horem demanded. "Do you now set yourself up as mightier than Mafdet, dispensing justice over all of us?"

"I do...when you refuse to listen to reason and act so stupidly." Senset couldn't believe she was speaking back to her brother in such a brazen way.

Truly, I've gone mad. Did the beast somehow bewitch me?

In that moment, all she could see were Aram's shadowy eyes, watching her in the dungeon's half-light.

"Why you..." The hand holding the sword pulled back. Senset braced herself, involuntarily shutting her eyes.

"Horem." Her father's quiet command cut through her brother's anger.

The sword swished as it was lowered to his side. Cautiously, she opened her eyes. Behind her, she heard the guards's soft sighs of relief.

"Why do you say this, daughter? What has my noble son, blessed by Sekhmet, done to warrant such brash accusations from you?"

"Horem told me the beast was a dumb creature, incapable of speech," she explained.

"It's true," Horem interrupted. "All he did once we

captured him was scream and shriek."

"Wouldn't you? If you were beaten with lances and clubs? And had clods of dirt and rotten fruit thrown at you?" she shot back. "He's not a beast. He's a man, as well-spoken as you, my brother." She couldn't resist adding, "Perhaps even more so."

"And you know this how?" Briefly, he bristled at that barely veiled insult as she compared the royal heir to a slavering animal.

"I spoke with him. He—"

"You *spoke* with the creature? You went to the dungeon?" Aseti-Ra was shaken out of his royal calm.

"Yes, Father. The dungeon master was absent on his meal time." She wouldn't say the man had gone for a little after-dinner gambling. He might yet escape punishment if she kept quiet about that.

"Foolish child!" Briefly, thought of her welfare overcame everything else. "The creature might've killed you."

"But he didn't," she retorted. "He was hurt. And hungry. I fed him a peach and we talked. And Aram told me—"

"Aram?" Brows scowling, Aseti-Ra interrupted.

"That's his name." She looked back at Horem, who was still silently seething. "It was what you should've done. Talk to him."

"So you talked to the creature. Did you have to let him go? You cheated Ra-Harakhty of the gift I promised him." He looked furious again. "What do you suppose he'll do in his disappointment?"

"Perhaps he won't do anything." She could only marvel at her own calm. By all rights, she should be shaking in her sandals at talking back so boldly to her royal brother and her father and king. "The gods never demanded human sacrifice before. Animals and birds always satisfied them. Did it ever occur to you that killing a man might insult Ra-Harakhty and he'd prolong the war instead of ending it?"

"He'd never do that," Horem blustered, "because my intentions were pure. For the good of my people."

"Oh, you insult the god with the right intentions," she snapped. "That makes a difference?"

"You—" Finding himself bested by a mere *female*, Horem began to shake with rage.

"Silence!" Once more Aseti-Ra broke in. "The deed's done, Horem. The beast's free and gone back to his people, and the war will continue. Perhaps Senset's right. Killing him might've been a mistake, but freeing him was an even worse one. That can't be undone, and you'll be punished for this, Senset." He gestured. "Seize her."

Without hesitation, the guards obeyed, grasping her tightly. Senset was so startled, she didn't attempt to struggle.

Idiot. Did I think he'd pat me on the head and send me on my way? What's he going to do? Oh, Nekhbet, protect me.

Aseti-Ra looked down at the cowering jailer, for a few moments forgotten. He raised the shepherd's crook, symbol of his role as protector of his people, extending it to the man.

"Go. Back to your own province. And be grateful for my daughter's honesty."

As the guards released him, the man scrambled to his feet. He backed away, bowing frantically. Once he was near the doors, he whirled and dashed from sight.

"Father, what'll you do?" Horem looked to Aseti-Ra.

"You've done a terrible thing, Sensete-Ra," her father said. His brows drew down. Beneath their lining of heavy kohl, his eyes held anger and a surprising sadness. That she had disappointed him by her actions? "This could be considered a treasonous act, one punishable by death."

Senset drew in a sharp breath, ready to plead.

"But since you're a foolish child, and female, I must consider that in rendering your punishment."

"I know what she deserves." Horem stepped forward, fist lashing out.

It struck Senset's cheek with such force she was knocked from the guards' grasp. Feet flying from under her, she landed between them, on her back on the tiled floor.

Briefly, she was stunned and could only lie there staring up at her brother, watching him suck in deep angry breaths, his bare chest heaving.

Truly, this is the way he must look in battle, flashed through her mind.

Her cheek was numb. Placing a hand on it, she clambered to her feet, to be seized again by the guards.

"Horem." The royal hand holding the flail pointed it at his son.

Horem walked back to the dais, taking the flail from Aseti-Ra.

"Five lashes across the hind parts. Don't mar the skin of her back."

Nodding, Horem advanced on his little sister. He glanced from one guard to the other. "Hold her. Tightly."

Before Senset could brace herself, he was behind

74

her, raising the flail and bringing it down across her buttocks.

Senset screamed. She'd never been beaten. Not by her mother nor her nurses. She'd never done anything to warrant any kind of physical punishment, and she was unprepared for the pain the thin metal strips inflicted, even with the protection of her linen skirt. As Horem raised the flail a second time, she struggled to get away, twisting her body, trying to make it as small a target as possible.

The second blow was worse than the first. She cried out again, heard fabric tear, felt something wet splash the insides of her thighs. The third brought a blessed numbness; she barely felt the fourth and final strikes of the whip.

Horem stepped back, coming around to stand in front of her. She was startled to see blood spatters on his chest and the wide triangle of sash at the front of his *shendyt*.

My blood?

The thought was dull, her mind now as numb as her body.

"The punishment's been carried out, Noble Father." He walked back to the dais, returning the flail to Aseti-Ra, who handed it to the advisor.

"Clean it of this child's disobedient blood."

The man, who had been silent as the little drama was played out, bowed, taking the flail.

"Take her back to the women's quarters. Senset, you'll remain in your room until the next new moon. All will be told of your transgression and none allowed to speak to you." Aseti-Ra raised his free hand, covering his eyes. "Take her from my sight, Horem. *Now*."

"Yes, Noble Father." Bowing, Horem gestured to the guards.

They released the girl, stepping away. She wavered, her legs crumpling. Horem caught her as she fell, hoisting her to his shoulder. Carrying Senset as if she were a bag of meal, he stalked out the door. Behind him, the two guards returned to their places, and the ones who had held the jailer took their stands to each side of Aseti-Ra's dais.

Horem took three steps into the hallway before Senset fainted.

They'd gone only a few feet more before she was shaken into consciousness again. She was hanging over Horem's shoulder, the braided tail of the *khat* covering his newly-shaven head caught between them, the knot digging into her breast. Her legs dangled against his chest.

"You deserve twice the punishment you got," he said. "I may never forgive you for this, Senset, and the gods only know if the people will when the war continues and we lose more men."

"Perhaps it'll be years before they attack again." She threw out the words hopefully, wishing he'd put her down.

"Don't count on it. When your precious Aram gets back and relates how we treated him, they'll probably come rushing back."

They neared the women's quarters. She heard the amazons straighten, saluting.

"General Horem? What—"

"Senset's being punished. I'll take her inside."

"Yes, sir."

It was unusual for any male to enter the women's

quarters. Generally, a wife or concubine was sent for, accompanied by Satis to her lord's quarters. Still, if the prince wished to go inside, who was a mere guard to stop him?

Horem pushed open the doors.

All sound stopped as he entered. No one spoke, all stared at sight of the king's son, standing there with his half-sister slung over his shoulder. Horem didn't speak either, just stalked through the groups of females, nodding to the secondary wives and concubines in his path as they jumped out of the way. He paused. They all straightened, looking hopeful.

"Which is Senset's room?"

Five forefingers pointed, each eager to bring herself to his attention.

He nodded, continuing on his way. The conversations started up again behind him, muted but curious. At the door, he went inside, dropping Senset roughly onto her couch.

"Stay there." He went back to the doorway. "Satis."

"Master?" The head slave scurried over, bowing and nodding.

"Senset's being punished. She's not to leave this room until the new moon's in the sky. She'll eat her meals here and bathe here, and no one's allowed to speak to her, except you. Is that understood?"

"Yes, master." It was plain Satis wanted to ask why but didn't dare. She bowed again, stepping back to allow Horem to pass.

He walked to the center of the room, clapping his hands. All sound died. Crouching on the bed, Senset listened as his voice carried back to her.

"Senset has done a wicked thing. She helped the

prisoner escape."

Loud exclamations greeted this announcement, falling silent again as he once more waved his hands.

"For her crime, she's to stay in her room for a month. None of you will attempt to see or speak to her, on pain of your own punishment. Is that understood?"

There were assenting murmurs.

"Good." With that, Horem stamped out, his sandals making a loud and angry *slap-slap* on the polished tile.

Immediately, the common room was filled with the rise and fall of their voices in speculation.

Chapter 9

Imprisonment was boring.

Senset discovered that the first day. She wondered how men confined for long periods retained their sanity. Certainly, after twenty-four hours passed, she was ready to beat her fists against the walls and scream.

The worst part was not seeing any other person except Satis. The slave came several times during the day, bringing her meals, and at night carrying water so Senset could bathe.

Senset looked forward to each bath. Horem hadn't tried to stay his hand when striking, and the wounds were so painful she was unable to sit or to lie on her back for the first week. All movement, even the soft brush of fabric against her hips, sent fire stabbing through her, and she spent those first days completely naked, lying on her belly on her bed, cheek resting on her forearms. Soaking in the tub Satis brought to her room eased some of the pain.

The slave also brought her apothecary basket, filled with its creams, distillations, and medicinals for any ailment the women under her care might suffer. For Senset, she brought witch hazel water and tincture of tree moss, pouring the liquid onto folded pieces of gauze cloth. While Senset lay on her couch, she swabbed the inflamed slashes caused by the flail.

Satis dabbed and patted the soothing liquids onto

Senset's buttocks, tutting under her breath as she did so.

"Ah…little mistress…your poor backside. There'll be scars, I don't doubt. If you get a husband, he won't desire to caress your flanks, I warrant. Well, it's no one's fault but your own. Be certain to tell him that when he complains."

"Since I don't have a husband as yet," Senset snapped, wincing as the slave pressed a little too heavily on a particularly deep cut, "I won't worry about that just now."

Satis made another little *tsk* under her breath. "Her Majesty objected. Said she agreed with you about the whole thing. Why does she have such a soft spot for you?"

Eventually, the pain went away as the cuts began to heal. And eventually, Senset got enough courage to stand before her beaten-metal mirror and turn her back, looking over her shoulder to view the damage. What she saw made her catch her breath sharply.

Five long, deep slashes criss-crossed the globe of each buttock, red and scabbing on her pale skin. There would definitely be scars. Senset didn't worry what some future husband would think but of what the other women would say when she was once more allowed to mingle with them, especially when they were bathing… *If* she were ever allowed in their company again.

Once she could move without pain, she began to explore the room where she'd slept every night of her life, certain she'd know every crack and crevice before the time was up. She'd never noticed how the tiles near the door were scuffed, the baked-in lotus flowers nearly worn white in the center, or how those under the lamp chest near her couch were spattered with candle-wax droppings and discolored with oil spots.

By the evening of the second day, she had gone through her collection of scrolls, silently grateful her royal father permitted his daughters be taught to read.

There were only four scrolls, so she read slowly, savoring every word and making each story last as long as possible...the love story of Isis and Osiris, with the bloody and treacherous evil brother Set...the tale of Maahes, the lion prince...and two scrolls filled with poetry, written by Horem shortly after his marriage to Asanath. Asa had been so proud of those two small scrolls, she'd shown them to Senset, and when the girl exclaimed at the beauty of the words—surprised by her brother's sensitivity and lyricism—she'd ordered a scribe to copy them, proudly making a present to her sister-in-law of this evidence of her husband's affection.

Now, as she read the lush and sensual words the prince had penned, Senset wondered what Horem would say if he knew his little sister—*his now-disgraced little sister*—was aware of the most intimate feelings between him and his wife.

He'll never find out from me. If Horem ever forgives me, I'll do nothing to get in his disfavor again.

She also had her paint set, sunbaked pots filled with crushed charcoal, pulverized beetle shells, and powdered clays and plants. Mixed with water, they became brilliant colors she stroked onto a parchment sheet with a bamboo brush.

She had only twelve pieces of parchment and wasn't certain if she'd be allowed more, so she drew pictures sparingly. Her drawings were all of Aram... One as she'd first seen him, being dragged through the streets. The second as he lay in the cage... The third a portrait…hairy, bearded…a fearful creature, until one looked at the eyes, where his intelligence shone through.

After the third picture, Senset hid the sheets at the bottom of the stack of parchment. She had no idea why she had drawn the pictures. Some emergence of her guilt? Though she truly didn't feel she'd committed a crime by setting Aram free, she nevertheless didn't want anyone seeing what she had drawn or how she depicted the beast. The sooner her transgression was forgotten, the better, and displaying drawings of her crime wouldn't help.

Setting aside her paints, she went back to reading, and when that also became a bore, she simply lay on her couch and slept. But one can only sleep so much, and soon she was lying awake long into the night. While it was quiet, with only muted snores wisping to her through her closed door, she thought of Aram, hoping he had managed to reach his people, and that he might think kindly of her even as he readied himself to begin a new onslaught against Ægys.

Satis never told her what was happening outside her room.

Senset had attempted to get the slave to talk,, but Satis feared Horem too much to tell her any news. Only once did she dare go against the prince's orders.

"My Lady Asanath is brought to her laying-in," she whispered as she set down the tray holding Senset's breakfast, a peach, a chunk of cheese, and a goblet of goat's milk. "Last night."

"Is she all right?" Senset seized the slave's arm.

"The general has another son." Satis didn't raise her voice or look at Senset as she gently extricated her arm from the girl's grasp. "He's to be called Seti-Horem."

She leaned forward, whispering her next words. "They say Her Highness doesn't do well, that the madness of childbirth visits her."

As if fearing the walls would somehow transmit her words back to Horem, she ran from the room.

The madness of childbirth...

Senset had heard of such, where a woman suffering the pain of birthing retreated somehow into herself and was never the same again, but surely Asanath, who had survived so many other births, wouldn't be so affected.

Senset was to have been present to assist Asanath during the birth. She hoped her sister-in-law would forgive her absence. Somehow, she doubted it. Either Asa would consider it a personal affront as well as a breaking of a solemn promise, or Horem wouldn't let her forget.

Early in life, she'd learned her brother could be petulant in spite of his age, and long held a grudge. This was definitely something he'd remember.

That night, Senset had another dream.

This time, she dreamed of the night she'd looked into the mirror seeking her true love...

Once more, she again saw the cat's furred face reflected behind her.

"Go away, Bubash. I won't let you spoil it for me this time."

The animal didn't move. Its face came closer, green eyes enormous in its golden face.

But Bubash's face was black, dark and soft as sable...why had it changed? She could hear the soft pad, pad of its paws.

"Bubash, I said...go away."

Movement behind her. A soft brushing against her

shoulders…as if…as if someone stood close.

She stiffened, "Bubash?" She raised the candle…slowly turned…

He was less than a foot away…white-robed and tall…a man, surely, but…Senset's startled eyes eagerly sought his face…

The lion's roar made her stagger backward, thrusting the candle before her as if it would protect her from what stood there. A man with a lion's head…mouth snarling, fangs gleaming, and while she cowered, putting one arm up to shield her face, he spoke.

"Come, Senset, my bride, I await you…"

Before she realized what she was doing, Senset reached out. She couldn't stop the movement of her hand…it reached for that furred, taloned paw of its own accord. The candle tumbled from her grasp, striking the tiles, guttering before the flame snuffed…

…and Senset awoke, sitting up in bed, reaching into the darkness.

Chapter 10

Once again there was a commotion in the common room. A chattering resembling nothing so much as a group of monkeys screeching in the trees. It quickly receded into voices rising and falling, not in consternation but in excitement.

"Rise, little mistress." Satis appeared in the doorway. "You must hurry and dress."

It was neither the hour for eating nor for bathing, so Senset hoped that meant her punishment was over. Since her room was an inner one, she had no way of seeing the sky or knowing if it was time again for the new moon.

"I'll be so glad to get out of here." She sat up, climbing from the couch and stretching. Arms over her head, she welcomed the deep pull of back muscles stiffened by lying in one position all night.

"Your imprisonment isn't over, little mistress." Though holding that same tremble of excitement coming from the outer room, Satis' answer was soft. "Your royal father sends for you. He's sent for all the women, in fact. We've an important visitor."

"Who?" Senset took a step away from the slave, listening to the voices. Hurrying to the door, she peered out, seeing other slaves scurrying about.

The common room was a hubbub of activity. Her father's lesser wives and concubines, as well as those of her six older brothers, stood in various stages of nakedness, slaves painting their faces, selecting gowns, offering jewel cases.

"He doesn't tell me why he does things, my lady." Satis helped Senset into her robe.

As the girl slid her arms into the voluminous sleeves and secured the girdle, the slave went to the dressing table to pick up a sheshamwood cosmetics box.

"It's said that, around dawn, a messenger arrived carrying a white banner. That's all I know, so don't ask me more."

"Odd." Senset returned to the couch, pushing aside the sheets and sitting upon it. In the common room, the noise grew more frenzied and hurried, the sounds of chests being opened, slave feet pattering, water splashing. "Why did the messenger carry a white flag?"

"That I can't say, mistress. The gate guards sent word to the palace, and the messenger was received by His Majesty and then returned the way he came. Within a few hours, the visitor arrived. A representative of a foreign prince. With him, he had two dozen guards and other attendants plus two carts, one carrying a litter grand enough to convey a noble lady, though it seemed to be filled with gifts. Truly, he's from a wealthy country." The slave opened the box and took out the little jars of lip color, face powder, and eye dust. "That's all I know, so don't ask me more."

"What country?"

"I'm not told. His Majesty merely sends word everyone is to paint her face, put on her most beautiful gown, and wear her best jewels."

"But why send for all of us?" It was rare for Aseti-Ra to gather his entire family, especially the female members, to receive a visitor.

"His Majesty appeared most impressed by the visitor's retinue and wishes to receive him formally and with the most respect, as soon as the royal family's assembled." Satis removed the lids of the jars, arranging them on the couch's side table. "At present, his soldiers are housed in the guest barracks and he and his attendants refresh themselves in one of the palace's suites. That's all I know, so don't ask me more."

"Truly this prince must be a very powerful ruler for Father to be so lavish to his representative." Only someone whose military might and ruling strength equaled Aseti-Ra's own rated a calling-out of the entire royal family.

"Truly, I believe it's so, little mistress," Satis agreed.

"Soldiers and attendants and wagonloads of gifts…"

Senset allowed herself to speculate. Where was the visitor from? Who could he be? As far as she knew, none of the allied kingdoms to the south were engaged in any conflicts requiring Ægys's assistance.

There were few tribes to the east and west, and most were too small and weak to be considered important enough to be given such royal accord. As for the north—little was known of the people existing there, though that was the way from which the Ægysians themselves were said to have come before settling this side of the Plain of Arriah.

"Satis, from what direction did the messenger come?"

"I'm not certain, mistress. North, I think. The only other thing I know is they rode horses. Can you imagine? Only the two pulling the wagon didn't have men on their backs."

Tutting as if this were a shocking thought, Satis selected a feather-tipped brush. She dipped it into a compound of crushed beetle wings—turquoise blue and fine as dust—and rice powder, and began to smooth it across Senset's left brow.

"They…rode horses?" Senset started slightly.

"Did I hurt you?" Satis asked in concern. "Sorry, mistress. I selected the softest quill."

Occasionally, a stiffened bit of feather would accidentally slip into those making up a cosmetics applicator, and that single bristle could be painful when stroked against sensitive skin.

"It's all right." Senset settled herself again. "It's just…that startled me. About the horses, I mean."

Into her mind flashed the image of Aram struggling onto the mule's back, the creature galloping into the dark with him clinging to its short mane. And now…a strange prince arrives from the north on horseback…

Don't be foolish. No one knows who lives in the north. Perhaps they all ride horses there.

"I agree it *is* odd. I mean, everyone knows a chariot or cart is safer for traveling, but…" Satis shrugged, repeating for the fourth time. "That's all I know, so don't ask me more."

"For someone who know so little, you've certainly said a lot," Senset commented.

Satis looked down at her with a smile. "Do you expect a lowly slave to be your most revered father's confidant, mistress?"

Senset allowed herself an answering smile and didn't reply. As Chief Attendant of the Women's Quarters, Satis was no lowly slave no matter what she said. The girl settled herself to the slave's ministrations.

Sometimes it seemed those who were the lowest in caste were the ones knowing the most of what went on in the palace.

Whatever information they gleaned, however, was always accompanied by that phrase Satis had parroted to her with each morsel she related: *That's all I know, so don't ask me more.* It was a mantra to any slave's speech, used as an escape from punishment when relaying gossip or rumor.

With a sigh, Senset closed her eyes, sitting quietly as Satis applied her makeup. Inside her chest, however, her heart began to beat a little faster at being included in greeting this foreign visitor, because it was a sign her royal father had forgiven her...a little.

Satis worked quickly and expertly, first on the girl's face, brushing colored powder over her eyelids and outlining her eyes with kohl. She dusted her cheeks with cochineal, covering everything with a fine layer of rice powder to make her complexion the requisite paleness so liked by Ægysian men. She stained Senset's lips, nails, and toenails with henna so they were a sensual dark red. As a finishing touch, she placed a dot of perfumed cream just under each ear and in the hollow of her throat.

Opening the clothes chest at the foot of the couch, she brought out the white linen gown Senset had worn at Horem's wedding ceremony. Senset slid off her robe, dropping it onto the couch.

"Stand up, my lady."

Wrapping the girl's breasts with a linen band, she helped her into the gown, then set about folding the pleats and making certain the wide shawl sleeves overlapped in front. Bending again over the chest, she brought out an ornately-carved cedar coffer, setting it upon the bed.

Selecting bangles of turquoise and carnelian for each wrist, she carefully removed Senset's little earplugs and inserted earbobs through her lobes, heavy droplets of jasper, malachite, and turquoise, strung together on fine gold wires. They dangled, swinging slightly and striking her shoulders as Satis brought out a heavy gem-studded collar and placed it around the girl's neck.

Once again, she adjusted the part of the sleeves forming the neck of the gown, making certain they were tucked neatly into the top of the golden girdle holding the front of the gown together.

As Senset slid her feet into thin-soled leather sandals whose straps were studded with green-striped malachite and translucent rose-colored carnelian, Satis placed a many-braided, many-beaded wig on her head, then straightened the lanyard resting between the girl's shoulder blades, making certain it kept her collar in place.

"Beautiful." Nodding in satisfaction, the slave stepped back, bowing slightly, forearms crossed over her chest. "You are ready, little mistress." She touched Senset's arm. "Come, your royal father awaits."

In the common room, the other women were gathered in an array of white gowns, elaborate wigs, fragrant perfumes, and jewelry opulent enough to dazzle any visitor. As Satis and Senset walked across to the doors, the girl heard whispers behind her…excited speculations and questions.

"My ladies…" Satis paused at the door. "Please come with me."

She pushed open the doors and went out. Senset and the others followed, a white-robed, excited surge into the corridor, leaving behind their offspring and openly pouting concubines.

The slaves herded their daughters to their breakfasts. Missing their mothers, a couple of the infants began to cry. They soon quieted as they were lifted and soothed by their nurses.

Moving in a group, the wives and Aseti-Ra's third daughter converged on the audience hall.

Chapter 11

They didn't enter by the main audience hall doors. That was only for honored guests and any having official business with His Majesty. Satis brought them to one of the many side entrances, a door concealed by a heavy tapestry depicting Osiris' triumphant resurrection.

It took several minutes to get everyone inside, where there was a confused milling around while each got her bearings. Standing still in the center of it all, Senset glanced over the heads of the others to the dais where Aseti-Ra sat.

Today, his prime wife, Hatasu, sat at his left hand, on a throne inches shorter, signifying her subservience to her royal husband and sovereign. Her eyes met Senset's and she allowed her stern visage to break into a brief smile, signifying she was glad to see the girl.

Does that mean I'm here at Hatasu's request?

Had her royal father wanted to exclude her because of her behavior, perhaps? It was as Satis said. For some reason, the prime wife had always liked this particular child of her husband's.

At Aseti-Ra's right hand stood Horem, in the place of strength, looking every bit the prince he was, his right hand wrapped around a lance. Today, he wore a low-slung long linen *shendyt*, its gilded leather girdle tied tight across his slim hips, triangular sash skimming the toes of his sandals. A pectoral of a jade-and-turquoise *kephera* covered his bare chest, banded by a triple row of malachite, jasper, and agate separated by tiny gold beads. The design was echoed on his golden wristlets and in the beaded earplugs showing beneath the hem of his gold and turquoise-striped *khat.*

Even more briefly than his mother's glance, Horem's kohl-rimmed eyes lingered on Senset, then looked away. Her brother was still angry over his lost sacrifice.

Behind Aseti-Ra hovered his chief advisor, Hasta, and the three others, and behind them stood Aseti-Ra's six other sons, each dressed appropriately for his age and place in the line of succession. Above them, the gigantic statues of the gods protectively looked down on the king himself—Aseti-Ra, Lord of Ægys.

He was also dressed in linen, a pleated long-sleeved robe gathered at the waist by a gem-studded girdle. There were gems on his sandal straps and on the half-dozen bangles on each wrist as well as the rings adorning the fingers wrapped around the shepherd's crook and judge's flail.

Like Horem, he wore a *kephera* pectoral, with a heavy gold-and-gemstone collar under it, its edges covering his shoulders. Aseti-Ra wore a crown similar to his son's battle helmet, a round-domed gilded cap of woven reeds, encircled by the sacred snake and a falcon's protecting wings. The royal false beard, braided with turquoise ribbon, hung from a leather band stretching from just above one ear to the other, attached under the edge of the crown.

There was a minor clatter as a door on the other side of the Hall opened and the male children poured in…Horem's other two full-brothers, and the ten half-ones plus several grandsons. Much younger than he, they galloped into the room only to skid to a stop and bumble into each other as they attempted to look solemn. That lasted only long enough for some to spy their mothers and for all to turn wide grins on the king himself.

Hasta brought order by stepping forward and pounding the butt of the staff he carried. That brought a hasty silence from all.

"Pay homage to your king and take your places."

There was a group bowing, arms crossed and heads ducking quickly. The wives ran up the steps to their husbands' sides. With brief kisses of greeting, they stepped to the left and dropped to their knees. Once they were settled, each brother also knelt, hands pressed flat upon thighs in a position of royal repose.

The children were a little less decorous. The younger ones scrambled up the stairs, taking their places before their parents and assuming similar poses. The older grandchildren arranged themselves on the steps of the dais, again according to age and succession…Sapair, Horem's eldest son first, then his second, and so on. Across from them sat his brother, Seti-Phera's two sons, followed by his first half-brother's son, with other grandchildren seating themselves across the steps.

Aseti-Ra's glance flicked down to the bottom step directly in front of the throne. He looked at Senset, nodding. She ran to the spot, seating herself and arranging the skirts of her gown modestly.

Once there was quiet, Hasta again struck his staff against the polished floor. He looked at the herald standing at the entrance and nodded. The man disappeared through the door.

No one spoke; gradually, whispers and soft

murmurs swept the dais as they realized the herald had gone to escort their visitor into the king's presence. Hatasu glanced around with as much curiosity as the rest, Senset noted. And, if she wasn't mistaken, Horem appeared ignorant of their visitor's identity, also.

So, not even the prime wife and the heir have been told who our guest is?

She was brought out of her wondering by the herald's return.

Following him through the entrance were twelve soldiers. Not Ægysians, but foreigners, clothed in short, thigh-length tunics over which they wore woven leather chestplates studded with brass disks. The men lined themselves six facing six across from each other inside the doors. Their heads were covered by rounded helmets secured by wide chin straps, a thick noseguard extending from the browpiece, faces obscured by so much beard their features were barely visible. Each carried a rectangular shield and a lance, and…

Senset went cold. They wore gauntlets of animal skin with fur capes thrown over their shoulders.

The herald stepped forward and the twelve men snapped to attention.

"Announcing his majesty, General Arambengurion…" He garbled the name, making it into one word. "Brother to Michael, sovereign of Habir."

Senset, who'd been looking up at her father, glanced around, startled.

Did he say Aram? *It can't be.*

The answer came striding through the door…in a tunic over which a white long-sleeved *galabia* flowed and parted, revealing long, tanned legs in leather sandals. A cloak was slung over his shoulders, red, the royal color. He was tall, his dark curly hair barely shoulder-length, and his face was bare except for a narrow strip of beard stretching from one jaw to the other, as if in imitation of the false one worn by Aseti-Ra.

Briefly, Senset's dream-image swam before her eyes.

He moved as if he'd never been touched by a soldier's spear or sword, walking past the soldiers to midway of the length of the chamber before stopping. Senset's eyes were riveted to the white cloth—the sign of truce—tied around his right forearm. It waved like a banner as he crossed his arms over his chest, bowing to Aseti-Ra. As he raised his head, his eyes met Senset's...for one brief, heart-stopping moment.

It is.

It was as if all the breath went out of her. She couldn't inhale as she stared at the man standing there looking up at her father. A man nothing like the filthy, hairy beast she'd seen in the cage in the dungeon...but it *was* Aram. She was certain.

General? Brother to a king?

"My brother sends greetings to you, Mighty Aseti-Ra. Long life and a prosperous reign be yours."

"We thank you, noble general." Aseti-Ra inclined his head slightly in acknowledgment, looking past the general as two other men appeared, stopping a few feet behind him.

The two were dressed similarly. The older man held a set of narrow, hinged boxes, while the younger one's hands were empty.

"However, we must confess we're puzzled—and intrigued—by your visit. Wishing no disrespect to our honored visitor, but...where is Habir? And why have we not heard of it before? Or of its sovereign?"

"We accept the question in the spirit with which it's asked, Your Majesty." Aram's smile was guileless and friendly.

Senset felt fear coil inside her.

Is this a trap of some kind? A prelude to another battle? To be fought here in the Audience Hall?

The most important members of the royal family were present. If they were all dispatched… But there were only fifteen men, counting the twelve soldiers.

How much damage can they do before our own guards kill them?

"However, you've heard of Habir, Most Royal King." Aram was still speaking, his voice drawing her back from her fear.

"When, General?" Aseti-Ra frowned. "We recall no mention of your people. Ever."

"That's because you don't know us as *Habiru,* sire." The smile quirked upward, a lilt of triumph in his voice. "You know us better as *Beast Men.*"

"Beast Men?"

One of the wives near-shrieked the word, and others took up the cry, a loud protest sweeping the dais. Horem stiffened, taking a step closer to his father and raising his lance. Even Aseti-Ra look startled.

Before anyone could move, however, Aram continued as if no one had reacted.

"However, we accept it and consider it no insult, just as my brother acknowledges that some kingdoms call him the Beast King. Be assured we're here with no threat in mind, Noble Aseti-Ra, even if we weren't standing under a flag of truce." Aram held up his hand to again display the white banner. "To that end, and to show the sincerity of which I speak, my brother sends you these gifts…"

He gestured and the second man who'd followed him into the room, turned, clapping his hands together sharply.

Immediately, people began streaming through the door…bearers hoisting large, carved wooden chests on carrying litters…two men and two women, young and dressed in simple white robes. The slaves carrying the chests set them in a row at the foot of the dais, kneeling behind their burdens. The four stood behind them, heads bowed, arms folded at their waists.

"Gifts for Your Majesty," Aram went on. "Products of Habir…for your pleasure."

He gestured and the first two litter bearers got to their feet, opening the chest. One held the lid while the other took out a bolt of crimson cloth. Several others were visible inside.

"Linen," Aram explained. "Colored with the cinnabar our country has in abundance."

There was a murmur at that. Cinnabar was difficult to come by. It was brought by caravans traveling from the far north and costly, and for that reason only royalty were allowed to utilize it to dye their clothes. To have so much that entire bolts of cloth could be given as gifts was unheard of.

The slave held up the bolt, and Hasta came down the steps. Briefly, he fingered the fabric, inspecting it closely, then accepted a scroll the slave handed him. He nodded, and returned to his place, bending to speak to Aseti-Ra as he did so. The slave replaced the bolt in the chest, and the other replaced the lid.

"Gems from our mines." Aram pointed at the second

chest, whose contents were displayed as he spoke. "Malachite, turquoise, and jade." A slave held up gigantic cylinders fashioned from each gem. "For your artisans to employ as they see fit."

No murmur this time. The royal family seemed transfixed with awe.

The next chest contained jewelry. "Our own artisans have fashioned these for your prime wife's enjoyment."

A slave lifted out a tray holding bangles and ear-ornaments. Hatasu straightened, eyes gleaming. She beckoned, and the slave climbed the steps, bowing before her as he offered the tray. Her hands hovered, fingers stroking and caressing various pieces before selecting one, a bangle covered with large, irregularly shaped white stones glistening and gleaming iridescently in the light.

"What are these gems?" Her voice held the joy of a woman looking at something precious. "I've never seen such."

"Pearls, most noble queen. Tears of the moon falling into the river and solidified by the current's cold."

She slid the bangle onto her wrist, holding up her arm and admiring the way the pearls glowed in the light. Dismissing the slave, who returned the tray to the chest, she sat back, smiling, as the lid was closed.

The next chest held fruits—peaches, grapes—and bottles of wine. "Made in our vineyards." And the fifth chest...

It wasn't a chest so much as a large basket, woven of canes with openings in the weave of the lid. As the slave took off the top, there was a high-pitched *yip* and a shaggy golden head appeared, looking around with bright eyes and a lolling pink tongue.

"Ohhh…" came from Sapair, whose eyes were suddenly as bright as the pup's. Since his last natal day, he'd been pestering his father for a dog of his own.

"The prize of our hunting litters," Aram explained. "Our hounds can bring down a gazelle without becoming winded." He nodded at the first young slave standing to one side. "Aharon will train him to be Your Majesty's finest hunter."

The slave lifted the little animal out of the basket, setting him on the polished floor and stepping back with a bow. Overjoyed at being freed from its confinement, the puppy barked…he dashed about to adoring murmurs from the children and women…he wagged…he wiggled…he piddled on the polished marble floor…

Sudden silence.

"Unfortunately, he hasn't yet learned the proper way to show his master respect," Aram went on with aplomb.

Scooping up the puppy, Aharon held him under one arm while taking a small bag from the basket. He sprinkled its contents over the yellow puddle, waited a moment, then took out a handful of linen rags, dropped it over the mess, scrubbed a moment, and returned them to the basket. The spot on the floor appeared clean and unstained.

Another surprised murmur. Hatasu straightened again.

"Let me have the pup." She held out her arms. The puppy was placed in them. He wiggled a moment, squirming around to face her, tongue swiping at her cheek. She laughed and looked down at Sapair. "Here, my grandson. That dog you've wished for."

Sapair didn't need a second urging. Darting to his grandmother, he took the puppy and returned to his seat, stifling giggles as his face was thoroughly cleaned by a pink tongue. He settled himself, hugging the puppy, who sighed, placed his chin in the crook of Sapair's elbow, and went to sleep.

Like eager children, everyone looked back to see what other treasures the Habiru king had sent. Aram gestured at the three remaining slaves. "Benyamin's trained in horsemanship. My brother sends you a dozen of our finest horses—a stallion, eight geldings, and three mares. They await your inspection in the courtyard. Benyamin will assist in their care and in teaching how to ride them."

In spite of himself, Horem looked interested as he heard that. Senset remembered the things he'd said about the Beast Men and how they could handle their steeds and fight at the same time. She knew he was thinking how his grandfather's attempts to teach his men had failed. He glanced down, saw her staring at him, and as if reminding himself he was still angry at her, flicked his gaze away.

"Rachel's adept with cosmetics and is trained as a lady's handmaiden…to serve your Lady Wife," Aram went on. The girl he indicated bowed. He looked at the last slave. "And Dalilah…" He smiled slightly. "Trained in music, singing, dancing, and the ways to please a man. My brother offers her to you, Great Aseti-Ra…for your concubine, if you accept her."

Aseti-Ra nodded, unable to hide the tinge of eagerness before he heard Hatasu's little sigh, as if to say, *As if he needs another one.* He leaned back against the throne, assuming a stern expression.

"We thank your brother for his gifts…and truly marvel at his generosity. However, before we can accept these gracious offerings, we must ask: What does King Michael want in exchange? Don't be affronted, but these presents are too costly and precious not to require something equal in return."

Immediately, the air in the hall became tense, heavy with anticipation, as if everyone were thinking the same thing and fearing the visitor's answer.

"We see no insult in the question, sire, for it's the wise king who errs on the side of caution before committing himself and his kingdom to a promise." Aram paused a moment.

Once more, his gaze went to Senset and, this time, held hers, as if he were recognizing her for the first time since entering the chamber. His eyes were the brown of a hazelnut, flecked with green and gold.

Like the eyes of a lion, she thought, realizing it had been so dark in the dungeon she'd never seen their color.

He took a deep breath, and went on, "My brother wishes no further aggression between our peoples."

Again, he held up the arm bearing the white banner, gesturing to bring it to everyone's attention.

"He wishes peace, mighty king, and has sent me as his ambassador to sue for such with you and your advisors."

That was met by an even louder murmur, one which Aseti-Ra didn't protest as he looked back at Hasta and quietly asked a question of his own. The advisor said something, nodding. Aseti-Ra looked back at Aram.

"Peace is always devoutly to be wished by any kingdom, General. Forgive me for being dubious as to your noble brother's intent, but…our peoples have been enemies for many generations."

"Reason enough to call a halt to this never-ending

war, sire." Aram spoke up again. Once more, his eyes met Senset's. "I was your prisoner, sentenced to die, and one of your people freed me."

There was a murmur. Not many knew the truth of what had happened. Horem had made certain of that.

"I returned to my brother, asking the question: If one Ægysian can show mercy to a Habiru, why can't we all? Why can't our people stop this war and become allies? Because of that one act of mercy restoring me to him, my brother heeded my words. He wishes peace, Your Majesty, and he wishes it now." Aram nodded to the man holding the boxes. "My brother Gideon would offer you the *Articles of Peace* King Michael has proposed."

Gideon turned, handing the boxes to the young man next to him, who, in turn, walked to the dais. Hasta came down to meet him, taking the boxes. As they resumed their places, Hasta opened one box, taking out a scroll. He unrolled it, cleared his throat and began to read.

"Greetings to thee, O King of the Ægys and all lands south of the Plain of Arriah under your protection, this missive is sent to you with the help of Heaven. May Long Life and Prosperity be yours. I, Michael ben-Gurion, king of the Habiru, do send my brother to you as my ambassador, suing for peace and an end to the hostilities between our peoples. To this effect, we offer the following terms to be negotiated: An immediate ceasing of belligerence between Ægys and Habir, the Plain of Arriah to be considered a neutral zone which no one may invade or claim. Habir will possess those countries to the north of the Plain as its own and settle there, never again venturing south in search of new territory, and Ægys will act the same in the south. Habir offers to become Ægys' ally, our men fighting beside yours should any other

kingdom offer you aggression, with expectation of Ægys reciprocating should Habir be threatened. Trade to be established between our two countries, each being welcomed in the others' cities in friendship and commerce…"

Hasta paused, looking at Aseti-Ra.

"This sounds a just and reasonable set of terms," Aseti-Ra replied. "Of course, we must discuss it with our advisors and determine if anything should be amended before we agree."

One of the other advisors spoke softly to Hasta. The elder advisor looked away, leaning back with a question. They and the other two conversed a moment before Hasta straightened, turning to his master. He said something to which Aseti-Ra responded in apparent surprise. The king looked back at Aram with a barely controlled quirk of one darkened eyebrow.

"It appears our advisors have already conferred. They recommend we accept your brother's offer of peace, General Aram. As it is. Now. In its entirety."

"In that case, Your Majesty, perhaps it may be best if your advisor finishes reading my brother's request," Aram answered.

Aseti-Ra looked even more surprised. Apparently, he thought Hasta had finished when the advisor stopped. He nodded. "Continue."

Again, Hasta raised the scroll.

"To erase any lingering doubt as to my sincerity in this request, I do further ask you to send me your daughter to take as my wife. As yet, I have no prime wife for my House and I will set her above all that is mine and make her my queen, ruling by my side. Grant this request, O Noble King, Live Forever, and may we both

end our days in old age with our great-grandchildren around us as peace settles over your kingdom and mine. Signed by Michael, of the Ruling House of ben-Gurion of the Nation of Habir from the Beginning to this Day."
Hasta lowered the scroll. "That's all, sire."

"We heartily accept your brother's offer, General. However…" Aseti-Ra looked perturbed. "We've no daughter to send to your brother as wife. My two daughters are already married to princes of our allies farther south."

"May I beg to differ, Your Majesty?" Aram smiled. He looked at Senset again. "You've a third daughter. She who showed me her mercy and saved my life."

"Senset?" For the first time, Horem spoke, and it was with such disbelief it sounded as if he shouted, though he barely raised his voice. "You wish Senset for your brother's queen? Great Ra-Harakhty save us!"

A gesture from his father prevented him from saying more, while Senset shot him a furious glare and Hatasu merely looked amused.

"Sensete-Ra's a lesser daughter, child of my seventh wife. Her claim to the throne of Ægys is scant. Further, she's headstrong and willful. Is your brother certain of his choice?"

"He's certain, Your Majesty." Aram bowed to underscore what he said. "Michael of Habir wishes Sensete-Ra as his prime wife."

There was a moment's silence, as if Aseti-Ra pondered this, no doubt thinking back over Senset's past sins and behaviors, and wondering if he dared let such an undisciplined creature become part of a pact for peace.

"Senset?" He looked down at her.

She got to her feet, feeling Aram's eyes and those of

her entire family upon her. She looked up at Aseti-Ra, meeting his dark gaze, seeing Hatasu smile slightly, as if something she'd always thought was now being vindicated.

If I say yes, I'll have a husband. At last. The thought was exhilarating. Her heart thumped so loudly she was certain all within the audience hall could hear. *And we'll have peace*, she added hastily.

"It shall be as you and His Majesty wish, Noble Father. I live to serve Ægys." Crossing her forearms over her chest, she bowed and sat down again.

"Then it will be done," Aseti-Ra said. At his side, Horem still looked dubious. "We'll hold a banquet in your honor tonight, General Aram. To celebrate the cessation of war. To celebrate our daughter's betrothal to your king. Criers will be sent throughout the kingdom and to neighboring domains, proclaiming the news. Immediately."

Getting to his feet, he gestured with the flail and crook, bowing to Hatasu and then his son.

"You're dismissed, my sons. Visit with your wives and children, then return to your dwellings." As they dispersed, sons with arms around their wives' waists, children trailing behind them, he relinquished the flail and crook to one of the advisors.

Hasta began supervising the removal of the gifts to the royal treasury. Sapair happily ran from the room, the puppy at his heels. Dismissing Hatasu, Aseti-Ra came down the steps. He stopped near Hasta and nodded to Dalilah, who stood demurely, eyes downcast.

"I'll speak to that one later tonight. In the meantime, take her to the women's quarters."

Behind him, Hatasu shook her head, gave Senset a

nod, and went out.

Aseti-Ra ignored his daughter, turning his attention to Aram. "General, walk with us in our private garden. There's much we must discuss before the banquet."

Bowing, Aram joined the king as he headed for the door leading into the garden.

The audience hall was nearly empty as Horem came down the steps. He caught Senset's arm as she started toward the side door, following the last of the children.

"I hope this king knows what he's doing, taking you as a wife." It was spoken through gritted teeth. "You'd better become circumspect in your behavior, Senset. Two kingdoms now depend on it."

Chapter 12

The others quickly left Senset behind as they returned to their quarters. She didn't try to catch them but walked slowly, as if she wasn't certain where she was going. She felt so odd, almost dizzy…the way she had that one time Horem had let her drink some of his beer…fuzzy-headed and detached. As though her body belonged to someone else and she was merely observing it, her legs moving her inexorably down the hallway but not doing what she wished them to at all.

By the time she reached the double doors to the women's quarters, she could hear the excited chattering coming from within. The others had wasted no time relaying the astonishing news to the concubines waiting eagerly to hear about the visitor and what had transpired.

The amazons crowded into the doorway, listening with amazement. As Senset passed them, they turned to gawk, then hurried back to their stations as if reminded they were hired by His Majesty to guard his wives, not eavesdrop on their chatter.

Senset was no sooner in the room than Xena detached herself from the others.

"Well, here's the blushing bride now," the concubine sneered, making her tone contemptuous to hide the anger she felt at her status excluding her from the excitement of seeing the royal visitor. "I suppose now we must bow down to you…since you're to be queen of the Beast Men, though I wouldn't consider that such an honor." She glanced around at the others as if seeking their agreement. "I certainly wouldn't relish being mounted by one of those horrible creatures. He'll probably do it from behind like real animals do."

"You haven't seen the general, Xena," Tetashera, one of Horem's other wives, spoke up. She sighed and placed a hand over her heart. "Merciful Ra...I wouldn't mind being taken by that one...behind or face-to-face."

"Yes," Tumerisy, second wife of Senset's half-brother Toth-Amasis, chimed in. "Who'd have thought under all that fur was such a figure of a man? Truly, you're to be envied, Senset."

"Don't let Amasis hear you saying that," Tetashera answered, and the others giggled while Xena glared.

Senset knew they were expecting her to join in. She'd always been good at foiling Xena's sharpest barbs, but this time she simply walked past them, running the last few steps into her room.

"Well...I guess she's too good to speak to lowly lesser wives and concubines, now that she's to be a prime wife." With a loud sniff, Xena changed the subject.

Too good? That's not the reason.

Senset sank onto the couch. She felt numb. The realization that within a few days she was going to be married to a stranger, a man who only a few weeks before had waged war against the entire kingdom, came crashing in. And she'd agreed so eagerly.

We know nothing at all of these people, not even how they look, for Aram's so different from the prisoner I felt pity for. Oh, Ra-Harakhty! What have I agreed to?

She wanted to burst into tears, find her father, and beg him to release her from the agreement, to send someone else instead…but there was no one else. Aseti-Ra had three daughters but only one free to marry, the one King Michael specifically requested. There was no way out, and she knew it.

"Mistress?" Satis appeared in the doorway.

Senset looked at her, blinking back the tears.

"Your Noble Father requests you come to his quarters."

Nodding, Senset stood and walked from the room. Ignoring the other women, she wondered what Aseti-Ra would now say to her.

****

Though he still wore his linen robes, Aseti-Ra had removed his crown and heavy jewelry. Without all his adornments, he was no less imposing, however…at least not to Senset's eyes. When he looked up and beckoned her closer, however, gesturing to a stool placed near his chair, it was a father and not a king who spoke to her.

"Senset, come, daughter. Sit."

As she settled herself on the stool, he lifted one foot, placing it on a richly decorated tussock. She wasn't surprised to see that his sandals had been removed. Aseti-Ra hated footwear and was known to walk around his private chambers barefoot. Now, at ease, minus crown, jewelry, and sandals, he uttered a quiet sigh and smiled at his third daughter.

"We've some things to discuss before your wedding," he said.

"Yes, sir." Senset's hand went to her belly, trying to quell its sudden quiver.

"General Aram and I had an interesting conversation in my garden," Aseti-Ra went on, accepting a goblet of grape squash offered by a slave.

110

When the tray was held out to Senset, she took the other goblet, though she didn't drink. She wasn't certain her stomach would allow her. Aseti-Ra paused, as if expecting Senset to respond.

"Yes, sir?" was all she could think to say. She tried to make it sound encouraging.

"It seems King Michael's very anxious to receive back his *Articles of Peace*, signed by myself. In fact, his signature's already affixed. Truly, that's a sign of intense faith…expecting his offer to be accepted so readily."

Senset didn't answer, and Aseti-Ra sipped his squash before continuing. Slowly, the girl raised her own goblet and forced herself to take a swallow. The tart liquid clogged her throat. She barely managed to keep from gagging.

"He's even more eager to be married, it appears…so much so that the General's requested the marriage ceremony be held in the morning."

"Sir?" Senset looked up, startled. "H-how can that be? With His Majesty absent?"

"The General suggests a proxy wedding ceremony."

"How does that work?" She'd never heard of such a thing. Whenever her brothers married, the ceremonies were carried out after their brides arrived in Ægys. Likewise, her sisters traveled to their betrothed's kingdoms where they became wives.

"The ceremony'll be held in the temple, with our priests presiding, and the general standing in as his brother's representative." Senset didn't realize she'd paled until her father said, reassuringly, "It's perfectly acceptable. I understand royal marriages are often carried out that way in the North."

"I-I see." What else could she say?

I'll be Michael's wife before I even see him?

"You'll leave immediately after the ceremony. It's a two and a half day journey to Habir, and your husband-to-be wishes you there as soon as possible." Aseti-Ra managed to look thoughtful. "Do I dare say he sounds as if he's smitten with you, sight unseen?"

"I… Perhaps the General let his relief at being given back his life cloud his judgment and made him freer with his praise of me than he might otherwise have been?" Senset suggested.

"Whatever the reason, he wants you, daughter…and soon." Aseti-Ra set down the goblet, reaching out to pat her hand. "Please him, Senset, and cement this newfound peace for our peoples."

Senset nodded obediently and bowed, and was sent on her way, not back to the women's quarters but to Asanath's suite.

"She wishes to tell you goodbye," Aseti-Ra said.

She didn't spend much time with Asanath, just long enough to be hugged and told how brave she was for marrying the king of the Beast Men, and then being allowed to hold Seti-Horem a moment. He was a beautiful baby, resembling her handsome brother even more than the others, and good-natured for one only a few days old.

As she cradled him in her arms and he caught at the swinging beads of her wig, Asanath spoke up. She appeared to be having a good day, and was remarkably lucid and talkative.

"Horem tells me His Majesty's most eager to marry and has asked noble Aseti-Ra for a proxy ceremony."

Senset nodded, forcing herself to concentrate on the happy baby in her arms.

"I think the whole thing's very romantic," Asa went on.

Briefly, her fingers plucked at the fabric of her skirt. She'd been doing that since the moment Senset arrived, keeping up that incessant motion except when she was holding her son. It bothered Senset, for it was such a foreign movement for Asanath, but she forced herself to ignore it, thinking to speak of it might not be the wisest thing.

"Like one of those fairy tales the children's nurse reads them at night. Just think, Senset. Before the year's out, you may have a child of your own…like my darling Seti."

If she noticed the sudden tremble of Senset's shoulders at those words, Asa didn't comment on it.

A child of my own…

Senset studied the baby. He was beautiful, with his father's black eyes instead of Asa's brown ones. That tiny snub nose would eventually lengthen with a hawklike curve like Horem's, and she had no doubt he'd have the Prince's height and breadth of shoulder eventually, also.

But my baby… What'll he look like? I've no idea how Michael looks. The only beast I've ever seen is Aram and the two accompanying him. Will my child have hazel eyes and curly black hair?

"Y-yes," she managed to stammer. "I daresay you're right."

"I mean…" Asa went on, giggling a little. "He's a *beast* after all, and he'll probably be as amorous as one. Oh, Senset…" In a spasm of delight, she hugged the girl. "I'm certain you're in for some very vigorous lovemaking."

She couldn't know how those words, meant to be encouraging, filled Senset with cold dread.

****

On the way back to the women's quarters, the extent of what was happening descended as Senset realized that, in the morning, she would be leaving Ægys…as well as her mother, siblings, Asanath, and Horem…forever. Never to see them again.

By the time she reached the doors leading into the common room, she was nearly in tears.

The fact that the common room was a flurry of activity distracted her.

Eighteen chests sat on the floor, five with their lids off. Under Satis' supervision, slaves were hurrying back and forth, filling the chests.

"Your noble father sent word about the ceremony, mistress," the slave explained. "I took the liberty of beginning the packing for you." She placed a hand on the girl's shoulder. "You're pale. This excitement's too much for you, I fear. I've prepared a goblet of wine to calm you. Drink it, then go to bed. I'll tend to packing your clothing and jewels."

"Thank you, Satis." Truly, Senset didn't want to have to personally pack anything. She didn't know if she could bear it. She started to her room, then stopped. "Be sure to pack my painting set."

"Of course, mistress." Satis bowed, then stood watching the small figure walk to the bed chamber, shoulders slumping.

She gestured to one of the chests, telling a slave to place inside it the jeweled collar she held.

Chapter 13

In her room, Senset drank the wine Satis had poured
for her, undressed, and lay down, forcing herself not to
think about the morning. Tonight, there would be
feasting… She felt more than a little anger at being
denied the distraction and excitement of the banquet with
her royal father and Aram.

*It's to celebrate my betrothal as well as the ending
of the war. I should be there.*

It wasn't fair that she, who should've been the guest
of honor, wasn't invited. Though women were expected
to arrange such celebrations, they were never present. If
Aram or his brother had brought wives with them,
Hatasu would've entertained them at a private dinner in
the women's quarters. Only concubines and female
slaves were allowed at the men's banquets, and they
never spoke of what went on there.

Briefly, Senset wondered what it would be like to
attend.

****

The slave girl selected a honey-dipped grape from
the bowl on the banquet table, offering it to Aram. He
opened his mouth, letting her deposit it inside, then
licked the sweet and sticky residue off her fingers,
trailing his tongue to her palm. She smiled and giggled
slightly, dipping her head so the pat of solid incense
attached to her wig, and now melting from her body heat,

115

wafted acacia scent over him. Chewing enjoyably, and even more so after discovering the grape had been de-seeded, he gestured to her to get another as he relaxed against the couch's soft wool draperies.

Next to him, Gideon also reclined, fed almond halves by another slave.

Aseti-Ra's banquet was in its early stages and the guests were still settling in, though it had begun bizarrely enough, at least to Aram's way of thinking.

No sooner had they been seated on the couches than a slave appeared carrying what looked like a miniature corpse wrapped in linens. Walking up one side of the table where the princes sat, across to Aseti-Ra, and down the side where the guests reclined, he intoned solemnly, "Gaze upon this and heed, O noble men. This is the end for all, so enjoy this feast as if it may be your last."

"A most unusual opening to a celebration, Your Majesty." Aram hoped that didn't sound critical, though it chilled him slightly and momentarily cooled his anticipated enjoyment.

"A mere reminder that all men's days are numbered and we should live each as if it's our last and enjoy it to the fullest." Aseti-Ra's hand hovered over the dish of candied fruit. "After a while, one comes to ignore it."

Aram was glad of that. Being reminded daily how short one's lifespan could be wasn't a cheering notion. To distract his thoughts, he turned his attention to the end of the room where a quintet of female musicians provided music. One plucked a dulcimer while another strummed a cyther. A third blew gently on a flute, its reedy notes floating over the heads of the diners, accompanied by the shaking of a sistrum and a drum's slow beat.

At the head table, Aseti-Ra's gift knelt beside him. Changed from her Habiru garments, Dalilah was now clad in an Ægysian gown of pleated form-fitting linen. Above the wide, bejeweled collar, her comely face had been painted and kohled, though her hair remained uncut, hanging past her shoulders, beaded and beribboned locks framing her face. At the moment, she was holding a small saucer of candied jujube fruit, ready to serve her new master.

Aram, Gideon, and their younger brother Yeshua were seated on Aseti-Ra's right at a separate table reserved for honored guests, in this case, the relatives of his soon-to-be son-in-law. As Michael's proxy, Aram had been given the place of honor, and—Aseti-Ra informed him—his most beautiful slave. Facing them at the table on the left were Horem and his other adult brothers. Though the prince still appeared a little reticent in showing his feelings in the matter of the truce and the coming marriage, the others had wholeheartedly embraced the event. Aram generously acceded since Horem had spent most of his adult life fighting the Habiru, just as he himself had fought the Ægysians, he supposed it might take more than a day to rid himself of those feelings.

Aseti-Ra's cooks had truly outdone themselves for the feast. Gideon and Aram were both taking in their exotic surroundings with enjoyment, managing to contain their awe, but Yeshua reminded Aram of the puppy Horem's son had claimed. The boy was watching everything with the excitement of an ungoverned child in a marketplace full of free sweets. His dazzled gaze roved the lavish table, the glorious paintings and mosaics decorating the walls and floor, and above all, the slave women serving them.

I pray the boy can keep his body under control.

Yeshua was the youngest brother, and had begged Aram to allow him to accompany him on this mission. Their mother, Rebekah, argued otherwise, of course, and the boy fumed rebelliously at what he called her attempts to keep him a child. Aram agreed; after all, upon reaching the age of thirteen, Yeshua had undergone the ritual admission into manhood, and now, at sixteen, was chafing to join his older brothers in serving his king.

Aram agreed to take Yeshua along, in the capacity of Gideon's aide. Thus, the boy had been the one handing the scrolls to Aseti-Ra's advisor.

At the moment, the slave girl assigned to him was feeding him wine-soaked candied figs and he was eating as if he were famished. He had one arm around the girl's waist, holding her closely against his own body.

Aram hoped he had enough self-control not to do more. *Yet.* He didn't want Yeshua committing the equivalent of the puppy piddling on the king's marble.

Uncertain how undisciplined Ægysian men were at their banquets, he didn't want the boy becoming overexcited and committing a public error. At the present, however, he was watching his elder brothers from time to time and copying their behavior.

If he continued to do that, there would be no mounting of a slave girl before the king's eyes, though Aram might have to intervene when it came to the boy's wine consumption.

So far, the wines served had been light ones, slightly dry, to whet the appetite and create a thirst, making a desire for more. Aram was certain Aseti-Ra would break open one of the gift bottles for the main course, and it was then he'd have to keep an eye on Yeshua, for Habiru wine was deceiving. Pleasing to the palate but deceptively strong, allowing a man to drink many goblets as harmless, then suddenly find himself face down on his dinner plate. He and Gideon had consumed enough of it to be aware, but Yeshua still hadn't had that dubious pleasure.

The girls were another matter. Each man had a companion for the evening, Aseti-Ra's sons inviting their favorite concubines to the feast. The slaves supplied for the guests were a temptation to the eyes, especially to a still-uninitiated youngster like Yeshua. Dressed only in bib-like necklets of many rows of jasper, carnelian, and jade, and wide girdles—barely groin-width—tied with golden knee-length tassels, they selected from offered trays of candied fruit, assorted baked and honeyed nuts, and fresh slices of melon, feeding them to their guests.

"Your Majesty…" Hasta stood before his king, and his words pulled Aram from his sweets-laden reverie.

The advisor placed a silver tray upon the table. It held the two boxes containing the scrolls as well as a quill and a small pottery cup holding a sponge, and two ceramic oblongs. He opened the boxes, taking out the scrolls, and unrolling each to its end. Setting them before Aseti-Ra, he picked up the cup.

"The treaty's ready for your signature, sire."

Goblets were set down. Fingers peeling fruit stilled. The servants stopped in their passages between the tables. All watched as Aseti-Ra reached for one of the ceramic rectangles. He rubbed it against the sponge, then pressed it onto the scroll at the spot the advisor indicated.

When he removed it, his cartouche containing hieroglyphs spelling out his name appeared where the rectangle touched. He did the same to the second scroll and Hasta lifted the tray, walking over to where Horem sat. The prince repeated what his father had done, using the other oblong to ink his own cartouche onto the scrolls.

There was no hesitance in his movements, and he smiled slightly. A favorable sign because it showed a lightening of his attitude, Aram thought. Abruptly, the prince looked up, his eyes meeting Aram's.

The smile broadened.

Aram returned it with a nod.

The advisor carried the tray to him and Gideon. Each took the quill, thrust it into the sponge and inscribed their names and rank under Aseti-Ra and Horem's signatures.

As Gideon placed the quill on the tray, the advisor re-rolled one of the scrolls and returned it to its box, then handed it to Gideon. He bowed, put the second scroll in the other box and offered it to his king.

Aseti-Ra took the box. As Hasta bowed and gave the tray to a slave to take away and returned to his place beside the prince, the king clapped his hands.

"Now that the formalities are out of the way, let our celebrating of these two joyous events begin."

A line of slaves bearing the main courses streamed through the door, each accompanied by the cook who had prepared the selection. Aram was reaching for a slice of melon offered by his attendant as the first of the slaves stopped before him. Gideon also stopped eating, looking eagerly at the platter.

"Our honored guests will be served first," Aseti-Ra announced.

The cook who had prepared that particular dish was

waiting, his carving knives ready to cut as many slices as the honored guest required. Aram turned his attention to the platter borne by two slaves, and stiffened. Besides him, Gideon did the same. Yeshua was too engrossed with his slave girl to notice what the platter held.

A whole suckling pig, spit-roasted to a golden brown, garnished with grapes and peaches.

Aram was silent. Aseti-Ra, however, saw there was something amiss.

"Is there a problem, General? The offering isn't to your liking?" There was puzzlement as well as a sincere hope in his tone that nothing was about to spoil the evening.

"Not at all, Your Majesty…"

How to say it without offense?

He'd not thought to mention it, and there was no way the Ægysians, much less the kitchen help, could've known. Well, the only thing to do was to say it outright but without accusation.

"I regret, and apologize for my omission, but…Habiru aren't allowed to eat the flesh of swine."

"Not…" Surprisingly, it was Horem who spoke up.

That one word rising, then dying away as if he couldn't believe it and thought perhaps his father's guest was making a rather tasteless joke. His brothers simply sat and stared.

"It's a divine law, laid down by our God," Aram went on. "I beg your indulgence, Most Noble Aseti-Ra, but we must decline this dish though it appears to be prepared most appetizingly."

There was silence as the king absorbed this information. At the second table, his third son Potifar studied the platter and licked his lower lip.

"Does your God allow you to eat beef, mutton, and fish?"

"Yes, sire, except for certain shellfish."

"I'm not surprised. Can't say I like those either." A royal hand waved. "Take it back to the kitchen and distribute it to the house servants at their evening meal."

"But, Father," Potifar protested. "That's my favorite."

"And you'll have it again, my son," Aseti-Ra replied smoothly. "Just not this night. What's the next item?"

The next slave held out his platter for Aram's inspection. Fish baked in a savory rosemary sauce garnished with lemon slices. He nodded, pointing to the top fish on the dish and the cook took a plate from his assistant, deftly scooped the fish onto it, carefully filleted and cut it into bite-sized pieces, poured a spoonful of sauce next to it, and handed it to the slave girl. There was a tiny pick resting on the edge of the plate and the girl used it to spear the fish, dip it into the sauce, and offer it to Aram.

He ate, nodded, and took the plate from her, helping himself as the cook beamed and Gideon was offered his choice.

The wines changed now, a bottle of Habiru wine opened and goblets filled. Ægysian wines accompanied the pit-cooked beef, basted with pungent honey and vinegar, as well as a mutton shank marinated in fig and lemon jelly. Bowls of artichokes, pickled beets, and peppers were passed around as were rounded loaves of wheat and rye bread with accompanying bowls of aromatic basil oil in which they were to be dipped.

Desserts were fruit breads and a compote of mixed fruit in a wine sauce. By this time, Aram was close to being sated and more than a little drunk.

He was beginning to look on his attendant with a completely lecherous eye, and sternly told himself he'd better drink no more or he'd do himself out of the way he planned to end his evening. He'd wanted the girl from the moment she bowed and sat down meekly beside him, and hoped he was right in assuming she was also offered to him for the night. That was generally the way a betrothal feast ended in Habir, and he already had plans of exactly what he was going to do once he got her back to his suite, envisioning her naked upon the soft cotton sheets of his couch and he just as bare beside her, enjoying her ministrations.

Horem, he noticed, was already absent, having made his excuses to his royal father. He'd left, taking the concubine with him, though the woman looked anything but pleased.

"She didn't appear happy," Aram commented to Aseti-Ra, raising his wine cup but taking a bare sip this time.

Have to start tapering off now.

Aseti-Ra sighed as he selected a morsel of mutton and swirled it in an aromatic red dipping sauce. "My heir—fortunately or unfortunately as the case may be— is in love with his prime wife and spends every free moment with her except when duty calls. Xena there is jealous because she hoped to have him to herself tonight, but she'll go back to the women's quarters and he'll go to the Princess Royal's suite to be in her company, though Asanath's still being purified from recently giving birth."

"A son, I hope?" Aram set down his goblet. That was an interesting fact about the prince. It showed he had a gentler side.

"My fifteenth grandson and sixth heir to the throne after his father," Aseti-Ra confirmed. As if he'd just thought of it, he raised his own cup. "Our family's a very fertile one, General Aram. Your brother won't lack for heirs."

Aram considered that, nodded, and lifted his own cup in a salute to the king's statement. He got to his feet. *Staggered* would be a better description.

"I should retire now, Your Majesty. Since I'm to represent my noble brother at tomorrow's ceremony, I don't wish to do so while still in wine's embrace." He looked around, as if seeing the girl for the first time. "However, I fear I may need some assistance in finding my way to the rooms you've so graciously offered me. May she—?" He gestured at the slave.

"You'll guide the general to his apartments," Aseti-Ra told her, adding, "and stay with him until he no longer requires your assistance."

Aram smiled. That was plain enough.

Bowing to the king and whichever of his sons were looking in his direction, he spoke to Gideon, whispered a word of caution to Yeshua, and, reaching out to draw the slave girl near as if to lean on her, walked out.

Chapter 14

The cart lurched sideways as one wheel struck a solid object in its path, tossing Senset from her doze. Gingerly, she shifted on the padded seat, trying to find a comfortable position. Though the overstuffed cushions were filled with feathers enclosed in lamb's wool, to someone having sat in one spot for nearly five hours, it was uncomfortable; to a backside still recovering from a flailing, their touch was more than near-excruciating. Thinking of having to sit this way for two more days brought a gigantic shudder.

It's so hot.

Accustomed to the cool limestone and marble interior of the royal palace with its wide windows and airy hallways, she was finding her present surroundings anything but pleasant.

The Plain of Arriah was arid and nearly treeless. The sun beat down on the litter in which she was riding. Though its roof protected her, it also held in the heat, making the interior hot as an oven.

A drop of sweat trickled between Senset's eyes, sending a liquid streak of kohl down her nose. She wiped it away.

By the time we get to Habir, I'll be as well-baked as a loaf of bread. She rubbed her hand on a thigh, leaving a dark smear. *Now I've ruined my gown, and who knows when we'll stop so I may bathe and change.*

If they were going to stop at all. For all she knew, with the haste they had left Usaset, the caravan might keep going until they arrived in Habir.

From the floor of the litter came a soft snore. Orora, the slave given to her as a handmaiden, lay asleep at her feet. She'd been that way since five minutes after they'd gone through Usaset's gates, curling up on the floor and promptly falling into a doze.

How can she look so comfortable? Senset sighed. *If only I had someone to talk to.*

She'd planned on Orora keeping her entertained, going over the girl's duties with her…speculating about their destination…any number of things to keep her mind off the journey. As yet, the slave's only distraction was the varying pitch of her snores.

Where's Aram?

She hadn't seen him since he'd escorted her from the temple after placing the wide marriage band around her wrist.

He'd arrived at the ceremony dressed for traveling, in wide-sleeved white robes whose crimson headdress draped cloak-like over his shoulders. Once the rites were completed, he helped her into the litter perched upon the cart—the same litter previously filled with gifts for her father, now filled with an even greater gift for her husband—fastened the door, and turned to speak to Horem and her father.

She hadn't heard what he said, except for the words, "The Plain." Whatever it was, her brother and father agreed, for they both bowed, raising their hands in the symbolic movement denoting acceptance.

Nodding, Aram mounted the horse Gideon held for him, saluted his new relatives-by-marriage, and rode to the head of the caravan. The slave driving the cart called to the two horses. It lurched forward and they were on their way, leaving her father, Hatasu, and Horem—still looking slightly skeptical and still unreconciled with her—standing on the temple steps along with the other witnesses in the royal retinue.

Senset wanted to lean out the door of the litter, look back, and watch them become smaller and smaller as she was whisked away.

Away from Usaset…away from Ægys…to Habir and her still-unknown husband…

She forced herself not to. Instead, she leaned back against the padded seat and watched Orora begin her five-hour nap.

The sun was now directly overhead and they were showing no signs of slowing or stopping. Senset was thirsty, hot, and bored. Surprisingly, she wasn't feeling any regret at leaving Usaset, however. Once the gates of the city were left behind, a slow excitement set in, followed by an eagerness to get to her new home.

It had now become more than eagerness. She was *impatient*.

Shutting her eyes, she concentrated on the sounds outside the litter. The thud of horses' hooves on the hard-baked, dried grass…the squeak of wagon wheels…a snort or two from one of the horses.

Slow…monotonous… She let it lull her into a fretful doze.

When the cart stopped and the door opened, she jerked awake.

Aram climbed in, falling onto the seat beside her…bulky and masculine, his face covered by an edge of his *tarna* tucked into the opposite side of its headband.

He struggled to fit himself into the small space she and Orora so easily occupied.

Senset scrambled upright, reaching up to smooth her wig, which had slipped slightly as her head tilted backward while she slept.

"It came to me I'm being uncaring of my new sister," he said as he secured the door and leaned back.

The cart rumbled forward again.

"Generally, I wouldn't be allowed alone with you, but as your proxy husband, I can take exception to that law until we reach Habir. I imagine you're bored, so I thought perhaps we might talk. I'm certain you've many questions you want to ask before we reach our destination."

"More than a few," she admitted, "but I've one question of more importance than any other at the moment."

"What's that?" His eyes smiled at her.

She wondered how he managed to look so cool when she felt like a cake thrust into an oven. Granted the hem of his robes were grayed, as was the flowing headdress, and his sandals and feet appeared dusty, but he looked surprisingly relaxed. She supposed he was accustomed to long rides in the searing heat.

As he spoke, he loosened the tucked-in corner of his *tarna*, letting it drop, revealing his smile.

"You were my husband's stand-in at my wedding. Will you also take his place at my wedding night?" She managed to ask that without blushing.

"I didn't expect that." He burst into laughter. "Are you always this blunt?" When she didn't answer, he went on, "No, Senset. Calm yourself on that score. Only your husband will celebrate your marriage night with you."

She relaxed, visibly, and knew he saw. Somehow, it didn't embarrass her as she'd expected it would.

"When we arrive in Beth-Gurion, there'll be a second marriage, performed under Habiru law. Then and only then will your husband come to you and make you his wife."

"Why do I have to be married again?" It seemed a silly thing, and redundant, at that.

"My brother wishes there to be no doubt of his sincerity, so he's marrying you under the customs of both your people and ours."

Senset considered that. "Thank you, Aram. I hope you don't think my question that of a silly girl. I'd never heard of a proxy wedding before my father informed me I was to have one."

"To tell the truth, neither had I, but my brother's advisors have, and they were the ones suggesting it to him." He sighed slightly. "Now that your mind's laid to rest, have you anything else you'd like to ask?"

"Of a certainty." She settled herself, turning to face him. "Horem told me that during the battle, he saw a man wearing a gold mask, and he thought that man was your leader." Briefly, she wondered if it was wise to mention their former hostility. "Was that Michael?"

He nodded.

"Why does he wear a mask? Is he so ugly he hides his face?"

"It's the custom for our leader to wear a mask. Michael has worn one since he was a few minutes old. It's never been removed."

"For the gods' sake, why?"

"I think my brother should explain that himself." His expression closed as if he wanted to say more but was forcing himself not to.

"I'll never see my husband's face?" Dismay twisted within Senset. "I'll never know what he looks like?"

"You have only to gaze on me, little sister." Aram caught her hands, holding them tightly between his own. His words were earnest as if to impress them upon her. "Michael and I are twins. He's five minutes older than I—something I daily thank the Good Lord for."

She thought she saw a flash of shame as he said that. For his good fortune in not being the older twin and sentenced to hide his face forever behind a metal mask?

What kind of barbaric custom forces such a thing on a man?

She stared at Aram's face, at the straight slash of his brows, the aquiline strength of his nose—*almost like Horem's*—the way his lips curved slightly even when he wasn't smiling.

"If I look at you, I see him?" She was asking to be reassured she hadn't married a monster.

"Michael's eyes are green," He nodded. "Otherwise, I believe we're exactly alike."

"And he never takes it off?"

He shook his head.

"Not even when he sleeps?"

"What's the meaning of the word *never*, little sister?" He was laughing at her. "If it bothers you, thinking of a faceless man making love to you…" He shrugged. "…put my face in your mind and call it his."

Senset didn't answer that. *If I put your face in my mind, Aram, I won't be thinking of my husband.* That thought startled her so, she nearly gasped.

"What's the matter?"

"Nothing." She wasn't about to tell him *that*. "I was

thinking he must be uncomfortable sometimes…as hot as the weather gets." In an effort to change the subject, she hurried on, "Do you have any other brothers? Or sisters?"

"More than enough." He didn't seem to notice anything odd about her manner. "The two accompanying me… Gideon's my brother's scribe…"

So that was why he had carried the boxes of scrolls.

"And Yeshua." He smiled. "He's the baby, and our mother tries to shield him from everything. He begged to be brought on this trip—mainly to get away from her, I think—and Michael agreed, much to her unhappiness. My other brother's Shemuel."

And the king has a mother. One who pampers her youngest child.

"I've also two sisters. Meryam and Rachel. Rachel's a year older than Yeshua. Meryam's the eldest of us all. She's married to Adonijah, my brother's chief advisor." Aram stretched out his legs, crossing them at the ankles. "Glad I don't have to ride in this thing for long. It's not constructed for a man, is it? And it's uncomfortably hot."

"It certainly is," Senset agreed. She shifted on the seat. "Sitting in one spot all day isn't doing my backside any good."

Aram stifled a laugh. "Perhaps I should order Yeshua to ride with you. He's smaller and could fit more easily into this contraption than I do."

Having been introduced to the pleasures of physical love by the slave girl who'd sat with him, the boy'd been pouting since the moment he arose because he didn't want to leave Usaset. Didn't want to go back to Beth-Gurion where he'd again be watched over by his mother and older sisters.

"Rachel's looking forward to having another female in the household close to her own age." Aram swiped the back of his hand across his chin before returning to his subject.

For the first time, Senset noticed that the strip of beard was beginning to glisten with sweat.

So he isn't as cool as he looks. She felt a sudden desire to touch the hair on his face, wondering if it was as soft as his dark curls or stiff and bristly.

"I hope you and she will be friends. She's—"

"Aram?" Gideon appeared next to the litter, leaning down to peer through the open window. He placed a hand on the edge of the doorframe. "The watering hole where we made our last camp before arriving at Usaset is just ahead. Do you wish to stop there for the night or travel farther?"

"I think we should stop," Aram decided, giving Senset a smile. "I imagine our little sister's had enough traveling for one day. Are you weary, Senset?"

"Yes, I am." She didn't even have to think about it.

Looking more closely at the man riding beside the cart, she studied him as he nodded in reply. She could see a strong resemblance between the two. Gideon also had hazel eyes, though his nose wasn't quite as curved. In her mind, she tried to combine their features, making a new face—Michael's—to carry in her memory.

Gideon called out and the cart came to a halt. Aram climbed out. He'd tied his horse to the back of the cart, and she heard him walk around to it, fumbling with the reins before swinging onto its back.

Within an hour they arrived at a grove of trees surrounding a small lake, and stopped.

****

"I'm afraid you'll have to dine on soldier's fare tonight," Aram apologized as Orora brought her a plate. "We don't eat very grandly while on a campaign."

"Do you consider taking me to Beth-Gurion a campaign? I thought that was a term used only during wartime."

"You're right. Wartime no longer exists. I stand corrected, little sister. 'While we travel.' There, does that sound better?"

She studied the contents of the plate. "What is this, anyway?"

"Smoked beef, dried pitted apricots." He pointed at each item. "We don't use much fresh food when away from the city. It spoils too fast in the heat. And..." He reached beside the stool on which he sat, lifting what looked like a wineskin. "Sweet well water to drink."

She selected an apricot, studied the wrinkled golden oval a moment, then put it into her mouth. It was tart, not too sweet, and surprisingly juicy in spite of being dried.

"Do you smoke other meats, too? Fowl...mutton...pork? And take those with you?"

"Not pork." He smiled slightly, remembering the scene at Aseti-Ra's banquet. "We're forbidden to eat that."

"Why?" She finished the apricot and bit off a strip of beef. It was tough. She began to chew with great difficult, one jaw bulging slightly.

"Our God has declared it unclean." Aram stifled a smile.

Like most of his people, he'd never wondered about that specific canon, simply accepting it, but Senset was already questioning that he took for granted. Briefly, he wondered if he was going to have to justify everything he said if it involved something their God forbade.

"I suppose they are." She looked thoughtful. "The way they wallow in all that mud. And they'll eat anything."

Aram didn't bother to correct her and say that wasn't the type of *unclean* he meant.

"So I'll never have pork again?"

He shook his head., wondering if that made her sad.

"Good. It always gives me an upset stomach. I won't miss it." She held out the plate to the slave. "Get me some more beef, Orora."

The girl got to her feet, taking her mistress' plate and scurrying to where the wagon containing their provisions was stopped. A soldier standing at its dropped tailgate smiled at her and dipped into a basket, bringing out a handful of beef strips he dropped onto the plate. Orora dipped him a curtsey and hurried back to Senset, placing the plate in her hands.

"Get some food for yourself and then get to bed," Senset told her.

With a bow, the girl ran back to the wagon. The soldier was walking away. She called to him and he turned back. Rummaging around in the back of the wagon, he found another plate, filling it from the baskets. He said something, and Orora answered with a toss of her head. As she walked toward the tent she shared with her mistress, he studied the girl appreciatively.

"That soldier's watching my slave." Senset looked at the figure leaning against the wagon, a piece of smoked beef in his hand.

He was chewing slowly as his eyes followed Orora's progress across the grass.

Senset looked back at Aram. "And so are you."

"A comely woman's always a delight to behold," he answered, as if that was enough of an excuse. He also considered the sway of Orora's hips, the white linen a contrast to her darkness. "She's like an onyx figurine."

And you are as fine as a statue carved from alabaster, he wanted to say. He got very busy studying the contents of his plate.

"She's Amasulu. Father paid a trader from the south five bars of turquoise for her. He gave her to me for my twelfth natal celebration. She's my handmaiden and isn't to be touched." Senset put as much firmness into that statement as she could. "I didn't bring her for my husband's pleasure."

"Nor your brother-in-law's, either, I suppose."

It was muttered so low she wasn't certain she'd heard correctly. He looked up, those hazel eyes meeting hers.

"You'll protest if Michael claims the girl?"

"Yes. Even if it *is* acceptable." She thought of the handmaidens brought with Horem's other wives as well as those women marrying her father.

The slaves had gone to their husbands' beds as well. An image of the woman Dalilah brought as a gift to Aseti-Ra, came into her mind's eye.

"He can have his pick of any of the others my father sent with me, but not Orora."

"My dear Senset, Michael has enough concubines that he isn't going to need one more, I assure you."

Senset looked away.

Should I tell him?

"I didn't have to bring her. I imagine Michael will supply me with enough servants I won't even miss her."

"Why did you then?"

135

"Because…" She hesitated, then plunged on. "If I'm barren, I wanted my substitute to be someone of my own choosing. She'll go to my husband and have his child for me."

That made a dark eyebrow go up. "Do you doubt you can give Michael sons?"

He looked as if he might have made a mistake lauding her virtues to his brother, before he remembered what Aseti-Ra had said.

"No." She got very busy eating the last of the beef. "But the gods may decree otherwise, and if that happens, he'll still need an heir. Orora will sit on my thighs and give us a son."

"I'd no idea your people followed that custom, too," he spoke slowly, as if thinking about that.

It was an acceptable way for an infertile wife to give her husband children, sending her handmaiden to his bed. During the birth, the wife held the new mother on her lap, so the child passed between her legs and symbolically she also gave birth to the baby, claiming it as her own from that moment on.

"Perhaps we're more alike than we both know." Senset handed Aram her plate and, as he took it, went on, "However, I've no doubt as to my ability to produce heirs for your king, so don't tell him of this little conversation." Another thought struck her. "How many children does Michael have, anyway?"

"None." Aram gave her a startlingly direct stare. "So far, the Good Lord has prevented his concubine's wombs from accepting the king's seed. My brother sows in infertile soil."

"I see."

Does he blame his God for his king's inability? Is

136

Michael sterile? Dear Ra-Harakhty, have I entered into a barren marriage?

Senset didn't let her dismay show. "I daresay I must be the one to end the drought."

Getting to her feet, she walked to the tent, leaving him sitting there.

You are a very surprising female, little sister. Aram was a little shocked by the admiration in that thought.

****

As the litter door swung open, Senset looked toward it eagerly, expecting Aram to appear, though the cart still moved. Instead, she saw he was on his horse, again wrapped in that face-shrouding headdress and leaning over to peer in at her as Gideon had.

"Is anything the matter?" She imagined bandits storming out of the foothills, brandishing swords. Foolish thought…she'd have heard them.

"Not in the least. I thought you might like to ride with me," he said.

"Ride with you?" Senset repeated. "On that horse?"

"It'll be something to ease your boredom." He loosened the headdress, flashing her a brilliant smile, as if to say he understood how uninteresting, and uncomfortable, sitting all day in a cart-carried litter could be. "A change of scenery. For you and your…backside."

I should never have mentioned that.

Senset blushed, hoping he'd think it merely the heat inside the litter making her complexion high. "I don't know how to ride a horse."

"It's not difficult. Come." Dropping the reins onto the animal's neck, he twisted in the saddle, holding out his right hand.

When Senset slid across the seat, reaching for it, he

grasped hers tightly and pulled her out of the litter, his left arm going around her waist as he swung her up and onto the horse's withers.

He lifts me as if I weigh nothing.

She settled herself quickly, glancing down. The sandy soil seemed very far away. "It's a long way to the ground."

"Don't worry. I have you." His arms tightened, pulling her against his chest, rock-hard and steady. "You won't fall."

After that, he was silent and they rode along without speaking until he asked, "Well? What do you think of your first horseback ride, my lady?"

"I'm not sure." Senset was certain he wasn't going to like her answer. "Having something moving between my legs is a disturbing sensation. I don't know that I like it."

"Hah!" His laugh was throaty and coarse in her ear, rumbling through his chest. "Better change that attitude fast, little sister. Else your nights as Michael's wife are going to be miserable." At her gasp, he hurried on, apologetically, "I'm sorry. I've been spending too much time in the company of my men. I've forgotten how to speak gently to a female."

"No," she corrected him. "You're right. I must change my way of thinking. Understand, Aram, it's simply a…maiden's…thoughts."

That was the most delicate way to tell him she was a virgin and relatively ignorant of men's way…as if he didn't already know.

"I'm certain my husband will be nothing like a horse."

Again, his chest shook but this time he didn't laugh

out loud.

Oh, dear Ra-Harakhty, have I said the wrong thing?

When Aram didn't reply, Senset hurried on, "I'd like to learn to ride one of these creatures. Do you have someone who can teach me?" She remembered the young slave brought as a gift. "Is there another Benyamin in Beth-Gurion?"

"There is, and he'll teach you, if Michael permits."

"Why wouldn't he?"

"Riding can sometimes be dangerous. He may consider you too precious to risk."

Senset thought about that. It would be nice to be thought *precious*. Silence fell again. She lay with her head resting against Aram's shoulder. The steadiness of the horse's gait and the gentle swaying of her brother-in-law's body as well as the rise and fall of his chest against her shoulder blades was lulling her into sleep.

She forced herself to sit up, saying, "Tell me about your God, Aram."

He took a deep breath as if that surprised him. "What would you like to know?"

"What's his name? Is he a good God? What does he require of His worshippers?" All things she'd thought about since the night he told her his people had only one Deity.

He took a little longer to answer than she expected. "Our God doesn't have a name, Senset."

"Then how do you know how to speak to him?"

"He has no name," he repeated. "He simply *is* and that's how we've been instructed… *I AM*…that's what we say…*Yahweh*. As for His being a good God, it isn't for us to judge the Lord but for Him to judge us. He's given us laws to live by, and if we follow them, He

139

allows His face to shine upon us." He paused, holding her a little tighter. "The first law is that we'll worship no other gods but He who is the True One."

She thought that over. The concept of one God over everything sounded so...foreign.

Well, the Habiru are *foreigners, aren't they? Just as the land on the other side of the Plain of Arriah is foreign territory.* In the same country as Ægys, but vastly different.

"Will I be expected to worship Him, too*?"*

Give up Ra-Harakhty and Bast and all the others for a God with no name?

"It would be best, don't you think?" His answer was gentle, as if giving her a choice.

Senset was certain there was really none to be made.

"Of course." She put as much enthusiasm as she could into her answer. "I'll learn all I can. I'll read your Sacred Texts, and..."

"I'm afraid our Sacred Writings are in an ancient version of our language, little sister."

"Then I'll have someone teach me. One of your scribes can read them to me and I'll learn. I'll have to learn your language, anyway. So I can speak to my husband, at least. Gideon can teach me, can't he?"

"If Michael allows."

"Do you think he won't wish his wife to be able to read the Scriptures?" Senset was beginning to wonder if her husband would have more control over her movements than her royal father had.

Will I have to ask permission from Michael for anything I wish to do?

Hatasu has certainly never gone begging to Aseti-Ra like that. The prime wife had her own mind and opinions.

"Once he sees you, Senset, I think my brother'll find himself desperate to grant any wish you make." Aram's laugh reverberated against her shoulders. "If he doesn't fall madly in love with you, he's not the man I know him to be."

He couldn't know how that statement made a glow in her heart.

"When you spoke to Horem and my father, just before we left…what did you say?"

"I simply gave them a *mizpah*," he said it off-handedly, as if it signified nothing.

"What's that?"

"I told them my God would be watching them and us from now on. *May the Lord watch between you and me when we're absent one from the other*… The Plain of Arriah is the barrier between our kingdoms. If either Ægys or Habir crosses it in aggression against the other, the Lord will know and act."

"Truly?" That gave her an internal shiver, knowing that Unnamed God stood as a sentry, making certain the peace between their kingdoms held. She wondered what He'd do if either broke the truce, then decided she didn't want to know.

A short time later, Aram returned her to the litter, and a little while after that, they reached the second oasis and set up camp for the night. This time, as Senset slept, she dreamed again of Aram in kingly robes, but now he placed a golden mask upon his face, and as his hazel eyes looked out at her, they filled with tears running down his gilded cheeks.

The following day, with the noonday sun beating down, they arrived in Beth-Gurion.

Chapter 15

"Hurry, Orora." Senset jerked her foot from the slave's grasp, sending the painting quill flying. "You're too slow. My husband's waiting."

"Don't fret, mistress."

Orora reached for a strip of cotton cloth lying on the floor and carefully wied away the henna smear across Senset's toes. Retrieving the quill, she continued stroking the dark red dye onto her mistress's toenails.

"His Royal Highness can wait a little longer. He's waited weeks as it is, hasn't he? Besides, he did forego that *yuchid* ceremony, didn't he?" The slave shook her head. "I asked what that is, and one of the other slaves told me that's the time when the newlyweds are expected to consummate their marriage." She looked disapproving. "In a curtained-off space, with everyone waiting outside? I truly hope all their customs aren't so strange."

Senset didn't answer. She'd also been a little shocked when she learned what a *yuchid* was, and disturbed when she'd heard Michael state there would be none, though grateful she and her new husband wouldn't share their first intimate moments together with a listening audience.

Nevertheless, she was impatient.

She was now Michael's wife, and, if Orora ever finished her ministrations, her bridegroom would soon come to her.

Does that make me wanton or bold? That I'm looking forward to being in his bed, though he's still a stranger to me?

"There." Orora wiped the quill on the piece of cloth and returned it to the cosmetics box. "Finished. Now, for your wedding robe."

Barely listening, Senset stood. She was thinking of all that had happened. The hours since they'd entered the city were a whirl of images and faces…

****

She was startled by the joy greeting her. Lining the main street leading from the guardian gates and winding through the city until it reached the entrance to the palace itself, Beth-Gurion's inhabitants called out words she didn't understand.

Shlama…shlama…

"Peace…" Aram translated as she leaned out the litter window. "…and welcome." He'd once more loosened his face-covering so its veils hung about his shoulders, stirred by a brief wind into trailing draperies.

"Are they really that happy to see me?" Truly, their reaction was even more joyous than the Ægysians' to Horem's return.

"They're happy their king finally has his queen."

He rode ahead, taking his place at the head of the caravan, leading it through the palace gates. More shouts rang out as the people recognized their king's brother.

"It's so noisy, mistress." Orora, wide awake for once, asked timidly, "Are they angry?"

"According to General Aram, they're happy." Senset laughed. "They're glad I'm here, Orora."

She hoped Michael would be as joyous. Her belly

trembled as she realized that, in a few moments, she'd be in her betrothed's—no, her *husband's*—presence.

She hadn't met Michael, however. When the caravan stopped in the palace courtyard, Aram dismounted, throwing the reins to a waiting slave. He pulled open the door to the litter, holding out his hand.

"Come, little sister."

As Senset looked around, overwhelmed by her first view of her surroundings, he turned back to help Orora also.

Unlike its Ægysian counterpart, the palace was long and sprawling, the main building a great rectangle of granite cut from the mountain at whose feet it rested. The connecting structures on either side were handmade brick, plastered and whitewashed, reflecting the sun like a sheet of silver. The brilliance of those white walls made Senset blink, putting up one hand to shield her eyes. Though plain and undecorated compared to her father's palace, it had steep steps rising at its entrance to a portico supported by impressive, rounded pillars.

On the steps stood two men and four women, accompanied by guards armed as those riding with the caravan. Senset's attention was immediately caught by one man who took a step toward them.

Is this Michael? She felt sinking disappointment as she saw his face was uncovered.

He was dressed in a brilliant blue *galabia* over a white robe. His dark hair was held back from his face by a jeweled browband. Like Gideon and Aram, he also had a beard, though his was much fuller and covered more of his face.

Senset forced herself not to stare.

Apparently, once they were old enough, all Habiru

men allowed the hair on their faces to grow. She supposed even young Yeshua, who already had dark, downy shadows on his cheeks, would soon have his handsome face half-hidden by a heavy brush of hair.

That's going to take some getting used to.

The women wore white gowns girded at the waist by woven beaded belts, their heads covered by long shawls hanging over their shoulders and arms. Beaded necklets and golden earrings adorned throats and ears. Two of them whispered to each other while their eyes darted from Senset to Orora and back.

She saw the older woman's gaze slide past her to the slave Aram was lifting from the litter. As he released the girl, she looked back at Senset, frowning.

Senset understood. They were both wearing simple, unadorned gowns for traveling, and…

They don't know which of us is their king's betrothed. Oh, what a joke! Orora and I must laugh at this when we're alone.

Gideon and Yeshua, who'd ridden in before them, joined the others. Immediately, the older woman went to them.

That has to be Rebekah, Michael's mother, Senset thought. She studied her future mother-in-law carefully.

Small, gray-haired but pretty, the curve of her chin was like the brothers'. Gideon dutifully kissed her on the cheek and received an embrace in return, but when she held out her arms to Yeshua, the boy recoiled slightly, as if embarrassed to publicly show his mother affection.

At the look of sadness on her face, however, he caught her hands and pulled her toward him, kissing her forehead. Senset felt tearful, remembering a time when Horem acted the same way toward Hatasu.

Will I someday see that look in my own son's eyes?

"Come, let me introduce you to your new family." Aram held out his hand, she placed her own atop it, and he led her to them.

The blue-coated man stepped forward. Aram moved his hand from under hers and the man caught it, touching it to his forehead before releasing it. He said something as he bowed. With dismay, Senset realized she didn't understand, and looked helplessly at Aram who spoke a little sharply.

The man bowed again, and said, in Ægysian, "My apologies, Your Majesty. I made the error of assuming you already spoke our language. Welcome to Beth-Gurion. I hope your journey wasn't too unpleasant and your life with us will be a happy one."

"Thank you." Senset gave him her most winning smile.

Is this the older sister's husband? What's her name? Meryam? Is that she, standing behind him?

"I don't speak your language yet but, as I told Aram, I learn quickly and hope a teacher can be found for me immediately."

His answer was another bow. Senset hoped this wasn't the way they punctuated their sentences. She had a sudden vision of bobbing up and down every time she spoke.

"I'm Adonijah, His Majesty's chief advisor and husband to his sister, Meryam." He nodded to the woman beginning to hover. She held a folded bundle of white fabric and stepped forward, also bowing.

Senset didn't understand what she said, though the words sounded similar to those Adonijah had first spoken.

"My sister welcomes you also," Aram translated.

He took over introductions…the other man was the fourth brother, Shemuel, who gave her a shy smile and a nod…the younger woman was the other sister, and, as she'd thought, the older their mother. He ignored the third woman, so Senset assumed she must be a slave.

Once he spoke her name, Rebekah caught Senset's cheeks in her hands and kissed her on the forehead. She rattled out a long, convoluted sentence before stopping breathlessly.

"My mother says she's overjoyed you've finally arrived and she rejoices to see you're comely and young and hopes you'll give her many grandchildren to tend." As Senset blushed and struggled for an appropriate answer, Aram muttered, "And she's frank in what she says and delights in embarrassing all of us. Even her son, the king."

"Please tell your mother—and all of them—I'm as happy as they to be here and eager to begin my role as Michael's wife." Looking directly at Adonijah, she went on, "And I wish to learn to speak Habiru as quickly as I can so I won't need an interpreter."

When Aram translated that, there were smiles all around.

"Where's my betrothed?" Senset made a great show of looking around.

Should I have referred to Michael as my husband? After all, technically, we're already married.

"Why isn't he here to meet me?"

"Michael's at the Temple, praying and preparing for the wedding." Adonijah's reply was so quick she was certain he'd been expecting her question. "You'll see him there."

Aram smiled, saying so quietly the others couldn't hear, "He's probably been there since sunrise, meditating and altogether acting the impatient bridegroom. What did I tell you, Senset?"

"This is Helene. She speaks Ægysian." Adonijah beckoned to the third woman and she took her place beside him. "She'll be your interpreter at the ceremony."

Is she a slave? Helene…that doesn't sound similar to their names.

Helene silently walked around Senset, positioning herself behind the girl.

Meryam said something else, offering the bundle to Rebekah. The older woman took it, turning to Aram. Nodding, he took the bundle from her, unfolding it and shaking it out.

A shawl? No…a long, lacy veil…

Turning, he draped it over Senset's head and shoulders so her features and upper body were obscured. "With this veiling, I cover you, for none to see until you're my brother's bride. My sister, may you increase to thousands upon thousands; may your offspring possess the gates of their enemies."

Senset shivered. *It almost sounds like a curse.*

"And now, Your Majesty…" Adonijah bowed one more time. "If you're ready…?"

"What does he mean?" Through the lace, Senset looked at Aram for guidance. Foolishly, she wanted to cling to him.

"Your bridegroom awaits, Senset. We're to escort you to the temple."

"*Now?*" She didn't mean for her voice to hit such a high note of shock. "I-I mean…I need to prepare…my bridal robes…freshen my makeup…"

"You look fine…" His eyes said he understood her surprise at this haste, even as he reminded her, "Your betrothed's becoming an impatient man… He's not even allowing us to wash our feet or shake the dust from our clothes as is proper."

There was a sound from Rebekah.

Does she disapprove of her son's eagerness to claim me?

A murmuring came behind her as Gideon spoke to Yeshua.

Are they saying something vulgar and salacious concerning their brother?

Feeling dismayed and eager by turns, Senset forced herself to smile as she held out her hand. "Of course."

Aram placed his own under it and, in a moment, Adonijah took her other hand . With Senset between them, they went back through the gate and into the city street.

So the temple isn't within the palace grounds? And they were to walk to it. *I'm still traveling to my husband. I haven't reached him yet.*

"How far is it to the temple?"

"Not far." Aram was encouraging. "Don't worry. You won't be exhausted."

To her surprise, people still lined the streets. Obviously, they'd been informed of the swiftness of the ceremony and had stayed to once more cheer their soon-to-be queen as she walked to it. The wind was a little stronger now, sweeping over the rooftops of the small, whitewashed square buildings. It dipped over the crowds, fluttering Senset's veil, rising underneath and lifting it slightly.

From one of the taller buildings, a cloud fluttered

from an upper story, falling to surround her in white petals. Senset glanced down as she stepped through them. Acacia blossoms. She remembered how someone had thrown them at Horem. And now…a shower of fragrant petals for Michael's bride. She smiled, looking up at two young girls leaning out of the upper-story window, and the crowd cheered.

Ahead of them loomed the temple, larger and simpler in its lines and design than the palace, but more imposing and even a little frightening because it was where the Nameless God was worshipped.

Again, someone waited on the steps, a figure in rich robes and headdress, but again with his face unmasked and bearded.

Not Michael.

With her features now hidden as they were, Senset hoped no one could see her disappointment.

They stopped in front of him. Adonijah released her hand, though Aram still kept his under hers. He bowed to the man who raised his own in benediction.

I see. This is the priest, the one who'll perform the marriage ritual.

She should've realized it. Though he looked much different from Ra-Harakhty's priest, who like all Ægysians was bald-shaven, jewel-bedecked, and wore a white linen *shendyt*, there was that same sanctified air about this man indicating he was one communing with his God.

"He comes!"

The shout made Senset spin around, jerking her hand from Aram's.

"The bridegroom comes!"

Someone else walked toward them, but from a side

street running parallel to the temple itself. He strode confidently, surrounded by a group of children, boys and girls running around him laughing and tossing flowers and green leaves into the air. The crowd cheered and some were also throwing petals. He laughed and held out his hands.

The sun gleamed off his golden mask.

Michael. Senset felt her knees weaken. *At last.*

As he neared where Senset and Aram stood, the children flung the last of their flowers. Their laughter stopped as they ran into the crowd to waiting parents holding out their arms to hug them tightly.

"My brother..." Aram stepped forward, offering Senset's hand. "I bring your bride to you."

Michael held out his hand and Aram placed Senset's in it. He stepped away, placing himself in the background, so no one would be distracted from the young couple standing before the priest. Helene took his place by Senset's side.

Senset began to tremble. Michael's hand was warm and firm against hers, but he didn't speak. Behind the mask, his green eyes stared at her. He was as tall as Aram, his hair beneath his jeweled crown as dark but perhaps curlier, actually twisting into tight spirals touching his shoulders. The mask was only a half-shell, covering the upper part of his face, leaving his jaw and chin bare. It was clean-shaven and she thought it resembled Aram's also.

She remembered what he'd said. *Michael's his twin. See Aram's face and I see my husband's.*

She envisioned the general looking down at her with green eyes instead of hazel ones and smiled behind her own obscuring veil.

"Come , my bride."

His first words to me... His voice was deeper than Aram's, holding a breathless quality, but it might easily have been the General speaking. He nodded to the priest who led the way up the steps. Helene moved with them, timing her steps to Senset's. Behind them, she heard Aram and the others following.

At the porch, a pavilion had been set up, a billowing canopy of bright blue, held upright by sturdy wooden staves with thick heavy bases. Two men in robes similar to the priest's stood at the back of the canopy. One held a small salver; the other carried a tray containing a large wine chalice. Stepping under the canopy, the priest turned to face them. Michael reached the top step and looked down at Senset, waiting...for what?

Helene leaned forward. "You must walk around His Majesty three times."

"What?" Senset looked at her. "Th-three? Why?"

"To symbolize the virtues of marriage...righteousness, justice, loving-kindness...that you both give and accept them."

Nodding, she pulled her hand from Michael's. He stood very still as she began the first circuit, his eyes behind the mask following her movement as she disappeared behind him and reappeared at his left side. She thought she could feel the weight of his gaze upon her as she circled him the second and third times. When she once more returned to her place beside him, he took her hand again, reaching out and capturing the other also, holding them tightly.

As if he can't bear the time he wasn't holding them. That thought thrilled her a little.

The priest spoke and Senset looked to Helene, but

the slave didn't translate so she waited, ignorantly watching the others to see if she could determine what had been said.

At the priest's gesture, the two men stepped forward. One held out the tray with the chalice. The priest took it, murmuring something over the goblet before offering it to Michael.

Is it a prayer?

Reluctantly, he released her hands, taking the chalice. He held it while the priest spoke again, intoning another prayer. Then, he raised the chalice, drank, and offered it to Senset.

"Just a sip," Helene whispered.

Raising the veil, Senset obeyed, taking the goblet from Michael. The wine was sweet but strong. From that single sip, she felt her senses whirl. Briefly, she couldn't catch her breath. She released the chalice into his hand again and he returned it to the priest as she let the veil fall.

The man holding the smaller salver held it out to Michael. He picked up the item on it. A ring…a plain gold band patterned after the bangle Aram had placed on her wrist two and a half days before, at the ceremony in Usaset. He held up the ring between thumb and forefinger, displaying it to Aram and Adonijah.

Taking Senset's right hand, he slid the ring onto her right forefinger. It felt cold and heavy. She thought she'd never be able to raise her hand with such a heavy weight upon it.

"Behold, my bride, with this ring you are now consecrated to me, according to the Laws of Moishe and our people, before these witnesses, my brothers."

Aram spoke. "We have witnessed the plighting of

your troth, my king."

Again Helene whispered, "Say this to him: *I am my beloved's and my beloved is mine.*" She repeated the words in Habiru.

Dutifully, Senset said the words, stumbling over the foreign sounds, hoping she pronounced them correctly.

I'm married now. Truly married. She shivered.

Michael must have felt the tremor through her fingertips, for he frowned slightly. She forced herself to smile. Briefly, his own mouth curved upward in answer.

Immediately, the chalice was handed back to Michael as the priest again spoke, gesturing at Aram.

"Seven guests are now called upon to give you blessings," Helene explained.

Aram's blessing was quick. As he finished speaking, Michael raised the chalice, drinking from it. The priest spoke again, nodding to Adonijah, and he delivered his blessing as easily as Aram had. Again, Michael drank from the chalice. Five other blessings followed in quick succession…from Gideon, Yeshua, Shemuel, Meryam, and Rebekah…and after each one, Michael took a sip from the goblet he held. After Rebekah finished speaking and he took his final drink, he held the goblet out to Senset.

"The last drop of wine is for you, my wife."

Once more, she lifted the veil so it cleared her mouth. He placed it against her lips and tilted it. She caught at the stem, studying it a moment.

It was a beautiful thing, decorated with a fine turquoise glaze, a raised design of vines encircling under the lip and trailing around the stem, festooned here and there with bunches of grapes. She raised it higher so the wine ran into her mouth. As she swallowed, Michael pulled it away.

What he did next happened so quickly, it startled her.

He raised the chalice, then smashed it against the granite porch. It shattered, bits of glaze, pottery dust, and a small portion of wine still inside spattering and puddling at their feet.

"Why?" she whispered. "Why did you destroy that beautiful thing?"

"The cup contained our hopes and joy for this day." The look he gave her held sympathy for her shock. "We mustn't keep them locked away, else they grow stale and die. Breaking the chalice releases them so they may thrive and grow."

A cheer rose from the crowds behind them. Senset thought she caught the words, "*Mazel Tov!*"

"See?" Michael gestured to the villagers as they shouted the words over and over. "They're wishing us luck in our new life." He seized her hand again, raising it to kiss the ring on her forefinger. "Come, my wife. Let us and our people celebrate."

"Michael?" Aram spoke up. "There's to be no *yichud*?"

His tone indicated this was an unheard-of occurrence. Adonijah and the others also looked surprised, though the priest seemed already aware.

"No." Michael's answer was so short as to be curt. With that, he led Senset down the steps, nearly dragging her as his longer legs covered the distance to the bottom.

Around them, the people still cheered, pelting them with flowers…petals and small blossoms and leaves. They began to chant, then sing, as they followed the wedding party to the town square where tables and benches were arranged in a rectangle.

"You aren't having the wedding feast in the palace?" Aram's voice held the same surprise as when he'd asked about the *yuchid*.

"I choose to have it here," Michael replied. He looked down at Senset as he spoke. "To share with my people the good fortune and happiness my bride brings me."

In that moment, as she looked up at him, Senset hoped with all her heart she could live up to everything he expected of her. She felt she should say something, deliver him some compliment to balance those he had given her since he first stood by her side.

"I pray *Y-Yahweh...*" For a moment her voice trembled as she spoke the name Aram had told her they called their God. "...will aid me in keeping happiness forever alive within our house, my husband."

The answer pleased him, she thought, and perhaps surprised him a little, too.

"Come." He led her to the center table, seating her on the bench and then settling beside her. Helene sank onto a cushion behind Senset. Aram and the others found their places, with Rebekah sitting closest to the newlyweds in the honored place of the mother of the groom, the rest seated according to their line of birth. Behind them, the townsfolk gathered in small groups, sitting on cushions and blankets.

The next hours were a delightful whirl of laughter, wine, good food, and complete joy. Servants appeared bearing platters of roasted meats, savory vegetables, and freshly baked loaves. Wine bearers filled goblets again and again, weaving in and out of the seated crowds. Music floated over them, played by slaves kneeling before the town fountain.

As the sun began to drop behind the rooftops, torches were lit, held by servants stationed at various places, lighting up the town square as bright as day. Aram, Adonijah, Gideon, and even Yeshua made speeches, though the boy stammered about a bit and blushed as he wished his brother and his bride a fruitful life together. Michael laughed, thanking them all, and when Senset echoed his laughter, he gave her a smile holding a spark of mischief, as if they were conspirators sharing a secret.

When Aram leaped to his feet and stepped into the clearing between the tables, pulling Adonijah with him, the most surprising thing occurred. The two began to dance, and it wasn't long before other men joined them. They formed a line, arms outstretched so their hands touched, moving gracefully in time to the music as it changed to a lighter note and a more whimsical rhythm.

Senset's mouth dropped open. She couldn't help it. Never would Ægysian men dance in public. That was the task of slaves and traveling mummers…to entertain their betters.

The dance continued, music again changing. Now, the women got to their feet, their movements more sedate than the men's but no less joyful. They whirled in a circle, and the men surrounded them in a larger one.

Michael was pulled from his seat and drawn into the mass of moving bodies. Laughing, he stood a moment, then picked up the beat of the music and began to dance, also, clapping his hands. Behind him, someone also began to clap and the sound echoed across the square.

As Aram on one side and Gideon on the other caught Michael's arms and joined in the leaping steps, Senset began to laugh and clap her hands as everyone else was doing.

How graceful he is...like a cat...his steps as sure as Bubash when she leaps from the ground to a tree limb... That was exactly what Michael reminded her of, she realized, a handsome, giant cat...a lion.

The lion came toward her, hands outstretched, pulling her to her feet and leading her around the table to the center of the swaying mass of dancers. They danced together, he slowing his steps to her halting ones until she began to move with more confidence. The others continued around them, women in the inner circle, men in the outer, each circle moving in the opposite direction, while they two stood in the middle, holding hands.

Slowly, the circles became smaller and smaller, closing in, trapping them in the center. With a clash of cymbals, a wild beating of drums, and a mad trilling of flutes, the music ended. The dancers stood still, all panting from exertion and sheer joy. Senset looked up at Michael while he stared down at her, their eyes meeting.

My husband, I think I love you though I've known you only a few hours.

How it could've happened, she didn't know. She only knew she felt something for this man she'd never felt for any other, and she wanted that feeling to continue forever.

Michael caught the edge of the veil, raising it and tossing it back so her face was uncovered. He placed two fingers under Senset's chin. It became very quiet in the square, as if nothing moved, all living creatures holding their breaths.

Now Senset saw what the obscuring veil and the dimness of the torches had preventing her from seeing before…Michael's mask wasn't a simple covering. It was fashioned like a lion's face, a roaring lion, brow wrinkled, nose flaring, lips curled upward in a snarl. Laid-back ears ending in leather straps curved around his head. On either side of his mouth, tiny fang tips lay against his cheeks. She understood now why he was called the Beast King…

Why did they choose such a face to cover their king's?

"Don't fear me." His whisper was reassuring but with a hint of a plea. "The man isn't the mask."

Senset shivered, forcing her mind to replace the lion looking down at her with the image of Aram's face.

Bending, Michael kissed her. The cold of the golden mask pressed itself against her forehead and her cheeks but the lips touching hers were warm…and gentle.

A deafening cheer broke out, and the dancing and music began again. Taking Senset's hand, Michael pushed through the crowd. It parted to let him out, and he headed directly to where Aram stood.

"Prepare my bride to receive me." He placed Senset's hand in his brother's. Turning to Senset, he bowed, catching her other hand and kissing her palm. "I'll come to you soon, my beloved. Go now and wait for me."

With that, he returned to his place at the table, lifting his wine goblet and calling for it to be filled. In a moment, Aram led Senset to the table where his mother and sister sat. He transferred her hand to Rebekah's.

"I'll leave you to your wedding-night, little sister."

"You're not going to escort me to my rooms?" She couldn't keep her voice from trembling.

"It would be a little unseemly, since you're now my

brother's wife."

"But how will I speak to anyone? How will I tell them what I need?"

He nodded to the slave who'd gotten to her feet when Rebekah did. "Helene will interpret for you. That's her task."

"If you'll follow me, Your Majesty…" Gesturing, Helene started down the street, two guards falling in behind them. Hemmed in as she was by Rebekah and Meryam, Senset could only stare at them. "Why do I need guards?"

"His Majesty assigned them to protect you." Helene continued walking as she answered.

The sounds of laughter and music got fainter as they neared the palace. In a few moments, it was completely silent as they entered the courtyard.

Senset waited until they were inside before she asked, "Is the climate in Beth-Gurion so dangerous I need such protection?"

"Beth-Gurion's our safest city, Your Majesty." Helene smiled. "But one never knows what danger lurks outside its gates, and this is one way to ensure it never enters to reach those most precious to our king."

Most precious. There it was again, that word used to describe her. Senset hoped the sudden warmth she felt was a continuation of the emotion she'd experienced as she danced with Michael.

She was shown to a set of beautiful rooms and began her wedding preparations. Neither Helene, Meryam, nor Rebekah stayed; they'd all been hurried from the room by a suddenly possessive Orora, determined not to let them have any say in the preparations she was ready to perform on her mistress. Only a single slave girl, carrying a basin of water and a towel, remained, stationed by the door.

"For my master," she replied, when asked, and didn't explain further.

****

And now, Senset was ready…bathed, painted, powdered, and perfumed…dressed in the robe made especially for her wedding night. Surveying her image in the beaten-silver mirror the little slave held for her, Senset admitted Orora had outdone herself.

"Do you think the bands needs tightening? I must look as flat as possible, Orora." She assumed Habiru had the same female ideal as Ægysians.

"You do, mistress." The slave gave one last tug on the wide band of linen encircling her breasts, then tucked it in. Through the thin fabric, nipples brushed with henna glowed faintly. "Truly, you appear to have no breasts at all."

She caught the waist of the robe, pulling it open to reveal the girl's shaven mound, also tinted with henna and accented by a heart-shaped design.

"There…perfection."

"I hope so." Senset breathed, handing the slave the mirror. "I'll have only one wedding night, and it must be absolutely flawless."

She had to please her husband in every way possible—sight…taste…smell. Frantically, her mind raced over the ways her mother explained to her a man enjoyed being pleasured, hoping she remembered all of them. She refused to admit she was frightened, but it was a wonderful kind of fright, full of anticipation and eagerness…

"His Highness will fall in love with you the moment

he sees you, mistress," Orora assured her.

"According to General Aram, he did that sight unseen," Senset retorted. "Truly, he appeared so."

"Then he'll be even more in love after tonight."

"My hair." Her hands went to her head, brushing the inch-long curls the wig had hidden, forgotten until that moment. "I've not had time to remove it. What if…"

The double doors to the suite were jerked open.

Chapter 16

Michael stood in the doorway.

Behind him in the corridor, Senset could see Aram. Her bridegroom removed his crown, handing it to his brother. The general accepted it, bowed, and drew shut the doors. For the briefest moment, his eyes met Senset's.

Suddenly, he seemed frightening…a giant in his wedding finery, the golden mask gleaming in the light of the lamps set about the room, the lion snarling though the human mouth below it smiled slightly.

Michael bent, removing his sandals and dropping them near the door. Immediately, the slave girl knelt and set down the basin. Michael dipped each foot into the water, then waited while she used the towel to dry them. Afterward, she stood, picked up the basin, opened the door, and fled.

Senset wanted to say something, speak to him and tell him how she felt. She couldn't utter a word, sudden fright making her timid. Dropping to her knees, she raised her arms, elbows tucked against her ribs in the posture one assumed when paying another homage. She directed her gaze downward, staring at the blue and white tiled floor,

She heard him speak to Orora. "You're dismissed."

Bowing, the slave scurried to the door, opening it enough to slip through. As it shut again, Senset had another glimpse of Aram, seated on a bench opposite the door, clutching the crown.

Why is he there? Is this another part of their marriage ritual, the groom's brother waits outside the wedding chamber? Does he wait for proof our marriage is consummated, since there was no yuchid?

"Rise, my wife." Hands rested on her shoulders. Their touch was so strong she was certain he could've lifted her from the floor with little effort. Trying not to be awkward, she got to her feet.

"What happened to your hair? Have you been ill?"

It wasn't a question she expected a bridegroom to ask. Especially not the first thing said once they were alone.

"We keep it cut short. It's the custom. As is the wearing of wigs as head coverings."

"Those beautiful bejeweled locks I saw before were artificial?" He fell silent.

She could swear she felt his gaze as it traveled down her body. Why else did her skin seem to burn, then go cold? She was certain his eyes lingered on the tightly tied breast-band, studied it a long time, as if absorbing what he was seeing, before he spoke again.

"You've no breasts." It was an accusation. "How old are you?"

"Seventeen…"

Another silence. He seemed to be thinking that over.

"If you're as old as you say, why are your female parts bare?"

"It's the custom." The spot where Orora had drawn the heart-shaped design seemed to burn.

"The same as this?" One hand brushed through the short curls above her ears. Briefly, he rubbed a lock

164

between thumb and forefinger as if testing its texture. "You shave your body also?"

She nodded.

"Do all Ægysian women do that?"

"Ægys's climate is much hotter than here. It's cooler...and cleaner...this way. We bathe frequently, too."

What demon made me say that?

"So do we." He laughed, not offended. "You'll find no one here with lice or fleas or any other parasite. Not even on our dogs. You'll stop that practice. Tonight. The shaving, I mean."

She didn't answer, merely nodded.

He stooped, picked up the robe, and draped it over her shoulders. "I'll send servants to prepare you for bed." Then he spun and strode toward the door.

He's leaving?

"Wait. Where are you going?"

"To my rooms." He paused to look back.

"But it's our wedding night." She dared raise her head, staring at him, meeting the green eyes surrounded by all that gold.

"Not yet. I don't bed children." He straightened, becoming even taller, as if steeling himself for something unpleasant.

Does he think I'll make a scene?

"Grow a little more. Look like a woman first."

"What about the treaty with my father?" *If our marriage isn't consummated...*

"You're my wife under law, if not in fact. Don't worry, Sensete-Ra. The treaty stands." He opened the doors and went through them.

Senset stood there, stunned. On the other side of the

door, she saw Aram look up.

"Brother? Is something amiss?"

Michael slammed the doors.

Shoulders slumping, Senset sank to her knees. Without warning, tears began to roll down her cheeks. She wasn't certain whether they were of relief or disappointment.

****

"Brother?" Aram spoke again.

"No, Aram, nothing's wrong. Wait—yes, there is."

"What is it?"

"You told me the girl was marriageable."

"She is. By her own people's standards, as well as our own. Overdue, in fact, by her own admission."

"She has no breasts."

"Odd." Aram managed to hide his surprise at that statement. He got up from the bench. "She had some when she came to me in the dungeon. Quite tempting ones, too. Could she have lost them somewhere on the way here?"

"She says she's seventeen..." The look Michael gave him said plainly he didn't appreciate his brother's humor.

"That's what she told me, also." Aram looked confused. "Michael, what's the matter?"

"I think the girl lied, Brother. That child isn't ready for a husband. With that wedding veil and the torchlight, it was difficult to see her, but now that I've gotten a clearer look... Our wedding night must be delayed. I'll sleep in my own bed tonight, but I've a task for you."

"Certainly, sire." Frowning, Aram bowed.

"Go to the women's quarters and select a female to slake this lust I'd built up for my bride." Michael looked away, muttering under his breath, "She's so tempting…and I want her, but…"

"I don't think that's wise." Aram didn't move. "Especially tonight."

"My taking a female or having lust?" Briefly, Michael allowed himself to regret being swayed by his general's glowing description of Senset to the extent that he'd foregone visiting any of his concubines from the moment he'd sent Aram back to Usaset.

Why did I let myself fall in love with that child, even before meeting her? Truly I'm a fool.

"Neither… Both. I'm suggesting you rethink that order. Go back to your bride. Make her your wife this night. She brought servants with her. They're probably going to spy for her father in spite of our treaty. You know as well as I do that's what would happen if we'd sent a bride to Ægys. We don't want word getting back to Aseti-Ra that his daughter's being ignored by her husband while he frolics with his concubines, do we? Especially after you specifically requested her?"

"I told you, Aram. I don't—"

"Wait here. Let me see exactly what the problem is. She can't have changed that much. Nor could she have gotten younger." Aran looked at the door, then back at his brother. "Do I have your permission to be alone with your wife, sire?"

There was a gesture from Michael, impatient in its brusqueness.

Turning, Aram headed to the bridal chambers, leaving his royal brother standing there.

****

Senset was sitting on the steps of the dais. She raised her head and he saw the tearstains on her cheeks.

"You're crying. Why?" He knew it was a foolish question, even as he said it.

"Why shouldn't I? My husband—the man I came so far to marry—has rejected me. We're married only a few hours and he abandons his bridal chamber. *He walked out*, Aram."

"Because you look like a child. What is this, Senset? Stand up."

Obediently, Senset got to her feet, the narrow-cut front of the robe gaping. At sight of her privates, Aram turned his head, one hand going up as if to shield his eyes.

"Merciful heavens protect me." Now, it came to him…the slave he'd bedded after the banquet, she'd been shaven also, but in his lust, he'd ignored that.

I should've remembered. I should've warned Michael.

"Why are you wearing such a revealing garment?"

"It's a wedding-night robe." Her explanation was tight-lipped and insulted. "To excite my husband's desires."

"Cover yourself before it incites mine."

There was a rustle of fabric. Aram turned his head to look at her.

"He says you've no breasts. That wasn't so when you visited me in the dungeon." He saw the binding showing through the bodice of the robe. "What's that? A bandage? Senset?" His question held horror. "Is this some heathen wedding rite? Did they cut off your breasts?"

"Ægysians like their women small-chested. My mother's foreign and she doesn't fit their ideal. Neither do I. We bind our breasts to look smaller."

"Thank the Good Lord that's all you've done. And may Michael forgive me for touching you."

Aram drew his dagger, placing the tip under the edge of the binding. He sliced it through with one slash, pulling the linen away. As Senset's breasts filled the bosom of the robe, he headed for the door.

"Prepare yourself, Senset. Your husband'll be returning shortly."

****

Michael was where he'd left him…pacing, an angry, impatient man. He stopped as Aram approached, immediately seeing the handful of binding.

"What's that? A bandage?"

"Your wife has breasts, sire. Beautiful and ripe as pomegranates." Aram bowed his head, holding up his right hand, palm outward in a gesture of supplication. "I beg you don't put out my eyes for seeing them."

He was completely serious. Michael had that right, for the body of a man's wife was sacred and for his eyes alone. He reached out, pushing Aram's hand down.

"Didn't I give you permission to sort this out for me? Don't worry, brother, just answer my question."

Aram held up the strips of linen. "This is a breast-binder, sire. Those foolish Ægysians prefer their women flat-chested, and your bride bound her beauties to appear thus, thinking Habiru wish the same." He placed a hand on Michael's shoulder. "Go to her, Your Majesty. A *woman* awaits you in that chamber."

"You're dismissed. Go, brother. Find yourself a woman and enjoy this night as I shall."

Trying not to appear too eager, Michael walked past him to the double doors. Without hesitating, he pulled them open and went inside.

Behind him, Aram continued standing there, holding the linen bindings. Abruptly, he envied his brother this night.

Chapter 17

Senset stood where Michael had left her. Below her waist, the wedding robe was closed, clutched together by her hands. Briefly, his gaze lingered on her face before seeking her bosom. He liked what he saw. Immensely.

"*My beloved greets me with joy. Her breasts tremble in greeting. Their nipples bloom red as cinnabar,*" he quoted from an ancient love poem and smiled. "I'm pleased to see you've grown in my absence, wife."

"We Ægysians mature quickly, my husband." Her smile mirrored his own, though shyer.

"And for that, I'm grateful." He came up the stairs, bare feet making no sound on the smooth stone. He'd not reclaimed his sandals. They still lay by the door.

"Forgive me, my husband, but now you truly believe I'm the age I say? You've now returned to claim me?"

"Please understand my caution, wife. I've seen too many child brides."

She thought she saw something in him tense again, as if he were still wary of her age.

"And too many fathers wishing to marry them to me in exchange for alliance. I swore I'd never bed someone who should be playing with dolls instead of caressing her husband's plums."

"I put away dolls long ago," Senset whispered.

"I thank the Good Lord for that, for I truly want you, Sensete-Ra. More, now that I've met you, than I did from my brother's description."

At that, Senset looked up at him, face raised to his. This time when Michael kissed her it wasn't the gentle kiss he'd given her in the dancing circle. This one held fire and some of that desire she'd seen briefly in his eyes during the ceremony. His tongue thrust into her mouth, breath warming her tongue.

Senset breathed out, sending her own exhalation into his mouth. She pulled away.

"You breathe your soul into my body, I breathe mine into yours. We're of one breath, one soul, one body now, my husband." She touched his jaw, marveling at the smoothness of his cheek, carefully stroking along its strong line and making certain she didn't touch the edges of the mask and its sharp metal fangs.

"Not yet…but soon."

The next thing she knew, he'd scooped her into his arms. Michael went up the last steps of the dais and entered the chamber, carrying her to the bed. Senset's heart pounded so loudly she thought surely he could hear.

He set her beside the bed. His hands caressed her face.

"Beautiful is my beloved. Her cheek blushes like the dawn, her lips are bee-stung, swollen with passion…" This time when he kissed her it held the passion he spoke of.

He slid the robe off her shoulders, letting it fall to the tiled floor. Senset trembled as he pulled her against his chest, crushing her nakedness against the soft folds of his surcoat and robe. His hands stroked and caressed, moving over her back, her ribs. They lingered at her buttocks, found the still-fresh wounds…

She winced and cried out.

"I hurt you." It was a question within a statement.

She shook her head.

"Then what—?" He turned her away from him, saw the stripes criss-crossing her skin. "You've been flailed. Who did this?"

"My father." She thrilled at the outrage in his voice.

If Michael'd been there, he would've defended me, protected me from this pain. But would I want him to fight my father?

"In the Name of the Almighty, why did he mar your beautiful flesh? Those marks'll become scars."

"For letting Aram go," she said, quietly, not wanting to rouse him to true anger. Not after she'd come this far for peace. "Horem was going to sacrifice him to Ra-Harakhty and ask the god to stop the war."

"By letting Aram go, you brought about the same result," he pointed out. "Without another death."

His fingers moved again, brushing over the cuts, gentle and featherlight and not causing pain this time. Rather, they were…*arousing*…

"Father couldn't know that." Senset shifted uneasily, forcing herself to speak matter-of-factly when what she wanted to do was let a shudder of desire shake her. She wanted to throw herself into Michael's arms. "I confessed—"

"If he didn't know you were the one, why did you tell him?"

"He was going to kill Aram's jailer for allowing him to escape." She looked up, meeting his eyes as they widened behind the mask. "I couldn't let the man die for something he didn't do."

"You suffered to save two lives. And gave me back

173

my brother. For that I must thank you, my wife. I and my people sorely mourned when we thought him lost. Truly the Lord's sent me a woman worthy to be my queen."

His hands went to the neck of his surcoat, shrugging it off his shoulders. His robe followed.

As it fell to the floor, lying beside Senset's gown, he asked, "Are you ready to become my queen, Sensete-Ra? And my wife?"

There was silence between them now.

He stands before me. My husband, baring his body to me.

There was a deep scar on one arm, a long-healed rosette under his collarbone. She let her gaze roam to a broad chest covered with dark hair, startling after the hairlessness of Ægysian men. *Startling, yet pleasing*...even with its scars. His nipples were almond-husk brown among that darkness. Senset glanced down, seeing the mat of hair narrow to a ribbon of curls, a love-trail widening as a tangled nest.

The first man I've seen naked. The only man. She stared at the thickness of manhood resting against his thighs.

"O-oh..." It was just short of a gasp.

"It pleases you, I hope." There was nothing tentative in his voice, perhaps a little conceit, in fact.

He knows he's endowed for pleasure.

"You're..." She thought of the many births she'd attended, of Asanath cuddling naked newborn sons, their tiny proofs of manhood wrapped in sheathing flesh...the ceremony held within eight days to remove it... "You've received the *God's Cut*?"

For some reason, it was a shock, seeing that full-grown organ minus its covering hood.

174

"I've undergone the Covenant *brit milah*."

She sensed defensiveness. He took a step away from her.

"Our God commanded it…to seal a promise to our forefather Abram. It's one of our laws."

"Ours—I mean the Ægysians'—also." She spoke quickly, briefly grateful she'd never looked at Horem when he received her while in his bath or as his slaves ministered to him.

My husband's manhood is the only one I'll ever see…and it's beautiful.

"Then it—*I*—please you?" he persisted.

"Most wonderfully, my husband." Gently, she rested her hand upon his staff amid that bristle of curls, feeling the heat flowing through it. "Truly, as I told your brother, we are more alike than one knew."

Heat washed over her, flooding her body with desire, passion pooling. She wanted to cradle his member in her hands, kiss it, tell him she would worship it as she worshipped the rest of his body.

Standing on tiptoe, Senset clasped Michael's face in her hands and kissed him, then let her hand linger on his chest, fingers thrusting into the tight curls. She bowed her head to kiss his breast before taking a nipple into her mouth, caressing it with her lips.

Michael's own shudder of pleasure was a slow drawn-in breath. She felt his shaft rise to greet her, brushing her belly.

"Let us lie together, my wife. Get into bed, Senset."

As she obeyed, he lay down beside her, taking her in his arms. When he kissed her again, it was a rougher kiss, leaving her breathless but wanting the next. Expecting it to be the same and surprised to find it suddenly gentle before becoming a surge of open mouths and tongues pressing in exploration as she returned his kiss.

Fingers trailed down her throat, teasing her skin. Senset shivered and clung to him, clasping her arms around him and pressing her face against his chest, nuzzling into the thick dark hair. That made him give a short quick laugh dying into a groan as her hands traveled downward. Her fingers grasped between muscular thighs, through the tangle of curls. He was aroused, rampant and…

Beastlike?

Her encircling hands hesitated. His whisper urged her not to stop, and she began to stroke…caress…tease…felt that wonderful flesh stiffen even more, pulsating within her grasp. His skin was burning, blood rushing.

Michael's hand touched her breast, fingers tightening on a nipple already peaking with expected desire. Fingers seeking inner softness came away slick and wet. He pressed her onto the pillows and settled himself against her, the crown of his cock nestled itself between her thighs as unerringly as if it had been aimed.

"Bear with me this one moment of pain, my wife, and I'll never hurt you again." The green eyes behind the mask bore into her own.

Michael thrust his body into hers.

Her cry was buried in his shoulder. She drew in a shuddering, deep breath as Michael's tongue licked away the tears on her cheeks.

He gave a sound oddly like a growl as he began to move, sliding in and out of her body. She felt little ripples of pleasure as his body penetrated hers, moving into her very center, then just as quickly retreating. Wrapping her legs around his waist, she imprisoned him within her, so he couldn't escape again. He began to push against her, faster…faster…

She had the sensation of being seized by a wild creature, a lion leaping on its prey, devouring it. Buffeted about by wild, frenzied emotion…huge paws roughly caressing, claws grazing soft, vulnerable flesh…

Michael's a lion and I'm the gazelle for him to feast upon…my Beast King…

His cry of climax was ripped from him, a roar at the ending of ultimate pleasure. Raising himself on his hands, he continued to thrust against her, body still spasming…

Michael collapsed against her, pressing his lips to her breast. Encircled by their golden frame, the green gaze glowed with satiation. Rolling over, he gathered Senset into his arms, holding her tightly against his side. He reached down, brushing fingers across his now-resting member, holding them up for her to see her blood upon them.

Senset shivered.

…blood on the lion's claw from its kill…

"We've shared breath and body and soul, and now, your maidenhood sacrifice to become my wife. I love you, Sensete-Ra." He hugged her, kissing the top of her head.

Senset touched his chest, fingers stroking against a short furrow of flesh across his ribs.

"Scars…" she murmured.

"One can't be a warrior without getting those," he answered. "…and yes, your kinsman presented me one or two of them."

177

"That'll never happen again," she promised, raising one leg and throwing it over his. Gently, she began to move her knee against his resting cock, pressing in…not enough to hurt, only enough to stimulate. His free hand caught her calf, stopped its motion.

"We must sleep now, my wife. I wish to hold you and let your soft body soothe me."

She let the steady *thud* of his heart lull her to sleep.

****

Lying on the throne was a lion…black-maned, golden-pelted…it lounged in the carved and decorated chair as if it belonged there, powerful haunches stretched over the cushions. Its head lay on one of the armrests, one foreleg dangling negligently.

It opened its eyes and saw her and in one motion leaped from the throne, galloping toward her. Senset didn't move, except to brace herself.

This is a dream. I've nothing to fear.

The lion slowed its headlong pace, approaching her in a graceful saunter. Stopping, it sat before her, green eyes meeting hers as it rubbed its ear against her arm. Senset plunged her hand into the tangled curls of its mane, and it rested its head against her breast and began to purr, an odd, rhythmic rumbling deep in its chest. Abruptly, it rose to stand on hind legs, towering above her, massive paws resting on her shoulders. It nuzzled its broad muzzle against her cheek.

Senset smiled and kissed the lion on the tip of its nose, and it opened its massive jaws and laughed…

****

When Senset awoke, Michael was still with her. She must have looked surprised because he said, "Did you believe you'd open your eyes and find me gone?"

"How long have you been awake?"

Did he lie here watching me sleep? Or did my waking rouse him?

He didn't answer, merely pulled her once more into his embrace, one hand idly stroking the short locks now tousled from sleep. Senset placed her hand on his chest, letting her own fingers comb through the tight curls around his nipples. She watched the hair spring into a tangle again. She rested her cheek against his chest, listening to his breath mingle with his heartbeat, his voice reverberating around those sounds.

Briefly, she couldn't speak, she was so happy.

"*My beloved's body fills me with joy. She sends out her passion like the rose its perfume. It surrounds me with desire as I harvest the bounty of love she offers.*"

"That's beautiful," she whispered against his skin. "Those other things you said...last night... Are they lines from a poem?"

"Some of it," he admitted. "The rest...I composed them myself, upon seeing you...you inspire me, wife."

So Habiru also write love lyrics to their wives. That fact pleased her. *But I'll never speak of it to anyone. I won't be like Asanath. Even if the entire kingdom knows my husband's a poet-king, I'll keep what he quotes to me our secret.*

"Are all Habiru so poetic?"

"I can't speak for everyone, but I am...and I freely admit it. Warriors need to be able to see beauty as well as the ugliness of this world. Otherwise, they can't forget the horror of war and appreciate the loveliness of peace when it comes." He kissed her forehead. "With you, I hope to see much beauty."

"You flatter me, Michael."

"Not flattery, the truth. In your presence, I feel I could write a thousand poems." He took a deep breath and hurried on as if speaking something he wished to say as quickly as possible. "Aram told me of the passion your brother has for his prime wife. Though we come to each other as strangers, I want to be your Horem, Senset, and you to be my Asanath."

Senset raised her head, kissing the underside of his chin. "I think we'll be more than that, Michael. Much more."

Through the open balcony doors, a gentle morning breeze brought the sound of voices. Outside in the corridor came the patter of footsteps, activity as the palace came alive.

"I'll have to leave you soon, but let me love you once more before I do." Placing a finger under her chin, Michael tilted Senset's head and bent to place another passion-filled kiss upon her lips.

Chapter 18

Alaph, Beth, Gamma, Dalath…

Senset quoted the letters to herself as her quill traced them across the parchment. She had proven an apt pupil, and only that morning, Gideon announced she had learned so much he felt he couldn't teach her anything more. They'd had a lengthy but simple conversation in Habiru…about the weather, the coming planting season, the things he'd taught her…and he'd declared her ready to speak their language with anyone.

"Now you'll understand exactly what my brother whispers to you in the dark." He turned his head as he said it and she thought she saw a faint tinge of pink in his tanned cheeks.

"Gideon, are you blushing?" She wanted to touch that cheek, turn his head back so he faced her, but knew that would be thought unseemly.

Unmarried men weren't allowed alone with married women except by the husband's permission, much less touch them, though a little more leeway was given to those within the spouse's family.

He looked back at her quickly enough, smiling. "I'm being the rogue, saying that to you, but I know how much Michael loves you—the entire city does—and I'm certain he sometimes lapses into our own language when he gets…passionate." He dared place a hand over hers. "Now, I'm being bold, too. I envy my brother, Senset.

Seeing the change in him since you became his wife almost makes me want to find a woman to marry."

"Almost?" She spoke with a quirk of an eyebrow, a brow now bare of any of the darkening makeup and powders she'd brought with her. Senset had seen quite soon that though Habiru women wore cosmetics, they were more subtle with them than as in Ægys, and she'd ordered Orora to adapt her own to copy their style.

"I'm afraid I've too many women." He gave an exaggerated sigh. "I can't choose between them."

She shook her head as if disparaging that remark. "Michael has other wives. How does my becoming another make such a difference?"

"Michael has no other wives. He made it plain to each king who came offering a daughter to seal a treaty that he'd marry only if the Lord willed it. Otherwise she'd become a concubine." Gideon shrugged as he gathered his writing implements and the scrolls they'd been studying. "Before he received each one, he spent an entire day in the temple, praying and awaiting Yahweh's answer. Each time, he returned with the same statement: *She isn't the one.*"

"Their fathers accepted this?"

"How could they go against what their proposed son-in-law's God decreed? Especially if, by doing so, war continued? Once Michael assured them he would treat each woman as he would a wife though she wouldn't have the power of a spouse, they agreed."

"When he decided he wanted me, did he pray then, also?"

Gideon nodded. "And fairly ran from the temple the next day. I don't think I've seen him in such a joyous mood…laughing, shouting… You'd have thought he'd been given a glimpse of heaven…" He let his voice trail away, then smiled. "Perhaps he had."

Afterward, when he was gone, leaving her to think over his words, she practiced her letters once more.

In the short time she'd been in Beth-Gurion, Michael had come to her every night, except for one week, in which he'd explained, in a surprisingly apologetic tone, that he had to visit his concubines.

"It's each woman's right to my physical affection, and my duty to give it. A man must keep all his women happy." Briefly, the apology changed to mischief. "Though they'd be happier if I came to them more often."

Their second night together, he'd made it plain that if it wouldn't cause recriminations and possible wars, he'd dispense with his concubines altogether and send them back to their fathers.

"You complete me, Senset. I've no need for other women."

That filled her with such a warmth she wanted to cry. Instead, she kissed him.

Now, thinking of that intimate little scene, she began to compose a poem, something to read to her husband in the privacy of their bed.

As the gazelle pants after the cooling waters, so does my soul thirst for your love. As the river runs through the plain…

"…so does my heart chase after thine, beloved," someone spoke behind her.

Senset started, the quill making a smudge on the last letter.

"I hope you aren't going to leave that in. It completely changes the meaning of the word, you know." Michael leaned down to kiss her cheek.

"Of course not." Senset placed the scroll aside and picked up another sheet. "I'll start over." She gave him a smiling yet accusing stare. "You weren't supposed to see that. It was to be a surprise."

"Now I've spoiled it. I'm sorry."

He looked more than sorry, however. At least that was the way she interpreted what she could see of his expression. It was a little vexing, being unable to see her husband's face, having to guess his feelings by the set of his mouth and the way he held his head.

She thought he was upset. Very upset. His next words confirmed that.

"Senset, I must speak with you about a serious matter."

"Is something wrong?" She tried to think of anything she'd done that might go against Habiru custom.

Gideon touched my hand, but surely... How would Michael have known about that, anyway? It just happened.

"Have I done something to—"

"You've done nothing but be the most wonderful wife in my kingdom." Dropping onto the bench beside her, he laid down the scroll he carried. He took the quill from her hand, placing it beside the ink pot. "This is something you must know, and I've delayed telling you."

He looked away slightly, giving a rueful laugh.

"I let my passion distract me from my duty."

Duty? That one word sent a twinge of fear through her. The only duty he'd mentioned so far was that business with his concubines.

"Michael, what do you mean?"

"Don't ask questions, Senset. It's the day of the full moon, and I haven't much time."

"Day of… Don't you mean *night* of the full moon?" *What do the phases of the moon have to do with anything*? "I don't understand."

"When you were traveling here, did Aram tell you about my mask?" He gestured at it. "Why I wear it?"

"Not really. I told him Horem spoke of a warrior wearing a golden mask and he thought he was the beasts's…I mean, the Habiru's leader." She was relieved when she saw his mouth twitch in a brief smile as she corrected her description. "You can laugh? At that awful name we've given you?"

"Why not? It's how I'm known, and I accept that. After all, it's true…though I doubt anyone knows the true reason. Aram didn't tell you, did he?"

"He explained you wore a mask and had done so since shortly after you were born. But no, he didn't say why, other than it's the custom." She paused, then went on, "He said you should be the one to tell me."

"And now, *I* must." He caught her shoulders, holding her so tightly she flinched.

That made her realize Michael, though he'd been gentle in touching her while they made love, was a strong man and the strength in his hands made his fingers seem like iron rods boring into her skin. As if realizing he was on the brink of hurting her, he released her and picked up the scroll he'd dropped onto the bench.

"Did you know that once my people were rulers over yours?"

Startled, she shook her head.

"It was long ago, in the land called *Ta-Sheme'aw*. We were called the *Heka Khasewt*, the Rulers of the

Foreign Hills, and we rolled across the desert in our war chariots and subdued the Ta-Shemans and became their sovereigns." He held out the scroll. "Read this. It'll explain much more quickly and more thoroughly than I can."

Senset took the scroll. As she unrolled it, he stood and walked away. With his back to her, Michael looked out over the courtyard. The lines of his shoulders under the richly-embroidered surcoat were tense with anxiety.

What can be in this scroll to make him so worried? What does the full moon have to do with it?

The scroll was ancient, its edges fragile and crumbling. Some of the words were archaic, their meaning obscure. Holding it gently, Senset settled it on her lap and began to read.

I, Malachi ben-Gurion, do now set down the facts of how this curse was visited upon me and my House, for the explanation to future generations of kings of the Habiru.

Once my people were kings of the people of the River Sihor, but eventually others came to power and after a few generations we who had been rulers became slaves to our new masters. While they worshipped their many gods, we began to find faith in only one, a nameless God who promised one day we would be free. That came to pass when a miracle happened and one of our own was raised as a royal prince by the sister of the then-king.

Moishe, his name was, and he believed himself a Ta'Sheman, having the power of the Royal House behind him, calling the prince and heir Cousin and the king Uncle. Eventually, Moishe learned of his true heritage and he fell under a shadow and left the Court for many years. When he returned, he had discovered the One God and, because of promises the Lord made to him, swore to free his people from their bondage. He presented himself before the new king, he who had been called Cousin in years before, and made this demand, but the king refused. It was only after Moishe's God brought many travails upon the king's House that he agreed to release the Habiru and they gathered up their belongings and their wives and children and followed Moishe from Ta-Sheme'aw into the desert.

Making camp, Moishe went up into the cliffs of a nearby mountain to commune with God and seek instruction as to where he should take those whom he had rescued. He couldn't know the ones he left behind would work against him. Now away from the country where they had lived for so long—some knowing no other home—they were afraid of the unknown awaiting them. 'We were fools to leave a place offering us food and shelter,' they said. 'Even if we were slaves there, at least we were protected. Here in this desert, we may fall prey to wild beasts or hunger or thirst.' Aharon, Moishe's brother, tried to reason with them, telling them Moishe was receiving words from Yahweh to guide them, but they wouldn't listen.

As sorry as I am to admit it, I was one of those who spoke loudest. 'We were better off in Ta-Sheme'aw, pretending to pray to their gods and secretly worshipping our own. What if Moishe dies while in the mountains? What if the Might of the Lord smites him when he's exposed to His glory?' I looked around at the faces of those who followed me, seeing a need for reassurance, and I gave it to them...in the wrong way. 'We would do better to pray to Ta-Sheme'aw's gods and ask them to look over us until Moishe returns. Our God can't keep us safe if He's busy with someone else.'

That was all it took. Immediately, the people accepted my idea, not just my followers but others in the camp. Though Aharon pleaded and threatened, they gathered the jewelry and metals they had with them, melted them down, and set about fashioning a likeness of Hastur, the cow-headed goddess, and prayed to her for Moishe's safe return and to keep them in good stead until that happened. At the urging of my own people, I also sought what little precious metals we owned and created an image of Bast the cat, and of her son, Maahdes, the lion prince, and we bowed down to them and begged safe passage back to AEgyptus and the security of slavery should Moishe perish while communing with God.

Moishe returned to that sight, and his fury was only less than that of the Lord Himself. Thunder and lightning struck the earth, trees and brush burned and were consumed, tents were blown away, and we were sore afraid, for we knew we had sinned with our lack of faith.

'You and yours will leave here,' Moishe shouted, waving a hand to include me and those around me. 'Never let the faithful see your faces again!'

'Why must we alone be punished'" I asked. 'The others were also unfaithful.'

'They will rue this day also,' he replied, 'but they are mere followers. You put the worm of doubt into their hearts, and for that the House of Malachi must pay.'

'Where shall we go?' I asked, my heart sinking at being alone in this strange land with no one to guide us.

'I don't care. Go back to Ta-Sheme'aw. Sell yourself into bondage again. But in the morning, you will be gone from this camp forever.'

'It is spoken, so be it.' I accepted our fate. Telling the others to begin gathering their belongings, I bowed my head and returned to my tent. Guilt was in my heart for being so weak in my faith, but it was now done, so what could I say?

Some might say Moishe was lenient with us; he had the sons of Levi punish the others and three thousand died by their swords.

For us, something worse than exile was to come.

In the morning, my ears were met with screams of terror, growls of wild animals mingling with the voices of people in fear. I stumbled from my tent to a horrible sight: bodies lay on the ground writhing in agony, the roars of beasts issuing from their throats. Men, women, and children were afflicted. No one was spared. As I raised my face to the sun, crying, 'Lord God, why is this happening?' I felt its rays strike my face and I also screamed. It was as if a firebrand pressed against my flesh. I fell to the ground, my body curling and twisting, my pleas changing to the screams of an animal. When the pain passed, I sprang to my feet, but I now stood on four legs. I knew myself to be a Beast but my thoughts were those of a man trapped within the creature's body.

In fear, the others tried to come to our rescue when the first screams were heard, but Moishe held them back. 'It is God's curse for their sin. Leave them be.' He set guards around our section of the camp to keep us away from his followers, and for an entire day, we roamed within that perimeter, fighting among ourselves as the Beasts took over, before falling exhausted into the sand.

When night came, we were ourselves again, though now bloody from wounds made by our claws, and fearful that it might happen again, and repentant because we understood why it had happened. Stumbling to my feet, I staggered to the closest guard and begged to speak to Moishe. He came quickly, not looking triumphant, as I'd expected, but sad.

'Don't ask to have this curse lifted,' he said before I could speak. 'Only Yahweh can do that, and he wishes you to suffer for your disobedience so others may heed.'

'What disobedience?' I demanded. 'We still acknowledge He is the One and Only God.'

'But you weakened. When your faith was tested, you chose to ask the gods of AEgyptus to protect you. The moment I wasn't here to remind you of God's sheltering shield, you turned away from Him. It is written: Thou shall have no other Gods but Me. *This has always been the first of the teachings of our people, Malachi, and you and the others knew it, yet you begged Bast to protect you.*'

'So we are cursed for that? Though we now repent?' My words were bitter.

'God isn't as forgiving as I, I'm afraid.' Truly, Moishe looked sad as he said those words. 'You chose to call to Bast and her son; now, with each day's sun upon your faces, you will become as they. As a lion, to tread the earth as a Beast.'

I knew what I had to do. 'Please, Moishe, intervene with Yahweh. Don't curse my people. Only me. I was the one who spoke up and placed doubt in their hearts. I fashioned the statue of the beasts. Place this curse upon me alone.'

He looked surprised at that. 'You'll accept changing to a Beast every day for the rest of your life, being caged and chained to keep from harming anyone...to protect your followers from the curse?'

'I will.'

'I must pray on that and ask Yahweh to accept your sacrifice, Malachi, for I can't do this on my own.' And he left me and went into his tent.

It was almost dawn when he returned. I was beginning to panic and I could see the others were also. They'd gathered around us and heard Moishe's words and set up wailing and beating their breasts. Some took ashes from the dead fires and covered themselves as if in mourning, and all were praying and begging forgiveness. Now, we looked anxiously at Moishe as he emerged from his tent, his face gray with concern.

'From this day forth, Malachi, you alone will bear Yahweh's punishment for your doubt. When the sun shines upon you, you will become a Beast. At night, you will become a man again, but on the night of the full moon, your transformation will continue and you will be a Beast for an entire day and night. And any who look upon your face will also be transformed. Otherwise, the curse is lifted from your people.'

'What if no one sees my face?' I asked, a sudden hope flaring inside me. 'What if I wear a mask to hide my countenance from my people? May I then walk among men without changing?'

'I have been told you would ask that question.' He shook his head as he spoke. 'This curse will follow your line, Malachi. Through you to your eldest son and to his eldest and so on through the generations. Covering your face and theirs will hinder the curse…but on the day of the full moon, you must separate yourself from everyone and remove your mask and for that day and night, suffer again by entering the body of a Beast. So it is spoken, so be it.'

'Is there no way the curse can be resolved?' I was sickened at what I had done, more so by how I had doomed my son and my descendants. 'I truly repent my actions. I fall on my knees, Moishe, and beg the Lord to forgive me.' Saying that, I knelt, hands crossed over my chest, head bowed.

'Do not think God is unforgiving, Malachi, for one day, the curse will be lifted.' As I looked up in hope, he went on quickly, 'But not by your actions. And not in your generation. Only by an act of unselfish love will your House be freed.' He made a gesture, impatient and sad at the same time. 'Now, gather your people and your belongings and leave here. I wish you many miles away before the sun rises. I want none of my people harmed when you change.'

'I won't change again!' I swore as he turned and walked away. I left also, hurrying to my tent to order my wives to fashion a mask keeping the sun from touching my face, and also to tell my eldest son what was now expected of him. He is an obedient boy; he merely nodded and told his mother to make him a mask, also.

When we left the camp, my face and his were covered by leather, and as Moishe had said, we remained unchanged through the entire day. From that time on, we never removed the masks, not even at night, for fear we might forget and walk from our tents into the sunlight. Later, when we reached a land far to the south where we chose to settle, they were replaced with metal ones, forged of gold.

We settled in a mountain land north of the desert they call the Plain of Arriah and there made our home and our kingdom. I became king and I consider I rule well and wisely, partly hoping one day Yahweh in his *mercy will relent and release me, and partly because that is my nature. Every month having a full moon, I bare my face to the sun and suffer alone the Torment of the Beast, and then I replace the mask and rule as a man again. Because of this, I have taken the name ben-Gurion—son of the lion—as the surname for my family, and now, I am called the Beast King, and it is thus we shall be forevermore known. The city in which I dwell is called Beth-Gurion, House of the Lion, and it is here I daily pray for that unselfish act of love, that final sign from Yahweh that we are truly forgiven, which will set my family free.*

(Signed by His Sigil) *Malachi ben-Gurion, first king of the Habiru.*

The scroll slid from Senset's fingers. It struck the bench, falling to the floor. Michael turned, coming back to where she sat.

"Now you understand."

"No, I don't."

"Don't you see, Senset?" Behind the mask, his eyes were bright and glittering, almost feverish. "You're going to free me from the curse."

"I? How?"

"By your unselfishness. When Aram told me what you'd done, I knew you were the one. I prayed and Yahweh agreed."

"Michael, I don't—"

"You've done so many unselfish things, Senset…freeing Aram, saving the jailer, marrying me to make peace…"

"Michael, I think you're wrong. I've done nothing selfless. Freeing Aram was done through pity. Preventing my father from killing the jailer was justice.

As for marrying you…though I truly love you now, that was mere duty."

"It may have been duty, but I think it was something more. Why else would you travel so many miles to marry a stranger?" He looked up at the sky. "It's time. I have to go."

Bending, he pressed his mouth to hers. His kiss was so full of hope, she wanted to weep.

"When I return, you'll be able to see my face, my wife. From now on."

With that, he went back into the palace.

"Michael!" Senset leaped to her feet, running after him.

He stopped, looking over his shoulder as she reached his side.

"Where are you going?"

"There's an enclosed garden. The walls are so high nothing but a gazelle could leap over them. I'll be locked inside and will stay there until the sun rises in the morning."

"What if you should manage to get over the wall?"

"The guards are instructed to kill anything escaping from the garden."

"And if that happens?"

"The curse continues in my son, but since I haven't one as yet… Once the eldest direct male line of Malachi ben-Gurion dies, so does the curse…but that isn't going to happen, for you're going to lift it from us."

Again, he started walking. She caught his arm.

"Let me go with you. Into the garden."

"That's forbidden. Only I—"

"Surely there's no danger? If I'm truly the one to break the curse?"

"Malachi decreed no one would accompany the king into the garden. That's the way it must be." Seeing her expression, he relented slightly. "Wait for me here. I'll be back as soon as I can, my mask in my hands. "

Chapter 19

As soon as Michael was out of sight, Senset found she couldn't sit still. In a moment, she was on her feet, pacing.

What'll Michael do when the curse isn't lifted? Will he blame me? Nothing I've done was unselfish. I left my father's house to marry him because I wanted a husband, though I do truly love him now. I can't let him go into the garden alone.

Flinging open the doors, she ran down the corridor. She remembered one day seeing a high gate set into a wall and asking what it held, of being told by Gideon of the garden existing behind it. He'd glossed over his answer, but now…

She arrived at the wall in time to see one of the guards stationed on either side push it shut and slide the bolt home. Immediately, she ran to him.

"Open the gate. I wish to go inside."

"I'm sorry, Your Majesty." He was startled, she could tell, his expression saying plainly, *Why would you want to go in there*? "It's forbidden for other than the king to enter the garden."

"I want to go in." She felt like a child being refused a treat, sensed tears stinging her eyes, was certain they'd soon be sliding down her cheeks and shaming her before this soldier.

As he shook his head, someone spoke behind her.

"Senset."

Turning, she saw Aram standing there, face darkened by a glowering frown. He held out his hand.

"Come."

Silently, she placed her own in his and was led away, up another set of stairs and onto a balcony.

"Why do you wish to go in?" he asked as he guided her to a stone bench near the railing.

"Michael believes I can lift the curse—"

"So he's told you." He didn't appear surprised.

"He had to, since this is the day of the full moon." Her answer was so sharp Aram frowned again. She caught the edge of his sleeve, clutching it tightly. "Aram, I have to be with him, to help him through his disappointment when he realizes I can't do this."

"Do you have so little faith in yourself?"

"I've done nothing that can be called selfless…whether it was freeing you or coming here… It's all been for myself. Did you know what he thought? Did you encourage it?"

"I hoped it was true, Senset, but I never said anything. I suppose the way I described you made Michael form his own opinions, but I never knew of that until this morning when he spoke of them to me. So you think he'll leave the garden as he entered it…still a cursed man?"

"I know so…and I'll be the cause."

"It's too late now to worry about it." He nodded, and she looked over the railing.

The balcony hung over the garden. She could see trees and an abundance of flowers, truly a beautiful place, except when one thought of its purpose…to imprison a king so he wouldn't kill anyone.

She saw Michael emerge from the shadow of the gate where he'd been standing. There was a stone bench in one corner of the garden, half-enclosed by a Rose of Sharon hedge. He paused before it. Lifting from his head the golden circlet serving as his informal crown, he placed it on the bench. Then, he removed his sandals and proceeded to undress, carefully folding each piece and placing it beside the crown.

When the last garment lay on the bench, Michael turned away. Senset held her breath. Even in the tenseness of that moment, she managed to appreciate the beauty of her husband's body, how the sun made his tanned skin glow as if reflecting off molten gold, how his dark hair gleamed blue-black in the sunshine. As he moved away from the stone bench, the muscles in his shoulders and thighs rippled, and she remembered the feel of their strength when he lay over her in their bed. She let her breath out slowly, shuddering at the memory.

In the center of the garden, Michael stopped, hands clasped to his chest, his head bowed over them. She could see his lips moving, realized he was praying and, without hearing what he said, knew he was begging Yahweh to let his wife be truly the one to free him.

Michael raised his head, looking up at the sun. He reached to the back of his head, unbuckling the straps holding the mask in place.

Aram placed his hand on Senset's shoulder. Unconsciously, she put her own hand over his, as if it might give her strength. She sat still, gaze riveted to her husband's figure.

Holding the mask, Michael's hand dropped to his side. Unblinking, he stared up at the glowing, burning orb directly overhead. Aram's hand tightened on

Senset's shoulder, making her stiffen.

For a moment, Michael didn't move. His face glowed as if absorbing the sun's rays. A bright nimbus of light spread from his head to his body, coiling around him in a sparkling golden spiral. The mask slipped from his fingers, falling to the grass.

Michael took a step backward, looking down at his hands, at the flame-like iridescence radiating from his fingers. When he screamed, disappointment, disbelief, and agony were in the sound.

"No...it can't be... Please, Lord, no!"

Abruptly, he twisted, bending double as if struck by sudden pain. With a second cry, he fell to his knees, clutching his belly.

Senset glanced at the gate. Beside it, the two guards stared stonily at nothing, their bodies visibly tense. They might have witnessed this event many times, but it was obvious it still distressed them to know what was happening on the other side of the wall.

Michael screamed again, falling onto his side in the grass. Body quaking, he tried to push himself to his knees. Instead, he toppled face down and lay still...and began to change. His spine curved and arched, body stretching, legs thickening and growing shorter. His hair lengthened, spreading to his shoulders, hanging tangled about his face. The tanned skin darkened, becoming as tawny as a lion's hide, and as furry. Michael cried out again, but this time, the sound ended in a deep-throated cough.

Senset had heard that sound before when the wild lions hunted near Usaset's walls. To hear it coming from a human throat was chilling. Each moment of transformation brought a new cry of pain, making Senset flinch and want to hide her face, to wipe away the sight before her. She forced herself to stay silent, but when Michael began to convulse, that brought her to her feet.

Releasing her brother-in-law's hand, she dodged his grasp, running to the stairs.

"Wait! Where are you going?" As if he didn't know.

"Michael needs me." She was down the stairs and through the corridor, at the gate before he could follow.

The guards threw their crossed lances before the door.

"Out of my way." She struck the lances aside, reaching for the door handle. "My husband needs me."

"It's forbidden, mistress." One dared reach out as if to stop her.

"Let her go." Behind her, Aram spoke. The guards looked at him. "Open the door. I'll take full responsibility."

Silently, one bowed, slipped the bolt, and lifted the handle. The door swung open and Senset rushed inside, stopping inside the entrance. The guards pulled the door shut, the sound echoing in her ears as she stared at that beautiful greenness, the colorful flowers…and the body writhing in the grass.

As she started toward him, Michael raised his head.

At first, she thought he'd again put on the mask, for she could see the tips of tufted ears. In a moment, she realized she was only seeing more of the transformation. Michael's ears had shifted. Nearly hidden by the thick black mane, they appeared as rounded tips near the top of his head, his face a broad-nosed muzzle.

He rolled to his feet, raising his head, mouth opened in a fang-filled snarl, roaring once more. In the sound, she thought she heard a warning: *Don't come near!*

Senset stopped. She and the Beast stared at each other. His green eyes gleamed ferally.

Is there any recognition in them? Or does he see me as nothing but prey?

The Beast growled again, softer this time. He steadied himself on thick sturdy legs, massive paws crushing the grass, tail twitching.

Then, he leaped…

…away from her, aiming himself at the wall. Rising onto hind legs, he flexed talons, clawing at the wall, scoring its plastered surface with deep grooves, sending flecks floating to the grass and dusting his shoulders with white. He leaped, raking at the wall as if to pull himself up and over, fell back, and tried again.

Again and again, the Beast threw himself at the wall, the thud of his body echoing throughout the garden while Senset winced. At last, with a growl, he turned away and raced around the garden's edge, crushing shrubs and flowers, clawing bark off the trees, while continuing to roar until she clapped her hands to her ears to stifle the sound…

…but through it all, he never came near or looked at her…until…

…the Beast stumbled, turned, and staggered toward her. He looked up, misery in his eyes. She could swear she heard Michael's voice in her head…*Senset, wife, help me…* Then, slowly, as if he were very, very tired, he lay down at her feet, panting heavily.

Senset fell to her knees, hugging the great maned head to her breast. The Beast sighed, body heaving with the sound. His tongue came out and he brushed its rough surface against her wrist before he burrowed his head into her lap and lay still.

With another sigh, he slept.

Senset stroked his head, murmuring soft, soothing nonsense. She thrust her fingers into the tangled mane, combing through it as she had the hair on Michael's chest on their wedding night. Once in a while, the Beast trembled, but he continued to sleep, while the sun rode across the sky and settled into the earth, and the moon rose to shed silver light upon the two figures in the garden…

…and Senset sat with the giant head in her lap and continued to caress it.

It was perhaps an hour before dawn when the Beast roused with a startled soft growl, almost a question. He raised his head, looked up at her, then struggled to his feet. Backing away, he again changed, the transformation of the night before reversing itself—much more silently—until once more her handsome husband, still beautifully naked, stood before her.

"My mask." The first words he spoke, lifting his head to the sky, seeing the first streaks of dawn.

Senset stared at his face.

Hurry. Before he can cover it.

Truly, he did look like Aram but with subtle differences—there were marks on his face, deep grooves in his flesh where the mask he'd worn for twenty-four years marked his skin. But…

…oh, he's so handsome…

She ran to where the mask lay, picked it up and handed it to him. With the quickness of long practice, he strapped it into place, then turned to the bench, hastily pulling on his robes and buckling his sandals. When his crown was once more settled atop his now tangled hair, he looked at her.

"You disobeyed my orders." He held out his hand.

"I had to." She placed her own in it.

He led her to the gate, calling out, "Open the gate. My ordeal's finished for another month."

No mention of his failure; only Aram knew, it appeared.

As the gate swung open, the soldiers immediately began excuses for Senset's presence.

"I ordered them to let her in." Aram's explanation overrode theirs.

Michael nodded and released Senset's hand, staggering as he stepped through the gate. Aram caught him about the waist and led him away, calling for a servant to bring wine. The soldiers followed, and Senset was left standing in the dark before the garden's gate as the full horror of what she'd witnessed poured over her.

Hands to her face, she fled to her quarters, where she waited until the doors were shut behind her before she burst into tears.

By the time Michael arrived, Senset had cried herself dry. With Orora hovering helplessly, she washed her face and removed the tearstains, then sent the girl away.

He didn't knock this time, as he usually did, but burst into the room, flinging the doors aside with such force they rebounded against the walls before swinging closed again. As Michael walked toward her, she was reminded of a lion stalking into its den, daring any to deny him entry.

They stared at each other. She swore she saw the wild gleam of a lion's gaze in her husband's eyes. He was panting slightly, not with exhaustion as the Beast had, but as if he'd run all the way from Aram's ministering hands to where he now stood.

"Can you forgive me?" Senset spoke first.

What little she could see of his expression showed surprise.

"It's I who should be asking forgiveness, wife. Of you…and the Lord. I was foolish to believe that because he'd sent you to me to wed, you were also to be my savior. *My* savior…I selfishly thought of no one but myself. Not my sons or the descendants to follow me…just my own redemption. Perhaps that's why the curse wasn't lifted. To teach me to think of others, to be unselfish."

He looked up as if he could see the blue of the sky through the bedchamber's ceiling, then crossed his arms over his chest and bowed his head.

"I thank Thee, Lord, for sending me this woman to be my soulmate. I thank Thee for giving me this treasure in spite of my selfishness." His eyes sought hers again. "I do love you, Sensete-Ra. Now and forever."

Senset managed a shaky smile.

"You're pale."

"I've just bathed my face."

"To wash away your tears? Don't deny you cried. For me? Or because you were afraid?"

'I can never be afraid of you, Michael. Otherwise, I wouldn't have gone into the garden. I knew you wouldn't harm me. You never came near me until you were exhausted."

"You're a remarkable woman, Sensete-Ra." He caught her shoulders, pulling her body against his.

When he kissed her, it wasn't the gentle yet passionate kiss of all their other nights but a demanding, harsh pressing of his mouth to hers, stifling the gasp she gave. His tongue thrust out—she was reminded of the way the Beast had licked her wrist—as it claimed hers boldly and savagely. One hand tore away her robe, tossing it to a far corner of the chamber, while his other ripped away his own garments and threw them on the floor. She was swept into his arms as he ran to the bedchamber and the drapery-hung bed.

She was dropped onto the bed, his own body following as he flung himself upon her with a sound so like the lion's growl it made her shiver. Into Senset's mind came the thought she'd had on their wedding night…of being loved by a lion…but now she knew that was nothing. This night, she truly learned what it was to be possessed by a wild, but loving, Beast.

Chapter 20

Languid, Senset floated in her bath.

She hadn't felt well that morning, not for days, in fact, but hadn't told Michael for fear of worrying him. As soon as they had finished the morning meal and Michael was gone, she ordered Orora to have the sunken marble tub filled and immersed herself in the water.

It feels so good. Leaning back, she rested her head on the little pillow the slave placed on the rim of the tub.

The water was warm; she felt as if she were surrounded by soft rainclouds, enclosing her in soothing dampness. Except for the slight uneasiness of her belly, she might slide into sleep again…

"Mistress, you should come out of the water." Orora broke into her drowsy thoughts. "Else you're going to be as wrinkled as one of those dried apricots you love so much."

Recently, she'd developed a taste for the deliciously tart fruit, eating them by the handfuls.

Perhaps that's the reason my stomach feels so rebellious? Senset shook herself awake, climbed the steps out of the pool, and then…

"Mistress!"

She raised her head to find herself in Orora's arms, the towel the slave had been holding clutched tightly around her wet body. As the darkness faded, she gazed into frightened brown eyes before pushing away.

"What happened?" She remembered stepping from the water and then...*nothing.*

"I don't know...you wavered and...f-fell." Orora's voice shook. "If I hadn't caught you..." She left the rest of the sentence unfinished.

"I'm all right now." On shaking legs, she allowed Orora to guide her to the marble bench near the pool.

As she sat and the slave rubbed the towel against her body to dry it, Orora asked, "Have you had these dizzy spells before, mistress?"

"Never. You know how healthy I've always been." Senset forced a shaky laugh. "Didn't Satis once say I had the constitution of a horse?"

"That she did, mistress," the slave agreed. She knelt to pat the towel against Senset's legs and ankles, looking up at her with a worried frown. "Perhaps it's your Time?"

"I hadn't thought of that. But I've never been faint or sickly before. Satis always commented on that, too."

The mistress of the women's quarters had thought it scandalous how Senset went through her courses with such ease when the others suffered cramps, weight gains, and general unpleasantness of temper.

"No...it can't be that." She paused, watching Orora's expression. "What can it be?"

"Think for a moment, mistress." Orora spoke softly as if to keep anyone else from hearing, though they were alone. "The Time of Women has come and gone for you with no issue. I think you know what caused your swoon..."

Their eyes met, and Senset knew, but she didn't want to know, didn't want to believe it...

I'm with child. The thoughts she'd had wondering if

Michael was sterile burst upon her. *The Lord was withholding children from him until he could marry me. So I could give him his first son. Now, probably all his concubines will quicken.* She gave a quick laugh of disbelief, then burst into tears. *And now I'll give him a child whose face I'll see only for a moment before they cover it with a mask like his father's.*

"There, there, mistress." Misunderstanding, Orora patted her back as she sobbed onto the slave's shoulder. "It's nothing to be frightened of. You'll probably birth this babe as easily as you experience every other function of your body."

"Yes, I will, won't I?" Senset sat up, blotting her tears with the edge of the towel.

"When will you tell His Majesty?"

"Not yet." She didn't want to tell Michael, didn't want to see the joy and the following sorrow as he thought the same thing she had, but something like this couldn't be hidden. Not for long. "In a little while. When we're alone."

"That's best," Orora agreed and giggled, plainly excited at the prospect of tending her mistress' child. "When you're alone and in his arms and he's sated with love, then, tell him…"

"Stop such talk," Senset forced a laugh and got to her feet. "It's not your place to speak of your master and myself in such a way. I might tell him tonight. Fetch my prettiest robes, just in case."

She *would* tell Michael. And soon. And they would rejoice in having a child, no matter what came after.

Chapter 21

At the moment, Michael was receiving a guest.

A short time before, he'd been brought a missive from the prince of a coastal kingdom, requesting an audience. A reply was given, and now, soldiers from the gates sent word the prince's caravan had arrived. His Majesty was duly escorted to the palace and the grand audience chamber where the king received visiting dignitaries.

They stood before him…the prince, clad in brightly colored, flowing robes, as were most garments made for traveling. Under the robe, he wore a loincloth wrapped around his hips, fastened with a wide belt from which hung tightly twisted pieces of antelope skin, interwrapped with narrow strips of colored fabric. Upon his head, there was a tight cap with a circlet of gold, evidence of his royal position, woven into the cloth. His dark face was handsome, unmarked except for a tattoo covering one cheek, denoting his caste. It was incised in shades of ochre and crimson, contrasting with the dusky color of his skin, as did the golden disks in both earlobes and the three strands of gilded beads around his neck.

Behind the prince stood his wives and, a little apart from them, a boy dressed so similarly to the prince Michael assumed he was the son and heir. On either side of them ranged guards, their weapons sheathed. Directly behind the prince, another man stood at respectful attention.

"M'Hina-Enzi, *mbwana* of the Kiswana." The prince bowed low, the sleeves of his traveling robe brushing the floor. He didn't appear the least uneasy at standing before a man whose face was half-hidden behind a golden mask fashioned after the countenance of a snarling lion.

"Welcome, M'Hina-Enzi." Michael nodded his greeting in return as the prince straightened. "We've heard of you here in Beth-Gurion."

"As we have of you in Kiswana…" Enzi met Michael's gaze. "I find the tales of the Beast King are, indeed, true. You do wear the mask of *simba,* but why? May one ask?"

"A family tradition," Michael answered easily enough. "As no doubt your own family has its own rituals."

"True enough." The prince bowed again, accepting the explanation easily, though his expression hinted he felt there was obviously more that could've been said.

"We were gratified to receive your request to visit our kingdom. To what do we owe this honor?"

"I've come to effect a peace treaty with the Habiru," came Enzi's surprising answer.

"A peace treaty?" Michael glanced at Adonijah, standing by his side in his place as chief advisor. "That suggests Habiru and Kiswana are at war, something I wasn't aware of. Are we at war, my lord?"

"No, sire, we are not." Enzi flashed a smile, teeth brilliant in his dark face. "And I hope we never are, for it truly would be a disaster for both our kingdoms."

"Do you wish a treaty to prevent that before there's even a suggestion of conflict?"

The prince nodded.

"Truly a prudent man, who looks to the future. We must talk more of this." Michael stood, gesturing at the women. "Your wives and…son…?"

Again, Enzi nodded.

"…will be escorted to apartments where they may refresh themselves and rest while we confer."

As if by magic, slaves appeared, bowing to Michael's orders and leading the prince's six wives away. The son looked as if he wanted to protest.

Probably thinks he should be allowed to stay and be part of the negotiations, Michael thought.

At a shake of his father's head, however, he bowed, and allowed the remaining slave to escort him from the room. Two of the guards went with them.

Once the chamber was empty but for the remaining guards and the man he assumed was the prince's advisor, Michael walked to an open door to the left of the throne dais. Inside was the council chamber, furnished with table and stools, and he seated himself on one, as Adonijah motioned for the advisor and the prince himself to sit, also.

When everyone was seated, Michael spoke again.

"Now…why do you feel Habiru and Kiswana need a treaty, Your Majesty? There's never been even a hint of aggression between our peoples."

"My country guards the coast, my lord, protecting it and the inner kingdoms, such as Habiru, from pirates." Enzi looked serious. "We stand as a barrier to their pressing inward and attacking countries here as they do others up and down the coastline."

"For that we thank you." Michael's expression showed he'd never thought of how important Kiswana was to his people and the others around the Plain of Arriah.

"Those attacks are now becoming more frequent…not yet to Kiswana, but several of the other kingdoms have been devastated, their people seeking refuge within my own. I fear it may not be long before my own country may be threatened in such a way. My capitol, Kishwahili, is strong, but when I'm gone, if an attack is made before the new prince—my son—is fully seasoned as a warrior, we may all suffer." He smiled again, spreading his hands as if the answer was plain. "Therefore, I come to you…"

"You wish a treaty of mutual defense," Michael supplied. "Should Kiswana be threatened to the point of being overcome, Habiru and its allies would come to its aid."

The prince nodded. "In return, Kiswana will help you defend yourself from aggressors to the west and south, should the need be."

"I pray none come from the south." Michael smiled. "Since I'm allied to them through marriage."

"It's always unwise to fight with in-laws," the prince agreed, dark eyes flickering with ironic laughter. "So…what say you, Your Majesty?"

"You make a good case for such a treaty," Michael agreed. "I admit I've never given much thought to a threat from the sea, since we're so far inland. Still, if Kiswana fell, it could happen, and I'm not so smug as to think my country could withstand, if it did occur." He glanced at Adonijah. "What do you think? Do we need to discuss this further, pray on it, perhaps?"

"Nay, sire." Adonijah had been watching Enzi while he spoke. "I think, truly, Prince Enzi has stated his case quite plainly, and an agreement between our countries would benefit both."

"Then we'll—"

"Before you make your decision, my lord," Enzi interrupted. "There's one concession I'd ask that you make."

"And what's that?" Behind the mask, Michael's eyes narrowed slightly.

"I wish to cement our alliance by more than a treaty. I wish to strengthen it by marriage."

"Marriage?" What little of Michael's expression the prince could see changed to a frown as he thought of his little sister.

The prince wants Rachel as his bride? On that thought came another. *Is this so different from what I asked of Senset's father?*

"Forgive my confusion, Your Majesty, but I had thought your religion only allowed you one prime wife and five lesser ones."

Does he want Rachel as a concubine?

A sudden twinge shot through him. Now he knew how those fathers felt when they'd offered their daughters to him.

Can I let my sister become less than a wife to another ruler? Do I dare let her be treated as I did those women?

It was truly different when the woman in question was of one's own family.

"Or do *you* have a woman you wish to offer *me*?"

Michael sincerely hoped that wasn't the case.

"Your knowledge of my religion is correct." The prince bowed slightly, revealing his approval of Michael's awareness of his gods' laws. "I wish a bride for my son, Zuperi. I understand you've a younger, marriageable sister."

That was met with silence as Michael thought of the young man wanting to be included in the treaty negotiations. The young man who might not be a tried enough warrior if pirates attacked when he became prince. The boy appeared about sixteen, old enough to be considered a man; he had the tattoos showing he'd passed the trials Kiswana required of those entering manhood. His indicating he wanted to sit in on the session showed he was already serious about duties concerning the throne.

"My son's successfully survived his rituals," Enzi said. As if Michael had requested it, he began to list the boy's qualifications as a husband. "He's being instructed in the strategies of warfare and has already shown himself a capable warrior in two battles against invaders. He's not ignorant of women—he was initiated in that knowledge two summers ago, and it was reported back to me that he's a gentle but vigorous lover."

For a moment, the prince's chest swelled slightly in parental pride.

"He'll make your sister a good husband and, as his first wife, she'll be given the place of honor as his prime spouse."

Michael relaxed slightly. "Recommendations to make a brother's heart lose its worry," he said. "I'll speak to my sister."

Do I want to marry Rachel to this stranger's son? Send her away to an unknown kingdom where she'll be the stranger in an even stranger land? Immediately the answer came back. *That's what Senset's father did. Sent her to a former enemy whose language she didn't even*

214

speak. And I've thanked the Lord each and every day that he did.

"Do your females have a voice in such matters?" Enzi's tone indicated perhaps he'd made a mistake in assuming Michael's strength of rule.

Adonijah visibly stiffened.

"My sister will do as I say." Michael chose not to take offense, making a slight gesture to Adonijah. His brother-in-law relaxed. "But—if you've daughters, my lord, you understand these things go easier if the bride is compliant."

"Of course." Enzi nodded. "But be assured, any woman would be honored to wed my son."

"No doubt so shall my sister." Standing, Michael bowed to the prince. To Adonijah, he said, "Fetch Gideon and have him prepare the proper papers for the prince and me to sign." He looked at Enzi again. "In the meantime, Your Majesty, you'll be shown to a suite where you may rest and await the banquet held in your honor tonight."

"My wives…"

"…will be entertained by my own prime wife in a separate dining hall," Michael assured him. Inwardly, he groaned.

Oh dear Lord, forgive me, but I'd much prefer dining alone with Senset tonight rather than indulging in merriment with this man, amiable as he seems.

That meant he wouldn't see his wife until much later, after the banquet was over, which, if these things went as they usually did, wouldn't be until the very late hours of the night. Perhaps not even then, if Enzi liked to imbibe and he, like a good host, drank along with him.

For the very first time in his life, in spite of the

advantages given him as heir, Michael wished Aram were the eldest, entertaining the prince while he hurried to his wife's waiting arms.

Chapter 22

Senset smiled at the prince's wife and held out her goblet so the slave girl could refill it. Orora had made certain the pitcher set at her table was filled with fruit ade, no different in color from the wine the others were served, so her mistress could drink it undetected. Lifting the glass and taking a sip, Senset glanced at Rebekah, seated on her left, nodding slightly as her mother-in-law also raised her wine cup.

Bashasha, the prince's prime wife, flicked her dark gaze at Rachel. "Your daughter's a quiet one, Rebekah. Is this her first attendance at a banquet?"

"Not at all."

Rebekah laughed as she set down her cup and reached for a stuffed date. Delicately, she picked out the roasted almonds packed inside and placed them on her plate before putting the fruit into her mouth.

She chewed, swallowed, and said, "She's usually quiet. It comes from having five brothers, I suppose. They overpower her."

"Hm...that's good in a maiden, but not so good in a wife." Bashasha looked past Rebekah directly at Rachel. "You'd better grow some determination, young woman, if you're to be my Zuperi's wife."

Rachel swallowed the apricot she was eating, choked, and began to cough. She was pounded rather forcefully between the shoulder blades by her mother.

"Best chew things well before you swallow," Bashasha cautioned. "We wouldn't want you to choke on a morsel of food going down the wrong way."

"Oh, it wasn't that," Rachel assured her. She took a deep breath. "I was thinking of marrying Zuperi."

"That caused you to choke? La! Not very flattering." The princess selected a peach slice, nibbling on it delicately.

At the other end of the table, one of the lesser wives giggled at her words. Bashasha gave her a friendly glare.

"Hush there, you."

The wife smiled and ate a second bite of melon.

"So…" the princess persisted, "your brother's spoken to you? What do you think of my son?"

"Is that a fair question?" Senset spoke up. "After all, she's never even seen him."

"Oh, but I have," Rachel protested.

"When was this?" Rebekah turned suspicious eyes on her, eyebrows raised. "Rachel, you know that isn't proper."

"I did nothing wrong, Mother," the girl answered, studying the piece of apricot she held. Slowly, she began to pick it apart. "I hid in the upper gallery over the audience chamber and peeped out at him as his father spoke to Michael."

"Well!" Rebekah looked aghast. "I'd never have been so bold as to do that when I was a girl."

"I suppose I must confess I'm bold, too," Senset said. "For I did the same thing, when I lived at my father's court. Though not on the day Aram returned to claim me."

"Yes, you were more than bold, I'm told." Rebekah's tone wasn't condemning, however.

"Sneaking down to the dungeon where my son was a prisoner and freeing him. Did I ever thank you for that, my daughter?"

"More brave than bold." Bashasha nodded. "We heard that tale, even in Kiswana…it's true then?"

"I'd no idea my infamous behavior had spread so far." Senset tried to look horrified and failed.

That made Rebekah laugh slightly. "In view of the presence of such scandalous company, I suppose I may confess a secret now and not be called a strumpet…"

The others looked at her, waiting.

"I lied…about being bold. When Michael's father came in person to ask for my hand, your grandfather was of a mind to refuse him, in spite of the honor it bestowed on his House."

"Mother, no." Rachel looked shocked.

"Your grandfather was a stubborn man, Rachel, and he wasn't sure he wanted his daughter married to a man placed under such a shadow by his God." She looked at Bashasha as she spoke, as if apologizing for mentioning the family curse. "I was beside myself. Like any other young woman, I dreamed of being a queen, and to have our king actually desire *me…*"

She sighed and raised her goblet.

"What did you do?" Rachel demanded. "I mean, obviously Grandfather agreed, but what made him change his mind?"

"*I* did." Rebekah smiled. "Father told him he'd give his decision on the morrow and His Majesty was shown to his rooms. As was the ritual, he was given water to bathe and…I…"

Senset was startled to see a sudden blush suffuse her cheeks.

"There was a creeper vine clinging to the wall outside his balcony. I climbed it and peeked in on him."

She set down the goblet, hands going to her cheeks.

"Dear Lord, he was such a figure of a man…and I was such an eager virgin…I went to Father and told him if he didn't agree, I'd refused to marry anyone else." She picked up the goblet, downing the rest of its contents with a flourish. "We were wed three months later."

"A woman with a mind of her own," Bashasha announced, nodding approvingly. "I admit I did something similar when it came to marrying Enzi."

"I think he has cow's eyes," Rachel spoke up again. She dropped the torn fruit to her plate. "Big and brown and gentle."

For a moment, they stared at her, before Bashasha said, "Zuperi, you mean? A bull's, more likely, for they can be *gentle* but when he's *passionate*—" She emphasized the words so that none of the women misunderstood her meaning. "—they fill with fire. His name means "strong" and he is that. My son's sixteen, Rachel, and you're…"

"Fifteen," Rebekah put in.

"It's always good for the groom to be a little older," Bashasha nodded, smiling broadly. It was plain she was proud of her son. "Zuperi has been a man two years now. He survived the rituals our people demand, and his father took him to a courtesan when he was fourteen so he might learn the ways to pleasure a woman."

She gave Rachel a direct stare.

"Are you aware of the ways to please a man, my dear?"

"My daughter's a maiden…" Rebekah began.

"My mother's taught me what to do," Rachel

answered calmly, adding, "My husband will rejoice when I show what I've learned."

Senset took another drink from her goblet, a loud gulp this time.

What frank talk.

Surely the others, even gentle Rachel, were letting their drinking get away with them, succumbing to the wine, to say such things. She remembered the way Asaneth spoke of Horem and how the other wives and concubines rambled on about their men in the privacy of the women's apartments.

How soon I've forgotten. Truly, that seems like another life, now. I wonder if I'm supposed to contribute something about Michael? No, I can't. I won't.

"So. What do you think?" Bashasha wasn't ready to give up the subject of her son. "Other than that my son has gentle eyes?"

"I think…" Rachel again studied her hands, selected another apricot to mutilate. "He looks to be as strong as his name…and…" She hesitated so long, Bashasha scowled. "I say I shall be honored to be his prime wife."

She bowed her head.

"Well said." Bashasha raised her goblet. "Let's drink to that."

****

It was late when Michael came to Senset's quarters. Not really expecting him that night, she'd gone to bed. Exhausted from her first experience at hosting a visiting dignitary's wives, she'd quickly fallen asleep, though Orora had insisted on staying.

"…in case His Majesty wishes entry."

Sure enough, sometime in the early hours, there came a knock at the huge gold-bound doors. Senset awakened, struggling to sit up as Orora pulled one door open, admitting the king.

A very tipsy king, it appeared. He wavered across the threshold, hanging onto the door and nodding to Orora as he asked in a husky whisper, "Is my beloved wife still awake?"

"Yes, Michael." Senset spoke as Orora bowed, slipped under Michael's arm, and bolted for the hallway. "I'm awake."

"Good." Pushing the door shut, he started up the steps of the dais, stubbed his toe and nearly fell, rapping out a curse as he regained his balance. "Damned steps…who made them so high?"

Gaining the top one, he stood on one foot, removing a sandal, and nearly over-balanced and fell.

"Michael!" She slid out of bed, running to his side to grip his arm.

"Not to fear, little wife." The sandal fell to the floor, followed by the other.

He was more than drunk, she realized, he was *soaked* in wine. The fumes floated around him, stronger whenever he spoke.

"I'm as sure-footed as a gazelle."

"Usually…but the gazelle has had his fill of several bottles of wine." She guided him to the bed and pushed him onto it, sitting beside him. "Michael, we need to talk."

"The last thing I want to do at this moment," he protested. "I haven't had so much wine my rod won't work properly."

Putting his arms around her, he pulled Senset close, attempting to kiss her. She dodged; he kissed her earlobe instead of her lips.

"Wife…are you refusing me?"

"Not exactly, but we need to talk." She touched the strong curve of his jaw, fingers caressing. "About something serious."

"Very well." He took a deep breath, pulling away and straightening. "I've been expecting this."

"You have?"

Was he so certain he could get me with child he's been counting the days?

"Of course. You've been here over a month, Senset, and while it may be indelicate—indeed, even forbidden—for me to speak of the subject, I'm aware of what has happened. Go ahead, say it: It's your Time and I have to absent myself from your bed until your course has run and you can be purified." He looked away and hiccoughed. "I'll be brave about this but I'll truly count the minutes until I've your lovely little body within my grasp again."

When she laughed, he whirled around, stiff with insult.

"You're laughing, as I tell you how much I love you?"

"I'm laughing because it isn't my Time, Michael. Quite the opposite."

"What does that mean? Senset, am I truly so drunk I can't understand what you're saying?" Taking a deep breath, he appeared to be making a valiant attempt to be as coherent as possible.

"I think you understand very well, Michael. Oh, my husband…" Senset couldn't stand it any longer. Throwing her arms around his neck, she kissed him, then sat back, smiling broadly.

"And that display of wifely affection means…"

"It means we're going to have a baby, Michael. I'm with child."

Briefly, it appeared he didn't understand. The green eyes within the mask simply stared at her, wide with what she could only describe as astonishment. A moment later, she was crushed in an embrace as strong as it was loving.

"Lord God, thank you," he breathed into her hair.

He raised one hand to stroke the stick-straight locks now grown to shoulder-length, combing his fingers through them before sliding his hand to the nape of her neck. He studied their color, dark as the wood of the mahogany tree, shot through with strands of coppery-red.

Like the fire within my Senset's heart.

"Truly, Yahweh has blessed me above all men, Senset. In spite of my curse, I'm happier than anyone in my kingdom tonight, for now I've a wife I love and will soon have a son." He was silent a moment, as if thinking what those words truly meant. "A son…"

If the Beast had been wild and passionate before, he was startlingly gentle in his loving that night.

Chapter 23

Three days later, Prince Enzi's caravan left Beth-Gurion, after the celebration of the betrothal of King Michael's sister Rachel to the prince's son.

Under the watchful eye of his parents and Rebekah, Zuperi and Rachel were allowed to meet in one of the walled gardens. Each sitting on the far end of a stone bench shadowed by a pink Rose of Sharon tree, the young couple spoke to each other—but weren't allowed to touch—for two hours.

Nevertheless, when they parted, whatever was said between them had cemented the proposed desire for the marriage.

Zuperi begged his father to urge Michael to agree; Rachel did the same.

The caravan left for Kishwahili, their capital city, built on the banks of the KubwaMto river. It was decided that, in three months, a wedding journey would be made, bringing Zuperi's betrothed to him. With Rebekah, Adonijah, and Meryam as the king's representatives and witnesses, Rachel would travel to the Kiswana capital to be married to Enzi's heir.

The entire palace was now in a mild uproar, as Rachel, her sister, and her mother, routed slaves and servants to begin preparations for the journey and collect the dowry of personal goods the girl would take with her, besides the small fortune Michael would send with his sister.

In a short time, however, everything changed…

Chapter 24

Death, in the form of an Ægysian prince, came riding through Beth-Gurion's gates on a near-exhausted horse…

Aram was there before the rider hit the ground. The horse staggered away on trembling legs, to be caught by one of the guards. Falling to his knees, the general lifted the man in his arms, staring at the dust-begrimed face beneath the tightly-tied *khat.*

"Prince Horem? What's happened?"

"General Aram…" Horem's eyelids fluttered and his eyes opened, staring dazedly up at Aram. A shaking hand caught his shoulder, fingers scrabbling. "I…come to…ask my brother-in-law…to fulfill his pledge…"

The hand fell away as the prince fainted.

"Get him to one of the bedchambers," Aram ordered, looking up at the soldier who'd cried the alarm. As the guard and another gathered up Horem's body and staggered to the steps, he said to Gideon, "Fetch the physician. And notify His Majesty."

He followed his men into the palace.

****

"How is he?" Michael demanded of Elijah as the physician came out of the bedchamber.

He'd been in his study, reading over the inventory of Rachel's dowry, when Aram's message arrived, and he had come straightaway.

"He's severely fatigued," Elijah replied. "But a few days' rest should…"

"No time for that." In the doorway, Horem teetered, clinging to the frame. He looked at the three men standing there, his fevered gaze settling on Michael. "You wear the Beast's mask. You must be Michael. I've come to—"

He started forward, only to waver and fall. Michael and Aram both caught him, keeping him from hitting the hard marble of the floor.

"He shouldn't have gotten up," Elijah said.

"Michael, we must talk…" Horem clutched at his brother-in-law's sleeve.

"There's nothing you can say to me that you can't say lying down," Michael replied. He nodded to Aram. "Let's get him back to bed."

Carrying the prince into the bedchamber, they deposited him on the sleeping couch. In spite of his determination to stay on his feet, Horem didn't protest and heaved a loud sigh as his head touched the cushions piled behind him. Once he was settled, Michael drew a stool to the bedside.

"I must say I was surprised to see you riding a horse," Michael began.

"No more than I." The prince managed a husky laugh sounding as if it were filled with sand from the Plain of Arriah. "We've learned to ride and also how to fight from horseback… your Benyiamin's a good teacher. I thought it might be swifter than taking a chariot. I've ridden for two days…"

"Lord in Heaven," Aram exclaimed. "No wonder the horse was on its last legs."

That prompted Horem to ask, "The horse… How is

he?"

"Doing better than you," Elijah put in, using his position as doctor to speak severely to the prince. "At least he has enough sense to stay in his stall and rest."

Horem laughed again, the sound just as harsh.

"Why have you come, my brother?" For the first time, Michael spoke that word, acknowledging his relationship to Horem through marriage. "What's happened?"

"Usaset's under attack." That brought a spasm of coughing.

Immediately, Elijah poured a cup of wine, offering it to his patient. Horem seized the cup, drinking greedily.

"By whom? Now that Beth-Gurion and Usaset are allies, who'd be foolish enough to attack…"

"The Misazula…" With a grateful nod, Horem released the cup into the physician's hands.

"But…they're a band of weakling tribes." Michael couldn't hide his surprise. "Scattered throughout the east. None strong enough to…"

"They may be weak separately, but combined they're dangerous. They've a new leader." Horem sounded stronger now.

He struggled to sit up and Michael caught him about the waist, lifting him. He nodded his thanks.

"He's gathered all the tribes together, filled them with zeal and pride in their people, and ordered them to drive out or slaughter all who are not Misazula. So far, they've attacked and destroyed the cities of the Siswati, the Chuluvale, and the Setswana. They've nearly decimated the populations there, and those who survived have descended upon Usaset, seeking refuge."

Horem leaned forward, seizing Michael's arms, as

if their touching might better convey the threat the Misazula offered.

"The city's overrun with refugees…we're running out of food, and now the Misazula are marching on us…"

The speech was too much. Horem released Michael and fell back on the cushions, breathing heavily. His eyes closed.

"Rest, Horem." Michael stood. "You need sleep now. We'll talk more on this when you've recovered."

"There's no time…" It was a feeble protest.

"We must make time," Michael replied. "Even if we could leave this moment, you're in no condition to ride. Be assured I'll hold up my end of the treaty, but we have to be realistic."

The way he spoke told his brother-in-law there would be no argument.

"You'll rest. I'll notify Beth-Gurion's allies. Then we'll go."

The prince didn't argue, his expression saying quite clearly he recognized Michael's authority and his own present incapacity. As Michael turned to his brother, he nodded and once more closed his eyes.

"Aram, send a rider to Prince Enzi. He may not yet be allied with our House through marriage, but I think we're going to need his assistance in this. Also to Izhmir and to Bawanda. Then have your men begin preparations for the march to Usaset."

"Where is he?" The cry came from the anteroom, sending Michael spinning around, looking in that direction. "Where's my brother?"

Leaving Horem in Elijah's care, Michael and Aram went into the anteroom where Senset confronted Caleb, the king's personal servant.

The moment she saw them, she demanded, "I was told Horem arrived...on horseback?"

As if that, and not his arrival, was the most important thing.

"Your brother's learned a few things from our Benyiamin," Michael explained. "He's brought us bad news, my wife."

"What news? Not my father?" She started past him, only to be stopped by Michael's hand on her arm.

"Your father's well...for now," he assured her.

His tone as he said it made Senset study his face, frowning at the way his mouth went stern under the mask.

"If it isn't Father, then what?"

"Ægys has been invaded and Usaset's soon to be under siege... Horem's come asking our help."

"You'll give it, won't you? You'll help them fight?"

"Do you doubt me, wife?" He struggled to keep his answer from being sharp. Or angry. "I made a treaty with Ægys. If they call, I'll answer. I simply didn't expect it to be so soon," he added, a bit ruefully.

"I need to see..." Again, Senset looked at the bedchamber door. Once more, Michael stopped her.

"Later. For now, Horem needs to rest." He turned her away from the door, propelling her to the one leading to the hallway. "You must go back to your own rooms. Aram and I've much to do and I've no time for even my favorite wife."

With a kiss to her forehead, he sent her through the door, watching her reluctantly walk away.

"Thank the Lord she didn't protest or cry," Aram said. "I don't think I could tolerate a woman's tears just now." He studied his brother's profile. "You do know you won't be going to her for a while? Not if we're to make war plans."

"I'm aware of that." Michael's answer was a little stiff, as if his brother were reprimanding him for being in love with his wife. "We haven't been at peace long enough for me to forget how it is when we prepare for a battle, brother." He smiled. "As for tears? In a short time, I think we may be grateful we've a war to distract us."

"What does that mean?" Aram demanded.

"Remember how Mother wept before Yeshua was born? A harsh word…my presenting her with a bouquet of flowers…seeing the rain fall… It seemed anything made her cry."

"I remember well," Aram replied and shook his head as if sometimes he didn't understand the way his twin's thoughts came together. "Her mourning notwithstanding, I didn't know whether to feel sorry for her or to chide her, and that made me feel guilty…to think such thoughts of our mother when she was carrying our brother so bravely after Father died. But what does that have to do with Senset? Or this coming battle with the Misazula?"

"Combine a breeding woman with the thought of her husband, father, and brother being in a war, and you've tears aplenty," Michael replied, and waited for the meaning of his words to sink in. As he saw understanding touch his brother's face, he laughed. "Yes, my brother! The Beast will soon have an heir."

"The Lord is generous." Aram allowed himself one moment of envy, thinking of Michael performing the act of planting his seed in Senset's little body, then thrust the thought away lest he let his affection for the girl show and be considered sinful. "Come, we'll drink a toast to your coming heir while we make our plans."

Throwing his arm across his twin's shoulder, Aram guided his brother through the door.

Part 2: A Time to Mourn

Chapter 25

Two weeks later, the combined armies of the Habiru, Ishwahili, the Shona, and the Luapala rode out of Beth-Gurion and across the Plain of Arriah.

Seven days before, having slept for two full days, then risen to bathe and eat, Horem greeted his sister. He rejoiced with her at news of the coming child, expressed his wonder at the tale of Michael's mask, and was impatient to return to Usaset.

"We'll leave as soon as our allies arrive," Michael told him calmly. "In the meantime, rest and enjoy our hospitality and regain your strength, my brother. From what you tell me, we've a terrible battle ahead of us."

Horem forced himself to relax in his sister's company while he waited. Having accepted Habiru clothing and armor, with the exception of his shaven head he now looked no different from the other men and found himself being accepted easily by them.

"Our father'll be glad to hear you're presenting him with another grandchild," he told Senset, hugging her tightly. All his animosity gone, the look he gave her held more than a little affection. "Little Sister…you've changed. Truly, you appear an adult now."

"And not just because of this?" She patted the slight mound of her belly visible under the flowing robe. "I've grown up, Horem…because I've a good man as my husband."

"And that…" He motioned to his face, finger encircling it to describe Michael's mask. "Doesn't it bother you? That you're wife to a man whose face you'll never see?"

"At first, it did," she admitted. "But not now. In a way, not being able to see his face makes me love him more. Now, I judge Michael by what he says, not by his looks."

They were sitting on the balcony of Horem's suite. Below in the courtyard, Michael was sparring with Aram, their swords flashing in the sun.

"Also by what he does. He'll help you drive back the Misazula, Horem, don't worry."

"I don't doubt that," Horem hastened to assure her. "It's merely that I fear this wait may work against us. The Misazulo move quickly. Even now, they may be nearing Usaset's walls. Still, I know the other cities are days from here, and even on the swiftest horses, Michael's message won't arrive quickly. Also, it'll take more days for them to come back."

To prevent his dwelling on that fact, Senset changed the subject. "I hope the food is acceptable. I know some of the Habiru dietary restrictions may seem odd…"

"Not at all. I was already aware of their prohibition on eating pork. Besides, at this point, I was so hungry, I'd have eaten boiled palm bark if it were properly seasoned."

The prince had plenty of time to familiarize himself with the aspects of Habiru life, as well as his in-laws, before the first of Michael's allies appeared.

****

Now they were on the march, and the first night, when Michael called for a halt and to make camp, Horem immediately voiced his anxiety.

"We mustn't stop. We have to keep going. To get there as soon as we can."

"We could do that," Michael agreed, "but if we push ourselves to the limit in travel, both our men and their mounts will be exhausted when we get to our destination. Tired horses can't run. Tired men don't fight, they die. They won't be any help to your lord father if they're too fatigued to lift their spears."

"You're right," Horem immediately capitulated. "It's just that…"

He looked away, shaking his head.

"I've never been in this situation before. Ægys has never had to seek help in defending its walls."

"I understand, my brother, but you *did* ask, and we've answered…even those with no bond to you but only to me," Michael took the plate Aram offered him and held it out to his brother-in-law. "Now, eat, sleep, and we'll be off again when the sun rises. By this time day after tomorrow, we'll engage the Misazula and end their terror."

On the morning of the third day of their march, the armies arrived at Usaset.

Chapter 26

It's too quiet." Horem stood in the stirrups, craning his neck as if he could see across the plain and into the city. "Usaset's such a bustling place, one can generally hear it, even this far away."

"Perhaps it's too early," Aram suggested, but he remembered how the sounds in the marketplace had stayed with the caravan even after they'd lost sight of the city. He didn't like this silence, and his expression mirrored the prince's. "They may still be asleep."

"The sun's full past the horizon." Horem gestured at the flaming orb. "The Plain acts as some kind of sound carrier. By this time, we should be able to hear any noise in the marketplace."

His expression, held something short of terror. Michael imagined he was probably silently cursing himself for allowing it to show.

"Something's wrong."

They were closer now and could see the walls of the city.

"There aren't any guards on the walls…" Michael began, and stopped as he saw something between them and the gates, a dark, undulating mass covering a quarter-mile of the Plain, wavering and moving like wind stirring the waters of a shining, black lake. "What in the name of the prophets is that?" His curse was a shocked gasp. "Water? Since when is there a lake before

Usaset's walls?"

"That's no lake." Horem kicked his horse into a gallop, sending the animal leaping toward the swirling darkness. "Gods of Ægys, no!"

The horse dove into the mass, sending it into the air in an opaque swarm briefly blotting out the sun. Briefly, man and mount were obscured, disappearing into its shadow. The swarm broke apart, becoming hundreds of wings, flapping and sending the sand into spirals around Horem's body.

"Vultures! Yahweh preserve us." Michael and Aram sent their own horses following the prince.

By the time they reached his side, Horem had reined in his horse and was staring around as if stupefied.

The vultures' feasts covered the ground…bodies, or what was left of them, for many were mere bones now, picked clean by the scavengers' beaks. On some, flesh still clung in ragged, bloody scraps to disfigured faces. Some lay under the corpses of the precious horses, evidence the Ægysians had ridden the animals to face their enemy. Here and there, war chariots rested on their sides, smashed and splintered, horses dead in their traces. Blown by a sudden upsweep of wind, a wagon wheel, its spokes broken, turned slowly, squeaking eerily in the silence.

"We're too late." Horem made a sound so close to a sob it made Michael's heart clutch to hear it. He looked around, his wavering gaze settling on a single chariot standing upright in the midst of the carnage, though its horses lay twisted and dead before it. "That… It's my father's chariot."

He rode toward it, sliding from the horse's back before the animal could stop, running to the chariot.

Horem placed one hand on the iron-rimmed edge, staring at the huddled body lying on the blood-splashed floor. Behind him, Michael pulled his own horse to a halt and jumped to the ground.

"Horem, is that…?" A glance inside made him choke on the question.

"It's Imtep, my father's charioteer, but there's too much blood…" He looked around frantically, scanning the mass of bodies. "I don't see my father's body."

"Perhaps he…"

"I smell smoke." Horem didn't give Michael time to finish.

Whirling, he caught his horse's reins and vaulted into the saddle, turning its head in the direction of the gates. Behind him, Michael did the same, gesturing to Aram. In turn, his brother signaled to the men behind him. As he galloped after the two, the columns behind them began a march toward Usaset's gates.

The marketplace was inside the entrance, the first thing a visitor to the city would see, convenient for traders and buyers alike, but there was little left of it now. The vividly colored canopies marking booths and pavilions were ripped and torn, some fluttering in ragged streamers from the splintered remains of their poles while others were burned and blackened, the remnants of cloth mere smoldering ashes. Flowers and garlands decorating the awnings lay in the dirt, smashed and ground into bright shreds.

Booths were broken and scattered as if a crazed horse had galloped through them; none were intact. Strewn among the ruins were bodies…soldiers, dying to protect the city, their corpses a near-barricade to the new arrivals…behind them lay the inhabitants of

Usaset…men, women and children, killed before they could take refuge in the temple's haven…

In the rubble of what had been a jeweler's shop, judging from the crushed small chests and coffers surrounding him, lay the body of the owner, his robes splashed with blood. In one hand, he clutched a broom like a weapon, the tip of its handle splintered. Nearby, a coffer spilled beaten copper bracelets into the dirt as if he'd dropped it in his flight and turned to protect himself with that pitiful broomstick.

A burned cart had been thrown into the well in the middle of the square, filling it with dirt and ashes, sullying the water so no one would dare drink from it again. Protruding from the water, the wagon tongue still flamed, sending a trickle of gray smoke into the air.

Other bodies lay in doorways, some half-buried in the debris of burned buildings, more in the streets. All faced toward the temple. The townspeople and shopkeepers had been heading there when the attack occurred, the soldiers closing in to form a protective wall between them and the oncoming enemy.

The horses were jittery, not liking the smell of fire and death, but Horem rode through it all, over bodies and debris, heading for the palace, Michael and Aram following. Behind them, their armies marched, faces impassive to the slaughter, though an occasional hand raised itself to make the sign of various gods, silently beseeching them to take those dead souls.

In the courtyard of the palace, it was the same. Dead guards, dead servants…all held weapons of some kind, even the house servants and slaves had been issued lances to fight the invaders, but it had done no good. If trained warriors couldn't fight the Misazula, how could a man who had never before held anything more deadly than a fly swatter be expected to survive?

Soldiers and slaves lay side by side in death.

One body drew their attention. A slave, near the body of a white horse, his hand still gripping the animal's bridle. The horse's throat had been cut, its blood splashing on the young man who'd tried to get it to safety before being cut down himself. Aram turned his head, saying a silent prayer for Benyamin, remembering how excited the slave had been when told he was being sent to train the Ægysians in horsemanship.

Lord, accept his soul, for he was a good man.

Horem was off his horse, running up the steps of the palace. He didn't wait for Michael and Aram to dismount but was inside and heading down the hall before they reached the top step.

"Where's he going?" Michael asked, drawing his sword. "Does he think to find his father here?"

"The audience hall where Aseti-Ra held court is that way." From his previous visit, Aram remembered its location. "Come on!"

They were halfway there when the scream ripped through the corridor. Not a mere cry of pain, but a shriek of despair, forced from a suffering throat…the sound of a man in the full throes of grief.

Ahead, they saw Horem, standing before the audience chamber doors. They were shut, the massive wood and gold panels dark in the shadows of the corridor. He was staring at what was attached to one door…pale and still, dripping blood in a thick puddle onto the white marble floor. Horem stood in it, his feet and the soles of his sandals spattered and sticky.

The Misazula had captured the king and brought

him inside to kill him before the door of the room where he'd reigned. Aseti-Ra's naked body had been pinned to the door, held by metal-tipped spears driven through his outstretched arms at the elbows and his thighs. Three spear slashes opened his belly, leaving his entrails swaying above the floor. It was from these wounds and his cut throat the blood had come.

"Holy God!" Michael skidded to a halt behind him, as did Aram. "What kind of human does something like this?"

Horem jerked as if slapped, as Michael's words brought the prince out of his horror-struck trance. Unmindful of the blood splashing his feet, he called over his shoulder, "Help me get him down."

Silently, they tugged on the spears. They were immovable, driven in so deeply they penetrated through the wood, the points coming out the other side of the door. Michael looked around, saw a statue lying on its side, smashed into fragments. Seizing one piece the size of a large stone, he began to strike one of the metal points, driving it back through.

"Get ready to catch him," he called as he continued battering the spike.

When the piece of statuary shattered, he found another and continued beating. With a clatter, the spear fell to the marble, two more following. Legs and one arm freed, Aseti-Ra's body tilted, dangling by the other. The stone Michael held dissolved into gravel. He found another. The last spear was freed; the king's body slid from the wall into his son's arms, Aram catching his legs.

Tossing aside the remains of the broken statue, Michael came around the door in time to see Horem sink to his knees in the blood, clutching his father's body.

Bowing his head, he pressed his face against Aseti-Ra's slashed neck. When he looked up, his eyes, stark in a blood-smeared face, met Michael's.

"Asanath...my sons..." Letting his father's body slide to the floor, Horem got to his feet. He turned, running toward a set of stairs at the end of the corridor.

"Aram, come on." Michael turned to follow, but Aram held back.

"What about..." He gestured at the king's body.

"We can honor him later. Right now, we must see if any of Horem's family survived." Michael ran after his brother-in-law, and after a moment, Aram followed.

Chapter 27

It was an unsettling feeling, Michael thought, as they went up the high marble steps. Like walking in the halls of the dead, for truly that's what the palace had become…with bodies everywhere. Not just the king's but any and all in the palace. As in the city itself, none had been spared.

There's little chance of Horem's children or his wife—any of his wives—having survived, he thought, and an image of Senset, belly rounded with his child, appeared in his mind. *Merciful God, how would I feel if it were she I searched for?*

Nevertheless, he didn't hesitate but hurried after Horem, attempting to keep the prince's running figure in sight.

Horem stopped before a pair of doors. One was open, the other ripped from its hinges, lying in the corridor. He stepped over it, rushing inside.

"Asanath? Wife?"

The unspoken pleading in those words—*be here, be alive*—stabbed into Michael's heart. Together, he and Aram clambered over the ruined door and entered the room.

It was the common room of a lady's chamber, if the fragments of the decorations were any indication. Scenes of flowers and birds, though hacked and shattered, were still visible on the walls. All the furniture had been destroyed, and most of the draperies were in shreds, but for one pair in front of doors opening onto the terrace.

A high-pitched bark cut the silence.

"Yine?" Horem whirled, looking toward the terrace. "Yine!"

A flurry of gold dashed from the shredded draperies. A silky fuzzball streaked across the floor, launching itself into the prince's arms. Wet tongue slathering his face, the puppy's body wriggled in happiness.

"Yine." Horem dodged the tongue and allowed himself a bare smile.

"It's the pup you sent as a gift," Aram said in explanation as Michael glanced at him.

"So one creature has survived, and if it managed to…"

"Gods, I pray so." By now, Horem had calmed the puppy, stroking its head and murmuring to it. Gently, he set it on its feet amid the broken furniture. "Sapair…where's Sapair, Yine?"

The puppy looked up at him, cocking its head and wagging its tail.

"Find Sapair.

With another bark, it dashed back through the draperies and onto the terrace, Horem following. As he pushed through the slashed sheer fabric, he looked back. "Come."

"Horem, do you truly think that creature can lead you to…" Michael began a protest.

"Yine was being trained to hunt. Even if my son doesn't live, he'll take me to him." Horem disappeared through the drapes.

The two Habiru followed. They came onto the terrace in time to see Horem going up an outside staircase to the palace's next level. Running to keep up, they took the steps two at a time, following the prince along the terrace where the puppy paused and barked again, then darted inside an open door, Horem behind him.

They followed and found themselves in another common room.

This one was large and lush. Both men immediately realized this had been the women's chamber, where concubines and wives whiled away their time awaiting their men's pleasure. Piles of destroyed cushions lay amid slashed draperies, some floating in the bathing pools. Bodies lay in the water, others sprawled on the floor. Some huddled together at one end of the room, as if they'd clutched each other for protection as their killers descended on them.

The puppy didn't hesitate but dashed across the room, leaping over the hurdle of bodies, heading for a hanging tapestry at the other side of the room. He stopped before it, yapping loudly.

Tail wagging, he looked back at Horem and barked again then fell silent. Clumsily, he balanced on three legs, nose nearly touching the tapestry, one front leg raised, tail straight, the perfect posture of a hunting dog indicating it had found the requested prey.

Horem picked his way after the pup, pausing before the tapestry. There was a whimper from behind the heavy ruglike hanging.

Yine snuffled slightly, looking up at the prince, who touched his head, whispering, "Good dog."

He swept the tapestry aside.

Hands over his head, the little boy crouching on the other side squealed and leaped to his feet, trying to run past Horem. As the prince caught him, clasping him tightly, he began to shriek, "Let me go! Let me go!" kicking and struggling against his father's embrace.

"Sapair…Sapair…" Horem hugged the child tighter. "It's Abba, Sapair."

He tightened his hold and kept it that way until his words penetrated the boy's fear and Sapair stopped struggling.

"Abba?" He looked up at Horem, recognition appearing in the dark eyes, and abruptly went limp. "Oh, Abba! You've come back." He began to cry.

Horem held his son, swaying with him and murmuring words the two other men couldn't understand, nor would they want to if they could, Michael reflected. He could see the relief in Horem's body, the way he rocked the boy, the way he held him gently but firmly, every movement rejoicing in the fact that at least one of his children had survived.

Presently, Sapair's tears stopped and the child gulped, hiccoughed, and looked up at his father through watery and apologetic eyes. "I-I'm sorry, Abba. I kn-know a warrior m-mustn't cry…f-forgive me…"

"You're six years old, my son. I imagine you've seen things no child should," Horem spoke sharply, though the words were heartfelt. "You're forgiven."

He set the boy on his feet, kneeling beside him.

"Wh-who are they?" Sapair immediately saw Michael and Aram and assumed the worst. He cowered against Horem.

"These are your Aunt Senset's husband and brother," Horem explained. "Come to help me avenge our family." He caught the child by the shoulders. "Tell me, son, did anyone besides you and Yine survive?"

Before the child could answer, there was a patter of sandaled feet and a figure rushed around the wall hanging and at them. They only had time to see the upraised dagger in her hand before it descended, aiming at Horem's neck.

"Die, Misazula dog!"

Pushing Sapair aside, Horem dodged, throwing up one arm. Michael and Aram sprang forward, dropping their swords and seizing the woman's arms. As Aram pinned them to her sides, Michael wrested the knife from her hand. Subdued, she began to sob, eyes screwed shut.

"Kill me, but spare the boy, I beg you."

"Xena?" Horem got to his feet, once more picking up Sapair, who'd begun crying again. Hugging the child, he faced his attacker, forcing himself to smile and say in a startlingly gentle tone, "Gods, woman, I never knew you could be so fierce."

She opened her eyes and looked from Michael to Aram, who still held her, before directing her gaze at Horem's blood-smeared face and going paler than she already was. Like Sapair, she collapsed. Aram's arms were all that held her on her feet.

"Horem! My master, you're alive?"

"As you can see, Xena, and I thank you for trying to defend my son." Horem looked past her to the doorway through which she'd come. "Are there others still living? My other sons? Asa?"

"My Lord…" Zena turned her head and began weeping again. "Your lady has gone to the Underworld, may Isis protect her and Anubis judge fairly…"

Horem's reaction to that was a harsh and visible trembling, but all he said was, "Where?"

"I laid her body in her chamber." Xena nodded at a

third door on the other side of the room.

Setting down Sapair, Horem started to it.

"Master, no." Pulling from Aram's grasp, Xena caught his arm. "Don't. You shouldn't see her like this."

Horem didn't answer, just pulled away and walked into his wife's bedchamber.

It was silent in the room as they waited. With a muttered apology, Aram released Xena, who accepted his words with a shaky smile. Sapair had picked up Yine, cuddling the puppy in his arms. After a moment, he crept nearer Michael, and timidly reached up and touched his hand.

Surprised, Michael looked down at the little boy and smiled, studying the sturdy little body in its linen *shendyt*, his head shaved except for a single dark braid hanging from his right temple to his shoulder. His prince's lock.

You're a prince of a dead city now, child.

Briefly, he wondered if his own child would resemble Sapair. After all, they'd be cousins. He tightened his hold on the boy's fingers and was relieved when Sapair smiled back.

In a few more moments, Horem reappeared. He didn't speak until he stood directly before Xena again. His face was wet, eyes red and strained, but his voice held no evidence of the tears he'd shed, unseen by the others.

"Are there any others besides you two?"

"Five others." She touched his cheek, fingers gentle against his wet skin. Horem placed his own hand over hers, pressing it against his face. "Your newest born."

The relief on Horem's face at that statement made Michael look away.

"Prince Potiphar's prime wife and her second son, Satis, and the dungeon keeper."

"And my lady mother?" he asked without a tremor.

She shook her head.

"They must pay for this." Horem directed that statement at Michael. "For my family and my people and all the others they've slaughtered, the Misazula must pay. We must discover where they've gone. Who they'll attack next…"

"My trackers will find that out soon enough." Enzi spoke from the doorway. He'd followed their trail through the palace, arriving in time to hear Horem's last words. "I've already set them to the task."

Coming to where the little group stood, he nodded to Horem and made a gesture meaning *I share your grief.*

"Don't worry, Brother of Michael. We'll avenge everyone."

"Show us where the others are," Michael said to Xena. "Let's get them out of here."

****

"When Granabba gave orders for us to hide in the temple, Mama wouldn't leave," Sapair told his father his version of what had happened. "She said the great Aseti-Ra couldn't be overcome by a bunch of savages."

He still held Yine. The silky pup had been cradled tightly in his arms since Horem carried him from the palace. Horem set him before him on the horse, and they rode through the charnel house of bodies now rotting before the gates, to where the armies had set up camp. With the others, Sapair, wrapped in a blanket, huddled before a campfire. When Horem sat beside him and offered him a waterskin, the child accepted it, then began to talk.

"She just sat there feeding the baby." His eyes were wide with remembered shock. "We could hear the men shouting, and swords and lances hitting together, and people screaming. It kept getting closer and closer…"

"I went to her, Horem," Xena took up the story. "Begged her to come with us, but she still refused. I think it was the illness. She'd been so well until you left, and then… She went into that odd state again…" She shook her head. "She said you'd come back and save us all. I stayed until I heard the screams in the palace halls. Then I snatched the baby from her, grabbed Sapair's hand, and ran…" She looked away. "Forgive me…I knew I couldn't handle her and the children, too."

He caught her hand, squeezing it, though he didn't speak.

"I met Satis, who was helping Nofret with Nekh-Toth. By then, it was too late to get to the temple, so she took us into the under-rooms where the dungeon keeper hid us in one of the cells. He took one of his lances and stood guard at the door, promising to die before they would get in."

"I must remember to reward him for his bravery," Horem muttered, thinking how, but for Senset's interference, that same man would have been executed for letting Aram escape and his replacement might not have risked his own life to protect his king's family.

"I'm truly sorry, master," Xena went on. "Asa and I had our differences, and I admit I was jealous of the love you had for her, but I never wished such a thing to happen."

She began to cry, but this time, her tears were silent, slipping down her cheeks. She didn't brush them away, as if she were unaware of their presence.

"Don't worry, Xena. I understand," Horem assured her. He stood up, pulling her to her feet. "You need to rest now." Turning, he picked up Sapair, who was beginning to nod, the pup already asleep in his arms. "As do you, my son." He looked at Michael. "Let me settle these two and I'll be back."

Michael nodded, and Horem walked away, leading Xena and carrying his son.

"This is a terrible thing." Aram took the stool Xena had vacated. He raised the waterskin, taking a long drink from it.

Briefly, he wished it held good Habiru wine, but Michael didn't allow any strong drink on a campaign. Only the army physician and his aides carried wine, and that was for surgical purposes.

"Have the trackers come back yet?'

"They have." Enzi had been silent since they returned, listening to the story told by each of the survivors. "They say the marauders have gone northeast, and are only a few hours ahead of us. Not more than a day."

"We should've run directly into them then."

"They must've circled around us so we missed them," one of the other chiefs spoke up.

"Perhaps it's as well. If we'd come upon them and there was a surprise attack, we might not have fared any better than the Ægysians," Enzi replied. "We need a meticulously planned attack and go into it with the idea of taking no prisoners. At all."

"I disagree." Aram raised the waterskin again. "After seeing what those bastards did, especially to Aseti-Ra, I'm thinking they'll do the same to any man they believe a leader of his people." He looked around at the ring of faces. "We—you, I, Horem, any of us—run the risk of a similar fate, so I say we catch them by surprise, wipe them out, and don't give them a chance to slaughter anyone else."

There were murmurs of agreement, dying away as Horem reappeared.

"They're both asleep already." He smiled ruefully. "I couldn't get Yine out of Sapair's arms. Guess it won't harm him to sleep with his dog. I think he was sneaking him into his room at night anyway." He looked at Michael. "Tomorrow, will you spare a few of your men to escort them to Beth-Gurion?"

"We all will," Enzi answered. He looked around. "Each of us will send two men to protect your people all the way to Michael's palace."

"Seeing Senset will help, I hope," the prince murmured. He took a deep breath. "So, King Michael, I follow your lead. What do we do now?"

"Tomorrow, we appoint a burial detail to send your people to their Afterlife," Michael began. "I'm not aware of your death ceremonies…"

"They're not important now," Horem interrupted. "The rituals can come later. For now, let Anubis judge them without ceremony. Burn the bodies. Where they lie."

"Even your father?" Aram asked. "Surely a king should be given respect."

"Even my father. He loved his people. He died for them. Why shouldn't he join them in their journey to the Underworld?" Horem looked over his shoulder at the dark shape of the city gate, barely visible in the distance.

The wind chose that moment to shift, blowing over the mounds of bodies lying before it, and sweeping the smell of decay to them, causing coughs and quick gasps. "Burn the city, too. Let Usaset be a gigantic funeral pyre for its inhabitants."

"If we destroy the city, you'll have nothing to rule," Michael protested.

"What do I have to rule now?" Horem's words were bitter with anguish. "A city of the dead? With two subjects…a dungeon keeper and the caretaker of the royal women. She's a caretaker for corpses now."

In a sudden, violent movement, he ripped the helmet from his head, dropping it to the ground. Horem bent, fingers clawing at the dirt. He smeared the soft, silt-like soil across his face and head, rubbing it on his chest and arms. His eyes, bleak and burning in that dust-covered face, stared into Michael's.

"Behold a man in mourning, my brother…for I've lost everything. All my family's gone but my sister-in-law, my nephew, and my two sons…my kingdom is ashes, and after me, my son will have nothing to rule, either." He shook his head. "Burn the city and its people, Michael. I call upon our relationship by marriage and place myself under your rule. As far as I'm concerned, the Ægysians no longer exist."

"Bitter words, Horem," Michael spoke soothingly, understanding his brother-in-law's grief, and wondering if he could have been so self-contained if it had been his own people.

If Senset or my mother,or Yeshua or Gideon were lying dead, slain so cruelly, would I grieve so quietly, or would I become the Beast in my mourning?

"I'll accept your request. For now. Once this is over and you've time to lay your heartache to rest, you may change your mind. At that time, we'll speak on this further."

Horem didn't answer, merely nodded and fell silent.

Chapter 28

Aram was right when he said a well-planned attack would be of no use in fighting the Misazula.

The country through which they were traveling was vastly different from the Plain of Arriah. Greener, lush with grass and trees hung heavily with vines and foliage, it spread before them like a verdant meadow before slowly giving way to rougher terrain, eventually becoming the northern mountains. Rocks and huge boulders dotted the upward slant of the trail as it cut through the foothills. The way was darkened, the branches of trees meeting and blotting out the sky. Even with the sun directly overhead, they were surrounded by what appeared to be early dusk.

Somewhere nearby, they could hear the faint roar of water rushing swiftly past inside a canyon gouged out of living rock.

It happened quicker than they could've imagined.

The marauders were lying in wait, hidden among the rocks at the mountain's base, so silent even the scouts they'd sent ahead hadn't detected them. It was only as a spear sailed through the air, driving itself into a horse's chest, that they were warned.

There was a meaty *thunk* as the metal head tore into the animal's body. The horse died without a sound, toppling onto its side, its rider leaping from the saddle in time to keep from being crushed beneath it. Drawing his sword, he looked around frantically, trying to see where the spear had come from as Michael and the others also drew their weapons. Behind them, Enzi gave a frantic signal to his men, the other chiefs copying his gesture.

A single scream rent the air, made by many voices, ululating and high-pitched. Then the Misazula were on them in a streaming horde of waving spears and upraised oval shields.

Three footsoldiers were cut down before they could move, the others assuming protective huddles with shields making a barrier before them. Spears bounced off the surfaces, one sailing through to sink into a soldier's throat. As he fell, the others tightened their ranks, bracing for the assault. The Misazula were on them in a wave. The soldiers waited until they were within striking distance, then each man raised his lance and charged.

Aram found himself near Horem, who was fighting Ægysian-style. Even in the frantic chaos, he noted the prince's skill with both the sword he held in his right hand and the lance in his left as he fended off an attacking warrior. After that, he had no time to watch the prince as he raised his own sword to stop the downward slash of the oversized blade another Misazula aimed at his skull.

It was a mad, frenzied maelstrom of bodies and weapons. The Misazula were evenly matched in skill and numbers by those they attacked, but Horem's allies were slowly winning, spurred on by a desire for revenge and the memory of the atrocities committed on the bodies of those in Usaset.

Some of Enzi's men were forced toward the cliff where the river ran. Another chieftain's warriors came to their aid. The attacking enemy was caught between them, cut down before they could recover. Gradually, the Misazula numbers were whittled away.

If we can last long enough, we have them, was Aram's thought, and the next was for his brother. *Where's Michael?* In the frenzy of battle, they'd become separated.

In the next moment, Aram was unhorsed by a Misazula throwing himself against his mount's side and knocking him out of the saddle. Scrambling to his feet, he drove his sword into a charging warrior's chest, feeling the satisfied shudder of impact through his hand as the blade penetrated the hardened antelope-hide shield and sank into flesh. He stepped back, looking around frantically and saw his brother, still on horseback, only a few yards away.

Like Enzi's men, he'd been maneuvered to the cliff. His opponent was obviously a chief, if the streaming lion's mane neck covering and bright yellow body symbols glistening against his dark skin were any indication. The man was as fierce as the lion whose hide he wore wrapped around his body, and he was driving Michael backward to the cliff's edge. Slashing with his two-foot knife, he struck right and left with a frenzy Michael was having difficulty defending against.

They were as two beasts facing each other, each wearing the hides of the creatures they'd emulate.

Aram dodged, fending off another warrior. The Misazula rushed him, thrusting out the spear. The point sank into Aram's shoulder and the sudden pain was so sharp and burning he nearly dropped his sword. With a roar of rage, he caught the weapon in both hands and swung it, putting every ounce of weight he could muster behind the movement.

Blood spattered Aram's face as the warrior's head went flying, his body staying upright a second longer before collapsing to the ground. Aram wiped away the blood and looked back at his brother.

They were at the edge now, the horse hesitating as it sensed nothing but empty air behind it. Michael pulled on the reins, bringing it to a standstill. He struck at the chief, their blades connecting in a sharp, high clang echoing over the sounds of the fight.

The warrior lunged, throwing the spear in his left hand. Michael dodged and the spear sailed past, falling in a downward arc into the canyon. The horse took a step backward... One hind hoof wavered a moment in the air. It reared, body overbalancing as the hoof came down and found nothing to stand on. Michael leaned forward, trying to help it regain its balance.

Spear gone, the chieftain leaped, thrusting out with his knife. Michael twisted to bring up his sword and the horse staggered, swinging around so his body was exposed. The knife sank into his side where his armor laced over his ribs.

"Michael!"

Aram's shout was lost in the screams around him as the horse lost its balance and toppled backward into the ravine, carrying his brother and the warrior, still holding onto the knife, with it. He whirled to fend away another attack.

And then, as abruptly as it had begun, the battle was over.

There were more Misazula bodies upon the ground than there were those of Michael's men, or of Enzi's and the others. When it was evident the battle was lost, those surviving the fight decided living in shame by fleeing was better than dying. They ran through the trees as fast as they could, loincloths fluttering.

"Shall we go after them?" Aram asked.

Horem shook his head, wiping a bloody hand across an equally gore-smeared face. "My people are avenged. Let those cowards live and think themselves lucky to have escaped."

He smiled, teeth white in all that red, and looked around at an exhausted Enzi, whose sword arm was badly slashed and bleeding.

"Thank you, Friends of Michael." He raised his voice so all could hear. "Thank all of you for your help." As he spoke, Aram, hand clutching his shoulder, headed for the cliff. "Aram, where are you going?"

When Aram didn't answer, Horem ran after him. He caught up with him at the cliff's-edge. Below, they could see the horse's body…and what had happened.

Michael had leaped free as the horse fell, landing beside it on a narrow ledge some twenty feet above the rushing river. Both the horse and the Misazula warrior had died in the fall, their bodies twisted together, but Michael had managed to crawl a few feet away before succumbing. He lay face down in a puddle of blood slowly soaking into the dirt.

"I'm sorry." Horem put a hand on Aram's arm.

"What in the Lord's Name will I tell Senset?" was all Aram said. He was trembling, blinking to keep back his tears.

Michael…it can't be.

"That her husband died as a warrior should. Bravely." Horem answered. "As we all expect to."

Pulling away, Aram stepped over the edge onto the sheer slope. Horem reached to stop him.

"Wait, what are you doing?"

"I can't leave him for scavengers." Aram started down the slope.

The soil was soft and pebbly, giving under his sandals. He sank to one ankle and slid several feet, wavering with arms upraised to keep his balance and grunting with pain as the movement pulled against the wound in his shoulder.

Again, Horem reached out to pull him back.

"You can't go down that. The slope's too soft and that ledge looks none too steady. Leave his body, Aram. His soul's gone. It doesn't matter what happens to his corpse. We'll give Michael his honor with the others."

"I won't leave my brother here." Aram pulled away, his gesture making him slide another foot. More fire slashed through his shoulder.

"You'll never be able to get his body back alone," Horem protested. He started to follow, then hesitated as he saw the rocks dislodged by Aram's movements rolling toward the bodies, making the ledge tremble. "That shelf won't hold two of us."

Aram didn't answer, just continued sliding to where the bodies lay. He bent to touch his brother's body, pressing a hand against his neck. He felt no pulse, nothing to show life still moved inside him. Falling to his knees, he rolled Michael's body onto its back. There was an answering tremble of the rock shelf as he very carefully pulled him into his arms. Sliding his hand through the knife tear in the armor, he touched Michael's chest.

No heartbeat. Nothing. His hand came away bloody. "Oh, Merciful God, Michael…"

Bowing his head, Aram hugged his brother's corpse,

his own blood mingling with that on the torn armor as he sobbed softly, tears spattering the golden mask. He brushed a hand across his face, slinging away the tears as he stared at the mask.

"At least now you're free of the curse, my brother." Frantically, he worked the buckles holding the mask in place. "I won't let you stand before our God wearing *this.*"

With a jerk, he pulled the mask free, baring Michael's face. For one moment, Aram stared at his brother, looking at the face he'd never seen in all their twenty-four years of life together. It was the same as he saw in the beaten metal mirror when he shaved each morning, the face reflected in water when he bathed, with subtle differences.

Mighty Lord, he does *look like me.*

In a spasm of grief, he struck the mask against the ground.

And now I'll succeed you as king, Brother, but I won't have to wear this mask. Because I don't carry the curse. Why did this happen? Why has the Lord taken you from me...from Senset? Before God, how will I tell her...or our people...that their king is dead?

He pounded his fist into the dirt. "God help me, how can I do it?"

There was an answering tremor beneath him as his movements caused the shelf to shudder. A crack appeared in the ledge, running from a point where it hung over the river. Aggravated by Aram's blows, it widened, and the ground continued shaking as the ledge separated, the crack going under the horse's body to where Aram knelt.

The ledge crumbled.

Aram jumped to his feet, dragging Michael backward, but as the ledge fell away, the weight of Michael's body pulled it from his arms. As it tumbled into the river below, the horse's body followed, and Aram could do nothing but watch as his brother's body struck the water, disappeared into it, then surfaced and was swept away by the foaming current.

The ledge continued to shake, more falling away. The Misazula warrior's corpse joined the others in the water. Aram scrambled out of the way, clambering back up the slope on hands and knees, scrabbling in the soft soil until he reached the top.

"You were lucky." Horem caught his bloody hand, pulling him to safety. "You might've fallen with them."

Lucky? Aram didn't answer. At that moment, he considered himself the most unfortunate man in the entire world.

Chapter 29

In a rain of dirt and stone, Michael's body and the horse's plunged into the river, sending spume into the air. The animal's heavier body immediately sank to the bottom, while Michael's was thrown back to the surface and swept downstream by the surge of current. Aram's cry of despair was lost in the splash of the Misazula chieftain's corpse when it tumbled after them, then swirled and followed his brother's body in the rushing torrent.

They were swept away from the broken cliff, downward past more overhanging ledges and sheer drops. A violent eddy spun both bodies, flinging them outward and sending them spilling over a waterfall into a wide pool trickling into a slower-moving stream where fallen logs and leaves floated, with cattails and reeds growing near the shore. The water was quiet, almost stagnant, scum and tiny water plants mingling on its surface.

Disturbed by the gentle undercurrent, the two bodies drifted slowly toward the bank. An uprooted palm tree lay half-plunged into the river, its branches wafting back and forth in the moving water. The current brought them nearer, the palm's fronds entangling in the water soaked animal skin cloak tied over Michael's shoulders. Guided by the water, his body was soon securely enmeshed in the palm's embrace, the animal skin washing forward so it covered his head and shoulders and was all that was visible.

The chieftain's body was also snared, though nearer the palm's top. It wavered back and forth as the current sloshed around it with a lapping gurgle.

From the opposite bank, something slithered into the water. A thing appearing as a floating log opened yellow eyes, becoming the scaly body of a crocodile. Another joined it and the two river monsters aimed themselves for the chieftain's corpse.

Gracefully, they swam closer.

Without a sound, one of the crocodiles sank. A moment later, the chieftain's body was jerked from the palm's clutches, disappearing beneath the surface with a bare ripple. The second creature submerged also, appearing moments later a few feet away, an arm smeared with yellow symbols dangling from its jaws. Blood dripped slowly from the ripped-away limb, floating on the river's surface before spreading and drifting downstream in a crimson-frothed billow. The crocodile raised its head, tossing the arm into the air. It caught the falling limb and gulped it down.

By now, its companion was rising to the surface, the rest of the Misazula's body between its jaws. The other crocodile swam toward it, seizing a floating leg. The second creature tried to swim away. For a moment, there was a horrendous tug-of-war as each tried to wrest away what the other's mouth had claimed.

They were so enmeshed in their struggle, neither heard soft footsteps sounding from the bank. On a well-worn path leading to the river's edge, an old woman appeared. Dressed in a woven palm fiber shift and carrying a water pitcher, she immediately saw the matted animal hide caught in the palm tree.

"Gods above! What's this?" Startled, she stared, her leathery old face screwed into a scowl. "What poor creature's been drowned?"

The wild thrashing in the water pulled her attention away. Seeing the two monsters fighting over parts of another corpse, she dropped the pitcher and dug quietly into the pouch slung by a wide belt over her shoulder.

"You aren't going to take this one, you *mamba* devils. Even if it is some poor animal." Taking a small jug from the pouch, she shook its contents—a dark gray powder—onto her palm. She flung the powder onto the water near Michael's body, watching with satisfaction as it clumped on the surface, then spread in a wide circle around him. "You got the hunter, but you won't get his poor dog. One sacrifice a day to you is enough."

As the powder floated nearer, the crocodiles ceased their struggles. One swam toward the opposite shore. The other followed, keeping as far ahead of the oncoming gray scum as possible. They lumbered onto the bank, one dragging the chieftain's corpse that still dangled from his jaws. He dropped it, issued a threatening sound somewhere between a hiss and a growl. The first answered with a soft grunt and shambled away.

With a satisfied nod, the old woman raised her skirts, tucking them into her waistband. Approaching the bank, she cautiously waded into the water, muttering to herself.

"Damned lizards. Eat anything. First the hunter…probably even swallowed his spear…what's a Misazula doing hunting, anyway?" She'd seen the markings on the body, recognizing them as from the tribe currently terrorizing the countryside. "Isn't it enough they're killing us all? And what they don't kill, the river monsters do. Come here, you poor creature."

She reached for the water-logged, matted pelt. Grasping a handful of wet fur, she jerked it out of the tree's grasp. The body rolled over in the water and the old woman staggered backward, splashing and waving her arms. Nearly losing her balance, she stared at the pale face, scratched and bleeding from contact with the tree's jagged bark.

"Merciful gods of the river! It's a man."

****

"How can I do it? How can I tell my people they no longer have a king?"

It was momentary confusion, with men milling about shouting orders while others ran to obey. Some rounded up the horses, preparing a makeshift rope corral. Others pitched tents. The physicians they'd brought with them tended the wounded in a cleared area where sleeping bags were spread on the ground to hold those recovering. A few feet away, blanket-covered mounds silently testified to the casualties.

At the top of the cliff, away from the camp, Aram and Horem sat on stools, watching the hurried movements. Thus far, no one had missed them or asked where they—or Michael—were, and Aram agonized over what would happen when someone found out.

"Though I had so short a time to know him, I saw Michael was a brave man." Horem's voice trembled at the injustice of death. "He probably expected to die in battle, as does anyone who protects his people, but..." He paused, then burst out, "Bodies are to be recovered, to take home so we may bury them properly...they aren't

267

to become food for river-dwellers. Is there no way we can find his corpse and return it for your people to give the homage it deserves?"

"It's probably washed far downstream by now." Aram's voice echoed Horem's despair. "I agree. It isn't a proper ending for a king, but… Neither was being burned in a mass grave." His eyes met the Ægysian's sardonically. "As you said, Brother of my Brother, rituals can come later. If you can give up your father to the fire, then I may give up my brother to the river. Let Michael join your people in the Afterlife. For now…"

Shaking his head, he fell silent.

****

Once away from the water's buoyancy, the body was much more difficult to move. Somehow the old woman managed to drag it far enough from the river's edge to be safe. Besides, she was confident the gray powder would keep the crocodiles at bay.

"Who are you?" she asked aloud as she knelt beside the sodden body, studying the scratched and dirtied face. "Why were you with a Misazula? Did you fight with him…or against him?"

She'd heard the battle, had cowered in her hut, hoping whoever was the victor wouldn't decide to come downstream. Her people had already fled before the Misazula, but she, being old and alone, was left behind.

"No matter now. I've gotten you out of the river. Let's see if I need to get any of the river out of you."

Leaning over the lax lips, she pressed an ear against them, listening with relief to the barely audible hiss of breath. She nodded, seized one arm, and tugged, rolling him onto his face. Then, she began to pound his back under his shoulder blades, the *thumps* of her fists loud in

268

the silence.

Other than to give under the blows dealt it, the still body didn't move, until… Abruptly, a gasp and a cough was heard, then a ragged inhalation. Catching a shoulder, she hauled him onto his back again, watching the regular rise and fall of his chest with satisfaction. He didn't awake, however, eyes still closed.

"So you didn't drink any river water." The old woman looked back at the crocodiles on the far bank.

They glared back at her as if to say, *We're waiting…we'll come after the rest of our feast soon…*

Shivering slightly under the gaze of those malevolent yellow eyes, she muttered, "I hate those river monsters."

They'd claimed both her husband and her son, as well as others from her village who came to the river for water. *But not this time*. Straightening her shoulders, she scrambled to her feet and untucked her skirt from her waistband.

"You're not getting this one, you devils. I won't let you." Seizing Michael's wrists, she struggled to pull him down the worn footpath away from the water.

****

"You're your brother's heir, aren't you? Until Senset's child is born?" Horem was being practical to cover his own sense of loss for the brother-in-law he'd known only a few weeks. "If it's a daughter…"

"If she has a daughter?" Aram didn't even want to think about that. If Senset had a son, the curse would continue. If she had a daughter, his House would be free. "I'll sit upon the throne and she'll be an honored widow."

"Will you take her to wife? Make her your queen?"

"No." Aram looked away.

If this conversation were taking place shortly after he first met Senset, he might've answered differently, for he'd felt a stirring when he looked at that curious young girl in her nightshift, peering at him through the bars of his cage.

Now…?

He was fond of her, loved her as a brother should, but the thought of taking her to bed and performing the most intimate of acts as her husband… He couldn't. Since there would be a child, there was no need for him to marry his brother's widow so Michael's line would continue.

Besides, he couldn't do that, not with Senset. He'd heard tales of men refusing to do such, spilling their seed rather than create a proxy heir, and of how the Lord sentenced them to eternal fire for their sin. Aram was certain he'd be joining them in everlasting punishment if he were forced to make love to his sister-in-law.

"I couldn't. It'd be adultery. Senset loved no one but Michael. She belongs to him. Forever."

He broke off with a stifled gasp. His shoulder was paining him, fire coursing through it in deep, pulsing flames, making it difficult to concentrate.

"I have to think how to tell my family Michael's dead…how my people are going to react. Everyone loved my brother, and he was a good king. As for my becoming king…" He was still holding the golden mask. He held it up, looking at it. "At least I won't have to wear this, though I'd gladly do so if it would bring Michael back. They're going to be lost without him to guide them. If only I'd been killed instead…"

His voice trailed away and for several moments,

Aram was silent. He remembered how Michael had told him the people mourned when they learned he'd been captured, how their mother cried because she believed him as good as dead since he was taken prisoner. He was certain everyone's grief would be a thousandfold more if they knew their king had died…

He continued to stare at the mask, but now he wasn't seeing it. Now, he was on the balcony outside his mother's apartments.

****

It was on his second day back in Beth-Gurion, after riding into the city on the mule, both of them dusty, thirsty, and exhausted. His wound tended by Elijah, he reveled in the joy everyone showed at his safe return from the Ægysian dungeon, that the king's brother had escaped certain death. That was when he heard Rebekah's voice raised in grief.

"Truly the Lord will punishment me, for I'm a terrible mother."

Aram wasn't one to eavesdrop, but in this case, Rebekah's vehement statement made him stop. What could his mother have done to make her say such a thing?

"Mother, what do you mean?" Apparently, Meryam wondered, also.

"I swear, my daughter, I tried not to show favoritism between my eldest sons, though one would become my king."

Aram leaned against the wall outside the open window. At that angle, he could see into the apartment, where Rebekah sat on a couch, his sister Meryam beside her. His mother had seized Meryam's hands, squeezing them tightly as if to convince her she was speaking the truth.

"Mother, I know this. You've never shown partiality to Michael over Aram," Meryam assured her.

"That's just it. *I have*," Rebekah protested. "In my mind, in my heart, if not in my actions, Michael has always been my favorite." She was near to babbling, as if recounting her sins against Aram, accusing herself. "I cringed with fear whenever he was injured as a child, and when he became a man and made war, I prayed fervently for his safety… When he returned, telling me Aram was captured, when he gave up his brother for dead…Yahweh forgive me…I rejoiced."

Rebekah jerked her hands from her daughter's, pressing them to her face.

"I was glad it was Aram and not Michael who was lost…" She began to sob, deep wracking sounds seeming to tear themselves from her heart. "How could I think such? That I would feel joy a child of my body was dead if it meant his brother was alive?"

Meryam didn't answer; Aram could see his sister staring at their mother in disbelief. He felt his own hands clench into fists at this confession. *Truly she hid it well*, he thought. He remembered how joyful she'd appeared when told he'd returned, how she'd personally fetched Elijah to treat his wounds and stayed behind afterward, holding his hand until the soporific the physician gave him took effect.

Were the tears she shed then more of shame than happiness? He'd never thought about his mother loving one of them more than the other. He had always believed her deference to his brother was merely because he was their father's heir, destined to carry the Curse.

It seemed only natural.

"I thanked the Lord Michael was spared." Rebekah

lifted her head, wiping at her eyes. "Because I remembered the Scriptures: *For when the beloved King is lost, there will be gnashing of teeth and beating of breasts and a cry of sorrow will go throughout the land. The people will mourn; they will be lost though his Brother reigns in his stead. Like sheep without a shepherd, they will not obey the new master but will mill in confusion and grief and the throne will topple and the kingdom crumble because of their love for him who is no more...*" She took a deep breath. "So I rejoiced that the younger of my sons perished and his brother lived, and surely God will punish me for that."

"That Scripture was written during the reign of Malachi's son." Practical Meryam spoke up, trying to reason Rebekah out of her fear. "It's centuries old. It could refer to any king..."

"The Lord gives the gift of prophecy to some to warn others of the future. Do you dare not believe? If something happens to Michael, the kingdom will fall. God has said so. He should never place himself in harm's way. Michael must survive to die in his bed of old age with his grandchildren and great-grandchildren around him."

Aram couldn't bear to hear any more, didn't want his mother mentally flailing herself like that.

It's only right that you wish our king unharmed, Mother. Even I understand and don't fault you for it.

No matter what, he loved his brother and would readily die to protect him. He wanted to say that to her but didn't dare let her know he'd heard her confession, for that would shame her more. Quickly, he hurried away to a quiet spot on the terrace where he sat on one of the stone benches and thought of what she'd said...

****

In the long scheme of things, Michael was more important than he. Aram had known it all along, though it was never blatantly pointed out to anyone. They both simply accepted everyone's worry as concern for any soldier preparing to fight, each ignoring how important Michael was, how he should never be placed in such jeopardy.

Now I must return and say to them those words they've feared to hear…and the Scriptures will come to pass…

Abruptly, he knew what had to be done.

****

The old woman dragged Michael as far as the entrance to her hut, the deep marks his body made in the footpath revealing their wavering course from the river. When she stopped, puffing and panting to regain her breath, it was only for a few moments before renewing her efforts. Eventually, the inert body lay inside the hut, rolled onto her sleep mat set to one side of the doorway.

"Now." Sitting back on her heels, she pulled a short knife from her waistband. "Let's get these animal skins off you. Why do you wear the hide of *simba*, anyway?"

Still talking, she deftly inserted the tip of the knife under one of the fur gauntlets, and sliced it apart.

"With claws still in place, too. Did you think the lion would give you its fierceness?"

She tossed away the cut-up pieces, untying the hide from around his neck. It landed atop the others, a sodden pile soaking into the hut's pounded dirt floor. With the cape out of the way, the cut in his leather chestplate was visible, as was the blood still leaking through it.

"What's this? You were stabbed? So you and the

Misazula weren't allies? Good." She cut through the strings holding his armor together, fingers probing into the wound. "Hm. Shallow enough. I don't think it'll kill you. But I'd better bathe away the river's scum, else you may get an infection because of it."

Laying aside the knife, she touched his face, fingers exploring the bruises and torn skin on his forehead and temple, frowning at the depression on his cheeks where the mask had rested for so many years. At the back of his head, hidden in the thick hair, she found another cut, this one deep. Her fingers came away smeared with blood. She reached for the knife again, to cut away Michael's tunic.

"Need to get you as clean as possible... Oh, damn, I need my pitcher!"

Leaping to her feet, she hobbled from the hut and back to the river, retrieved the pitcher, and scooped up enough water to fill it. Back inside again, she poured the water through a piece of palm cloth and into a large copper kettle, straining out the dirt and filth from the river, then set it over the cooking fire in the yard.

While the water boiled, she cut away the rest of Michael's clothing, adding it to the wet mass in the doorway. When the water was ready, she let it cool, poured it into a large basin, took a clean piece of newly woven cloth and dipped it into the water. Wringing out the cloth, she began to wash the wound.

Chapter 30

Aram was quiet for so long, Horem finally asked, "Are you all right? Your shoulder…"

"I'm fine." Aram raised his head, looking at Horem. The prince was startled when he smiled.

"I know what I must do, Horem."

"What do you mean?"

"It's good we're out of sight of the others."

Taking a deep breath, Aram placed the mask against his face. It wasn't difficult to fasten the buckles. They slid easily into the grooves worn in the leather. He closed both, then dropped his hands.

"What are you doing?"

"I'm taking Michael's place." He looked up at Horem, who'd gotten to his feet and was staring at him. "My people can more easily lose the general of the king's army than they can their king, and Senset won't miss a brother-in-law half as much as she will her husband."

"Aram, that's insane." Horem caught his shoulders, staring into the eyes looking out of the golden mask.

His hands tightened as if he was going to shake him. When Aram grimaced, he let him go.

"How's that going to help? You might be able to fool the people, even your family, perhaps, but not Senset. Besides, you'll still have to…"

"No, I won't," Aram interrupted. He wasn't going to let Horem say it. "I'll proclaim mourning for my brother's death to take me from her bed. By the time it's finished, she'll be close to giving birth. I'll stay away because of that. Once the baby's born…"

He took a deep breath.

"If it's a son, I'll tell her Michael's dead, and continue my charade until the boy's old enough to rule. Then I'll abdicate in his favor. If she has a daughter…"

"You'll be expected to sire another child," Horem argued. "And another, until you get a son for the throne."

"I'll never touch Senset," Aram's reply was so positive Horem shook his head. "There's a purification period after the child's born. During that time, I'll find some way to keep from going to her bed. Permanently."

"This is a fool's act, Aram, and I see nothing good coming from it."

"Do you intend to denounce me?" Aram challenged. He got to his feet, waving a hand at the tents and the moving men at the other end of the clearing. "Go ahead, tell them I'm not really Michael. That *his* dead body and not mine was washed away when the cliff fell into the river. If a man saying he's their king calls you liar, who do you think they'll believe? They won't dare unmask me because of the curse. Even if they did, since we're twins, how can they say which I am?"

"I won't betray you if you truly believe this is best for everyone." Horem shook his head in a defeated gesture, as he realized argument would do no good.

"I do." Aram looked toward the clearing and back at Horem. Brushing a hand over his eyes in a formal gesture of grief, he made his next words a formal declaration. "My brother Aram died today as a warrior should, fighting to help an ally. Come, Horem, let's tell the others and mourn him."

"Aram was truly a courageous man." Swallowing loudly, Horem stepped to Aram's side and caught his arm as he stumbled. "And you, my brother. You must have that shoulder wound looked after."

Chapter 31

The ride back to Beth-Gurion was a slow and sad one. A rider had been sent ahead to notify the sentries of their approach, but no one seemed in a hurry to reach the city.

As soon as they were notified of their general's death, all Michael's men braved the steep slope to the river. While several kept watch for crocodiles, spears at the ready, the others dipped their hands in the water, then scooped up handfuls of dirt, and smeared their faces with mud, mourning their fallen comrades as well as their lost commander.

In sympathy, the others did the same.

It took longer to return than it had to leave, their riders' grief slowing the horses' hooves. After all, there was no urgency now, no lives to save. Aram didn't order them to move faster. Truly, he had no desire to get to Beth-Gurion any sooner than was necessary, for he needed time to think—of what he was going to say to his mother and his brothers—and to pray, asking Yahweh to forgive him his deception and aid him in bringing it about.

At the forking road leading into the city as well as to points east and north, their allies' troops took leave of them, the leaders staying behind with an accompaniment of a dozen men to continue on to Beth-Gurion for Aram's funeral.

Teetering now on the edge of fever, Aram thanked them all for this last gesture of homage before leading the way to the city. His right arm was in a sling, shoulder heavily bandaged under his armor, white strips showing through the neck and armhole of the leather breastplate. In spite of the physician's ministrations, the wound continued to open, and he'd had to stop many times for the bindings to be changed. Even now, blood spotted the skirt of his tunic, and the pain when he moved his arm was heavy.

Beside him, Horem said, "Only a few more miles. Then the real grief begins."

Aram didn't answer, simply turned his horse's head toward the road leading home.

****

The people rejoiced to see them, flinging flowers intermingled with cheers, as was their customary greeting to their returning king. Eventually, the silent attitude of the soldiers and their lack of response, as well as the significance of their mud-besmirched faces sank in, and the joyous calls became more subdued. A murmur swept through the crowd, loud enough for those on horseback to hear.

"Where's the General? Where's General Aram?"

The question swirled around the marching men, an insect humming above the cries of welcome, making Aram want to wheel his horse and ride back into the desert.

Most Holy God, help me.

In the palace courtyard, Adonijah waited as always.

Nothing's changed, Aram mused sadly. *The chief advisor waits to greet us, the king's family stands beside him…*

Horem's horse snorted and Aram looked over at him.

Before, Michael returned from war with the Ægysians. Now an Ægysian rides with us and we return without our king...and no one will know.

Senset was absent, her condition preventing her from greeting her returning husband.

Thank the Lord, was Aram's only thought as he saw his mother and then turned away, as if he couldn't bear to look at her.

He was so tired, almost exhausted. Though the doctor had bound it tightly the last time, packing the wound with fresh herbs, his shoulder had hurt for a good part of the journey, the pain growing to such a persistent burning that every step the horse took brought a jolt of agony, and with it the heat of illness rushing through his blood.

Merciful God, don't let an infection be starting. I mustn't become incapacitated. Beth-Gurion has to have a king standing on his feet.

He reined in his horse, waiting a moment before sliding from its back. He nearly fell; the moment his feet touched the ground, his knees threatened to buckle. Only his grip on the pommel of the saddle kept him upright. He clung there, forehead resting against the blanket-covered leather.

"You're hurt." Rebekah cried, running to him. "Michael, where's Aram?"

Aram raised his head and stepped away from the horse. He could feel the blood leaving his face, briefly was thankful for the mask, though nothing was going to prevent them from seeing how his legs trembled. He wasn't certain he could stay on his feet much longer and wished he might avoid this meeting with his mother until he was recovered. Unfortunately, she'd already noticed her other son's absence and nothing short of his dramatically collapsing at her feet was going to delay what was coming.

"Mother…"

With his uninjured hand, he caught hers and brought it shakily to his lips. Behind him, he heard Horem step closer and knew the prince had seen how weak he was and was readying himself to catch his body if he fell.

Rebekah looked up at him, lips trembling as if she knew what he was going to say. He forced himself to get on with it, made that damned gesture of bereavement for all to see and spoke loudly enough for the others to hear.

"Once again, I regret to be the one bringing you grief…"

He didn't go on, didn't get the chance.

"No…"

Slowly, quietly, she began to cry.

Aram put his good arm around her, crushing her against the dried blood, dirt, and mud on his battle-worn chestplate, feeling the bandages soak up her tears as Rebekah wept against his shoulder.

"My son…my son…why?"

Behind her, the others, seeing her tears, looked to Horem, reacting to his words.

"The General was slain… We were unable to recover his body."

"*Barukh atah Adonai Eloheinu melekh ha'olam, dayan ha-emet.*"

Blessed are You, Lord, our God, King of the universe, the True Judge.

Adonijah chanted the traditional response to the

news of a death, intoning the blessing. The cries of bereavement, the ritual gestures of mourning began, and from somewhere came a barely heard whisper, *Thank Yahweh it wasn't our king...*

More people thinking as Rebekah did? Aram hugged his mother and wondered if he'd really heard those words.

****

Will he never awaken?

It had been three days now since the old woman had rescued the unconscious man from the fate of being a crocodile's feast. Three days since she'd cut away water-soaked clothing and bathed the blood and dirt from his face and body. The river had washed away most of the blood from the stab wound in his ribs, and she'd cleansed it and rubbed a fragment of bloodstone over the slashed flesh to stop the bleeding. Then she'd packed the wound with herbs known to have healing properties preventing infection.

Afterward, she covered him with a soft blanket and sat back to wait, beginning a chant to her gods to keep bad spirits away and let him live. Other than to occasionally dip a cloth in water and press it to his lips, or dampen his face and chest as his skin went dry and hot from fever, she didn't leave his side, continuing to pray for the life of the stranger who'd come into her own life so dramatically.

****

After he'd relinquished his mother to Meryam's care and she'd been escorted to her suite and Elijah called for, Aram turned to a more emotional and even less pleasing chore.

Telling Senset.

Explaining to Adonjah and his brothers, "I'll speak with you on this later. Now I must inform my wife of my safe return. Please see that Horem's given water for bathing, as well as food and drink."

He hurried into the palace, leaving Horem speaking to them, the Ægysian's words following Aram down the corridor.

"My heart weeps at the grief I've caused your House…"

Chapter 32

The halls were strangely silent, as if the very walls knew their king had died. Aram swore he could hear whispers echoing after the scuff of his sandals on the marble floors...

Liar... false king... do you think you'll fool anyone?

He walked faster, until he was nearly running. Most would think him simply eager to see his wife again. None could know he was running from his conscience and the accusations he imagined he heard.

At Senset's door, he paused, knocking out of habit, striking the door with a visitor's fist, requesting entrance. When Ororo's call came, "Who disturbs my mistress's rest?" he forced his answer.

"Her husband. May I enter?"

The door was opened, the slave's surprised face peering at him. "My lord, you needn't ask. My mistress eagerly awaits you."

She flung open the door, stepping back. As he hesitated one more instant, then forced himself to step across the threshold with authority, she moved into the corridor. When the door closed, he felt as he had the day they'd thrown him into that cage in Aseti-Ra's dungeon.

Trapped.

"Michael?" Senset called to him from the bedroom.

Though his steps were firm as he went to her, his mind screamed, *This is wrong... you don't belong here…it isn't right for you to be in your sister-in-law's bedchamber…*

Forcing himself through the door and to the bed, he looked down at her. "I've come back to you, my…wife." He prayed she didn't hear that slight hesitation.

She'd just awakened, was sleepy-eyed and still somnolent, hair mussed and tossed about the shoulders of the sleeping rail she wore. He wanted to brush the hair back from her shoulders, kiss her cheek, and place his head on her breast and beg her forgiveness for the masquerade he was about to perpetrate on her.

"Michael."

The smile she turned on him held sunshine and warmth and love, and it stayed any words he might have said. Made him mute in its happiness. And even more guilty.

"My husband, welcome home."

She held out a hand. Automatically, he took it, steadying her as she pulled herself to her feet. She smoothed the robe about her and raised her arms to hug him.

"Don't." He put up a detaining hand. "I'm covered with battle dirt and travel dust."

"It doesn't matter." She put her arms around him.

He nearly recoiled as he felt the curve of her belly like a small but solid barrier between them. Taking a normal step backward, he pushed her away but kept his arm around her shoulders. Gently, he kissed her forehead.

"You were asleep. Is everything well with you? And the child?" He hoped that was the proper thing for a husband and father-to-be to ask.

"We're both fine." Her hand touched the little

mound. She looked up at him, this time throwing herself into his arms. "Oh, Michael, I'm so glad you're back. Unharmed."

"Not exactly unharmed."

He winced as he raised his arm to hug her, and it was then she saw the bandages. He'd begun bleeding again—from raising his arm, no doubt—and she gave an exclamation of dismay at the fresh spots on his tunic skirt.

"I'm all right," he assured her, wanting to get the rest of the unpleasant business said and done. "It's not a serious wound."

"Thank God for that." She brushed a hand over the binding, jerking it away when he forced a second false flinch. "And my brother? He's unharmed, also? The soldiers arrived with Xena and the others. They'll need to be notified. Sapair's been anxious since he got here, worrying about his father. "

"Horem's fine," Aram said. "Untouched. I imagine he's even now assuring his son of his well-being."

I left Horem in the courtyard. Walked away and left him to his own devices. A king wouldn't have done that. How can I ever keep up this charade?

"Senset…"

"I'll see him later then…and Aram, too. They told me about my parents. Michael, I can't believe it. I know I should mourn, but I don't feel anything. Nothing except hollowness inside. I thought to delay my mourning until you returned. I don't know if that's proper but… I should get dressed," she went on. "Did you send Ororo away? Oh, Michael, who'll help me get dressed? Unless…"

It seemed to him she was babbling, as if words would stave off the desolation she should be feeling at loss of her parents. She untied the cords at the neck of the night rail.

"I know I should've been more prepared, as soon as we were told the sentries had been notified, but I was so tired… Having a baby's a heavy burden in more ways than one. Are you hungry? Don't worry, there'll be a celebration tonight in your honor, and everyone'll be there… you and Horem and Aram can tell us how you routed the Misazula and slew them."

"Senset…"

"Sapair says he wants to live here." Again, she interrupted, as if now that her husband was back, she was determined to say all the things she'd thought of while he was gone.

She had the robe-front open, turning to look back at him. Aram averted his eyes from that pale, rounded bosom. He'd swear it was larger than he remembered, swelling in preparation for the child's birth…*my brother's child*, he reminded himself.

"I told him he'd have to discuss that with his father. Do you suppose Horem will want to go back to Usaset? From what Xena told me, there's no one left and the city was almost destroyed in the attack and Horem…did he really order it burn—"

"Senset!"

The harshness of his voice made her stop, staring at him, as if not believing her beloved husband had raised his voice to her. By the stiffness of his posture and the way he looked away, she sensed something more was wrong.

"What…what is it, Michael?"

"Senset…Aram…" A lump lodged in his throat. He couldn't say it.

Mighty Yahweh, give me strength. Don't let me give myself away.

He swallowed, forced the lump down, felt a desire to gag, and whispered, "Senset, A-Aram's dead."

Now, she *did* stare. Like a child being told something unbelievable, something she'd never expected. "But...how can he be... It isn't so... Don't joke about such a thing, my husband."

"I'm not joking. He..." That was as far as he got.

Her face twisted, mouth opening in an ugly square. The tears splashed down her cheeks as Senset began to sob, burrowing her face against his chest.

Unmindful of the dirt and mud, Aram held her tightly, letting her cry and feeling every tear and tremor as it shook and trembled through her. No mouthed responses now. She probably didn't even know what their bereavement practices involved, he realized. All he knew was that, in that moment, he held a woman needing comfort.

"Shh, little one...oh, Senset..." They stood that way for several minutes, until he picked her up and walked back to the bed. "You should lie down. I've shocked you."

"No more than I'm already shocked." She didn't argue as he placed her on the bed but clung to his hand when he started to move away. "Please, don't leave me. Hold me, Michael."

Gingerly, he sat on the bed, hoping she'd mistake his hesitancy for his own inner turmoil at his grief.

She pressed her face against his chestplate. He felt the dried mud break away, falling between them onto the bed.

"How did it happen?" she asked into the stained

leather.

"We don't need to speak of that now. Later, when things are quieter."

"Very well."

He was relieved she didn't argue.

She looked up at him, face smudged from contact with his filth. "Tonight, when you come to me…"

"I…I won't be doing that, m-my wife." Gently, he brushed fingers against her cheek, wiping away the dust as he forced himself to speak that word. Tried to make it sound as if he'd said it many times before and it wasn't one strange and new to his tongue.

"Why not?"

In the question, he heard others unsaid. *I need you now more than ever, to calm me in my grief, and you'd abandon me?*

"Michael, you've come back from war safe but you won't come to me?"

"My brother's dead, wife. I must mourn. Indeed, the entire kingdom must grieve the loss of their general, their protector, the leader of my army…my family has lost a son, and I my brother, and because Aram was my twin, I've also lost part of myself."

He stood and turned away, feeling his excuses were lame and insincere, though he wanted to shriek out his pain and beat his breast with grief and shame.

"We must all lament Aram in deepest bereavement…the House of Gurion will be draped in black…and we'll not touch again until our mourning's over."

Without giving Senset any time to protest, he spun and walked out… *"Escaped" would be a better word,* he thought, and marveled at the vast rush of relief sweeping through him once the door to the suite swung shut.

Horem was waiting for him outside the door. He'd removed his dirtied armor and bathed and was now wearing Habiru robes. Aram was startled to see that the newly-grown shadow of hair on his head, shaven by one of the palace barbers before they left Beth-Gurion, had been smeared with oil so the short bristles were forced into a thin cap.

"You intend to let your hair grow?" It seemed such a mundane subject on such a sad occasion.

"Adonijah tells me a man may neither shave nor cut his hair while mourning." His answer was quiet. "To all intents and purposes, I'm Habiru now, my brother, though I don't follow the tenets of your One God. Do you think He'll consider me a hypocrite if I mourn as Habiru without believing in Him as yet?"

He asked the question in complete earnestness.

"A man who mourns with his friends can never be considered a hypocrite, Horem. Yahweh sees into a man's heart and knows when to judge and when not."

Horem nodded and fell into step as Aram went down the corridor. As they passed one of the high, unshuttered windows, he heard the cry welling up from the city like a wind sweeping from one end of Beth-Gurion to the other. It meant word was spreading of General Aram's death, and the people were beginning their own mourning.

A weeping and a gnashing of teeth and cries of grief…

Chapter 33

With a sigh, Michael turned his head and opened his eyes. The first thing he saw was a bit of blue sky directly above him, sunbeams shining through a hole in a thatched roof. The sun was so bright, it dazzled his eyes, making him blink.

His face felt odd, his head light, as if a heavy weight had been taken from it.

Surely if I move, it may float off my neck.

He forced himself to lie still, when he wanted to roll over and get to his feet. His skin was so warm, as if the sun shone directly upon it, not blocked by the heavy shield of the mask.

The mask…

He put up one hand, touching warm flesh instead of cold, heavy metal.

"My mask! Where's my mask?"

"What?"

He started as the old woman jerked awake, scrambling from where she'd been slumped against the wall in exhaustion after sitting beside his unconscious body for so long.

"Be calm, my son. You've been ill."

Michael twisted to face her.

"Why did you take off my mask?" Hands flailed as he tried to push himself off the pallet.

"You weren't wearing a mask when I pulled you

from the river."

"Find it. You mustn't see my face." Spreading his fingers, he covered his face with his hands.

"Why would you want to hide that handsome face behind a mask, *mto farisi*?" She pushed him back onto the folded blankets.

"You think I'm handsome?" He stopped struggling, looking at her through his splayed fingers, green eyes staring into her rheumy mud-colored ones.

The thought flashed through his mind: *Why do I wish to hide my face?* He had no answer, but was certain it should be covered before the world.

"Like one of the gods, my son..." she answered, with complete sincerity. "Truly, my young river horse, you're one of the most handsome men I've ever seen."

"You call me *son.*" He seized on that one word, letting it drive other, more confusing thoughts away. "Are you my mother?"

"The gods bless you, no." She managed a dry croak of a chuckle, pulling his hands away from his face so he could see hers grasping them, how dark they were against his paler, though tanned, flesh. "Can't you see we're not the same color?"

"Why was I in a river?"

"That I can't say. There was another body, a Misazula," she scowled at the memory. "The *shetani mambas* got him. I pulled you out."

Gently, she released his hands, brushing back the damp hair on his forehead.

"You've been sick quite a while."

"Misazula..." A sudden memory...*a brown arm painted with yellow symbols...a knife flashing out...pain...* "He stabbed me...in the gut... I remember falling…" He shook his head. "And…nothing else." He stared up at her. "I-if you're not my mother, who are you?"

"My name's UmRawa. What's your name, *mto farisi*?"

"My name? I'm…" He looked panic-stricken. "I-I don't know." One hand went to his head, wincing as he touched one of the bruises on his forehead. "Why don't I remember?"

It was a soft but fierce cry of frustration and approaching fear.

"Don't let it worry you, *mto farisi*," she soothed. "You hit your head, probably when you fell. No doubt that knocked your name right out of your mind. It'll come back to you." She nodded as if to affirm what she was saying. "After you rest a while."

"Rest…yes…I'm so tired…" Muttering, Michael closed his eyes. "So…tired…"

As he fell silent, UmRawa nodded with satisfaction. "Rest, my young river horse, my man without a name. I'll get supper ready. I think next time when you wake, you'll be hungry."

****

"There's already a problem, as far as the interment's concerned." Aram was explaining to Senset the intricacies of a Habiru funeral ceremony.

"In what way?" Her question was subdued, almost listless, as if she didn't care one way or another but was simply replying to what he said because it was the duty of a wife to show she was attentive when her husband spoke.

They were at the evening meal.

Aram was aware Michael always ate with Senset,

generally staying with her afterward through the night, and though he didn't intend to carry out that part of his brother's habit, he knew it would arouse suspicion if he avoided her completely, especially since he'd walked so abruptly out of her bedchamber earlier.

Most credited it to his grief over losing his brother, though they still thought it odd a husband wouldn't seek out his wife for comfort when she was also stricken by losing her brother-in-law, as well as her parents.

"There's no body to prepare," he said flatly, trying to hide the tremor in his voice.

At the moment, he wanted nothing more than to seek his own bed, stretch out in its comfort, guzzle down a jugful of the most potent wine, and fall into a drunken, dreamless sleep. Escape for a little while the pain of his wound and this masquerade.

Elijah had re-bound his shoulder, scraping out the herbs and replacing them with more, cautioning Aram to be careful and use his arm as little as possible.

There's a fever starting, my lord. I'll leave a februgia elixir for you to drink before you sleep... He'd wedged some of the herb's blossoms into the wound as he gave his warning.

"We've a very complicated ceremony for preparing our dead for burial, my wife...prayers to be said, bathing and purifying and dressing the corpse...choosing *shomrim* to sit with the body until it's taken for burial..."

"And none of that can be done b-because..." Senset's own voice broke as she finished for him. "Because Aram's body lies at the bottom of that river...or in the belly of one of those river monsters."

At her urging, he'd reluctantly told her what happened, though he exchanged himself for Michael in the story…of the Misazula lunging with his knife…the horse falling over the cliff…the ledge breaking away as he attempted to retrieve his brother's body… It felt so odd to speak of himself as another person.

Senset had listened dry-eyed and hadn't cried since, though occasionally when she spoke her voice sounded full of unshed tears.

"That won't stop you from giving Aram the honor he deserves or prevent him from entering the Afterlife, will it?" Her question was anxious.

"Not in the long run."

No more than it'll prevent your most noble father, or so Horem thinks.

The determined set of his chin told her all she needed to know.

"The Lord will welcome Aram into his Paradise if I have to demand it of Him."

"Michael, don't dare speak such sacrilege." The look she gave him was horrified.

"Don't worry, my wife." He managed a slight laugh to show her he wasn't serious.

Is it improper to joke in the midst of such sadness? Blasphemous, perhaps?

"The Lord God and the House of Gurion have an odd relationship, and I doubt he'll prevent one as brave as my brother from receiving his rewards. And also forgive me my impudence, " he added.

She visibly relaxed.

Aram bowed his head. "For the honor of the deceased, we're delaying the actual burial ritual to allow time for those from the other cities to get here, so they may pay their respects."

Within hours of the announcement of Aram's death,

messengers had been sent to the five other Habiru cities, notifying the leaders of what had happened.

"I've spoken to the priests. Since there's to be no preparation, the ceremonies will begin with the *kevura* itself."

"But if there's no body…"

"There'll be a funeral procession. We'll go to the place of burial and perform the funeral service there. I've had a marker placed where A-Aram's body would lie."

Damn it, got to watch that. I've got to stop stumbling over saying my own name.

He went on as if making a decision. "I don't know of your people's burial customs, but if you wish your father to have a marker also…"

"My father…" She turned her attention back to her plate. "I've barely thought of him. Why is that, Michael? Is it because he's been so far away and out of my sight? Like my brothers and sisters-in-law, and my nieces and nephews? Is that the reason the only one I mourn is Aram?" Her voice trembled. "Am I being an ungrateful child because I feel nothing when I think of my father and mother and the others, but grief claws at me when I think of Aram?"

"Don't worry yourself on that," he urged, thinking frantically for a cause.

I'm no physician. How do I know why the heart grieves for one it loves and not another?

"You were in my brother's company often, so his memory is sharper in your mind. Pain for the others will come when it comes, Senset. And it will, in time."

While he talked, Senset picked at her food, cutting a slice of melon into tiny bits, then pushing them aside, selecting the smallest morsel to nibble on. She'd done the same to the other food on her plate…a portion of mutton, a slice of bread…

"Finish your supper. You haven't eaten much."

"Neither have you," she pointed out, gesturing at his empty place.

The silent servants hadn't even put a platter before him.

"It's the custom for the bereaved to fast during the first two days of their grief."

"Why didn't you say that before?" She dropped her knife, pushing her plate away, and calling out, "Remove this."

Obediently, the slave waiting by the door darted forward, reaching for the plate.

"Leave it," Aram ordered.

The slave wavered, looking from him to Senset, then decided the king was the one to obey. He bowed and returned to his place.

"An exception's made for breeding women. You've yourself and my child to nourish. You'll not fast, wife."

"As you will, my husband." Nodding, Senset, stabbed the knife into one of the melon pieces and brought it to her mouth. "Know this doesn't reflect my grief, however." She chewed as if eating were a duty.

Indeed, it was.

This tastes of ashes and dust…as my parents and my people and Aram are now. I hope Michael's right in saying that my mourning for them will come in its own time.

"No one believes that, Senset." Before he realized it, Aram was out of his chair, coming around the table to take her in his arms. "I most of all."

She pressed against him, face nuzzling his chest as

he fell to his knees beside her chair. Abruptly, she pulled away. "I'm sorry. I know that's unseemly, especially now, but I long for you, my husband."

Aram released her, returning to his seat. He gestured to a slave holding an ornate pitcher.

"Water."

He might fast in his mourning, but he was allowed drink, providing it was non-alcoholic and merely for the purpose of preventing dehydration.

After his goblet was filled and he'd drunk part of it, he set it down, saying, "You may have cause for more longing before this is over."

****

The sun had sunk behind the palms when UmRawa heard faltering footsteps behind her.

She squatted by the cookfire, stirring a stew in her copper kettle. Secure in her knowledge of her ability to heal, she was certain her young visitor would awaken with an appetite, so she'd set about preparing food as soon as he fell asleep, daring to leave him long enough to rummage through one of the baskets in a corner and select some dried tubers.

A quick trip to the traps she'd set at the edges of the forest yielded a young monkey caught and killed. She skinned and filleted it, dropping the thick meat into the pot, then took the bloodied pelt and entrails to the river.

Throwing them as far from the bank as she could, she shouted, "Take that as your tribute, monsters," and scurried back to the hut as they dove into the water.

Seasoned by her herbs and spices, the stew bubbled, sending an appetite-tantalizing smell into the air. UmRawa'd been so intent on her task, she didn't hear movement behind her until those final halting steps.

Startled, she spun on her knees, reaching for the knife at her belt.

"Be calm, UmRawa." Michael took a step backward. He started to raise both hands in the gesture of peace, then decided against it as that let slip the blanket he was pressing against his privates.

"You startled me." She returned the knife to her belt and nodded at the kettle. "I'm preparing supper. Are you hungry?"

"Hungry?" He considered that, as if it were the most important question in the world and his answer equally crucial. "I think I am."

"Then you should return to your bed and lie down." She could see he was wavering on his feet and she didn't want him falling, perhaps into the fire. She didn't believe she could catch him if he began to topple. "I'll bring you a bowl of stew when it's done."

He nodded and turned to go, then hesitated, fumbling with the blanket. "Clothes…I need something to wear…"

"I had to cut away your garments. They're ruined, I'm afraid." She nodded to the pile of fabric and fur by the door.

Turning only his upper body, he glanced over his shoulder. She brightened as she saw his scowl.

"Don't worry. I'll make you new ones, *mto farisi*."

"Why do you call me that?" he asked. "It means *river horse*, doesn't it?"

"Because you came to me out of the river." She laughed, wondering why she was surprised he knew the meaning of the words. *He's speaking my language, isn't he?* "You *do* need a name."

"True, but I don't know if I like that one." He started

to gesture, then grabbed at the blanket again. "Do I look like one of those huge creatures?"

"What would you like to be called?" He was visibly wobbling now, and she was certain in a few moments he would truly collapse. Might even be too weak to walk back into the hut. "You wore a lion's skin. Would you prefer *Simba*?"

"*Simba*..." He looked thoughtful, clutching the blanket tightly, as if it were the only thing keeping him on his feet. "I don't know why, but... For some reason, I think that might be more appropriate."

"Then, get to your bed, Simba, and let old UmRawa return to her cooking."

Nodding, he staggered back to the doorway, belatedly reaching behind him to hold the blanket's corner against his backside. UmRiwa had a glimpse of taut buttocks only a shade paler than his back, muscles playing tightly under his skin as he gained the doorway and disappeared inside.

Ah, gods preserve me...such a handsome boy, and me so old and useless...

****

"What do you mean?" Senset had eaten several cuts of the melon, but she paused now with the final piece halfway to her mouth.

"The *avelut*—the mourning—required by our canons is a week-long bereavement, but a man may mourn longer if he chooses. In view of what my family, Beth-Gurion, and the Habiru in general have lost, I've chosen to extend our *avelut* for a year." He looked down as he said it, not wanting to see the dismay in Senset's eyes as she realized her husband wouldn't touch her with any form of intimacy for twelve months.

"If that's how it must be…"

He was startled by her quiet acceptance. He looked up to find her staring at him.

"Poor Michael, you truly do miss him, don't you? I loved Aram like a brother, and I've tried to imagine how I'd feel if Horem hadn't come back from one of those times he fought the Habiru, but…I can't really know how you feel, can I?"

"He was my other self, Senset. The part of me free to view the world without a mask." He said the words Michael had once spoken to him, when they'd been younger and allowed themselves one evening to come under the power of strong Habiru wine, allowing it to free their tongues for thoughts otherwise best unspoken. "That other piece without a curse to be imparted to his children. I was Aram, and Aram was *me*."

And now, more than ever, that was true.

****

Gratefully, Michael took the crudely-carved wooden bowl UmRawa filled with his second helping of stew. His appetite had returned with a vengeance and he'd devoured the first portion as if ravenous. Now, he ate a little more slowly.

"What's in this, anyway?" he asked, gesturing with the wooden spoon.

"Monkey." UmRawa threw the word at him as she gulped her own portion.

Pausing a moment, he studied the chunks of meat, as if inspecting them for fur or vermin, before thrusting the full spoon into his mouth and chewing determinedly.

"It's good," he said around it.

"I'm glad you like it," UmRawa replied. "It's my specialty. My husband and son always enjoyed it."

"Where are your husband and son? Why aren't they here to eat with us?"

"The *mambas* got them." As he looked up, she went on. "Not at the same time. My son was almost old enough to be called a man."

"I'm sorry." He avoided her eyes.

"I've mourned a long time. I still miss them both." She fell silent, studying him as he continued eating.

Facing her across the fire, Michael sat cross-legged on a woven-reed mat. He'd managed to wrap the blanket discreetly about his hips, carefully tucking it in as he sat. Intent on his food, he was eating with still-apparent enjoyment when he suddenly stopped, spoon to his mouth.

"Why are you staring at me?" He sucked the morsel off the spoon, then raised the bowl and drank the last drops of stew directly from it. Lowering it, he swiped at his mouth with the back of his hand.

"I'm wondering where you come from," UmRawa replied. "I've never seen anyone with skin as pale as yours, though I've heard those from my village who've traveled say there's a tribe south of the Plain of Arriah with skins that are pale gold and not black."

He didn't answer, just scowled as if considering her words and thinking them over.

"There's also a tale that if you follow the River-that-Flows-North as far as it goes before pouring into the Great Ocean, you can see people even paler, some with yellow hair, but I don't believe that." She laughed. "How could anyone have hair the color of dried grass?"

"Does it matter where I came from?" Michael's tone made the question important.

"Not really, I guess." She was a little shaken by the

way he looked at her, as if he thought she were about to turn him out.

"I'm your son now, UmRawa...Mother. If anyone questions my skin color...tell him my father was a river god and I resemble him." He lurched to his feet, careful to make certain the blanket didn't slip, and leaned across to hand her the bowl. "The stew was good. I feel much better with my belly full."

"You still need rest. I don't want that wound re-opening. My bloodstone was broken when my people fled, and the piece I have isn't too potent."

"What caused your people to leave?"

He put one hand against the door frame. UmRawa glanced at his face, to see if he was tiring and bracing himself. He appeared to be merely touching the wall, so she relaxed.

"The Misazula," she explained, reaching for the soup ladle and pouring a bit more stew into her own bowl. "It's so odd you were fighting that one and still can't remember. They banded together and were attacking and killing everyone. It's said they want to rid the world of everyone but themselves, and when my people heard they were coming this way, they ran."

"Why didn't you go?"

"I tried." She studied the bowl, stirring slowly. "They chased me away."

Taking a deep breath, she looked up at him.

"I'll be truthful, Simba. They think me a witch. Oh, they come to me for elixirs to stop bellyaches and want my herbs to heal their wounds and ask for love potions, but otherwise, they stay away. They didn't want me coming with them." Her voice dropped bitterly. "Lest my wickedness draw the Misazula to them." She looked away. "I'm just a lone, old woman, and they left me here to be killed."

"But you weren't killed," he reminded her, releasing his hold on the wall and walking around the fire. "And now, you've a son to protect you."

UmRawa was so touched for a moment she couldn't speak. She poured the stew back into the copper pot, then got to her feet.

"There's not much left. It won't keep in the heat. I'll get rid of it."

"What'll you do with it? Do you have pigs to feed it to?" For some reason, speaking of swine made an odd jitter in his belly. He hoped it wasn't a reaction to eating monkey meat. "Do you throw it out for scavengers?"

She shook her head. "The animals are too smart to eat cooked food, and I don't want to lure hyenas or vultures close to my hut. I dig a hole and bury whatever isn't eaten."

"I can do that," he said, stooping to lift the kettle.

"You'll do nothing to re-open that wound, son."

Reluctantly, he released the kettle's handle into her hand. UmRawa smiled. She could see he was a man who thought females were to be protected. His next words confirmed that.

"Will you go to the river to wash the kettle? That's dangerous if there are crocodiles about." He looked around. "Do you have weapons? I'll go with you."

"My husband's spear, shield, and long knife are in the hut." She got to her feet. "And my shovel. Fetch it and wait while I dispose of what's left of our meal. Then you can guard me while I wash the kettle." As he nodded and disappeared into the hut's darkness, she smiled. "My *simba*."

****

The rest of their meal was eaten in silence. Aram felt there was nothing else to say at this point, and Senset looked as if she had no wish to speak to anyone, not even her beloved husband.

She had forced herself to eat, he could see that, so after she'd finished the piece of melon and managed to consume a portion of mutton, he said, "If you don't wish to eat any more, it's all right. I simply don't want my child to suffer…"

His voice trailed away as she looked at him.

"Be assured I'll never do anything to hurt our baby, Michael, no matter how much my grief." Her eyes were thoughtful as she laid down the piece of bread she held. "I had intended to talk to you about what we should name our child… Would it be permissible to call him after Aram?"

That question made him want to weep, but this time for another reason. "I think it would be very acceptable, my wife, to honor my brother that way."

****

Later, after they came back from the river and UmRawa returned the kettle and bowls to their places on the shelves in the hut, Michael gathered the pile of rags and animal skins and the pieces of leather breastplate. Seating himself once more on the reed mat by the still-burning fire, he pulled the remnants apart, holding up each and studying it while frowning fiercely.

"What are you doing?" UmRawa asked.

"I thought looking at the garments I wore might help me remember."

When he glanced at her, his dark brows were drawn down into a scowl so deep it made the old woman tremble slightly. He'd chosen his name well, she decided, for truly she felt as if a real lion stared at her.

"Does it?"

He shook his head. "I feel nothing when I look at these." He let one of the gauntlets fall to the mat. "Except curiosity as to why I'd wear the paws of a lion over my own hands." He looked up at her. "There was nothing else? For some reason, I thought there should be more."

"That was all." She shook her head. "No amulets or arm bands. You've scars, but they're not ritual, more from other battles, I think."

He looked down at his chest as she said that, a hand going to the binding over his ribs.

"Other than that…"

"No matter. As you say, after I've rested, knowledge should come back to me." He got to his feet. "In the meantime, I need something to wear, Mother. Other than this blanket."

Cautiously, he touched the faded cloth wrapped around his waist, as if fearing the brush of his fingers might make it part and fall.

"Of course. I've been an inconsiderate parent. Wait there, my son."

As fast as she could hobble, she went inside the hut, reappearing with a folded length of fabric. Kneeling on her own mat, she shook open the cloth and laid it on the dirt, smoothing out the wrinkles.

"I've been saving this piece of cloth I made. Guess now I know why."

Michael watched her silently as she pulled the knife from her waistband and cut away a large square. Getting to her feet, she walked over to where he stood, holding out the square. Before he realized what she intended, her fingers went to the tucked-in top of the blanket, pulling it loose. He caught it as it slid past his thighs, tried to cover himself, but she pressed the square against his belly.

His cheeks reddened, flushing through his chest and downward until his skin held a rosy glow. UmRawa ignored his embarrassment, holding the square with one hand while the other wrapped it around his privates.

She nodded. "That looks as if it'll fit."

Pulling the cloth away, she returned to her place by the fire while Michael hastily re-wrapped the blanket. He dropped to the mat, legs drawn up, arms around them. With his cheek resting on his knees, he watched as she took a bone needle from the basket and a long, narrow string of leather. Threading the string through the needle's eye, she folded the cloth and stabbed the needle into it.

"What are you doing?"

"Making you a *doti*."

The bone needle went in and out as she spoke, fashioning the square into what appeared to be a large pouch. He didn't ask anything else, and she cut off two more pieces of cloth, twisting them deftly into long, narrow strips, and attaching them to the larger one. At last, she held up the finished garment.

"Done. Here, my son."

Getting to his feet, he took it from her, studied it intently a moment, then whirled and disappeared into the hut.

UmRawa waited patiently.

Eventually, Michael emerged, minus the blanket. Stopping before her, he turned self-consciously.

"Am I wearing this correctly?"

He'd tied the top band around his waist. It hung low on his hips, the *doti* just under his belly, his privates tucked into the pouch. The second band, attached to the bottom, went between his thighs and up the separation of his buttocks, tied at the back to the waistband.

When UmRawa nodded, he went on, "Is there nothing else to wear with it?"

"That's all the men of my people wear, except for a cape when they travel, to ward off the sun." Sensing he was accustomed to wearing quite a bit more, she turned back to the remaining piece of cloth. "I think I've enough here to make you a *domo,* too."

"Please." Michael's hands went to his bare flanks, open palms hovering as if to shield them. He looked as if he wanted to bolt back into the hut and retrieve the blanket. "If you would."

Quickly, UmRawa fashioned the rest of the fabric into a large rectangle, trimming away the section where she'd cut out the square.

This time, as she offered the garment to Michael, he said, "Would...you mind putting it on me? To make certain I wear it correctly?" As if he wasn't sure how such a large piece of fabric was to be used.

"It goes this way." She wrapped it around his shoulders, then under his right arm, pulling it across his chest and tying the two ends together. The unsmiling stare he gave her reminded her so much of the solemn way her son used to regard her when he was smaller, as she bathed him, she was shaken.

Such an old memory to remember because of a pair of serious green eyes.

Giving him the same smile she'd given her lost child, she reached for the spear he'd propped against the hut wall, placing it in his hand. "There. Now you truly look like one of my people."

"Only with lighter skin." The smile he flashed her made her heart seize its warmth. "Thank you, Mother. I'll wear these garments with pride."

Chapter 34

The burial ceremony wasn't held for two weeks, and in that time, Aram thanked the Lord more than once that the five cities were no further distant from Beth-Gurion. While they waited, he settled more into his disguise, finding it becoming easier and easier to speak as the king and not as himself as he entertained with proper bereaved restraint Enzi and the others staying behind to pay their respects to their fallen ally. Only with Senset was he still hesitant and distant, uncertain how much to say and do lest he let some gesture or word of his own betray his identity.

Horem adjusted quickly, which was surprising. Currently, he was paying visits to the temple and speaking to the priests, asking questions and requesting copies of the Scriptures, that he might learn more about his brother-in-law's God. His intention to become Habiru appeared more than mere lip service, and to that extent, he took Sapair with him on his visits, asking that the boy be instructed also.

Rebekah was hardly ever seen. She'd taken to her bed and rarely left it. As far as her family was concerned, she was in *aninut*—such a state of shock over her lost child that she was incoherent. Meryam and Rachel spent a good portion of their days with her, performing the prayers and reciting the blessings she should have been saying. Aram visited her frequently, but her grief was more than he could bear, and he only managed to prevent himself from telling her the truth by realizing that to know her son *the king* was dead, not her son *the mere general*, might be more than her mind could accept.

He continued taking his meals with Senset, though he ate little, consumed by his continued guilt as well as by sorrow. Nevertheless, he made certain *she* was well fed and properly nourished, determined nothing would threatened his brother's unborn heir's welfare. Sometimes, he kept her company as she sat on the terrace or walked in one of the gardens, but he always made certain Orora or another servant or family member was nearby so he was never alone with her, especially as evening approached. To his surprise, after her initial protest, she accepted this, and never objected when it came time for him to give her a gentle kiss and leave.

He also was grateful that the current month was one without a full moon. He had enough to worry about without that problem also.

She had told him she would combine her bereavement for her parents with that for Aram and would continue it for the same period of mourning. What Senset didn't say was that Aram's death affected her more than losing Aseti-Ra and her mother; their dying still seemed distant and unreal, as if happening to relatives she hadn't seen in quite some time.

Eventually, when everyone from around the country had assembled, Aram led his family to the temple verandah to pay their last homage to their lost brother and son.

****

"*Hamakom y'nachem etkhem b'tokh sha'ar avelei.*"
It was one of the many phrases said to Aram as the

men governing the other cities, those appointed by his father and some by his grandfather, filed past him and his mother as the funeral drew to a close.

The Omnipresent will comfort you among the mourners.

It had been an odd ceremony. Aram had been present at only two others, that of his father, occurring when he and Michael were seventeen, and his uncle Yaacov's, appointed by his father to govern Bethbasar. Yonatan ben-Gurion was buried with complete ceremony, awarded all the honors available, as had been his brother. But now...

Such a poor offering for the son of a king, Aram thought. *Even if they knew it to be Michael and not me they are mourning, it's still a pitiful observance, with no body to put in the grave.*

If anything, today, he felt worse than he had before. Though he'd taken the februgia as Elijah ordered, the fever kept returning, each time getting worse. He'd staved off Elijah's ministrations, telling the physician he was healing and sending him to tend those soldiers needing him more. He told himself he'd survive his wounds on his own; that was part of his promise to the Lord.

Yahweh, aid me in my masquerade and I'll heal myself.

Nevertheless, he felt leaden-eyed, would swear he could feel illness surging through his veins, making his skin burn. It had taken all his will power to stand straight and unwavering on the temple's verandah and announce to those gathered before it that the entire ceremony would take place at the burial site.

To Aram's amazement, it appeared every adult in

Beth-Gurion had come to say farewell to their beloved General. In spite of his guilt, he was touched at the sight of so many of his brother's subjects kneeling with covered heads and darkened brows before him. As he spoke, there were obvious nods, as if they understood the extraordinary circumstances of this particular death and agreed with what had been decided.

When Aram walked down the temple stairs, supporting Rebekah by his uninjured arm, with Senset beside him, her hand resting on his wounded one, the silent crowd parted before them, heads respectfully bowed. Behind them, Shemuel and Gideon walked with Horem, the Ægysian accepted now as a proxy brother. Yeshua comforted and supported a weeping Rachel while Meryam and Adonijah followed them. Enzi and Michael's other allies followed, each with his face or clothing marked with his own particular form of mourning.

As they walked, Rebekah began to sob more loudly, Rachel's a soft accompaniment to her tears. Behind them, there came more weeping as the townspeople took up her grief. A second sound came, fists being beat against chests. Even without the presence of a body, it became a *levayah*—a funeral procession—in earnest, continuing with soft wails and pounding against hearts as they walked through the streets of Beth-Gurion and out the gates to an isolated and leveled-off plot beyond the city walls where engraved headstones dotted the soil like silent stone flowers.

The ben-Gurion graves were isolated from the others, cut into the mountain itself, behind a wall of carefully stacked stones expertly chiseled into squares and fitted together.

314

Silently, Aram led his mother to a large, cloth-covered object. He waited until his brothers and sisters were gathered around before releasing Rebekah long enough to look back at those following them.

"My brother's no longer with us. We don't even have his body to prepare for his journey to the Afterlife, but I'm certain in my knowledge that Yahweh accepts and greets him there. Nothing about this *levayah* has followed the proper order, so I now take it upon myself to change it even more."

A murmur arose at that, then swiftly died as Aram held up a hand.

"The priests will pray for my brother, but now, I ask you, people of Beth-Gurion, to give his *hesped*. If any of you wishes to say something in his behalf, speak. I ask it of you."

There was silence. Heads turned as people looked at each other, murmuring among themselves. It was customary for eulogies to be given at the start of the graveside ceremony, but generally, one of those bereaved didn't stand and invite just anyone to participate.

"I…I would speak."

Someone spoke from near the gate. The cemetery was crowded with townspeople, a stream of bodies stretching the width of the road and back to the city's entrance.

Aram swiveled to look in the direction of the voice. His brothers also peered anxiously. Even Rebekah ceased her tears, raising her head.

The crowd shifted to reveal a man holding the hands of a little boy and girl. He took a couple of steps forward, then stopped as he realized everyone was staring at him.

He looked as if he wished he hadn't spoken.

"I… I met the General once…" he began, gripping the children's hands tighter as if they gave him courage.

Aram frowned. *Do I know this man? I certainly don't remember him.*

"I'm a potter," the man went on. "I've a small shop on the other end of town. Some of you may know me." He looked around as if for confirmation and a few heads nodded. "My daughter has a cat. You may know it, too. A pest of a thing, catching birds and bringing mice into the house, but she loves it…"

His voice trailed away, then rallied.

"One day the creature fell off the roof of my shop. It was clumsy for a cat."

There were a few faint smiles at that, quickly hidden as if their owners realized a funeral was no place for levity.

"Broke a leg. I'm no doctor. I didn't know anything to do but kill the thing, but my daughter was crying so and begging me not to." He looked down at the little girl, who squeezed his hand tightly. "I was standing there holding that cat and trying to console her at the same time, when someone said, 'What's happening here? Why's the child crying so?' I looked up and it was the General…he'd heard my Esther's sobs and stopped his horse."

The potter paused, swallowing loudly.

"Well, I explained what was happening, and he climbed off his horse and held out his hands and said, 'Let me see.' I placed the cat in them and he sat on my potter's bench, looked at it, and said, 'If you get me some wythes and a strip of cloth, I think I can repair that leg.'"

I do remember, Aram thought.

Into his mind came an image of the struggling cat, fighting in its pain to get out of the man's arms. It had already clawed him terribly, yet he held on to it tightly while with the other hand, he stroked the crying little girl's head, attempting to soothe her...and then that bloody, clawed hand had shoved the squalling animal at him.

"So, I found a couple of flat pieces of palm wood I'd saved to repair a stool, and tore a strip from the end of an old robe I planned to use to clean my wheel, and brought them to him. I can still see him there, sitting on that stool, stroking the cat's head. It was so still... He said to me, 'You need to hold it now,' and returned the cat to me, and before either I or the cat realized what he was going to do, he caught the broken leg, gave it a twist, and it snapped back into place. Then he splinted it with the wythes and wrapped the splint with the cloth. 'Don't let him climb on any roofs for a few weeks and he should be all right again,' he told me, and then he got on his horse and rode away."

"Kitty didn't even scratch him," the little girl announced as if still awed by that fact.

The potter smiled gently and released her hand, brushing his own over her head.

"Well, the cat got well, though he can't climb trees or hop onto roofs now, but he still catches mice and birds. I took an urn to the palace—it was all I had to repay the General for what he'd done. I didn't get to see him, but he sent me a message that he accepted my gift but I didn't really owe him anything because he couldn't stand to see a child cry."

Aram looked away. He still had the urn. It sat on a table in his chambers. It was a utilitarian thing, with a flat base and rounded sides, fired and glazed a cinnabar red, made to hold water, and not sit amid the other decorated and bejeweled vases and bowls in his suite. Rachel had often asked him why he kept such an unattractive piece of pottery with the other more beautiful ones. *Because it was given in appreciation*, he'd told her.

"The General was a generous and good man to do such a thing for my Esther and...I'm sorry he's gone..." The man's voice trailed away, winding down his story. "I'm glad I got to meet him face to face, and though I met him only that one time, I'm going to miss him."

He stepped back, pulling the children with him, passing another man who pushed out of the crowd.

"I met the General also," he said. "At the well in the city square. It wasn't about a hurt cat, though. I'd had too much wine to drink..."

Before they were finished, a dozen people had stepped forward to tell of things Aram did for them or words he'd said that helped or made a moment a little easier. Most of them were events Aram himself had long forgotten. Some had happened when he was barely out of childhood, but they'd remained in the memories of the people he'd spoken to, and he was astonished how, for even a moment, he'd interacted in so many lives.

Gradually, the *hespeds* were all said, the assurance that General Aram was truly going to be missed stated quite plainly. The priest intoned several prayers, drawing the ceremony to a close. There was no grave for the mourners to close, but one custom was followed by everyone there.

Reaching out, Aram pulled the cloth off the upright object so they could see it was a granite pillar. "This would've been my brother's *matzevah*. In the proper time, it'll be engraved so all will know whose memory it presents."

"My son, my son!" Pushing away from Aram, Rebekah rushed to the stone, throwing her arms around it. "Oh, my child! I cry for you, I weep for the days you no longer have. For the time you no longer will spend with us."

Seizing an embroidered cloth medallion sewn onto the left breast of her overgown, she ripped it violently downward, tearing a gaping hole in the fabric.

Immediately, Aram seized his own robe, tearing it also, his movement almost vicious. Besides him, he heard Senset do the same. As if that were a signal, Gideon, Yeshua, and Shemuel rent their robes and placed their hands over their eyes.

Behind them, Horem copied their action.

"I mourn with you, my brother."

The air filled with the ripping of fabric as everyone accompanying them to the cemetery performed the same act.

"We all mourn with you, my king." More voices than Aram could count echoed Horem's.

As Aram gathered his weeping mother against his chest and his other hand sought Senset's, the followers filed past, bestowing the last blessing upon them.

May you suffer no more pain...you should have only good luck from now on...may we be told only good things about you...I wish you and your other brothers long life...

General Aram's funeral was over. Now his mourning would begin.

The imposter's reign had started.

****

Once back at the palace, with Rebekah again given a soporific to ease her misery, Aram and his family began the month of *shloshim,* thirty days of mourning in which he would each night pray for the strength to carry on in his brother's name…to resist the temptation to become Senset's husband in earnest…and to be as good a king as Michael.

And then…then we'll begin shneim asar chodesh. *A full year of more mourning. Michael deserves it.*

Aram's intentions were brought to an immediate halt, however, as the false king kissed his brother's wife chastely on her brow and turned to leave her to her lonely bed. He made it down the dais steps before he stumbled once, then fell to the floor. Senset's screams brought the guards who gently lifted him and carried him to his own chamber while another ran to summon Elijah.

Chapter 35

With a groan dying away into a sigh, Aram regained consciousness.

What happened? Where am I?

He felt soft sheets beneath him, his movements sending a sweet herbal scent wafting from them.

Surely I'm in my own bed… I remember now. I felt so hot…a fever…I gave in to it as I was leaving Senset…

"Senset?"

"I'm here, my love." A soft hand squeezed his fingers. "Oh, Michael, I was so worried. Why didn't you tell Elijah your wound had become infected?"

"There were so many others needing him more. And truly…I didn't believe it was serious…" He broke off, opening his eyes and seeing her tearstained face. More shame washed over him. "I'm sorry, my wife. I didn't intend to…"

"No matter." She didn't let him finish but raised his hand and kissed it. "He's cleansed the wound and applied a healing poultice and says that *this time*, if you promise to follow his orders, you may rise and carry on with your duties."

"Good."

He sat up, wincing a little as he felt a pulling in his side. A glance down told him the bandaging wasn't stained, so he wasn't bleeding again. This time, Elijah had stitched the wound together after scraping out the infection and applying medicinal salve. Someone had also undressed him.

"You must leave now, Senset."

"Why?"

"I have to get up and clothe myself."

He didn't dare get out of the bed while she was there, wouldn't risk her seeing his body. They were both scarred from previous battles but he had wounds in places Michael didn't, and he was certain she'd notice.

"You can't do that before your wife?" She gave a disbelieving laugh. "Michael, truly I know your body well now. There's no need for modesty between us, husband."

"I'm bruised and battered. I don't want you to see what fighting has done to me." Her knowledge of Michael's body was his fear. He forced a sheepish smile. "Allow me a little vanity, wife."

"I worship your body, my husband, whether it's beaten and bloody or unmarked and pristine, but..." Senset stood and returned the stool to its place. "If you insist, I'll humor you. This time."

She leaned over, kissing him on the mouth before he could turn his head, then straightened, looking directly into his eyes.

"Michael?" Her expression was confused. "What happened to your eyes?"

"What do you mean?"

Lord, please, no. A chill ran through him. It was too late to look away. Nevertheless, he turned his head. *She's found me out.*

"My eyes weren't harmed."

"They certainly weren't." Senset's voice became hard. She caught his chin, forcing him to look at her.

"But they've changed color."

"You're mistaken, wife. My eyes are the same color they've always been."

Damn it, How could I forget Michael's eyes aren't the same color as mine? He'd thought so about their similarities but completely ignored their difference in eye color.

"Yes…for Aram. Michael's eyes are green." It was an accusation. "Is that why you've avoided me? Why you've never let me be close to you? You knew I'd see, and…"

She caught at the blanket, jerking it away and staring at the wound on his shoulder. The wound made by her brother's spear. A scar his brother didn't have.

"Aram—where's my husband?"

No need to pretend further.

Silently, he reached behind his head, unbuckling the mask and letting it fall into his lap. When he looked at her again, his eyes were as full of guilt as they could be without being those of an assassin. She looked from the mask to his face, at the fresh abrasions caused by the lining rubbing against skin unaccustomed to its touch.

"Michael's dead, Senset. It was he who went off the cliff and not I."

"Why have you done this?" She looked as if she wasn't certain whether to be angry or to burst into tears. "Why not tell us the truth?"

"You can ask that after seeing how the people mourn when they think *I* died? My mother prostrate with grief? She's in severe *aninut*. Elijah thinks it may be years before she recovers. What do you think would happen to her if she knew the *king* had died? Senset, it'd probably kill her."

"Rebekah doesn't love you any less than—"

"Yes, she does, and the people, also, but I don't care about that. I'm not so selfish I'm jealous of the affection felt for my brother. But the love they have for him will destroy them if they learn he's the one who perished. So—" Picking up the mask, he rebuckled it. "I've become Michael, for everyone's sake."

Once the mask was secure, he looked at her, eyes imploring.

"Will you now renounce me and tell everyone of my deception?"

It was a long moment before she spoke, her own eyes boring into his as if she could see into his soul and the sincerity of what he'd done, as well as the guilt he suffered.

At last, with a sigh, she asked, "Why hasn't someone else noticed?"

"People see what they want to see. Only a wife would know her husband even if he does wear a mask."

"Yet I almost didn't. So no one else knows?"

"Only Horem, and he swore to keep my secret."

"Then I shall also." She smiled slightly. "Can I suppose this is the reason you've avoided my bed, and demanded the *shneim asar chodesh*?"

"I can't be your husband, Senset. Surely you can see that." He caught her hand.

"Yes, I do, and frankly, Aram, I wouldn't want you to be." She pulled her hand from his. Touching his cheek, she patted it gently, then let her hand drop to her side. "I'll leave you to dress, my…husband. It's almost time for the evening meal. If you feel up to it, will you join me?"

"I… Yes, m-my wife. I will."

"Good. In the meantime, I've more mourning to do. *True* mourning this time." Turning, she walked out.

****

Within a few days, Michael's allies returned to their own kingdoms, to help their wounded recover and begin taking up their own lives again.

"My son's wedding will be postponed, of course," Enzi told Aram. "When the year of mourning for your brother has passed, send me word. Then we'll speak again of the marriage and happier things."

"Thank you, my brother." Aram extended his hand in farewell.

Enzi touched his palm to Aram's, nodded to Horem, then rode to the head of the column and gestured to his own men.

"Senset knows, Horem." Aram didn't take his eyes off Enzi's departing figure as he spoke.

"And…?" The prince gave no reaction to that.

"She's agreed to go along with my deception. She understands why I had to do what I've done."

"Then may Yahweh look over us all." Horem bowed his head.

Part 3: The Time of the *Shneim Asar Chodesh*

Chapter 36

"It looks like a fine day to do the planting." Michael glanced up at the sky, shading his eyes with one hand.

The sun felt good; he welcomed it but, as always, felt a sudden tremor as it touched him, as if he should run and hide from its warmth. Even after all this time, the feeling stayed with him, as it had from the moment he opened his eyes to see that bit of sky through UmRawa's torn roof.

Somehow, he connected it to thoughts of a golden mask...the mask he'd demanded when he'd first awoke...sometimes of the odd dreams he had on occasion, of the woman with hair the color of mahogany, a woman looking at him with sad eyes, though who she was and why he dreamed of her he had no knowledge. He hadn't mentioned those dreams to UmRawa, certain she'd tell him it was a sign from the gods that he should find himself a wife.

Once recovered enough to use his arm without tearing open the wound, he was kept busy with tasks UmRawa's husband and later her son should have done, now long neglected once they were taken from her by the *shetani mambas*. As if to show her his gratitude for taking in a river foundling, he set about taking their place in the old woman's life.

His first project was the garden, and he told her his intention one night as they ate their supper.

"This squash is good," he said, using his knife to cut a slice off the baked half in his bowl.

In the center of the circle of stone UmRawa used as her cook fire was a round hollow lined with water-smoothed river rocks. UmRawa baked the squash by wrapping them in palm leaves and placing them on the rocks and covering them with another layer of stones. Then, she built a fire over them and the heat made the stones glow red and bake the vegetables in their center.

He stuck the still-hot portion into his mouth. Um-Rawa had made him a gift of her son's hunting knife. Michael now wore it in a sheath tied around his waist atop the band of his *doti.*

"I see one of those baskets in the corner is nearly full, as is the one holding the squash. Where did you get so many? I've seen no garden."

"The chief," she told him, pausing in her own eating. "His youngest wife was with child, and he asked me to make a potion ensuring he'd have a son. I mixed my best elixir and poured it down her throat." She laughed slightly. "She didn't like it. Truly, it's a foul-tasting concoction. When she gave birth to a healthy boy, I was rewarded with three baskets of vegetables."

She looked suitably satisfied.

"An elixit to guarantee a son..." Michael spoke thoughtfully. He swallowed and cut off another mouthful. "What if your elixir hadn't worked and she'd had a girl-child?"

"Then I'd have blamed it on all the figs she ate beforehand, and remind the chief I'd warned him about that. Everyone knows fig tree fruit is female and causes girl babes." She snickered slightly. "Truly, Simba, there's nothing to ensure whether a child will be boy or girl…that's in the hands of the gods. But our chief didn't believe that."

"Well, since your people are gone now and there are no more chiefs or anyone else for you to dupe, we're going to have to work for our next crop of vegetables." He finished the squash and picked up the pomegranate he'd plucked from the tree growing at the corner of the hut.

UmRawa had told him her husband planted it for her when they were first wed. Now the tree was taller than Michael and laden with fruit.

As he thrust his thumbs into the spiked end and tore it open, he went on, "Those vegetables aren't going to last forever, so I think I'd better get a garden started. That area behind the hut should be a good place."

The pomegranate came apart with a spray of juice, staining his fingers. He licked it off and began to bite into the tiny arils, chewing and swallowing seeds and juice.

"What'll we use for seeds? It's been a long time since I've had a garden. After my son was killed, I began trading my herbs and potions for food."

"We'll sort some out of the baskets, take the best. Since the vegetables are still fairly fresh, there should be enough fertile seeds among them."

So it was settled. As soon as he finished eating, Michael wiped his pomegranate-stained fingers on his thighs, rummaged through UmRawa's late husband's set of tools, found a spade, and began to break the ground behind the hut.

It was hard work; in a short time, he was sweating under the exertion and the heat of the sun and discarded his *domo*, to continue work wearing only the *doti*. He'd already dug a few holes, tossing aside the huge, dry clods of dirt, when the old woman appeared with a hoe. Though he protested, she insisted on helping, using it to break the lumps apart. They worked the rest of the day, stopping only when the sun went down and it was time for the evening meal.

"Here." UmRawa poured water into a basin and handed it to Michael, who was rubbing his thumb over the blisters on his palm.

As he took it from her, she sprinkled in some herbs, stirring them with her finger.

"You may be a warrior, but I can see you've never been a farmer."

"I've calluses," he protested, holding out a hand to show her those on his palm.

"Aye, but holding a sword is different from wielding a hoe. Those raw spots are going to hurt tomorrow unless you soak them. The herbs'll ward away soreness."

Leaving him with both hands immersed in the water, she went inside the hut.

****

Before UmRawa began cooking, she had Michael go through the potatoes, beans, and squash and select those he wished to use for seed, waiting until he'd chosen six handfuls of beanpods and set aside some squash and melons, cutting them open. While he separated seeds from pulp, spreading them on a bamboo mat to dry, she chose a melon and some beans to cook. He'd gotten the squash and melon prepared and was busy shelling the beans and arranging them on another mat when she called him to eat.

Michael seated himself on his mat. Once again, he

found UmRawa watching him, but by now he was accustomed to it. Even after all these months, she still appeared a little awed and disbelieving that the river gods had blessed her by sending a replacement for her dead husband and son.

"Why do you stare, Mother?" He teased, accepting the slice of melon she offered. "Is my face dirty?" He bit into the melon, letting the juice run down his chin.

"How can I tell with all that sticky nectar on your face?" She laughed.

She'd easily fallen into thinking of him as her son, rejoicing with his easygoing manner, and doting on the gentle way he treated her and seemed to care. UmRawa had taken the young stranger into her heart and her life, happy once more to have someone to care for, to cook and sew for, and…to worry about. To think of his welfare, and his future, as she was doing now.

She became serious. "Simba, I've been thinking."

"About what?" He looked up, smiling. "Don't worry, I promise I'll wash my face when I finish eating." Then he saw her expression and his own changed. "What is it, Mother?"

"I…" She looked away, then took a deep breath and raised her gaze to his. "You're a young man, Simba. Handsome…and a vigorous one, I don't doubt."

The slight smile he gave her was so much like a smirk, she nearly laughed.

"It's lonely here, with just an old woman for company. I'm thinking you need a wife…"

"A wife?"

She thought he was going to laugh out loud.

"Mother, I don't know who I am or where I come from. I'm a foundling rescued from the *shetani mamba*

330

by the good luck of your needing water at the right time. For all I know, I may truly be a river god's son. Let me accustom myself to life here before I think of something *that* serious. Besides, at the moment, I don't want a wife."

He frowned slightly. Saying the word *wife* sent another of those strange little twinges through his belly, similar to the one he felt when he looked at the sun.

"But…"

"Let's you and me live here and enjoy the peace, Mother. Later, when I'm well, and settled, and the season changes and the wind stirs my blood…then we'll talk of my taking a wife." He shook his head. "Where will we find one anyway? With your people gone and all the other tribes scattered who-knows-where because of the Misazula?"

He concentrated on the melon, taking another bite and saying through a mass of pulp and juice, "Besides, would any female of your people want someone as pale as I?"

"Any woman seeing your handsome face and body would be a fool not to want you, my Simba," UmRawa breathed. Briefly, she felt as proud of him as if he truly were her child.

"Thank you, Mother. Then when I'm ready to marry, I'll take you along to give *me* a recommendation, and *her* your approval. We'll go to those golden-skinned people you told me about…the ones south of the Plain of Arriah, and see if we can find there some woman foolish enough to marry a river god's son."

He laughed in earnest, and UmRawa joined in.

"You're a good boy, my Simba." It was all UmRawa could think to say as she cut her own melon off the rind and ate it.

The next day, they planted the seeds. Michael then set about devising a way to bring water to the garden.

"I don't want you going to the river alone, Mother. I won't always be here to guard you if I'm off hunting."

UmRawa looked on with pride as he used her husband's long knife and hacked down the long bamboo growing at the edge of the forest. The larger canes were wide and rounder than a man's hand's could encircle, and hollow. Slicing them in half, he shoved smaller ones inside larger ones, binding them together with rawhide thongs. After digging a narrow canal reaching from the river where the ledge of the little waterfall lay and stretching to the garden, he lined the cavity with pebbles gathered from the riverbank, then placed the bound-together canes atop them, letting one end extend under the falling water. While the old woman watched with delight, the water flowed from the river through the bamboo to the garden.

"How do you know to do these things, Simba?" she asked as the water spilled from the last piece of caning, flooding between the rows of little mounds holding the seeds.

"How?" He tilted the last piece of bamboo downward, so the water flowed out of it and trickled downhill back to the riverbank. "I... I don't know, Mother. I just do."

He looked uneasy, as if the fact he had no explanation for his knowledge worried him.

"No matter." She seized his arm, hugging it tightly. "It's enough that you know."

Chapter 37

In Habir, life slowly returned to normal. In the far cities, things became as they had been before. Within Beth-Gurion itself, people once more went about their chores and duties, perhaps a little more subdued than usual, though children now played in their yards or ran through the streets laughing. The sun shone brightly, flowers bloomed, and the winds blew gently, as if to comfort them for their loss. Peace and contentment were once more with them.

The palace was a quieter place, however. No music was now heard within its halls. The harpers were silent, their instruments collecting dust on shelves where they would lie until the *shneim adar chodesh* fulfilled. Servants and slaves went about their tasks quietly, speaking in hushed tones, with downcast eyes. Occasional laughter or light conversation was heard, but it was always subdued. Everyone still wore their rent garments over their other clothing, though the ashes of mourning were now mere smudges on foreheads.

General Aram's presence was missed more than any wanted to admit.

Rebekah had eventually emerged from her bedchamber. Though outwardly recovered from the shock of losing her son, she now became obsessively attentive to the king and in her concern for the health of Senset and the coming child.

Alone in his quarters at night, Aram silently prayed nothing would threaten either, fearing what it might do to his mother's slowly healing emotions. Senset, however, responded to Rebekah's excessive care. With the loss of her parents, she bloomed under her mother-in-law's attention, for which Aram was grateful, though she still mourned. Her admission to Rebekah that she wished to name Michael's son after his brother brought tears of joy to the older woman's eyes.

Accepting the confines of continued mourning, Rachel was nevertheless impatient for the time to end so she could become Zuperi's wife. Surprising himself with his sympathy for young love, Aram gave her permission to carry on a correspondence with the Kiswanan prince. Daily, couriers left the palace carrying missives to him expressing her devotion and impatience, while others arrived bearing scrolls laden with equally flowery phrases of professed love and faithfulness. In the meantime, the contents of Rachel's marriage chest grew higher.

Eli ben-Gurion was chosen to take Aram's place as general. Cousin to the brothers and son of their deceased uncle Yaacov, he'd ridden with them to fight the Misazula, as well as in their wars against the Ægysians, and had distinguished himself with his bravery and skill.

The days and nights of the full moon came and went. With each one, Aram allowed himself to be locked inside the garden while Senset and Horem sat on the overlooking terrace, silent witnesses to this further falsehood. Seated on the bench under the Rose of Sharon, he spent the entire time praying, his cries not those of a man anguished by the transformation of the Curse, but of one asking Yahweh to forgive him the sin of perpetrating such a hoax upon his people. Each following morning, he emerged, greeted by his partners in deception, to continue his ruse.

In a ceremony in the temple, Horem was accepted into the Habiru community. Presenting himself as a proselyte, the Ægysian prince stood before the interrogation of the temple's rabbinical council, while Gideon and Aram testified to his progress in studying the laws and customs as well as his knowledge of the Scriptures. Though he was too old for *bar mitzvah*, Horem underwent the rituals of conversion. Beginning with the *mikvah* to spiritually bathe and purify his body, he suffered the *hatafat dam brit,* a single pinprick of blood symbolizing his previous rite of circumcision, and was proclaimed henceforth to be known as Horem-Adam.

"Now I'm fully Habiru," he said to Aram as he emerged from the temple. "The Ægysians are no more."

Thus, slowly, life resumed around them.

Part 4: The Return of the King

Chapter 38

"It looks like we may soon have rain," Michael commented, nodding at the sky. "It'll be good for the garden, but I don't relish waking in a puddle of mud. I think I'd better repair that hole in the roof. I've delayed it long enough."

The weather was changing. Soon, the rainy season would be upon them. Already there had been dark clouds on the horizon, and the thunder from far-off storms rumbled over the trees. The river was getting higher, once or twice actually overflowing its banks as it sped past, filled with rain from cloudbursts farther upstream.

"We'll put out all the vessels we have…" he went on. One hand stroked his beard, an act becoming a habit whenever he was lost in thought.

Since UmRawa had no razors, he'd let his facial hair grow, though he kept it trimmed with his knife. It was an odd sensation but not altogether unpleasant. Still, it was easier to have a beard than attempt to shave with only his hunting knife.

"…and catch rainwater. Then we won't have to go to the river so often or spend so much time straining it to get out the dirt and insects." He smiled at UmRawa and put his arm around her. "Some time soon, Mother, you must use your witchery skills and see if we've any springs around here."

"I'm no dowser," the old woman denied. "I've never been able to find anything with a forked stick, not even one of my own water pitchers."

"Too bad." He feigned disappointment, then kissed her forehead, hugging her tightly, as she gave what sounded like a giggle. "Guess that means I'll have to keep lugging those pots of water from the bamboo canals."

From far off, there was a distant rumble. Michael looked up again. Across the river, the sky at the horizon was darkening.

"That storm's getting closer. I'd better get started on the roof."

"It's still far away," Umrawa protested.

"It might get here faster than we expect. You know how unpredictable storms are, and how fast they can travel."

"*I* do." She gave him a curious look. "How do you? There haven't been any storms since you came to me."

He shook his head. "Another thing I know without knowing how, Mother. Come, let's get busy. It'll be dark soon."

****

I'm so sorry I had to leave you, Senset. I wish I could've seen my son before I died…

Michael stood encased in light, but he looked so odd. His body was wrapped in a flimsy cape, his face bare and bearded, hair loose and flowing over his shoulders…and he held a spear of a kind she'd never seen before.

Wife, take good care of my child, and…

His body began to gleam, the light growing brighter

337

and brighter until she could no longer see him. Abruptly, there was an ear-shattering crash of thunder and the light disappeared so only a dark silhouette remained, its arms outstretched.

"Senset…"

"Michael, please. Don't go."

"I want to come back…"

At least that's what she thought he said. Senset reached out…and awoke, sitting up in bed, arms outstretched.

It was just a dream. The happiness within her disappeared as Michael had. Elbows resting against her knees, Senset put her hands to her face.

They say the dead speak to us in our dreams. Take care of our child. *Was that all Michael wanted to tell me? He should know I'll do that. As will Aram. Was there something more he wanted to say?*

She forced herself to lie down again, closed her eyes, and concentrated on sleeping, but sleep had fled for the moment. It was early evening, still light enough to see, but she'd gone to bed early, burdened by the heat and the baby's extra weight. A worried Aram had escorted her to her chamber door, though both Elijah and the midwife assured him her fatigue was nothing of concern.

He's a good man, and if he had children of his own, he'd be a good father. Truly, I think he couldn't take care of me better if I were really his wife.

Closing her eyes to blot out the light trickling through the shuttered windows, she continued thinking of her dream, of her husband's figure, surrounded by that brilliant, heavenly light, and then the awful sound of thunder.

He said he wants to come back to me, but I thought once the soul left this world, it was content to abandon earthly longings. Can that mean Michael's dissatisfied with Paradise? That he loves me more than being with the Lord? Surely, it's blasphemous for me to think such a thing, that a man would love his wife more than his God, so much he'd wish to leave Heaven. Oh, Michael...

As if in reprimand, the baby chose that moment to kick, a drumroll battering the inside of her womb, and she touched her belly, patting it gently.

"Quiet, little one. I know your father isn't coming back, but oh, I do miss him."

It was then she realized something else had been strange about Michael in her dream.

His face had been uncovered.

****

"I don't like your using that thing," UmRawa protested. "It's old and rickety."

Setting the ladder against the back wall of the hut, Michael put a foot on the bottom rung. He pulled himself up onto it, the other foot dangling, testing his weight.

"Don't worry, Mother. It's sturdy enough."

He examined the rungs.

Hm. This one's much like an assault ladder. Now, how do I know that?

He could see it had been constructed by an unskilled hand. Probably UmRawa's husband.

The rails were simply two saplings stripped of their bark, their branches hacked off.

There were no animal hide footpads to keep the butts from slipping but rather the ends themselves simply dug into the dirt. Each rung was lashed by leather strips wrapped around and around the rails in a figure-eight and then knotted with a long woven rope running the length of the rails, looping around each rung and attaching all of them together.

Still, the thing looked steady, and he wasn't going to be on it any longer than it took to secure a reed mat over the hole in the roof.

Grabbing the rails, he hauled himself up, saying, "Once I get to the roof, hand me the nails and hammer and the bamboo mat, Mother."

Obediently, UmRawa hobbled over to the little basket of nails and the stone hammer and picked them up. The basket held three dozen nails.

Michael had made them all. He had worked for nearly a week, each night fashioning them painstakingly by hand after he finished weeding the garden and watering it, or returned from hunting or fishing. While UmRawa cooked, he squatted before a flattened rock her husband had used as a work table and cut slivers off an ironwood tree, shaping them into four-inch wedge-shaped spikes. After pounding them into further hardness with the little hammer made from an oval rock secured with leather in the Y-crotch of a short but thick tree branch, he placed each in the basket until it was needed.

It was a tedious task but a necessary one, for nailing or tying were the only two ways to keep the hut repaired.

He'd now reached the top, looked back at UmRawa and, bracing his knees against a rung, leaned over slightly. She stood on tiptoes, holding the basket with the hammer inside, over her head. Catching the basket by its handle, Michael hauled it upward and rested it on the roof. Then he reached down and took the piece of bamboo matting from her.

"Looks to be just the right size," he commented, placing the mat over the hole. "How did this happen, anyway? Did you get angry and throw your copper kettle through it?" he teased.

"There was a storm with hail," she called up to him. "Pieces as big as a man's fist. Truly the gods were angry with us that day. The animals fled, and I hid inside the hut and didn't dare come out. I was afraid if one of the stones hit me it'd kill me."

"Wise of you, Mother." A breeze blew across his bare legs, tickling up his buttocks. It swirled, sending a whistle inside the *doti* and a cool caress against his stones.

Michael jerked slightly. Whenever he thought he was accustoming himself to walking around practically naked, something like that happened to remind him he wasn't. The wind didn't care. Abandoning its insinuation against his privates, it ruffled the edge of the matting, lifting it. He pinned it into place with an elbow while reaching for a nail with his other hand.

"The wind seems a little stronger."

"Hurry, Simba." UmRawa sounded anxious. She was looking over her shoulder at the horizon. "The sky's getting darker. I think the storm'll be here very soon."

"As fast as I can, Mother." Holding the nail while resting his arm against the matting was awkward but he managed. Michael tapped the wooden head, gently driving the nail through both mat and roof. "I want this done well so the wind won't blow it off."

In short order, he'd attached the bamboo mat over the hole, the edges overlapping. As he studied his handiwork, however, he saw that the canes were loosely woven. There were large spaces between the intertwined strips.

Surely rain'll be able to seep through. Not immediately, but eventually.

The wind moaned as if impatient, wanting him off the roof.

"Mother? That hide I was wearing, it's still around somewhere, isn't it?"

Just the thing. *It'll be waterproof. The rain'll run right off.* How did he know that?

"I hung it out to dry. In the branches of the pomegranate tree. It's still there, unless a monkey stole it." Her voice receded as she went around the corner of the hut. In a few moments, she returned, "Here," and held up the now dried and dusty lion skin.

Michael bent to take it. At that moment, the wind whipped over him, sweeping between the ladder and the roof. Everything trembled. Clutching the closest rail, he straightened, hoping UmRawa hadn't seen.

She had.

"Simba, come down. *Now*. The wind's stronger and it's shaking the ladder. I saw it move." She didn't try to hide the fear in her voice.

"In a moment. I want to make sure the roof doesn't leak…" He spread the hide, pounded more nails, dropped the hammer into the basket, then handed it down to her.

By now, the wind was howling around him, tossing his hair in his face. Turning his head, Michael saw the trees were swaying, the pomegranate branches flicking back and forth against the wall of the hut like a whip's lashes. A drop of water struck his arm, then another.

"Not a moment too soon. Here it comes. Get inside, Mother."

It began to pour, in torrents, drops hard as stones.

"You, too." She was soaked but didn't move, and he knew she wouldn't until he was safely on the ground again.

"I'm coming down. Right now," he assured her, and began his descent.

The wind was fiercer now. He could feel the ladder shaking, air buffeting his body.

Truly, I'd best get myself on the ground. He glanced downward. UmRawa was braced against the hut's wall. *These gusts are almost strong enough to sweep her away.*

There was a loud *crack* and Michael saw a limb break from one of the trees at the edge of the forest. It whirled across the clearing, striking the wall on which the ladder rested. A clatter from the other side of the hut told him the copper kettle had been ripped from its cooking stand and was probably rolling away to parts unknown.

"Simba, hurry," UmRawa wailed.

"Get inside, Mother." Michael quickened his downward progress, tightening his grip on the rails.

Twice he had to stop. The wind was so strong now it actually lifted the ladder away from the wall. Water ran down Michael's face, getting into his eyes, soaking his beard. He released the ladder long enough to swipe a palm across his face. There was another crackling sound, but this one wasn't from a breaking tree branch.

A streak of lightning struck the edge of the garden. Thunder boomed. Dirt sprayed upward.

Startled, UmRawa screamed, covering her head with her free arm.

The rain was now a downward flood, water falling in opaque sheets. Another crack of lightning, then another, followed by a deafening thud of thunder.

Michael put his foot on the next rung, felt it slip on the soaked wood. He clung to the rails, legs dangling, and the lightning flashed once more.

With the following crash, the entire hut shuddered, and the ladder bounced…away from the wall, far enough that it was caught and twisted by the wind.

Michael grasped futilely at the roof, fingers scrabbling against the woven matting and sliding away. Overbalanced by his weight, the ladder fell backward, toppling toward the ground. With an overwhelming sense of complete helplessness, he could do nothing but fall with it…

****

Once more, Senset found herself jerked from sleep. No dreams this time, just an ache in her back. With a groan, she floundered onto her side, wishing Michael were beside her. He'd help her roll over…

Then she remembered Michael was gone and Aram had taken his place, and Aram would never come to her bed. She was to be alone forever. There would never be a loving husband to help his clumsy, big-bellied wife hoist her bulk onto its side so she could sleep better.

Somehow, she managed the maneuver, putting her hand behind her and rubbing the small of her back.

Oh, it hurts so…a burning ache, growing worse by the minute. It had been hurting before she went to bed. While she sat at the table it had ached, though not so much. Indeed, it had been so slight she hadn't mentioned it to Aram. He was becoming prone to worry whenever she showed the least discomfort.

Senset moaned and, abruptly, the sound changed into a short, bitten-off cry.

Truly, it feels as if my bones are…she

344

gasped…*coming apart… Oh merciful Lord…*

Lurching around in the bed, she sat up, swinging her legs over its side. As she lunged to her feet, she felt a warm trickle down the inside of one thigh, traveling to her knee. Immediately, there was a flood of liquid and a puddle on the marble floor and she was standing in it.

"Orora!" Stumbling, Senset stepped away from the puddle, clinging to the bed's footboard. "Orora, wake up."

"Mistress?" A small form appeared in the doorway. The slave, pulled from her slumbers on the couch in the common room, rubbed her eyes.

"Get the midwife, and Elijah." She choked out the order. "I…ohhh!"

"The midwife?" The slave stared at her. "Mistress? You mean…?"

"My baby's coming, Orora." Senset spoke through gritted teeth, fingers digging into the wood of the bedstead to keep from screaming. Now that she was on her feet, the pain increased threefold, so rapidly she was shocked. She shut her eyes. "Hurry."

She heard the patter of Orora's bare feet to the door, the sound of it opening. Senset bit her lip as the slave spoke to the guard. There was the heavy clatter of sandals down the corridor.

"Don't worry, Mistress." Orora was back, putting arms around her waist and throwing back the covers as she helped Senset back into bed. "The midwife and Mistress Rebekah will be here soon."

They can't come fast enough, Senset thought as she lay down.

****

A frantic pounding on the door jerked Aram from

sleep. He rolled over in bed, reaching for the naked sword lying beside it. When in their own rooms, both he and Michael had always slept with their weapons within reach. Only when his brother entered Senset's bedchamber had he slept unarmed.

"Majesty!" The pounding continued—hard, sharp thuds, caused by the butt of a spear striking the door. If he wasn't mistaken, the voice was familiar, one of his men, though he wasn't certain which one.

He heard a door open. Voices, loud and hurried. Footsteps came toward his own shut door. When it opened, he recognized the silhouette as Michael's servant, Caleb.

"What is it?" He realized he was holding the sword as if to make a death-dealing thrust.

"Her Majesty's guard, sire. With a message."

Senset's guard?

Aram was out of bed in an instant, disregarding his nakedness to rush past Caleb to the outer door. "Why are you here?" Dismay flooded through him. "Has something happened to Her Majesty?"

"The Lady Senset is in travail, Majesty." The guard was breathing heavily, as if he'd run the entire distance from the queen's suite. Seeing Aram's bare body, he averted his eyes.

"What? When?" He was so shocked he asked stupid questions.

Senset's in labor...now Michael's son'll be born... the thought went through his mind as swift as a lightning strike.

"Now, sire." The man glanced back down the corridor. "I was sent to fetch the physician and the midwife, and Lady Rebekah, and now I'm notifying you." As he looked back, he swallowed loudly, and smiled and the effect was so brilliant, it was startling to Aram's still sleep-clouded brain. "You'll soon be a father, Your Majesty."

Not I. My brother… who didn't live to see this moment.

"Wait there for me." Turning, he went back into his bedchamber, stumbling to a lamp and lighting it, then standing a moment as if uncertain what to do.

Get dressed, fool. I'm General Aram. I fear nothing. Why can't I move?

While he dallied like a man turned to stone, mentally berating himself, Caleb busily gathered garments for him to wear, putting them on him. Aram lifted an arm, sliding it into the sleeve of his *galabia*, feeling as if someone else inhabited his body.

"Thank you, Caleb." With that bare murmur, he left the suite, running beside the guard down the passageway, to where Elijah waited.

"The midwife and your mother are with her now," the physician said. He was never present at a birth, except to examine the child and pronounce it normal and in good health. He looked as calm and cool as he always did.

Because it isn't your wife giving birth, Aram thought, angrily.

"I have to see her." Aram started toward the door, only to have Elijah catch his arm and pull him back. "I must…"

"That's forbidden, Your Majesty. As you well know." The physician's dark eyes were sympathetic, as if he understood his king's turmoil and concern. "Besides, what could you do? Truly, you'd only be in the

347

way."

He pushed Aram toward the padded bench across from the door.

"The women know what to do. She's in good hands. Sit, Michael, and wait."

Wait.

Yes, Aram thought, *that's all I can do. Now.*

Chapter 39

Through the night, Aram stayed outside Senset's chamber, listening to the sounds issuing from inside. The door was thick and strong, cut from the heavy oaks growing near the River-that-Flows-North. Words were muffled, but not their voices, and Aram recognized them in spite of their being two rooms away...the midwife's commands, sometimes spoken sharply, his mother's murmured prayers, but that other...

Surely it can't be Senset. Not that loud keening, breaking off to harsh grunting before spiraling into a choked shriek.

Like most men, Aram had rudimentary knowledge of childbirth. He'd witnessed animals giving birth...one of his own mares, some of the dairy cattle...and knew it was a long and tedious process, fraught with danger and pain—indeed pushing another being, even one so small as a newborn, out of one's own body had to involve pain and a threat to both mother and child. There was so much that could go wrong... But he'd never been witness to a human birth before, not in any form.

When his younger brothers and Rachel had been born, his father made certain he and Michael and Meryam were keep away from their mother's chamber. They'd merely been told Rebekah was bringing their new brother or sister into the world. Yeshua had been born during the night, so the older children actually slept through his birth. But this…

That Senset, his little sister, had to suffer so…

In his mind's eye, he saw her as she'd appeared to him that first night. A curious, disobedient child, peering at him through the bars, not knowing enough to be afraid of the fearsome bleeding creature penned inside. A child who'd saved him and married his brother, and become the young woman meaning so much to him now.

Aram thought of all the women he'd lain with. Reckless in his disregard of the commandment not to lie with whores and prostitutes, he'd taken advantage of slaves and servants who couldn't protest, refusing to take a true wife…

He'd used the excuse that he was a soldier and the brother of the king, could have whomever he wanted as long as the woman wasn't spoken for.

No more. I'll never again endanger a woman with the risk of bearing my child. I'll sin even more if I must, but I'll nevermore put my seed into a female, never allow anything of myself to grow within a woman…

He hadn't touched a woman since returning to Beth-Gurion, using the *shneim asar chodesh* and his deep grief as his excuse, though abstinence wasn't a necessary part of the ritual. Aram had found it easier than he'd expected and believed he might be able to accept it as a way of life.

Truly, I'll follow that path before I'll force a woman to suffer thus.

In this moment, however, all he wanted was for Michael's son to be born and for Senset and the child to be safe.

A single cry, louder and more pain-filled than all the others, floated through the door. He saw the guard wince, not trying to hide the movement. The man reacted to every sound as much as Aram did. Truly, he appeared no more accepting than his king of what was happened. Leaning his forehead against the shaft of his spear, his lips began moving in prayer.

Aram bowed his head, also, clasped hands pressed against his forehead. *Mighty God, Lord of my ancestors, spare Senset...spare her child...forgive me...*

There were no other sounds from inside. And then, a sudden bleating...like a young kid calling for its mother...

Elijah jumped to his feet so quickly Aram dropped his hands, staring at the physician. Hurrying feet sounded on the other side of the door, and Elijah ran toward it as if to meet whoever it was.

The door opened.

The midwife stood there.

Aram got to his feet also. Elijah stood in the way; he couldn't see past the doctor's shoulder. Couldn't see the midwife, except to note her head was bowed. Couldn't hear her softly murmured words to the doctor.

"What is it?" He dared break the silence, trying to keep the anxiety out of his voice and failing. They were taking too long, conversing together. *What are they doing?* A glance at the guard told him the man was still lost in his prayers for his queen. At least Aram hadn't shamed himself in front of one of his men with his show of fear. "My wife...is she...?"

He couldn't say the words.

Elijah spoke again to the midwife, who nodded and retreated into the chamber, shutting the door behind her. He turned. There was something in his arms, wrapped in a blanket. He came to where Aram stood.

"Your Majesty…" Cradling the thing against his shoulder, he opened the blanket. "Behold your son."

Aram went weak with relief, would swear he felt his legs tremble, worse than when he'd gotten off his horse to face his mother with the news of her son's death. Worse than when he'd collapsed from fever. He forced them to steady, looking down at the baby, at the little creature the cause of all the sounds of anguish he'd heard.

A son…Michael's son…

Small, surely not as big as his mother's babes had been…a mop of dark, damp hair already curling on its small skull…weak blue-mottled eyes peering around sleepily…a round, wrinkled face with a wobbling head… Aram's eyes swept over the naked newborn body…

The next king of Habir…

"My son…" He breathed the lie and held out his arms for Elijah to place the child in them, so he might accept and acknowledge his paternity, and make the child his heir. He studied the little face.

Look at it quickly. In a few moments, it'll be covered by the mask of the Beast, the first portion of its inheritance from his father.

Gently, he lifted the baby, brushing his lips against the soft skin of his forehead. "I recognize this child as my son and accept him as my heir. The Lord be praised. I thank him for being so gracious to me."

"The Lord be praised," Elijah echoed his response.

The guard was watching him now, smiling. Elijah was smiling, also. Clutching the baby against his chest, Aram pushed past the physician, eluding the hand reaching out to stop him. It might not be proper, it might go against custom, but he had to see Senset, had to know that she, also, had survived.

As if he understood, Elijah didn't protest but simply fell into step behind him. Neither paused until they reached the bedchamber door. The physician stopped; Aram ran through it.

Senset lay in the bed, her eyes closed.

They'd changed the sheets, and the air was filled with the sweet fragrance of incense, nothing of the bloody, pain-filled events of the night in evidence. Rebekah and the midwife were kneeling by the bed, hands clasped in prayer. The midwife got to her feet, bowing to her king.

Rebekah looked up and started to speak. To protest her son being there so soon after the birth?

He silenced her with a gesture. "Leave us."

"Michael." She got to her feet, smoothing the skirt of her gown. "It isn't prop—"

"My wife's just gone through more pain and suffering than one of my men after a battle. Don't tell me what's proper and what isn't." Later, he'd be horrified he'd spoken to his mother so. Now, he didn't care. He waved a hand at the door. "Out. Everyone."

Reluctant but not daring to argue, all turned to leave. Aram approached the bed.

"Senset?"

She still hadn't moved. Only the soft rise-fall of her breast told him she lived. She was so pale, so still... Aram fell to his knees by the bed, laying the child upon it. He stroked back the damp hair from Senset's forehead. When she opened her eyes, he gave a deep, pain-filled sigh.

"Isn't he beautiful?" Her gaze went from his face to

the baby. Her words were soft and breathy whispers, as if she couldn't get enough air to speak louder. "Our little Aram."

"Beautiful, my wife," he agreed and again studied his nephew's face. "Aram ben-Michael ben-Gurion…"

Before he realized what he was doing, he leaned forward and kissed her, out of joy, out of relief that the ordeal was over and his brother's heir was here and he now knew how the rest of his own life would go.

"Aram, you mustn't," she whispered as she pulled away. A pale hand went to his cheek, caressing its smooth line under the edge of the mask.

"Just a kiss, that's all," he assured her. "In my happiness. I won't break any other rules, but I had to see you. You understand."

She did, nodding, then looked past him as Elijah once more appeared, the midwife behind him.

"Majesties…?" He cleared his throat, lifting his hands.

They both saw what he held. A mask, leather-lined and gilded, a tiny thing barely covering one palm, to cover a tiny face.

Aram didn't speak as the midwife lifted the baby from the bed. He couldn't watch as Elijah placed the mask over the child's face. Shut his ears to the sounds of the whimpers of protest, bursting into a squall as the buckles were fastened behind the baby's head. Senset caught his hand, holding it tightly between her own as Michael's son's face was hidden forever from the world…

****

The first thing Michael saw when he opened his eyes was UmRawa's wrinkled old face, tears streaking her dusky skin.

"Mother?" He touched her cheek. "Why are you crying?"

"Why do you think, my son?" She caught his hand, kissing its palm and pressing it against her face.

He felt the dampness of her skin, evidence she'd cried long and hard while he was unconscious.

"You fell, Simba. And didn't move. I thought you were dead. I thought surely the gods had decided to take back their gift."

"Don't worry, Mother." He sat up, realizing he must've been unconscious for many hours, for his *doti* was dry and the hair hanging over his shoulders barely damp and already coiling into tight curls. He got up, stretching slightly with a little grunt. "I've a hard head. Once, when I was younger, I fell off a ladder while trying to climb a peach tree in my father's orchard, and Elijah told my mother the same thi…"

He stopped, as he realized what he'd said.

"Simba…?" UmRawa stared at him. "Wh-what are you saying?"

"My name isn't Simba," he answered, and there was wonder in his voice. "It's Michael ben-Gurion. I'm king of the Habiru."

Chapter 40

As soon as she'd recovered from the shock of his revelation, Michael told UmRawa everything—about the Curse and the Habirus's war with the Ægysians, of his marriage to Senset and coming to Usaset's aid, and the ambush by the Misazula…and how he had to return to his people.

"Do you have to leave, my Simba?" That was all she said.

"I must go back, UmRawa. Don't you see?" He didn't seem to notice how quiet she became or see the tears glistening in her eyes as she realized she was again losing her son, not to death this time, but to his real life.

She'd shown no awe that the man she'd dragged from the river, whose wounds she'd treated, for whom she'd sewn clothing to cover his nakedness, and cooked so many meals to fill his belly, was in truth a king. All UmRawa knew was that she'd be alone again.

"I'm sure my people think I'm dead…my wife believes herself a widow…my brother…Aram's probably seated on the throne and hating every minute of it. And my son's no doubt been born." He looked thoughtful. "Or my daughter. Perhaps that's why the Curse has been lifted. Because I've no son for it to be visited upon."

A daughter…

He walked to the door of the hut, looking toward the

horizon, now blue and cloudless, with no evidence of the fury that had swept over them. The day was as beautiful and peaceful as it could be.

Will she look like Senset, with those dark eyes and that straight hair the deep red of polished mahogany? Or will she have my eyes and these abominable curls? That thought made him smile. *My daughter…*

"I have to go back to Beth-Gurion…to my wife. I want to see my child."

A sob behind him made him spin around. UmRawa sank to her knees, head bowed, face in her hands. Her scrawny shoulders shook with the sobs wracking her body.

"Mother, why do you weep?" Immediately, he was at her side, pulling her to his feet.

"Why?" She raised a sodden face, blinking back more tears. "My son…whom the gods gave back to me…tells me he's leaving, and you ask me why I weep?"

She closed her eyes, crying even harder.

He pulled her old body against his, hugging her tightly against his chest. A hand touched her head, stroking the many braids.

"Cry not, Mother of men…weep not for your sons…for though they go to war or to pursue men's dreams, they always return to honor those who bore them…"

It was a quote, UmRawa was certain, and she wondered why her Simba spoke it to her.

His next words were more of a shock, as he went on, with a slight laugh, "Did you think I'd leave you behind? You saved me, UmRawa. You took me from certain death, tended, fed, and clothed me. You're coming with me, my mother. To Beth-Gurion."

****

Shielding his eyes, Aram looked up at the sky.

It's a good day to tell the people their king has a son. The Almighty sends bright sunshine to mark the time of my people meeting their next ruler. Blessed is He Who guides us.

It was the eighth day of Aram ben-Michael's birth, the day to announcement his arrival and the performing of the *brit milah.* Dropping his hand, Aram glanced behind him at the people gathered on the verandah. Proud grandmother Rebekah was there, and his brothers and sisters, as well as Elijah, in his best robes.

Though the physician would be in attendance, he wasn't allowed to perform the ceremony. The *mohel,* standing next to him, would do that, because he'd been educated in the proper ritual law and surgical procedure. Beside the *mohel* was the *sandek,* holding the infant as he would during the ceremony.

Aram and Senset had pondered for a long time over whom they'd ask to do this honor for Michael's son, for the one chosen had to swear to care for and guide young Aram should anything happen to his parents.

Finally, they asked Horem-Adam. Overwhelmed by the honor bestowed upon him, the former Ægysian stood proudly in his ceremonial robes, cuddling the little bundle in his arms.

Senset, of course, was absent, still being considered *niddah* until her ritual cleansing from the rigors of childbirth. Rebekah had explained to her she'd be marked impure for seven days after the baby's birth, then partially impure for another thirty-three, and during that time had to remain separated from her husband.

Senset accepted this explanation easily, making

only a small outcry of disappointment so her mother-in-law wouldn't be suspicious as to why someone so in love as she appeared to be wasn't anxious to be with her husband again.

Aram walked to the edge of the steps, looking out over the crowd.

Immediately, all conversation ceased, the usual buzzing of voices hushing as the people of Beth-Gurion, called to the temple by the blowing of trumpets, looked up at their king and waited for him to speak.

"Today is a day of rejoicing." Aram's voice was strong and firm and carried as far as the gate, loud enough for everyone to hear. "The throne of Habir has an heir, and the line of Malachi ben-Gurion will stand for another generation."

There was a cheer at this. Hands raised in affirmation, heads bowing briefly.

Aram held out his arms and Horem-Adam placed the baby in them. Aram pushed the blanket away so the baby's face in its tiny mask, as well as its naked little body, was visible. Eyes still that cloudy blue stared up at him. He marveled how the child had accepted him so quickly. Somehow, he'd expected the baby to sense he wasn't his true father, but young Aram seemed to feel secure in his presence.

Next came the part of the ceremony that worried Senset so. She hadn't batted an eye over her son's coming circumcision, but she feared that, once he was in Aram's arms, Aram might drop him. Making certain he had a good grip on the infant, he lifted the little bundle, raising him above his head so there was so doubt this was a man-child.

Little Aram waved his fists and cooed.

"People of Beth-Gurion, greet your future king, Aram ben-Michael."

Another murmur…blessings, exhortations to God to bless the child, prayers of thanksgiving for his safe birth…hands once more raised and heads bowed.

Aram released the baby once more into Horem-Adam's arms, and the procession into the temple was underway.

****

"Here he is, my wife. Your son, safely returned to you." Aram led the way into the common room of Senset's suite, the only place in her apartments where he could be in her company.

She sat in a chair near the open windows, basking in the sunlight, a light blanket across her knees, a woven shawl over her shoulders. Once again Aram thought how good the sun felt when it touched his face and how he would continue to miss it.

As Senset looked at him, smiling, he took the baby from Horem-Adam's arms and placed him in his mother's embrace.

"Did everything go well?"

"I didn't drop him, if that's what you're asking." He smiled as he said it. "So I suppose it went well."

Little Aram sniffled slightly, stuffing one fist into his mouth. Senset began to rock him, patting his bottom gently. Her face was rapt with love.

Aram swallowed quickly to force down the lump in his throat always seeming to appear whenever he watched her expression as she looked at her child.

"The *mohel* says he'll be uncomfortable for a few days. The…cut…will sting for a while. But all was done properly," he added hastily as he thought he saw a question in her eyes.

Her hand opened the blanket, seeing the binding on the tiny organ.

"The prayers were said, the wine blessed, a drop placed on Aram ben-Michael's tongue, and his name was spoken in the temple."

He wasn't going to tell her how the baby had screamed as the ritual knife removed his foreskin. No need to have her know that. It was to be expected, though such cries from the infant shook even Aram slightly. Briefly, he was glad the mother was excluded from the ceremony. Senset would probably have snatched the knife from the *mohel* and flung it away, then clutched little Aram to her breast and run back to the palace, locking herself and her son inside her suite.

"Now there's nothing to take him away from you until the *pidyon ha-ben,*" Horem-Adam added.

"I won't be able to attend that, either." Senset sighed.

The *pidyon ha-ben*, Redemption of the First-Born, was held on the thirty-first day of birth; she wouldn't receive her purification until the thirty-third day.

"Don't worry, I'll tell you all about it," Aram promised. He leaned over the baby, peering into the little face, surprised by how young Aram immediately had quieted when returned to his mother and was now drifting into sleep. "*The soul the Lord gave you is pure. Our God created it, He fashioned it, and He breathed it into you.*" He kissed the top of the curly head. "You're pure and without sin, little one. Rejoice in the Lord."

"If Aram ben-Michael's pure, why does he have to be redeemed?" Senset persisted.

She'd asked this question several times since

learning of the ceremony, as if she still couldn't comprehend the reason. She seemed to want to be doubly assured of everything these days, especially if it concerned her son, starting with the moment the mask covered the child's face. She'd demanded then and there to know if he'd accompany his father to the walled garden each month, and in the next breath informed Aram she'd be going also, for everyone knew a lion cub was never safe in its sire's presence.

It had taken Aram some minutes to calm her and convince her that while the child's face had to be uncovered during those times also, he would be kept in the nursery, though no one could be in his presence until after the full moon had passed. Leaving her child alone for a full day and night hadn't set well, either.

Briefly, he feared she was suffering the childbirth madness that had afflicted her sister-in-law but since he'd seen nothing else to confirm that, he decided she was merely afflicted by that other condition of young mothers…overprotectiveness.

"Why?" she asked again.

"Because we sinned with our doubt of the Lord and worshipped Bast." Aram smiled just a little sardonically. "Almost everything we do comes from that one moment of uncertainty. All who followed Malachi were cursed because of it, but our firstborn are still considered blessed. Thus, they must be redeemed before the Lord before they become corrupted by the world into which they've come."

"Five silver coins will do that?" Though she didn't mean to, skepticism crept into her voice.

"It's a small price to pay for redemption, Senset." Aram wished his own redemption or that of his brother's line could be bought so cheaply.

"Sometimes, Man must pay something tangible to the Lord," Horem-Adam spoke up. "Daily prayers of thanksgiving and the good guidance of parents and his *sandek* will keep young Aram on the proper path of righteousness, my sister, I'm certain."

She didn't answer.

"We have to go now." Aram caught her hand, kissing her fingers. That one kiss he'd given her on the night of the baby's birth had been a forbidden thing, another cause for more prayers of forgiveness, but a touch of his lips to her hand in leave-taking wasn't denied. "We couldn't have the usual celebration after the *bris* because we're in mourning, but—"

"So my son's cheated of the expected festivities." For some reason, Senset seemed determined to bring up anything pointing out how this joyous occasion was in opposition to the general air of bereavement still encasing the palace.

"We're having a quiet, family gathering," Aram went on. "Thanking the Lord for allowing my son—" There, he'd at last said the words without hesitation. "—to be born healthy, for my wife to survive his birth, and for the *brit milah* to be accomplished without complications." In an effort to forestall any more protestations, he added, "I'll send a servant with a platter of selections from the feast. That way you can partake and enjoy without having to endure the exhaustion of coming downstairs to the banquet hall."

Bowing, they left her still sitting in the chair, rocking the baby, and looking sad but thoughtful.

****

"Do you have everything we need?" Michael asked.

It had taken them several days to pick what vegetables they could from the garden and fill their packs. "I know we can't take much. We've a long walk ahead of us, and it's best to make our burdens as light as possible, but if there's something special you wish to take…"

"Nothing," UmRawa assured him.

She'd personally packed the bundle she carried on her back. Michael had insisted she take the lighter load, so she chosen the copper kettle and a small pitcher, their sleeping mats and blankets, rolled as small as possible, and her husband's tools. The *domo* was also folded in her pack, as was the other shift she owned, with the lion's-paw gauntlets and the pieces of Michael's armor.

"I can have new armor made from the old," he'd told her.

Michael carried their weapons, using his spear as a walking stick, while her son's knife and her husband's long-knife hung from the belt over his *doti*. His own pack held their food…beans UmRawa had dried in the sun, figs from some of the trees growing wild in the forest, a few of the smaller pomegranates, young bamboo shoots, and a couple of small squash and melons…along with three waterskins. He'd wanted to take more squash, but they were too heavy.

We'll have to eat sparingly and supplement our meals with whatever game I can kill.

He hated to leave the garden, especially with all its yield not yet harvested, but the urgency to once more be home and among his own people outweighed their waiting for the growing season to end. That was too far in the future. His return was more important and couldn't wait.

"Let the monkeys and wild pigs have the garden,"

UmRawa said. She waved a hand at the forest in a grand gesture, making Michael laugh. "They've left it alone and not stolen anything from it or eaten the new plants. I bequeath it to them."

The fate of the garden was settled.

It was UmRawa herself who brought up the one question he'd been mulling over in his mind. "How will we know which way to go? Where's Habir from here?"

"I believe it's northwest," he answered. "What we should do is go upstream and see if we can find the point where I fell into the water. Once we reach there, I should be able to get my bearings and find my way home." He looked around as if committing the little hut and the land around it to his memory before leaving it forever. "Are you ready?"

She didn't answer, only nodded.

"Let's go." Squaring his shoulders, Michael walked out of the yard, aiming himself for the little path leading to the riverbank where his life with UmRawa had begun.

Chapter 41

"This is madness," Horem-Adam declared. "Insanity."

"Madness or not," Aram replied. "I have to do it."

It was morning of the Day of Assumption of Guilt, the celebration of Malachi ben-Gurion's plea to Moishe for the Lord to allow him to take on the guilt of his people, removing the sin of their doubt, allowing him and his descendants to carry it from that time forward.

On the anniversary of that moment, the Habiru king entered the temple, and the small chamber housing the holy relics from that day. Opening the carved chest holding them, he would take out four objects…a small lump of melted gold vaguely resembling a cat's head…two pieces of wood once a tent's center support, one fragment scored with what appeared to be claw marks, the other holding deep indentations as if bitten by sharp fangs…a half-mask fashioned from a sheet of thin, beaten gold, lined with cracked and flaking leather, Malachi's original mask. Placing them on the altar, he would kneel and ask again for forgiveness and reaffirm his willingness to carry the burden of that long-ago sin.

"Brother, are you aware of what'll happen to you if you dare enter the Holy of Holies?" Horem-Adam had read the story in the scroll Michael showed Senset, as well as another in which Malachi chronicled other events pertaining to the Curse.

"Very aware, but what else can I do? Today's the Day of Assumption, and the people expect it to be done. Perhaps the Lord will be lenient." In spite of the hope in his voice, Aram knew he was doomed. The fury of the Lord would smite him the moment he set foot inside the chamber. "Perhaps he'll forgive my deception."

"You'll be killed for your blasphemy. That's what's going to happen," Horem-Adam interrupted. "You're tempting the Lord to allow you to commit a disobedience against His commandment. Yahweh will *have* to smite you…to show His might…to prove once more that He keeps his holy Word…only the king may enter that sacred place and live. There's no other way. He can't allow you to survive."

"The king's expected to perform the ceremony. If I refuse, I'll be exposed as an imposter."

"If you attempt it," Senset spoke up suddenly, "you'll surely die. That will also expose you as an imposter."

Twice before, others than the ruling sovereign had tried to enter the Holy of Holies. They'd both been blasted by the Lord's holy anger, nothing left of their bodies but charred bone.

"If that's what must happen…" Aram bowed his head in fatalistic acceptance. "So be it, if the Lord wills it…"

"The Lord isn't willing it," Horem-Adam flared. "You are. Don't do this, Aram. Think of Senset…of the child…"

"There's no way out. If the Almighty doesn't spare me…" He looked at Senset. "Tell the people I was punished for my own doubt. That I dared question the Will of God in my brother's death, and He smote me for my irreverence. As for Michael's son…"

He turned back to Horem-Adam.

"He'll have Adonijah and the other advisors to guide him, and his mother and you to guarantee he grows into a righteous man and walks in favor with the Lord."

Aram glanced at the window.

"I have to go. This is a morning ceremony and it's nearly noon."

"Don't…please…" Senset clutched at him, as if she had the strength to prevent him from committing this foolhardy act.

Aram caught her hand, kissing her fingers. She stared into his eyes.

"I love you," she whispered so quietly her brother couldn't hear.

"And I you." His whisper was as soft.

His arms went around her, crushing her against his chest. Aram kissed her, but it was like no other kiss he'd given her. Those had been careful and chaste, though affectionate. This was the passionate kiss of a man saying goodbye to the woman he loved.

As he released her, pushing her away, Senset said, "I won't be there. I won't watch you die."

She made it a threat.

"I wouldn't expect you to." Whirling, he stalked from the room.

She listened to the sound of his footsteps as they died away down the corridor, and then she began to cry, very softly, as Horem-Adam took her in his arms.

****

"Where is everyone?" Michael asked, as they came through the city gate and saw the empty marketplace.

He and UmRawa were nearly exhausted, their

backtracking trek long and tedious. The three-days' journey to Usaset he and the armies had made by horseback had taken them half a month on foot. Human legs could walk only so far and so fast, and they'd had to stop often so the old woman's enfeebled limbs could rest.

Though he was filled with impatience, knowing he could've made better time alone, Michael bit back his frustration, for he wasn't about to abandon the woman who'd saved his life. Whenever UmRawa admitted fatigue, they stopped; often they stopped even if she didn't. Michael insisted on resting, for he knew she realized how she was slowing him, and he feared she'd walk until she collapsed rather than speak up.

Once, they passed a small village, where a man was herding some donkeys. They swapped UmRawa's husband's tools and all the melons and squash for one of the little beasts. After that, it carried UmRawa and their packs, with Michael walking alongside. It was surprising how much faster they covered the miles, how swift a creature with such short legs could move, even when burdened with a rider.

On the morning of the twenty-fifth day after leaving the hut, they staggered through Beth-Gurion's city gate. Though they were a dusty and disheveled pair, the guards didn't try to stop them; it had always been their sovereign's order that all travelers were welcome within its walls.

In spite of the fact he'd hoped otherwise, Michael understood why the guards didn't recognize him, for he looked nothing like the beardless and masked king who'd ridden through Beth-Gurion's gates nearly a year before. No one would believe the long-haired, bearded, and sun-browned man wearing *doti* and *domo* could be the same person. Thoughts of seeing his family again, introducing UmRawa to them, and clothing himself once more in kingly raiment made his heart beat faster. Thoughts of holding Senset once more in his arms made it pound against his ribs.

It was only when they were inside and saw how empty and quiet the marketplace was that he returned to the gate to ask his question, calling up to one of the guards on the wall.

"You're Habiru, aren't you?" The guard shouted back.

"Yes."

"In that case, why aren't you aware today's the Day of Assumption? Didn't you come to take part in the Observation? That's where everyone is." The guard waved a hand in the general direction of the street leading to the temple. "At the temple. To verify that King Michael does as the Lord decreed."

"King Michael?" Michael took a step back, the words sending a jolt through him. "I thought Michael was dead."

"You think wrong, stranger." The guard looked somber. "It was our beloved general who was killed fighting the Misazula. Was the message garbled when it was sent to your city? Please the Almighty no one else thinks our king's dead."

"But…"

"We've mourned long and loudly for General Aram, since the day His Majesty returned from what was left of the city of Usaset. That was truly a terrible day."

"You say the ceremony's about to begin?" Michael's thoughts were frantic, the guard's words confusing and shocking. He knew UmRawa was staring at him, the guard frowning at his obvious agitation.

Aram, what've you done? You've let people think you were killed and not I? Why? And now you're about to ensure your own death by defying the Lord?

"Undoubtedly it's already begun." The guard glanced up at the sky. "The sun's fast climbing toward noon."

"Surely not yet…" Michael glanced in the direction of the temple.

Overhead, the sky was bright blue and cloudless. He could hear no screams of terror, no cries for mercy, or even prayers. He wasn't certain exactly how it would happen, but surely there would be some sound when the Lord discovered how his Holy of Holies had been breached…surely if Aram had entered the temple and been struck down by the Almighty's wrath, there would've been a tremendous explosion, possibly a great ball of fire falling from the sky to strike the chamber forbidden to all but the proper person. Even if the fire came from within the chamber itself, there would surely be some reaction the entire city would feel…

He whirled, clutching UmRawa's hand. "I have to leave you, Mother. I have to get to the temple and stop my brother."

With her "Go, my son," ringing in his ears, Michael ran up the street, heading to the temple.

"You'd better hurry, too, old woman, if you don't want to be late," the guard called.

UmRawa didn't answer, just tapped the donkey's flank with the little switch she held, urging it after Michael.

****

Almighty God, I'm only a woman, lowly in Thy

sight…only a foreigner, though I accept and worship You…My husband was Habiru, my son's Habiru, and I consider myself one of Your people now…I beg you, spare Aram…Don't punish him for daring to enter the forbidden place…Oh, Most Terrible Lord…don't let me lose him, too…

Senset was alone. Horem-Adam had left her, hurrying to the temple, hoping he might think of some way to prevent Aram from his self-destruction while allowing the ceremony to continue. They both knew it was useless. Nothing other than admitting he wasn't the king, that he'd lied about who had died, and that he'd taken his brother's place, that all ceremonies in which he'd participated since his return had been performed in deception.

Nevertheless, she prayed, remembering the miracles the Scriptures spoke of, the unbelievable things happening to those who truly believed and were faithful…

Our people need him, my son needs him…and so do I…

****

At a run, Michael sped through Beth-Gurion's winding main street. Briefly, he was thankful the Habiru had fought so many wars, that his being a warrior had kept him from becoming fat and complacent as those kings he and his soldiers conquered. It held him in good stead now as he raced toward the temple. He'd left UmRawa behind, the old woman forgotten in his haste to prevent his brother from destroying himself.

Nevertheless, from the marketplace to the temple was a long distance, and his side was beginning to hurt, a cramping stitch forming. He could feel the muscles in his thighs and calves protesting, though he forced himself to keep moving.

The gate came into sight.

Michael breathed a short gasp and reached the temple gate. Beginning to pant, he slowed his gait so he wouldn't crash into the kneeling figures inside the gateway, forcing himself to a walk.

The temple courtyard was filled with townspeople, as many as possible crowding into the open space before the steps leading to the wide verandah under the portico. As required, all knelt, hands clasped before them prayerfully, looking up at the man standing on the top step, his family behind him.

He was speaking the ritual lines of the Assumption, the words Malachi said to Moishe, and all were listening with rapt attention, but...

Michael felt his belief in his own identity tremble as he saw the mask covering his brother's face. Actually seeing Aram in kingly robes of state, golden crown reflecting beams of sunlight, he understood why no one questioned who lived and who had died, but again the question came, *Aram, why?*

Forcing himself to remain still, Michael strained his ears to hear what his brother was saying. Yes...he was giving Malachi's plea, begging the Lord to place all blame for what had happened on him... Words only the king should say. Words never to be spoken again, just as the Day of Assumption was never to be observed if the direct line of the king was gone.

Does he think the Lord won't strike him if he hides behind my mask?

Once more, he wondered what had happened to take the curse from him.

Did Senset have a daughter…Is that to be our only child…Senset…

The confusion of his mind, shaken more at seeing Aram, took a fantastic turn.

Is that the reason for his disguise? He thinks to take Senset from me? Aram wouldn't do that. He'd never covet my wife…he…

The thoughts flew through his mind, colliding against each other, but ceased as Aram dropped his hands, bowed his head, then turned and bowed to the little group standing behind him. Led in their replies by the priest, his brothers and sisters, his mother…all bowed in return, chorusing the words from the ritual, "The Lord protect us. Almighty, please forgive us."

Aram walked to the temple doors. All Michael could think in that moment was that he had to keep his brother from certain death.

Darting between the kneeling observants, he used the spear to propel himself forward. He struck a shoulder, nearly knocked a celebrant over. The man toppled, but caught himself, looking up with annoyance to see who was so irreverent as to be moving during the ceremony. Michael sped onward, leaping through spaces, springing onto a little path suddenly opening before him.

He was aware it'd be only moments before the guards would see him or, hearing the exclamations of those he was stumbling against in his haste, would attempt to stop the wild-haired man disrupting the solemn occasion.

He was almost at the steps, made a leap toward them, caught his foot under someone's, and nearly fell. The man he'd kicked let out a cry, seizing him to fling him away. Several others leaped to their feet, reaching for him. Eluding their grasps, Michael righted himself and gained the bottom step. Behind him, he heard footsteps and knew the guards were finally springing into action.

"Stop him!"

He was up the steps before those on the verandah could react, seeing his other brothers and the priest look around as if trying to determine what was causing the uproar.

Aram was nearly at the door now, reaching for the heavy handles, Michael a few steps behind him. His lungs were burning, suddenly refusing to let in air, legs abruptly cramping and tightening. With a desperate lunge, Michael caught his brother's arm, pulling him backward. As Aram staggered and regained his balance, he threw himself in front of the door.

"Back, my brother. I forbid you to enter this place."

"Michael?" For a moment, Aram stared at him, as if he couldn't believe this wild-haired, bearded, near-naked creature was his brother. Behind the mask, hazel eyes sparkled with abrupt but unshed tears. "Merciful Almighty, you're alive?"

Then the soldiers were upon him.

Chapter 42

"Let me go!" Michael shouted, beginning to struggle before he was touched. "It's I, Michael ben-Yonathan, your king. Release me!"

More moments of confusion as the soldiers started at his words, then stared from him to Aram as if seeking confirmation of this mad statement.

"Sire?" One of the men managed to gasp.

Michael was startled as his brother's mouth hardened into a brief, determined line.

Aram recovered from his shock. Taking a step back, he raised his hands, looking skyward.

"The Almighty be praised. My brother Aram has broken the chains of Death and returned to us. Truly the Lord is merciful."

That brought a response from the crowd as well his family...questions, exclamations of surprise from Gideon and Shemuel...a scream from Rebekah.

"Aram? My son's alive?"

"What are you saying? I'm not Aram." Michael jerked an arm from a soldier's grasp. It was immediately seized more tightly.

His spear was pulled from his hand. Over Aram's shoulder, he could see Gideon, Shemuel, and the priest hurrying toward them, Yeshua holding Rebekah back and gathering her into his arms. He continued struggling.

"Let me go. I'm Michael. I'm your king."

An outcry arose at that, the people in the courtyard repeating, questioning. Some began to pray. A few women burst into tears.

"Surely the wound causing me to think my brother dead has confused his thinking," Aram proclaimed, loud enough for everyone to hear. He half-turned as they reached his side. "We must get him to the palace and call Elijah."

"I don't need a physician." Michael's voice rose stridently over his brother's calmer, ringing tones. "I'm Michael. Aram, why are you carrying on this masquerade?"

"Take him to the palace," Aram ordered but as the men moved to hustle him down the steps, Gideon called out.

"Wait."

Immediately, there was silence. The soldiers stilled, the people falling quiet, watching their king's scribe walk toward the madman. Without speaking, Gideon studied Michael's face, reaching out to smooth the unkempt beard, looking into the green eyes.

Aram felt a tremor shake him, wondering if even Michael was aware of their difference in eye color. No one but Senset had ever commented on it. It was as if no one ever dared look into the king's eyes.

"My general, my brother, is it truly you?" The same tears Aram had so successfully banished appeared in Gideon's eyes. "We mourned your loss. Where have you been?"

"I'm not Aram." Michael's reply shot into the air like an eruption of water from a fountain. "I'm Michael." He nodded at the masked figure. "*He's* Aram. Gideon, he's played a most foul trick on all of you."

"Why would someone do such a thing?" Gideon looked from Michael to Aram in confusion. "Brother, what's he saying?"

"Surely, his wits are…" Aram began, only to have Michael interrupt.

"He isn't your king." Having gained a moment's attention, Michael spoke frantically, trying to get enough said to convince them before everyone was distracted again. "I am. Can't you tell?"

"How can I?" Gideon's answer was reasonable. "I've never seen my king's face. Besides, *he*…" He nodded at Aram. "…wears the mask."

"Then have him remove it," Michael demanded. "Take it off him."

"Remove my mask?" Aram's cry of horror was echoed as the spectators heard Michael's demand.

Behind them, Rebekah was now crying softly, all the grief she'd believed buried once more breaking free at her son's return.

"And bring the curse down on all those present?" Aram exclaimed. "How can you dare ask that of me? I refuse."

"No one will be affected by the curse," Michael retorted. "Because you're not I."

"You can't be our king," Gideon argued reasonably.

His voice, so calm in the midst of Michael's wild replies, seemed to soothe everyone, quieting the crowd's anxiety as well as those around him. Rebekah stopped crying, raising her head to stare at them. Even the soldiers were calmed, loosening their grips on Michael's arms.

"…else looking on you would already cause us to be transformed."

"That's just it…the curse has been lifted," Michael replied.

He forced himself to speak calmly, realizing his violent cries and demands were working against him. Affecting a stillness of body he didn't feel, he stopped straining against the soldiers' grasp.

"I don't know how it happened, but I no longer carry Malachi's burden." As a loud murmuring began, his words being repeated…doubtfully…as well as in hope, he went on, "Have *him*…" He nodded at Aram. "…remove the mask, and you'll see. His face won't affect you either."

"Michael?" Gideon looked at Aram.

"Don't listen to his ravings." Shaking his head, Aram took another step backward. "He was sorely wounded. Surely, his wits are addled."

"Why are you doing this, Aram?"

With a sudden, violent leap, Michael wrenched himself out of the soldiers' holds. The movement carried him into the air, past Gideon and directly onto Aram. Both he and his brother went down in a tangle, Michael reaching for the mask. While Aram struggled to fend him away, Michael's hands scrabbled at the buckles.

One came open; he pulled at the other, the strap slid loose…

Ripping the mask from his brother's face, Michael flung it across the verandah. A cry of horror followed its sail through the air, dying away as it struck the stone surface, slid a few more feet and stopped at Rebekah's feet, spinning slightly before coming to a halt. Fearfully, she bent and picked it up, staring at the object that had covered her son's face since his birth.

Scrambling to his feet, Michael seized Aram's

shoulder and jerked his brother upright as complete silence fell.

The people cowered, clutching each other in fear as they waited for the pain of transformation to strike them. Soldiers appeared stunned, their spears falling from lax hands. Gideon and Shemuel didn't move, staring at their two brothers while Yeshua pulled his mother's head against his chest as if to shield her from whatever was coming. Aram, more than anyone, appeared overwhelmed by what had just happened.

Slowly, he raised one hand to touch his face, as if to assure himself it was truly bare.

"You see?" Michael's question was triumphant, a vindication to their doubt. "Nothing's happening. You're untouched. The curse is lifted." He turned a furious glare on Aram. "And you, my brother, have some explanations to make."

****

The fierce knocking on the door brought Horem-Adam to his feet. Realizing his efforts were useless, he had returned to be with his sister.

Senset put her hands to her mouth. "Can…can it be…over? Oh, Horem."

"We've heard nothing, sister. Surely if Aram pursued this folly, his…punishment…wouldn't be a silent thing." He made a restraining gesture.

The knocks sounded again, heavier and more impatient this time.

"I'll see who that is." Striding to the door, he stopped before it. "Who seeks Her Majesty?"

"Her husband. Open this door before I break it down."

Senset gasped.

It sounds like… Surely it's Aram's voice, but why is he saying such a thing? Something's happened…

Horem-Adam looked back at her, brows raised, expression apprehensive.

"Go ahead, my brother. Let my husband enter."

Without speaking, he seized the heavy handle, but before he could turn it, the door was flung open. Horem-Adam staggered backward, nearly falling as he sought to remove himself from the path of the people storming in. They stopped inside the entrance, leaving the door ajar— he saw two sentries stationing themselves outside—and gathering around the two men in front of them. Neither spoke, they simply stood there, looking at Senset, who got to her feet.

"Michael?"

Who's that with him? Surely some holy man, come from a sojourn in the desert… Her gaze slid past the hairy, barely clothed figure to the richly dressed one beside him, only to stop as she realized his face was uncovered.

"Where's your mask?"

"He doesn't need it, my wife." The words came from the holy man. "Or can I still call you that?"

"What?" She looked back at him, took a step, then a second, before stopping again.

She studied the bearded face, stared as she realized what she was seeing…a face she'd thought she'd never see…green eyes gleaming in another mask, this one of tangled, wiry hair. Slowly, she touched him, fingers brushing across his beard-covered cheek. He closed his eyes, pressing into her hand.

"Michael…? Is it truly…"

Senset's eyes rolled upward and her knees buckled.

She fell into Michael's arms as she fainted.

****

When she awoke, she was lying on one of the couches in the common room, looking up into Michael's face…his handsome, dusty, bearded face.

"You're here," she whispered, as if daring to speak any louder might make him disappear.

Surely this is a vision…a spirit…sent by the Lord to remind me of what Aram and I have done… but Aram had been standing next to this wraith, hadn't he? They'd come through the door together, and one—the loincloth-clad man—had spoken to her.

"Michael, is it truly you, my husband?"

"It is, wife, and I…"

Whatever he'd been about to say was lost in Senset's cry as she threw her arms around her husband's neck and burst into tears. Putting his arms around her, Michael dropped onto the couch beside her, holding her tightly until her sobs subsided.

"I never thought I'd see you again," Senset whispered, wiping furiously at her eyes. "How can it be?"

She brushed the long curls back from his bare shoulder, fingers entwining in the thick spirals. They felt real enough, longer, perhaps, but as thick and crisp as Michael's hair had always felt…as her fingers remembered from caressing while they made love.

Glancing around at the others, who were standing a respectful distance away, she burst out, "Are you real? The Lord hasn't sent me a vision only to snatch you away again?"

"I'm real enough." Michael pulled out of her arms and stood, catching her wrists and pushing her hands away. "Real enough to ask why you called my brother by my name, and why, in the name of all we consider holy, Aram was pretending to be me to the point of risking instant destruction at the hands of the Lord by entering the Holy of Holies." He looked at Aram again. "Tell me, brother, and your story had better be a good one."

Aram didn't answer. Faced with the unbelievable, his façade of bravery had fallen away. In that moment, he appeared as nothing more than a man caught in a great deception, expecting the most severe punishment for his crime.

"You always said you didn't want to be king, though I never faulted you for it. I simply accepted it as Yahweh's will that I was the one unfortunate enough to be the first leaving our mother's body. That can't be the reason you did this." Michael looked from his brother to Senset, who sat staring at him, her hands clasped together tightly. "Was it Senset? I never thought you had more than a brotherly affection for her, but…did you fall in love with her? Want her for yourself, and saw my apparent death as a way to get both her and my throne? Truly, I can't see you doing that, either, brother."

There was a shocked gasp from his other brothers and Horem-Adam before Senset said sharply, "Don't be absurd, my husband. If Aram wanted the throne, he didn't have to pretend to get it. It'd come to him as the next in line. As for me…"

She left the rest of the sentence unspoken, shaking her head.

"What, then?" Michael didn't demand she finish. He studied his brother. "Why, Aram?"

By now, Aram had recovered some of his poise.

Raising his gaze to meet his brother's, he didn't falter, but said quietly, "I did it to protect our people, brother."

"How did pretending *you* had died instead of me do that?"

"If you could've seen how the people received the news of your—of *Aram's* death—you wouldn't ask that." It was Senset who spoke. "The entire city was in mourning…all Beth-Gurion attended the funeral service. Your mother…" She glanced at Rebekah, who still held the mask clutched against her heart. "She's only now emerged from her *aninut*…and I…I was beside myself in the knowledge that the man I loved was dead."

"Yet I'm not, as you can see…" Michael began.

"For that I'm truly grateful to the Almighty God for restoring you to us all."

"Yet you called Aram *husband*," he persisted. "You went to him when we entered the room. You knew of his falseness."

"Yes, I knew. Not at first, for he kept himself from me, first within the excuse of mourning, then with my *niddah* and my period of impurity…but a wife knows her husband, Michael, and I'd have known sooner had he dared enter our marriage bed. When I was able to see his eyes, I knew he wasn't you, and when he told me why he assumed the Beast's mask, I agreed to assist his deception."

"I couldn't let it happen, brother," Aram said softly. "I couldn't let anyone think you dead. I couldn't let the Scriptures be fulfilled."

"Scriptures?" Michael frowned, then his expression changed as he understood. "You mean that prophecy…?"

"If you condemn Senset for her part in this, "

Horem-Adam interrupted. "Denounce me also, for it was I to whom Aram first confided his plan, and I agreed to remain silent."

"I should," Michael snapped. "I should stand on the temple steps and accuse all of you, but once I said the words, I'd appear a fool. What would I accuse you of?" Looking around, he shook his head. "Having enough love for our people to give up your own self to become someone else? Of being unselfish in the extreme..."

He fell silent, staring at Aram for so long, his brother began to stir uneasily. "Michael, what is it?"

"*An act of unselfish love*... Truly, you've done more good than you ever expected." Bowing his head, Michael spoke more quietly. "Almighty, be praised. It wasn't Senset's love, as I mistakenly thought, that would free me from the curse, it was *yours*, Aram...the unselfish love of a man willing to relinquish his own identity to save his people from the grief of losing their king."

He threw his arms around Aram, hugging him and kissing him on both cheeks.

"Thank you, brother, for your devotion and your sacrifice."

Releasing Aram, he turned to look at his mother.

I must tell her how UmRawa cared for me. UmRawa... He'd abandoned the old woman at the city gate, left her to save Aram and hadn't thought of her since.

"Gideon, somewhere in the city, there's an old woman with a donkey..."

"Majesty?"

The call came from the open door. In their haste and excitement, no one had thought to close the door and shield the rest of the palace from whatever was to come, so the two sentries had been listening unashamedly. One stood in the doorway, someone behind him. One of the guards from the gate, Michael thought.

"What is it?"

The sentry stepped aside, nodding to the guard to speak.

"There's an old woman…" The young man appeared shaken by the fact that his king wore no mask. He bowed quickly. "It's true, then? The curse is lifted from the house of ben-Gurion?"

"True as the sun is shining." Michael affirmed. "About this old woman…?"

"The one with…you, my lord. She tried to keep up, but the donkey proved stubborn and wouldn't move. I've brought her to the palace, but she insists she wishes to speak to someone called Simba."

"Where is she?" Michael felt his heart leap slightly. *Dear Mother*. The guilt he felt over abandoning her fled.

"I told her to wait in the hallway, sire. Shall I—"

Michael didn't answer. Pushing past his family, he ran to the door. "UmRawa?"

She stood next to the other sentry, looked up anxiously, her wrinkled face breaking into a smile. "Simba? My son…"

****

"So, my wife…"

Aram and the others had departed. UmRawa had been introduced and her part in his survival explained. Rebekah cried again and clasped the old woman in a hug of gratitude, thanking her again and again for saving her son's life. Without waiting for Michael to order it, she took UmRawa to find rooms for her and establish her in their household.

Now, Michael and Senset faced each other in the otherwise empty common room.

"Yes, my husband?" In a posture of repose, Senset was again seated on the couch, though the tightness of her clasped hands revealed she had no idea what was going to happen now that she and Michael were alone.

"If only you knew how I missed you. From the moment I remembered who I am, all I could think of was returning to you."

"Yet now that you're here," she pointed out. "You accuse Aram and me of…"

"My mind was confused." He knelt beside the couch, taking her hands. "I couldn't understand what I was seeing at the temple. You've a king kneeling at your feet, Senset, asking your forgiveness."

He touched her fingers to his lips as he spoke. She jerked her hands away.

"If you could've known the torment I felt when I thought the man I loved was gone from me forever…" Senset studied her fingers before meeting his gaze. "When Aram turned away from me, I accepted it as grief, but when I learned the true reason, and that I'd never again know your love or the feel of your body… That your child would never see its father…it was almost more than I could bear. I'll forgive you, Michael, but only because I love you so."

"My child…" He breathed the words like a prayer. "I've waited for this moment until the others left. How is my daughter? May I see her?"

"Daughter?" She looked startled. "What makes you think you've a daughter? You've a son, Michael."

His heart leaped at that, for if he had a male heir but was now without his mask, it meant Aram's gesture had completely erased the curse and nothing remained to haunt future generations.

"May I see him?"

She led him into the bedchamber.

Orora stood beside the cradle. She'd been there during the confrontation in the common room, hovering protectively near its tiny occupant, in case the loud voices meant harm to her charge. She ran to Michael, falling to her knees before him. She caught his hands, pressing them against her forehead.

"Master! Welcome home."

"Thank you, Orora. It's good to be home." He pulled the slave to her feet.

"Go to your quarters, Orora. I'll take over," Senset told her.

Bowing, the slave hurried from the room.

"She has her own quarters now?"

"One of your soldiers has spoken for her. He was in the party escorting us here. I remember them flirting, and it appears they've continued to do so. I thought to free her so they might marry, if you'll tell me what I must do."

"We'll discuss it." Michael wanted nothing else to delay seeing his child. "Later."

Senset lifted the baby from the crib. Falling to her knees, she held out the child. "Behold your son, my lord."

Michael took the baby from her, thankful he'd been allowed to hold Yeshua and Rachel when they were infants so he knew exactly how to do it and wasn't entirely afraid of taking a babe in his arms.

This child was different, of course, because it was his own, and he still felt a tremor as he lifted the infant.

How light he is, no more weight than a blanket roll. His skin's so soft.

He hugged the warm little body close, fingers fumbling with the tiny buckles on the mask. "Let's get rid of this. You've been freed, my son, as have I."

He dropped it to the floor, and stared at his child's face before pressing a kiss on the baby's forehead. Aram ben-Michael didn't awaken but slept peacefully in his father's arms.

"I recognize this child as my son and accept him as my heir. The Lord be praised. I thank him for being so gracious to me." Michael spoke the same words Aram had used when he first saw the child, the blessing of a new father accepting his offspring. "What did you call him?"

"Aram. Aram ben-Michael. It was before I learned his deception," Senset sounded a little defensive. "I suppose…if you wish…his name can be changed?"

"He's called after a good man. He'll keep the name."

"What'll happen to Aram now?" Her question was anxious.

"Nothing, for I truly think there's no punishment for what he did. Surely there's no precedent for what's happened. My brother had no wicked motive in mind. He acted out of love and nothing more, and the people will be told that. The story of his loyalty to his king and his people will be sent to every Habiru city so all may know the bravery of what he did. I love Aram, Senset, and I thank the Lord for him."

Abruptly, little Aram awoke. Face crimping, he began to whimper.

"He's hungry." Senset held out her arms. "Let me take him." She settled herself in the nursing chair by the

389

cradle. "I have to feed your son, my husband."

She waited for him to leave.

He didn't move. "Let me stay…if I may."

Silently, she nodded, and he knelt beside her as she released her breasts and offered one to his son. The tiny pink mouth encircled the nipple, pulling on it greedily. There wasn't a sound in the room but the quiet whispers of Aram's breathing as he nursed.

Michael studied Senset's face, smiling at the look of love he saw as she watched the baby. Presently, with a sigh, Aram ben-Michael slipped again into sleep and was returned to his bed.

"Don't…" Michael caught Senset's hand as she went to close her gown. Clasping it within his own, he led her into the common room and to the couch where she'd been as they entered. "Sit with me, wife."

Still not speaking, she obeyed, and when she was seated, he slid his hand under one milk-filled globe, bending to press his lips against its rounded curve.

"*Blessed is the mother among women, for she nourishes us all…her kindness sustains her people…her milk sustains her sons…her love sustains her husband…* Nourish me tonight, Senset, as today you've done my child. Let me come to you when it grows dark."

"Our marriage bed awaits now, Michael." There was no mistaking her eagerness as she put her arms around his neck and pressed a kiss against his throat. "There's no need to wait until night falls."

"True."

Her body called to his. He could feel it, the blood in their veins rushing in a rhythm echoed by the beating of their hearts.

Truly, this woman and I were meant for each other,

and I thank you, Most Holy One, for returning me to her.

Michael forced himself not to move, when he wished nothing more than to lift Senset in his arms and carry her to their bed and make love to her.

A little longer I'll sit here, and then... It'll be much sweeter if we wait.

"For now, all I wish is to sit and hold you and thank the Almighty for all he's given me."

"Does any of the Beast remain at all? Is it truly gone forever?"

"You sound as if you miss it, wife." He smiled at the whimsy of that thought. "None of that Beast exists. The only animal in me now is the one rising in a man's blood when he's stirred by his woman...to protect her and to love her. The one who roamed the garden and cried out his torment to his God is gone forever."

"That one was gentle too," she murmured, moving closer to him. "He slept with his head in my lap and never offered me harm."

"We'll make the garden a monument to the gentle part of the Beast, then," Michael proposed. "Remove the gate to the garden, make it a place for our son...and our other children...to play."

"I love you, Michael ben-Yonathan." She lifted her face to his, her lips, those bee-stung lips whose color he'd once likened to that of the pomegranates, offered for his kiss.

"And I you, Senset, my wife. The Lord has blessed me and made his face to shine upon me. He's given me the love of my people, a loyal brother, a loving, most faithful wife...and a son..."

Michael kissed her, feeling his passion once more stir. They'd sit a little longer, let it burst into full growth, then seek that waiting bed.

"Praise the Almighty of Malachi, and I beg he allows me to dwell in His House forever."

Cradling Senset's head against his chest, he leaned back with a sigh. The feel of her warm body against his own was a delight, a reminder of the night to come. The clasp of her arms around him brought memories of other nights that had stayed with him in his dreams.

In his heart, for the moment, the now gentled and tamed Beast slept, waiting for his wife to awaken him.

Acknowledgements

This story is a work of fiction, and with the exception of the mention of certain Biblical/ historical characters, any resemblance to any person living or dead is not intended.

I admit to using a writer's artistic license in combining the chronology of some events: On the website, www.angelfire.com/nt/theology/06egypt.html, the first evidence of the Israelites in Egypt is stated as 1991-1786 BC (12th Dynasty); the Hyksos (*Heka Khasewt*)appeared in the 13th Dynasty, 1786-1567 BC; the Exodus occurred circa 1446 BC (18th Dynasty); and the Habiru invaded Egypt during the reign of Amenhotep III (1417-1379 BC). Other sources have identified the Hyksos specifically as Phoenicians but still others state they were a Semitic people of possible Israelite origin. The Habiru were believed to be barbarian invaders, or those Israelites led by Joshua, as evidence by inscriptions on the Tell el-Amarna tablets.

Though instances of Hebrew/Jewish Law and Commandments may be cited, it is to be supposed, for the purposes of this story, that some of the customs of the Habiru—in being separated from their brethren for so long—would, in the natural course of time, evolve along different lines.

Therefore, any divergence seen in how they conduct themselves as opposed to ancient or current Jewish custom/ritual is to be attributed to that fact.

Sources researched for this novel were:
Judaism 101: http://www.jewfaq.org
http://judaism.about.com/
http://www.my-hebrew-name.com/

http://www.brityy.org

http://en.wikipedia.org/wiki/Category:Aramaic_words_and_phrases

http://www.ancient-hebrew.org/

www.historum.com

www.jewishhistory.org/hyksos-or-hebrews/

http://tenthletter.com/Religious_Debates.html

www.wikipedia.com:

http://en.wikipedia.org/wiki/Mikvah

http://en.wikipedia.org/wiki/Tohorot

http://en.wikipedia.org/wiki/Onan#cite_note-15

www.angelfire.com/nt/theology/06egypt.html

A word about the author...

Toni V. Sweeney has lived thirty years in the South, a score in the Middle West, and a decade on the Pacific Coast, and now she's trying for her second thirty on the Great Plains.

Since the publication of her first novel in 1989, Toni has written 92 novels, with 89 of them being published. This includes several series.

Follow her at:

https://www.facebook.com
/profile.php?id=100048587829251

Thank you for purchasing
this publication of The Wild Rose Press, Inc.

For questions or more information
contact us at
info@thewildrosepress.com.

The Wild Rose Press, Inc.